# Can't Forget

A novel

by

James Gottesman

**ISBN-** 9 78099 1155712
**JayEddy Publishing**
This is a work of fiction and all characters appearing in this work are fictitious. Any resemblance to real persons, living or dead, is purely coincidental.

## ACKNOWLEDGMENTS

Thanks go to many. Gloria Brown Gottesman, my longtime co-conspirator, read it first and, like always, was brutally honest.

I need to thank the initial readers of the book, all friends, particularly Tony Wartnik, Chuck Caplan, Ruth Bunin, Karen Robertson, Greg Gottesman, Kim Boestom and Leah Formiconi to name a few, who gave me honest criticism.

My book editors, Aviva Layton and Kendall Geisel are amazing. Aviva's Anglo-Aussie-Canadian background can sniff out an overused Yankee cliché from fifty feet away – with a laugh. Always right on. Kendall insight was invaluable and her corrections of my punctuation and grammar made me feel like I was in the second grade again.

I always thank Diane Mackay Richie, the first person to teach me how to write. She may not remember, but I do.

Although I listened to everything and everyone, I didn't always follow all their suggestions. Alas.

DEDICATED

To no one else but Mrs. Brown's Lovely Daughter

*Mrs. Brown, You've Got a Lovely Daughter,* sung by Herman's Hermits, #1 on the U.S. Billboard Hot 100, May 1965

# Can't Forget

## Chapter 1

Hayley Green scanned the vacant waiting room in the 2-West Oncology Suite. Other than the soft breathing of her parents, only the whistling air-conditioning vent above her head provided sound. Empty of people at five thirty p.m., empty of color other than pale blue walls, but mostly, empty of happiness, the room exuded bad news.

Trying to focus on a procedure consent form in her hands, Hayley's thoughts were light-years away, emotionally tuned into a music-less merry-go-round in her head of unanswerable questions in her head – *Who is going to take care of my mother and father?... What happens to my job?... When do I start treatment?...Why? Why me?....*

Hayley's merry-go-round had no off-switch and the litany of whos, whats, whens and whys revolved unendingly, never reaching a conclusion, never having an answer to a single question. The spinning had begun sixty-two hours earlier after a two-day nosebleed prompted a three a.m. rush to the emergency department at Seattle Med, followed by a visit later that morning with her longtime family physician. Hayley's fleeting memory of that tearful meeting was '*...some form of leukemia. I'm so sorry. I'm so very sorry. ...get you to a specialist.*'

Hayley reread the form's header for the fifth time, 'Consent for Bone Marrow Biopsy.' She stopped as the page evaporated into blankness. She curled her knees up on the couch and remounted the merry-go-round.

Hayley sat with her parents, Rachel and Mel Green. That, in itself, was unusual. Since graduation from high school, Hayley had managed her health care independently of her mother. Rachel Green didn't deserve the exclusion but accepted her daughter's nuances. Hayley couldn't remember if her father had ever accompanied her to a doctor.

Although Hayley and Rachel talked daily and loved each other's presence, Rachel Green had long ago stopped questioning her daughter about almost anything medical. In fact, Hayley controlled most aspects of her life and Rachel rarely got an entire sentence of criticism finished before being interrupted.

"She's just wired that way," Rachel would tell friends and herself.

However, Rachel and Mel Green now sat with their daughter when the three came to the unsaid realization that this catastrophe of catastrophes was different.

Rachel gambled and said, "I thought Brad was coming?"

"I guess not," Hayley said, softly. "He's already missed work and you know law firms and new associates. They count every minute and second. He has to keep his billable hours up."

"This is important. You were going to announce the..."

"Stop, please," Hayley interrupted. "Be realistic. Brad's there, but not there. I didn't want to tell you just yet. We talked last night, or more honestly, he griped and I listened."

"And?"

"He suggested we take some time-off until I got my 'medical situation' straightened out. Now I have leukemia and something else called 'medical situation.' I was so wrong about him and I don't want to talk about it."

Small tears appeared and held tight to Hayley's eyelids, refusing to let go. Swollen lids and ruddiness hid large, youthful, olive eyes and satin ivory skin. She looked at her mother's lap, filled with semi-damp tissues under folded hands. Hayley grabbed a used tissue and caught the moistness.

"I'm sorry, sweetie," Rachel said, then quickly changed subjects. "Dr. Marshall was so nice to stay late to see you on short notice." Hayley's mother air-swept the room with her right hand, staring at the walls filled with framed awards and certificates.

Hayley looked at her own hands and then back to her mother's waving hand. *Used to be the same hands.* Tan colored age-spots dotted Rachel Green's parchment-like skin, along with prominent veins and knuckles. *She's getting older.* Hayley squeezed her mother's left hand as the right continued to wave.

Rachel added, "Look at all the awards he's won. He must be good. Everybody says he's the best. I know he took care of Helen…."

Hayley had already tuned out her mother's ramblings when a nurse came into the waiting area, looked at her watch, shook her head, then approached the couch and announced to the otherwise empty room.

"Hello, I'm Kelly Drummond, Dr. Marshall's nurse. I'm sorry it's so late." Drummond, turning to Hayley said, "I assume you're Hayley?" Not waiting for a response, Drummond continued, "Did you read and understand the form? Do you have any questions?"

"I'm good," Hayley lied, without hesitation, as she signed the consent.

Drummond looked past Haley's blank stare to the angst-painted faces of the older couple. When they said nothing, Drummond said, "Please follow me, Miss."

As Hayley stood and stepped to the middle of the room, Drummond turned to Hayley's seated parents. "Mr. and Mrs. Green, the procedure will take about thirty minutes and Hayley should be ready to leave in about forty-five minutes. The results will be back in forty-eight hours. Before you leave today, I'll have an appointment set up for you to meet with Dr. Marshall to discuss the findings and the next steps."

Rachel and Mel Green nodded simultaneously as Rachel added to her small pile of tissues.

Drummond ushered Hayley out of the waiting area and led her down a hallway.

As they walked into the hallway, Hayley said, "Nurse. So you know, I'm twenty-eight years old and have a Master's degree in Social Work and Psychology. I appreciate the conversation with my parents, but you need to address everything to me and only to me. I'll decide what they need to know. Clear?"

Drummond slowed her pace, turned and said, "I'm sorry. I couldn't tell if you were processing everything."

"I probably wasn't."

Drummond squeezed Hayley's hand as they walked through a door marked 'Procedure Room #2.'

Hayley stared at the over-lit, but still lifeless, pale green room. A large, padded mechanical table centered the room. Drummond walked ahead to a cupboard and removed a folded light-blue paper gown.

"Do I really need to undress again?" Hayley semi-whined, knowing the answer. "Dr. Marshall just examined me twenty minutes ago."

"I am afraid so," Drummond replied, handing Hayley a paper gown. "This opens in the back. You'll need to remove your long-sleeved blouse and everything below the waist. I'll be back in a minute so you can undress in private."

"You can stay. I'd like to get this over as quickly as possible."

As Hayley disrobed, Drummond repapered the procedure table's well-worn dull black padding. "Don't tie the waist string. I'd like you to lie here, face down on the table," Drummond added as she smoothed the paper.

*'Looks like butcher paper,'* Hayley thought but said nothing.

As Hayley mounted the table and lay prone, Drummond scurried around the room, gathering supplies to set up a biopsy tray. She applied a blood pressure cuff to Hayley's left arm, took measurements and announced the numbers to herself. "One ten over seventy, pulse seventy-two." Drummond artfully slung the stethoscope around her neck, then opened the back of Hayley's gown and placed a paper sheet over Hayley's bare legs. "Tell me if your legs get cold. I can put on another sheet."

Hayley watched as Drummond opened a package of gauze.

"Which bone do you use?"

Waving the iodine-soaked sponge in a circle, out of Hayley's view, Drummond said, "The iliac crest, it's part of the pelvic bone back here. Don't touch. It's sterile. Okay?" Drummond's 'okay' wasn't a question, but an order.

Drummond turned her head to the door as Dr. Harold Marshall entered the room. Salt and pepper hair and small jowls on a round face exuded confidence and experience, while the sagging lower lids made him to appear tired. He mumbled a few words to Drummond and then came to Hayley's side.

"I see we're ready. Do we have any questions?" Marshall asked.

"No," Hayley said, "but we'd like you to explain what we're doing as we go along."

"Sure," Marshall mumbled, disregarding the mild sarcasm.

"We're ready," Hayley whispered to herself, softly, then shut her eyes. *I'll never be ready. We, who are 'we?' Why do doctors always use 'we?' Do doctors use 'we' when they take care of other doctors? Doubt it. I need to promise that I'll never use 'we' with any of my patients.* Hayley opened her eyes to watch Marshall put on a pair of sterile surgical gloves and withdraw an anesthetic into a needle and syringe from a small bottle that Drummond held at chest level.

"This should sting a little, just for a few seconds," Marshall said.

Seconds later, Hayley responded, "Ouch. Thanks for the warning."

"The rest should be easy," Drummond added. "You may feel a deeper pain for a moment once Dr. Marshall enters the bone marrow. It's important that you remain absolutely still."

Drummond watched Marshall as he worked quickly and confidently. He made a small scalpel nick in the anesthetized skin over Hayley's right pelvic bone. Marshall examined an old-style, large bore, bone marrow biopsy needle that he had used over a thousand times in four decades of practice. The needle kit came with a cumbersome, screw-on, safety guard to prevent the needle from penetrating too deeply. Marshall felt the guard restrained his touch and feel and, per his custom, removed the guard. He then inserted the biopsy needle down to the outer cortex of the bone.

Bone marrow sits between an inner and outer layer of bone. Most marrow biopsies require a moderate amount of force to penetrate the outer layer, or cortical bone. Marshall tried gently first. The needle would rarely penetrate cortical bone with such little effort, but he liked to show a modicum of caution.

"Did you feel that?" Marshall asked.

"No, just a little pressure," Hayley said, her chin now resting on folded hands.

Marshall applied a bit more pressure, this time with a twisting motion. No movement, no penetration.

"You okay?" Marshall asked.

"Yep," Hayley mumbled. "Just some mild pressure."

Marshall then applied firm pressure with twisting, an amount of pressure to which he was accustomed. A unusual loud 'crack' resonated through the room as the needle advanced quickly and deep into Hayley's back.

Three inches deeper than Marshall had ever seen. Three inches past the mark on the biopsy needle where the safety guard had been removed.

Marshall and Drummond echoed the same alarm, "Oh."

At the same moment, Hayley's head lifted off the table and she screamed, "Ow. Ow. Oh my God, that really hurts. That hurts so much."

Dr. Marshall, at first stunned by the depth of the needle, withdrew it completely and held pressure over the puncture site. Drummond stood confused, mouth agape and unable to move.

"Hayley, I'm sorry," Marshall said. "You,... you,... you must have had significant softening to your bone at this spot and the needle went a little too far....Everything will be okay....We'll just try a different spot, a little bit lower, in a moment."

Hayley bit her lower lip, shook her head violently, while her hands clenched the side of the exam table. "Please don't do it again," she pleaded, "I'm in so much pain...I feel horrible..."

Drenched with sweat, Hayley's face appeared pale as faded linen.

"I think I am going to puke," Hayley said, as she tried to raise her head. "I..feel..so..."

Hayley's plaint trailed off as her head fell back to the table, her eyes rolled up, her lids closed softly and then her arms dropped limply towards the floor, dangling like puppet arms after the strings had snapped.

All was quiet.

*_*_*_*

"Dr. Marshall, I think she's fainted," Drummond said.

"Take her blood pressure, would you? She'll be fine in a minute," Marshall replied.

Drummond whipped the stethoscope off her neck and quickly inflated the pressure cuff.

"Eighty over forty and pulse one-O-eight and weak. What should we do?"

"She just fainted," Marshall said, attempting to regain his composure, "Take her pressure again."

Drummond immediately reinflated and deflated the pressure cuff. "Sixty-five, maybe. I can barely hear it. Her heart rate is one forty, if it's even a pulse I even feel." She watched Marshall standing stone still, eyes searching, as if an answer might be written on the walls.

"Well, I've never seen anything like this," Marshall said. "I don't know how that needle got so deep. I guess you'd better call an IV team to start some fluids and let's lower the head of the table."

Drummond stood speechless, unable to move. She had seen countless bone marrow biopsies over the past decade, most by Dr. Marshall and all without complications. She had never seen the biopsy needle track so quickly and deeply. Before taking the cushy, daytime clinic job, Drummond had spent twelve years as an ICU nurse so she had a good idea of untoward events. She had a sense of when something was bad, really bad or terrible.

*Terrible.*

"Kelly, I said lower the head of the table," Marshall repeated, waking Drummond from her self-induced trance.

Drummond now focusing, lowered the head of the procedure table and then ran out to the hallway phone to dial the IV-team pager. The line was busy. Dialed again, busy. Again, busy.

Drummond could hear Dr. Marshall's pleas for help, crescendoing through the hallway. "Kelly. Kelly. Come back, I can't use this damn stethoscope. I can't hear a thing. Kelly. Kelly."

Drummond dialed the IV-team pager once more – busy. *Oh God, this is terrible.*

Drummond made a decision, or more honestly, a gamble, without Dr. Marshall's opinion or approval. She dialed nine-one-nine-one, the hospital emergency paging system, and said, "Kelly Drummond, RN, here. Code Blue Two-West Clinic. Procedure Room Two."

Immediately, the loudspeakers erupted throughout the hospital, "Code Blue Two-West Clinic. Procedure Room Two." Three seconds elapsed and the loudspeakers repeated the message.

Drummond reentered the procedure room to find Dr. Marshall, hands trembling, attempting to take a blood pressure from the limp, pale, and unresponsive patient.

"This damn thing doesn't work," Marshall screamed at Drummond. "I need a better stethoscope, not this piece of shit." He flung the stethoscope over Hayley's body onto the floor in the corner of the room.

"It was working a second ago, Dr. Marshall. I'll get another."

"She just.. just.. fainted," Marshall said, angrily. "I did not authorize a Code Blue. You..you..shouldn't have done…. It's.. it's.. it's not needed. Go back and call it off… and get me an IV team, stat. She just needs some IV fluids. That's all,…. some fluids."

"Dr. Marshall, she's not responding and the head of the table is down," Drummond pleaded, "She's been this way for more than five minutes. I really think we need help."

Drummond knew Marshall would never allow a nurse, even a senior and seasoned veteran like Drummond, to direct him.

"Kelly, go out and call it off. Now, God damn it," Marshall screamed.

"I,…I really...," Drummond mumbled.

Marshall, interrupting, yelled, "Now. Now is now. Do what I tell you."

Drummond turned to the door and was immediately spun around by a team of physicians responding to the Code Blue. She looked to the ceiling, closed her eyes and mumbled to herself, "Thank you, Jesus."

## Chapter 2 – minutes earlier

Benjamin Hunt, M.D., Chief Resident in Surgery, along with two senior residents and two interns walked quickly over the second floor sky-bridge to the west side of the hospital complex to see surgical consultations on the medical wards.

Ben, despite movie-star looks, was not well liked by most of the hospital staff. The residents and nurses referred to him as 'Attila the Hunt.' Penetrating ice blue eyes, a softly chiseled face that appeared perpetually tanned and Charles Atlas build added to the characterization. The moniker was not a compliment and Hunt didn't care. The non-English-speaking staff had a similar 'nom de sonofabitch.' Ben had just started as Chief Resident in Surgery, an R6 position denoting his sixth year of surgical training post medical school.

Opposite the outpatient cancer clinic for private clientele of the medical school faculty, Ben and his team's attention turned to the added decibels of the hospital loudspeakers. "Code Blue - 2 West Clinic, Procedure Room 2." Code Blue denoted a cardiac arrest or some life-threatening emergency. Seconds later the loudspeakers repeated the emergency call.

Less than fifteen yards from the call's origination, Ben stopped for a second and then started to run down a short corridor into the 2-West Oncology clinic followed by his two senior residents and two interns.

"Where's the Code?" Ben shouted at the lone secretary seated behind a huge reception counter.

The young secretary didn't look up from her computer screen and used her left thumb to point over her shoulder. "Behind me, I guess. Dr. Marshall's the only one still here. Down the hallway to your left. Procedure Room #2. Second or third door."

Ben banged his hand on the counter hard enough to knock a box of appointment cards onto the floor, then screamed, "Get your God-damn ass out of that frigging seat and take us there now. I'm not playing hide-and-seek searching for a Code Blue. Move."

The now-frightened secretary sprang from her seat, repeating, "Sorry. Sorry....," opened a door to the clinic area, and scurried in front of Ben until she got to an unmarked open door that led into an almost empty waiting room.

An anxious older couple sat clutching the ends of a couch speaking frantically as the surgical team sped by. "What's happening? Stop. Please, what's...." Both had a hand in the air, waving desperately, like fourth grade students trying to show classmates they knew the answer to a question. Ben and his team took no note as they followed the secretary past the couple into a narrow hallway full of rooms on both sides.

The secretary said, pointing, "In there. In one of the procedure rooms."

As Ben entered the hallway, shouting echoed from an open door twenty feet away. He headed to the sounds, a room marked Procedure Room #2, and entered, running down a nurse trying to exit. Ben righted the falling nurse who looked to the ceiling and mumbled something unintelligible.

Ben yelled back at one of the two interns, Jesse Tavares. "Tavares, gotta be a crash cart somewhere. Find the secretary and get it." Looking to the other intern, Sally Boestom, he said, "Boestom, you stay."

Ben surveyed the room. A young woman lay prone on a procedure table, head tilted downward. He guessed five foot two or three, a hundred and five pounds, motionless and the pale dirty-white color seen in fresh corpses. For all intents, she looked dead, or close to it. Dr. Marshall, a well-known oncologist, stood at the woman's side trying to check her pulse.

"Talk to me. What's happening?" Ben addressed Drummond and Dr. Marshall together.

"You're not the IV team. I needed an IV team," Dr. Marshall, sweat staining the top inch of his white cotton collar, said, "They'll be here in a few minutes. Who, who the hell are you? This is my patient. My patient, do you understand. Where's the IV team?"

Ben disregarded Dr. Marshall's rambling and turned to face Kelly Drummond. "Nurse, talk to me. What happened?"

Drummond, fear pasted on her face, responded, "We were doing a standard iliac crest marrow biopsy on this woman with leukemia. The needle accidently penetrated to its hilt. She had intense pain and then passed out. I've never seen a needle go so deep. Dr. Marshall removed the needle and we thought she'd need just a moment to collect herself, but she's been unconscious and hypotensive since."

"How long?"

"Six, seven minutes. Pulse over one-forty. BPs less than sixty."

Pointing to a small punctate oozing hole on Hayley's right lower back, Ben said, "That's the entry point?"

"Yes."

"Where's the needle?"

She pointed to a six inch, large-bore biopsy needle sitting on a sterile tray. Blood covered the entire length of the needle shaft. The pristine, chrome needle guard sat, unblemished, on the opposite side of the tray.

*She's not eight inches front to back*. "Christ. The needle probably tore the right iliac artery or vein," Ben said, looking back to the patient and the entry point.

Dr. Marshall circled the table and inserted himself between Ben and the unconscious patient.

Marshall demanded, "I'd like you and your team to leave and..."

Ben, looking over Marshall's shoulder at the face of the young woman, disregarded the older man's ranting. Her deep blue lips quivered faintly as if trying to say, "Help me."

Ben, young, tall and running-back strong, overshadowed the

diminutive, seventy-five year old oncologist. Before Marshall could open his mouth to start another disoriented sentence, Ben spun him around, grabbed both shoulders firmly and led him, mouth agape, onto a chair in the corner of the room.

"Do not move, Dr. Marshall. I am sorry but you're in my way. This woman is going to die. She is no longer your patient. She is mine."

Ben turned to Sally Boestom, the remaining intern, and said, "Make sure he doesn't move."

"You have no right to barge in here," Marshall screamed, "You, …you're gonna pay for this and...."

Ben went into trauma mode and tuned out Marshall's ranting. The young woman was critically injured and would die quickly if left alone. She needed no name; wasn't old or young, skinny or fat, pretty or ugly, tall or short, Christian, Jewish, Muslim or atheist. Ben exhibited no emotion. The team had seen this before. Orders would be coming quickly.

Ben turned to his two senior residents, Roy Watson and Bob Feldmar. "Roy, Bob, let's get her on her back and get her head down thirty degrees."

The three flipped the unconscious Hayley onto her back and Watson cranked the table to give the table an additional ten degrees of head down to get more blood from her legs back into circulation. Feldmar unceremoniously pulled Hayley's paper gown off and removed her bra by cutting the bridge between the two cups.

Naked, pale as bone china, cold, clammy to touch and with an abdomen bloated like a woman in her seventh month of pregnancy, Hayley resembled many of the abdominal gun shot and stab wounds presenting to the emergency department. Many died.

"Her belly didn't get distended from fainting," Ben said. "She's bleeding big time." Turning to the nurse, Ben continued directives,

"Get to the other side and keep doing blood pressure checks and reporting the numbers." Drummond moved around the table as Ben continued giving orders and asking questions. "Is there an IV setup in the procedure room? We need access now."

Drummond pointed to the corner of the room behind the door where an intravenous stand held a bag of fluids.

"Roy, Bob, get an IV running with Ringer's Lactate in one arm or the other."

The nurse yelled, "Seventy-five over forty, pulse one thirty," as Jesse Tavares rolled a large, red 'crash-cart' into the room loaded with resuscitation equipment.

Watson yelled, "I can get a line in her left elbow crease. Tavares, what do you have?"

Tavares handed Watson a large IV needle from the cart.

"Seventy over forty. Pulse one twenty," yelled Drummond.

Moments later, Watson announced, "Line's in and IV running."

Ben looked quickly into the corner. "Boestom, leave Dr. Marshall and squeeze the IV bag. When the bag is empty, replace it with another bag of Ringer's Lactate. Don't ask, just squeeze and replace bags." Ben eyed the stunned Dr. Marshall and said, "Don't even think about moving."

Ben then looked to Kelly Drummond. "Nurse, we need bags of IV fluids from the cart. Help Dr. Boestom swap bags when this one's done." Ben turned to the other intern. "Tavares, we need a gurney. Then call the OR, clear a room, any room and get a full vascular setup and anesthesia. Tell them we're in the outpatient clinic and we've got a deep stab wound to the abdomen. We'll be rolling the patient into the OR in four to five minutes. Then call the blood bank. We need six units of O-neg blood, stat."

"Seventy over forty. Pulse one twenty," Drummond said, standing ready with another bag of IV fluids, then ran out of the room to help Tavares find a gurney.

"First liter in. Another started," shouted Boestom.

"Keep pumping, Sally," Watson and Ben said in unison.

The gurney arrived and Watson, Feldmar and Ben transferred Hayley as if she had levitated from the table. Boestom moved from the procedure table to the side of the gurney to keep pumping IV fluids.

"Seventy-five over fifty. Pulse one twenty-four."

Tavares returned. "Chief. Got the OR and blood bank working."

"Tavares, dial the OR front desk on your cell phone, leave it on speaker, and give it to me. 251 20 20," Ben shouted, "then get your ass to the elevator bank below the OR. Push the 'up' button and hold the first elevator until we get there. Get everyone off. Don't take shit from anyone. Move."

"Main OR, Peter Nelson," the speaker on the cell phone answered.

"Pete. Ben Hunt here. Listen, don't talk. I have a stab wound to the abdomen in the 2-West clinic. The patient is bleeding out. We'll be pushing the patient through the front door of the OR in three minutes. I want an OR room cleared, full vascular setup, two scrubs, two circulators and two anesthesiologists. Get them from anywhere. I'll take full responsibility. Three minutes and we're there." Ben looked around the room. "Boestom, can you move onto the gurney and keep pumping the fluids."

"I think so," Boestom said, and the five-foot-tall intern climbed onto the gurney, straddled Hayley's legs and continued to squeeze IV bags of fluids.

"Let's go. Boestom, duck your head at every doorway. Nurse, get a sheet over her."

Exiting the room, Kelly Drummond threw a sheet over Hayley's nakedness.

Watson and Feldmar pushed the gurney through the waiting room and past Hayley's speechless parents. Ben took no note of the man's cry of "Wait, what's happening? Hayley…Hayley."

The gurney sped over the sky bridge, down the hallway into the main corridor leading to the hospital and a bank of elevators below the operating rooms.

As soon as the group cleared into the corridor, Ben bolted ahead. "You guys push. I'll check that Tavares has the elevator secured and then take the stairs up to the OR. The gurney goes directly in."

Ben took off at full speed and reached the elevators to find Jesse Tavares arguing with a group of semi-irate evictees after he had successfully commandeered the elevator.

Ben hollered as he approached. "Everyone back off, this intern is holding the elevator for an emergency. Back off."

As the gurney approached, Ben turned to enter the stairwell next to the elevators, ran up one flight, opened the door and turned left into the OR.

"Pete, where are we?"

"7-North."

"The gurney will be here in fifteen seconds. Get them down there."

Ben ran north, then west and entered OR 7-North. Two anesthesiologists, Bob Fink and Harry Gordon were opening sterile bags of anesthetic equipment. Two nurses were dumping sterile trays of surgical tools onto two large tables. Ben knew both nurses, Polly Sawa and Diane Hopper, both excellent and experienced hands.

Already in scrubs, Ben put on a surgical hat and mask, washed his hands for ten seconds, instead of the usual two minutes, and then quickly backed through the swinging door into the operating room. Diane Hopper, acting as circulating nurse, had his gown and gloves ready.

Each second counted.

The gurney rolled into the room and Sally Boestom jumped off onto the floor, squeezing the IV bag all the while. Watson and Feldmar, still dressed in street clothes, lifted the unconscious patient onto the OR table.

"I don't feel a pulse and she's not responsive, but the EKG shows a rhythm," Bob Fink, the secondary anesthesiologist, shouted.

Ben painted iodine compound onto the still nameless patient's abdomen, threw sterile towels along the sides of her abdomen and placed a large drape over the entire area.

Harry Gordon, the primary anesthesiologist, exclaimed, "Give me a sec; I've got to get her intubated."

Ben and the nurses stopped working for ten seconds. "Done, tube in," Gordon announced. "She's deep and non-responsive. I haven't given her anything yet."

Hayley hadn't moved during the intubation, which confirmed the lack of sufficient oxygen to her brain. As soon as the breathing tube was in place, Bob Feldmar placed a large bore IV into the large vein in her neck and threaded IV tubing down into her heart.

Feldmar announced, "Central line in. IVs running wide open.""

"BP is sixty. Rate one fifty."

Hopper moved the surgical trays next to the OR table as Polly Sawa stepped up on a stool at the foot of the table. Ben, facing Watson across Hayley's abdomen, said, "Scalpel. Stand back. Blood's gonna be everywhere."

Ben made a skin incision from above the patient's belly button to the pubic bone. A second, deeper cut, of the same length opened into the abdomen. Blood, much of it clotted, spewed over the edges of the incision. Ben put direct hand pressure over the bleeding vessels shutting off all blood flow to and from her right leg and pelvis. Using suction, Watson freed the abdomen of blood.

Ben told Hopper, "Diane, keep time as of now. I need to know how long we have the circulation to the leg stopped. I don't think I can safely let go of the artery until we get her medically stable and get some blood in the room."

"Ninety over fifty. I can feel a pulse," shouted Fink. "Rate one ten. We're making progress."

The OR doors opened and Armin Cassetti, Chairman of Surgery entered the room. "Ben, what the hell's going on here? Get me up to speed."

Without looking away from the patient's abdomen, Ben said, "Young woman with probable leukemia. Dr. Marshall put a bone marrow biopsy needle through the right iliac crest into her iliac vessels. She's lost five to six units and should have been dead."

"Need help?"

"Thanks Chief, I think we'll be okay. I suspect Dr. Marshall's out front, screaming and hollering. I had to be a little forceful. You might check on that."

"BP is now ninety-five over sixty," shouted Dr. Gordon. "Pulse ninety-six. She's requiring anesthetic, so she's getting blood flow to her brain again. First unit of blood will be running in twenty seconds."

"You've had pressure on the vessels for eleven minutes, thirty seconds," Hopper announced.

"Bob, I'm going to let go," Ben said, "so we can get a better look. You'll need to be ready to hold pressure on the vessels above and below the injury. Here we go."

Ben released his hand pressure from the vessels as he and Watson got a quick look at the injury. "Bob, pressure now," Ben said.

Watson replaced Hunt's hands in position to compress the vessels and stem the bleeding.

"Ben, she lost another half of unit of blood in that fifteen second look," Fink said, looking at the suction container at the head of the table.

"Seems like the good doctor hath biopsied both the front and back of her right common iliac vein," Ben said. "I can see the exit wound on the front, so an entrance wound must be on the back wall. Get another six units of O-neg blood and two six packs of platelets."

"Here's the plan," Ben said after hesitating for a moment "First, I get the common iliac artery freed and Bob puts a vascular clip on it to stop all the blood flow to the leg. Next, we free up the vein above and below the injury and place tourniquets to stop all blood flow. Then open the vein in the front, suture the entrance wound on the back and close the vein."

Ben paused for a second to see if Dr. Cassetti or anyone had another idea. The room silenced for a moment other than the intermittent whooshing of air from the anesthesiologist's breathing machine.

Cassetti, who had yet to leave the OR, stood on a stool to get a better vantage point, broke the silence and said, "Ben, I agree. Go for it."

Ben quickly looked over the drapes to the anesthesiologists, "I need blood going in as fast as possible. We're likely to lose another couple units in less than five minutes. You guys okay?"

"We're set," Fink said.

Ben looked at Watson and Feldmar. "I'll need both of you suctioning blood until I get control. Ready...Go."

Ben freed the common iliac artery and Feldmar applied a temporary vascular clip. Next, Ben freed the injured vein, above and below the injury and circled it with elastic tourniquets. Three units of blood were lost in fourteen minutes. Ben opened the injured vein above and below the puncture wound.

"Four-O Prolene…."

Sawa, a step ahead, had already loaded a needle holder with the correct vascular suture and needle and slapped it firmly into Ben's palm.

"...on a RV-One," Ben said, finishing the sentence.

Ben closed the hole on the back of the vein, then used a fresh suture to close the front. Ben then released the arterial clamp and venous tourniquets. All bleeding had stopped.

Drs. Fink and Gordon, peering over the sheets, uttered in tandem, "Amazing."

Armin Cassetti had returned and watched the procedure over the anesthesiologist's shoulder. "Great work, Ben. I don't know that anyone, including yours truly, could have done what you just did. I'll go out and tell Dr. Marshall. He's not happy but I'll try to pull him away from the family and explain things. In my opinion, if you weren't in the hallway outside Marshall's clinic at the time of the Code Blue, she's dead."

"Not just me, Chief," Ben said. "Watson and Feldmar, Tavares and Boestom, Diane and Polly, both gas passers. All needed to be on their game. A one hundred percent team effort."

Everyone in the room stood a little taller.

"Great work, everybody." Cassetti said. "I'm going back to try and calm Marshall."

*_*_*_*_

Ben returned to the locker room, showered, changed into fresh scrubs and started towards the surgical waiting area. He stopped in the stairwell to place a call into the OR.

"OR 7-North, Diane Hopper."

"Hey, Diane, this is Ben. What's this patient's name? Never thought to look."

"Hayley Green. You need her record number?"

"Nope, thanks, I've got to find the family."

"Dr. Hunt. Great job today. I mean it," said Hopper.

"Diane, great job on your part and Polly's too. You make me look good. When I walked into the room and saw the two of you, I said to myself, we're going to be all right. I swear."

"Thanks, Dr. Hunt. I'll tell Polly too. Let us know how she does."

"Oh, another thing," said Ben. "When you guys are done, I'd like the whole team to come down to the surgical waiting area. I may need some backup when I talk to Dr. Marshall."

"Sure," Hopper said. "We'll come down when we've cleaned up in here."

Ben continued down two flights of stairs, entering the large surgical waiting area, usually packed during the day but expectedly mostly empty in the early evening. Ben re-approached the familiar receptionist at the surgical information desk. "Joni, where might the Hayley Green family be?" he asked.

"No one with that name on the schedule, Dr. Hunt," said the receptionist, scanning a large printout.

"It was an emergency. Did Dr. Cassetti come down and talk to a family?"

"He did. We put that family in Private Suite #4. There's a note here that you're not to enter until you talk to Dr. Marshall. He had me clear out Suite #6 about half an hour ago. He wasn't very pleasant."

"I would have guessed not," said Ben.

"You're supposed to wait there until he comes and not to see the family. I'll call him to let him know you're here."

"Thanks. Is Dr. Cassetti still around?"

"I don't think so. Let me ask Susan." Joni swiveled to the other receptionist, whispered something and the receptionist whispered back.

"Dr. Cassetti left five minutes ago," Joni said. "He told Susan to tell you not to lose your cool and that you aren't dealing with a resident. He said you'd know what he's talking about."

Ben entered Private Suite #6. Two couches, three chairs, some end tables and a small sink. A flat screen TV hung on the wall tuned to a children's cartoon. Ben turned off the TV, sat on a couch, put his head back against the wall and closed his eyes.

Dr. Harold Marshall entered the suite minutes later. Ben stood and put his hands behind his back. Ben knew Dr. Marshall but doubted that Marshall knew his name. Marshall didn't normally take note of residents outside of the Department of Oncology.

Dr. Marshall had been in practice at Seattle Med for more than forty-five years and was the pre-eminent medical oncologist in the region for most of his career. Marshall's clinical research into adjuvant therapy for breast cancer was seminal work and still quoted widely. He had been the invited speaker at various meetings around the world and had met with President Obama at a White House dinner honoring national leaders in cancer research.

"Dr. Marshall, I'm Ben Hunt and I just...," Ben started.

Marshall didn't hesitate a second to interrupt. He came within an arm's length of Ben and pointed a wagging finger at Ben's face. "Who the hell do you think you are? You, without cause or justification, took over my patient's care. In my book, that's assault. You had no permission. This is not going to go well for you."

"Dr. Marshall, I don't want to get into a battle with you," Ben said calmly. "First, let me tell you that I believe you to be an outstanding and caring physician, a leader and I respect your contributions to oncology and.."

"I don't give a shit about that, young man," Marshall interrupted again. "You assaulted me and you assaulted my patient. I will have you drummed out of medicine. I swear. Cassetti tried to sweet talk me out of reporting you. I didn't buy a word of his bullshit."

Ben said nothing as his jaw muscles clenched, vice-like, giving his head a slight tremor. He took a deep breath waiting for Marshall to finish his diatribe. "Dr. Marshall, medicine is medicine and surgery is surgery. When your patient sustained a stab wound with a biopsy needle through and through her common iliac vein, she was no longer your patient. She was mine. I did what I had to do to save her life. I am glad to discuss this at length, but you may feel that it would be my views against yours. Right now, I believe that I need to talk to this patient's family and get them squared away. We still don't know how she might do and what kind of recovery she'll make, particularly neurologically."

"She would have been fine if you had left her alone, as I demanded. She had merely fainted."

Ben heard a soft knock on the door and turned to see Watson and Feldmar through the tinted window. "I have asked my surgical team, anesthesia and nurses to come down and talk to you. I have not prepped them in any way. I would appreciate it if you'd talk to them while I talk to the family."

Ben turned away from Marshall and opened the door. Roy Watson, Bob Feldmar, Polly Sawa, Diane Hopper, and Bob Fink entered.

"Dr. Marshall, this is Roy Watson and Bob Feldmar, my senior surgical residents and assistants in surgery, Polly Sawa and Diane Hopper, the surgical nurses, and Bob Fink from anesthesia." Ben then left to find Hayley Green's family.

*_*_*_*

Dr. Fink spoke first. "Hello, Dr. Marshall. You may remember me. You took care of my mother, Helen Fink for ovarian cancer a few years ago. I want to thank you again for all you did."

Fink hesitated. Marshall had not acknowledged a single word Fink had said and continued glaring at the door though which Ben just exited.

Fink waited for Dr. Marshall to turn his attention back to the team of doctors in the room before continuing, "Dr. Marshall, what Dr. Hunt just accomplished is one of the most incredible surgical exercises that I have ever seen. Your patient was, in my view, as close to clinically dead as one could be when she arrived in the OR. We intubated her without an anesthetic. She received no sedation of any kind for over five minutes corroborating my statement that her brain was not perfusing. I think that Dr. Feldmar and Watson can fill you in on the surgical aspects of what Dr. Hunt found and did."

Ten minutes later, the surgical team left the consultation suite. Dr. Marshall slumped in a chair, beaten and wrong.

## Chapter 3

Ben entered Private Suite #4, standing in the doorway for a moment to let the three occupants gather their thoughts. CNN News played on the TV monitor with the sound muted to a whisper. The room occupants cared little about anything else in the world.

Ben quickly surveyed the room. On a large couch in the middle of the suite sat Hayley's parents, Mel and Rachel Green.

Mel, late middle age, burly-white-buffalo large, sat on one edge of a large couch. Ben surmised that Mel stood taller than Ben's six one. Mel sat leaning forward, elbows on his knees and head bent down between his legs. He did not look up, oblivious to Ben's entry.

Rachel, similar vintage, alert, very attractive and petite towards delicate, sat straight up and turned quickly. "Mel. Somebody's here," she said.

Deidre Williams, Hayley's best friend, a young, tall, athletic-looking black woman, sat across from the Greens, reading a magazine. She looked up but did not move, as if unsure of what protocol to follow.

Mel turned his head towards Ben and then stood quickly from the head-down position. Ben knew immediately that Mel Green had risen too rapidly, almost jumping off the couch. Mel wobbled and Ben rushed to his side and helped him regain his seat.

Rachel, now on her feet, realized Ben had prevented a calamity without missing a step. She said, "Thank you."

Ben kneeled next to Mel, took his wrist and casually felt his pulse. "Feel better?" Ben asked.

"I think I'm okay now. I got dizzy," Mel said.

"From that position," Ben said, "to stand up quickly, most humans, even in good shape will faint."

Ben then stood next to Rachel Green, her head coming to Ben's mid-chest, and shook hands with her. "I'm Dr. Ben Hunt and a chief resident in surgery. I assume that you are the parents of Hayley….."

"Please tell us, is Hayley okay?" Rachel interrupted. "I'm her mother. Is she okay?"

"I think so," said Ben.

"What does that mean? Think so?" Rachel asked.

"First, let's all sit down," Ben said.

Rachel and Mel sat back on the couch and Deidre moved next to them. Ben moved the chair vacated by Deidre and slid it in front of the couch and sat.

"As I said, I'm Ben Hunt. A Chief Resident in the Department of Surgery."

"I'm sorry. I didn't mean to be rude," said Rachel. She then introduced herself, Mel and Deidre.

"Your daughter is in the surgical ICU," Ben said. "She's not fully awake yet so I can't completely assess her recovery. We'll know more in a few hours and maybe not completely for a day or two."

"ICU?" asked Rachel.

"Intensive Care Unit."

"I think I knew that," Rachel said. "Can you tell us what happened? Hayley went into a procedure room to have what sounded like a simple biopsy of her bone marrow. Four hours later, we are sitting here in the dark, scared to death."

"Dr. Marshall was here earlier," interjected Mel, "but was very non-committal, other than she had some bleeding during her biopsy. He seemed very upset. A Dr. Cassetti or Carpetti did come in to say that Hayley was in the operating room for a bleeding blood vessel and that a surgeon, I presume you, would be down to talk to us. So, what happened? We still don't know."

"I'll try to explain," Ben said. "The bone marrow biopsy is usually an uncomplicated procedure, particularly when done by someone with Dr. Marshall's experience. The important word here is 'usually'. Unluckily, the outer layer of the bone, normally incredibly hard, even with leukemia, had thinned at the random spot Dr. Marshall had chosen to do the biopsy. The biopsy needle went through the entire bone into your daughter's abdomen. Just under that bone is a large vein, called the common iliac vein, which brings blood back from the leg and the pelvis to the heart. The needle penetrated the common iliac vein and your daughter started to bleed internally."

Rachel and Mel Green softly nodded in unison, as if to say "And?"

Ben hesitated, then added a small lie to the facts. "Dr. Marshall then called a Code Blue and my surgical team was fortunately nearby and responded. Once we understood the magnitude of her injury, we rushed her to the operating room and repaired the injured vessel."

"Why couldn't it be fixed where she was?" Mel asked.

"Although the biopsy was done from the back, we had to make an incision on Hayley's abdomen to approach the injury. She lost a fair amount of blood before we were able to operate but she's young and strong and we are hoping for a full recovery. Again, we'll know more in the next few hours and days about any side effects from the injury and the surgery."

The door to the room opened slowly and Dr. Marshall entered. Everyone stood and when Dr. Marshall sat in an unoccupied chair, all resumed sitting.

Marshall spoke to the Greens and their friend in a calm and soothing tone, surprising to Ben after their tête–à–tête minutes earlier. "I was being brought up to date by Dr. Hunt's team about Hayley's injury. I am not sure what Dr. Hunt has told you but we are hoping that she will make a full recovery."

Ben nodded. *I used the same exact words.*

Deidre Williams, Hayley's friend, spoke up from the side. "Dr. Marshall, what type of side effects are you exactly worried about?"

Dr. Marshall turned to defer to Ben, "Dr. Hunt."

"Well, there are two major things we are worried about right now," Ben responded. "Hayley lost a fair amount of blood, so her blood pressure was very low and she lost consciousness. She's still asleep from the anesthetic so we aren't able to assess any damage to her brain."

Rachel Green grabbed Mel's arm and emitted a low and breathy, "Oh, dear."

Ben continued, "Yes, but I am hopeful that her youth and general good health will have protected her. We'll know more when the anesthetic wears off. In these types of cases, we'll keep breathing for her awhile with a tube in her throat. 'Awhile' meaning hours to days depending on how she does on her own. We'll be able to assess many things in the next hour, but not everything until she's communicating. That won't happen until the tube is out of her throat."

Rachel Green was leaning on her husband and Deidre moved to hold Rachel's free hand.

"The other issue is the right leg," Ben continued. "We had to stop the blood flow to and from her right leg temporarily to repair the injury. We won't know her leg function, strength and sensation until she's awake."

The room was quiet as Hayley's family digested Ben's comments.

"Let me call up to the ICU and see what's happening now," Ben said. "I'll take you up there as soon as possible. Maybe Dr. Marshall can answer any questions you have for him."

Ben left the consultation suite, telephoned the ICU and asked the secretary to patch him into Hayley Green's room.

"Rose Onti, RN, here."

"Hey, Rose, it's Ben Hunt. You're taking care of Hayley Green?"

"Yep."

"What's happening?"

"Well, she doesn't like the tube, that's for sure. Vitals okay. Making urine. Pain's hard to assess. We've had to keep her sedated for the endotracheal tube. I secured both arms in soft restraints to keep her from yanking the damn thing out. I think you'll be able to extubate her by morning."

"Is she moving her legs?"

"Moving," Onti exclaimed. "She's tried to kick me with both of them, so I have to say a definite 'yes' on that score."

"Great. Is it okay to bring in the parents?" Ben asked.

"Give me five minutes to clean up some mess. Sure, bring them up."

Ben returned to the suite and all eyes, including Marshall's, turned to him – pleading for information.

Ben smiled. "Good news and good news. She's awake and fighting the tube in her throat. Very positive sign. The ICU nurses had to restrain her arms to keep her from pulling something out. Better yet, she tried to kick the nurse with both legs. I think you get the picture that her leg is working fine. If you like, we can all go into the ICU for a moment. Your presence might calm her a bit. There's a waiting lounge in the ICU after you see her."

Dr. Marshall said to Ben, "I'll let you go up with the Greens and I'll follow later. Thank you, Dr. Hunt." Marshall turned towards Rachel Green and said, "Hayley's in excellent hands with Dr. Hunt. We were fortunate that he was close by."

*_*_*_*

Once in the elevator, Mel said, "Hayley's our only child. She's a clinical psychologist with a Master's degree in social work."

Ben uttered a barely audible, "A psychologist. Hmmph. Really." *That's too bad.*

"She's a Washington State employee working for the Department of Social and Health Services or DSHS," Rachel continued, "and spends half her time counseling and the other half maintaining a large group of patients on welfare in the central district. We wanted her to be a concert pianist but she didn't have the fortitude to practice. Actually, she hated it. She is so smart and could have been anything. Anyway, always the do-gooder, she wanted to help people. She and Deidre went to UC Berkeley and Hayley came back here for her master's degree in social work and counseling at Seattle U. We were hoping that…."

The elevator door opening allowed Ben to interrupt. "Follow me."

Before entering Hayley's ICU room, Ben gave the Greens and Deidre thumbnail sketch of the myriad of tubes and wires attached to Hayley.

Hayley's ICU nurse, Rose, came out into the hallway, introduced herself and added, "Before you go in I need to warn you that I just gave Hayley some IV morphine. She's heavily sedated. I don't expect her to respond much, or at all. Don't be alarmed."

A white sheet covered Hayley from toes to chest. Over her head, three monitors in various shades of green, red, blue and yellow spewed out a constant barrage of waves, numbers, spikes and beeping noises.

Rachel approached first, as she took in the dense forest of tubes, monitors, machines and IVs surrounding her only child. Tears slowly ran down her cheeks. The morning's mascara had been washed away hours earlier.

Hayley, eyes closed, appeared to be sleeping. A breathing tube exited Hayley's left nostril, held in place by crisscrossing, distorting bands of white adhesive tape. A bright blue surgical bonnet and the glistening white tape offset her dull pallor, a skin tone her mother had never imagined on her daughter.

Rachel's shaking hand reached out to touch her daughter's face but withdrew it quickly and looked to Ben. "I'm afraid I might disturb something important."

Ben watched Rachel Green's hesitation. "You can't hurt anything," Ben said. "Everything is secure." He purposefully wiggled the tubes and wires surrounding Hayley randomly. "See?"

Hayley, apparently deeply sedated, remained still other than her chest rising and falling with the rhythmic, whooshing, breathing machine.

Rachel tried smiling as her right hand, still unsteady, started back into the maze of wires and tubes towards Hayley's face. Her hand stopped three-quarters of the way and pulled back. "I'm sorry, Dr. Hunt. I'm afraid."

Ben moved behind Rachel and gently held her right wrist. "We'll do it together the first time," Ben said. With that, he moved Rachel's hand toward her daughter's cheek, letting go when they were an inch away. Ben couldn't help seeing the resemblance between mother and daughter. *Both beautiful.*

"Thank you," Rachel said as she slowly brushed Hayley's left cheek, expecting her to remain asleep. Between her own deep breaths, Rachel pleaded, "Hayley, we're here for you, Dad and I… Be strong... You're going to be….."

Hayley's eyes fluttered, then opened. She blinked twice, unable to focus, but turned her head towards the comforting and familiar voice and then lipped the words, "Mom. Mom." Her left hand was moving under the sheets and Ben pulled the sheets down to uncover her wrist bound in a soft restraint. Hayley put her thumb up, the universal OK sign.

Rachel spun to Mel and Deidre. "She's going to be fine. She's going to be fine." She pulled her husband down to her height, grabbed him about the neck and started to bawl. "She's going to be fine." Rachel next turned to Ben, put her arms around his chest and said, "Thank you. Thank you, so much."

Ben remained emotionless. *They're forgetting she has leukemia.*

Mel took a tissue from his wife's hands, wiped the moisture from his eyes and leaned over the bed's handrail, through parted tubes, to give his daughter a kiss on the forehead. Rachel did the same.

Hayley's eyes closed again.

The nurse put her hand on Rachel's shoulder and squeezed gently. "Mrs. Green, I'm impressed your daughter was able to communicate. One tough girl. I'd be surprised if we have to keep the tube in her throat very long. You're right, I think she's going to be fine."

*_*_*_*

Hayley's vital signs remained stable throughout the afternoon and early evening. Rachel and Mel Green had returned home but Hayley's friend, Deidre, remained at the bedside.

Ben returned to the ICU at eleven fifteen p.m. Hayley, heavily sedated, remained asleep. Ben nodded hello to Deidre, then reviewed Hayley's progress on the bedside computer screens.

Looking at Deidre, Ben asked, "Could you please step out of the room for a moment? I need to examine her."

Deidre stood and walked into the hallway but could still see into the room through the slightly tinted hallway window.

She watched as Ben, without hesitation, pulled back the bed sheet. A loose cotton hospital gown draped Hayley to her knees. Ben pulled the gown up, uncovering Hayley from the chest down, listened to her lungs with his stethoscope, and examined her abdomen. Ben then logrolled Hayley towards himself, pulled the small bandage off the needle entrance wound, found no bleeding and allowed Hayley to roll back. He then pulled her hospital gown back down to cover her torso and examined her groin, legs and feet to check for skin temperature and pulses. Ben lowered the gown to cover Hayley's legs and replaced the bed sheet.

"Obviously, no one gives a shit about modesty in this place,"

Deidre mumbled, greeting Ben as he walked into the hallway.

Ignoring the remark, Ben said, "Her leg is warm and pink and the pulses are good. She ought to be okay from what happened today. Do you have any questions?"

"First, I'd like to thank you for helping Hayley. From what the nurses and residents have said, she's lucky to have lived. She's been my best friend since third grade. I don't know what I'd do if we lose her."

Ben hesitated then said, "I said she'd be okay from what happened today. I didn't say she'd be okay from her leukemia. They'll have to repeat the bone marrow biopsy when she's stronger. She's received seven units of blood and they'll probably have to wait for the foreign blood to get out of her system before doing the repeat biopsy. Then she's likely to need a bone marrow transplant."

"We knew all that. Who will do the repeat biopsy?" Deidre asked.

"That'll be up to Hayley or her family," Ben said. "Dr. Marshall has an excellent reputation and has probably done more biopsies than any two people at Seattle Med. That said, I think he'd understand if Hayley switches oncologists."

Deidre nodded acceptance. "Hayley will make the decision. That's her personality. How long will she be in the ICU?"

"If she keeps doing this well, maybe day after tomorrow."

"Thank you, Dr. Hunt."

"Hey, you're really tall," Ben declared, realizing Deidre was as tall as he.

"I played b-ball at Cal Berkeley."

Smiling, Ben added, "I assume that Hayley didn't play ball with you?"

"No. Not after fourth grade. I was already a head taller. We've been best friends forever. She's the smartest person I've ever known. She has a second sense about people and what makes them tick. That's the good."

"What's the bad?" Ben asked.

"She's a pig-headed, know-it-all, bulldog."

"Like most psychologists," Ben added with a touch of sarcasm.

"I don't know about that. She's really good at her job. More importantly, she's the most loyal friend anyone could ever have."

"That's good, I guess."

"Our freshman year at Cal, she picked a fight with a drunken fan three times her size. The guy wouldn't stop heckling me. She didn't care how big he was, so she poured a can of beer over his head."

"She lived."

"Luckily, the guy's friends kept him from strangling her," Deidre laughed. "Not that I haven't thought about doing it myself a few times.

"What do you do now?" Ben asked.

"Law school, then the FBI."

"You on duty?" Ben asked, smiling and holding both hands up.

"Always."

Ben nodded his respect. "Anyway, let's get your friend out of here in one piece. She's got a long tough road ahead of her."

*_*_*_*

Hayley had her breathing tube removed at six forty-five the next morning.

"What happened? Where am I?" were Hayley's first raspy words.

Standing at Hayley's side, Ben said, "You're in the ICU at Seattle

Med."

"My stomach is killing me."

"You started bleeding from a blood vessel in your abdomen and I had to operate. The bone marrow biopsy......"

Hayley, still sedated, dozed off before Ben finished the sentence.

Two days later, Hayley transferred out of the ICU to a regular surgical ward, 6-South.

## Chapter 4

Sue Taper, a senior staff nurse, aided Hayley into her first post-operative shower, six days after the surgery. Taper left the bathroom door ajar and returned to the hospital room to check medications when she heard sobbing mixed with running water. Returning to the bathroom, Taper knew enough not to intervene. Taper had seen and heard reports of Hayley crying intermittently for the past three nursing shifts.

"I'm sorry. I don't mean to get so emotional. I'm just scared," Hayley said, emerging from the shower.

Helping Hayley back into her hospital bed, Taper offered an ear, "I've got a little time. Wanna talk about it?"

Hayley wiped her tears with her hospital gown. "Thanks but no. Not now."

Taper stood her ground, not accepting the refusal.

After a long moment of silence, as the tears reappeared on her cheeks, Hayley held Taper's hand and said, "I don't know what's going to happen. I don't know what to do. I don't know how to prepare. Maybe later."

"Have you had a chance to talk to someone about all this? A professional?" Taper asked.

"I am a psychologist," Hayley said, emphasizing the 'am', "and whomever I talk to isn't going to make my leukemia go away. I've got to retake control of my life."

"Can't hurt to talk," opined Taper.

"I agree, but right now, I just feel like crying."

"I get it," Taper said, then changed topics. "By the way, the nurses and residents are still talking about your surgery. Amazing."

Hayley asked, "Dr. Hunt does this all the time?"

"No. Rarely, actually. Your situation was from a staged episode of

E.R. or some TV movie."

"What's Dr. Hunt like?" Hayley said, trying to be subtle, but failing.

"Which Dr. Hunt?"

"There are two Dr. Hunts?" Hayley asked, clearly confused.

"One person, two personas," Taper said. "There's the nice Dr. Hunt and the out-of-control Dr. Hunt."

Taper tied Hayley's gown in back, plumped up two pillows and continued, "The nice one is an incredible teacher, to the nurses and to the residents. He once spent an hour of his time, which he didn't have, teaching me the intricacies of chest tubes. He was so patient, making sure I understood everything. Few doctors do that kind of stuff."

"And the other?" Hayley asked.

"The out-of-control one is well, uh," Taper said then hesitated. "Let's just say he's out of control. I've seen him get mad at the simplest mistake and lose all self-control. Scary when he's like that. It's gotten him into hot water with the department on more than a few occasions."

"Wow," Hayley mumbled.

As Taper exited the room she turned. "You didn't hear any of this from me."

Taper called the OR and left a message for Dr. Hunt to call.

Forty minutes later, Hunt called the floor.

"Hey, Sue. What's up?"

"Miss Green in 642. She's doing great surgically, but she's an emotional firecracker. I think she needs to talk to someone."

"Sue, she's a psychologist. She'll figure out when she needs to see someone, as if that's going to help."

"You have something against psychologists?" Taper asked.

"Other than finding them self-serving and worthless, no. Never did much for me. She'll figure it out."

Taper added, "Ouch. Do you mind if I handle this?"

"Do what you want. I don't care. Gotta go."

The line went dead. "That's the one I don't like," Taper said to the phone.

*_*_*_*

Later that day, Hayley made a request to one of Hunt's junior residents, Dr. Ralph Yamamoto. Yamamoto seemed to take special interest in Hayley and often returned after rounds to re-explain her surgical status in simpler terms.

"From here on out," Hayley told Yamamoto, "I'd like all discussion about me to occur in my room, rather than the hallway outside. I can hear you talking about me. Even if I don't understand everything, I'd feel less out of the loop. I can ask questions later."

"I'll ask Dr. Hunt," Yamamoto replied. "Can't promise anything. It's not the usual way he does things."

That evening, Ben and his surgical team entered Hayley's room and discussed her status, which was improving quickly.

Hayley watched Ben closely. *He never makes eye contact with me and rarely talks to me directly.*

As the residents started to file out of her room, Hayley asked, "Dr. Hunt. Excuse me. When will I get the IV out?"

"One of the residents will be back later to explain," Hunt said, without facing Hayley.

Later, Hayley queried two other nurses about Hunt's behavior.

"Really nice except when he's really, really mean," summed up the totality of their impressions.

"Why does Dr. Hunt act so distant?" Hayley asked Yamamoto who had returned to check an IV. "Is he like that with everyone? Did I do something wrong?"

"I don't know that you've done anything wrong, but he's not like that with most patients," Yamamoto responded. "Dr. Hunt hasn't said anything other than he has a definite negativity against psychologists. He said they're useless. Not sure why."

"I know why," Hayley declared. "He's an idiot."

"Actually he's really smart. That said, when he gets angry, he doesn't have much control. Maybe he's seen psychologists before and didn't like what they told him. Just a guess and you didn't hear me say that, okay?"

*I've heard that before.*

*_*_*_*

Not unexpectedly, Dr. Marshall voluntarily withdrew himself from Hayley's care. Dr. Solomon Capland, a medical oncologist, with credentials as solid as Marshall's agreed to take over Hayley's care.

*_*_*_*

On the next day's surgical rounds after reviewing Hayley's progress, Ben announced, "When Miss Green is stable and eating, we'll need to transfer her to MedOnc and Dr. Capland. Day after tomorrow, maybe."

"Dr. Hunt, do you think I could talk to you alone for a moment?" Hayley asked, as the team was about to leave to continue rounds.

Ben told the team to wait outside. Shuffling out of Hayley's room into the hallway, the entire team, including medical students and nurses, gave a "Hmmm" collectively to razz Ben.

As Ben shut the door, Sally Boestom mumbled, "Little does she know."

Hayley started talking as soon as the door shut, "Thank you for hearing me out. First, I've heard from the nurses and the residents that what you did was extraordinary and undoubtedly saved my life. One resident said you were the only surgeon on the entire staff with the skill and speed to have done what was needed."

"You're welcome but there are other good surgeons here besides me," Ben said.

"Yes, I'm sure there are, but for some reason, as a clinical psychologist, and watching you run rounds, I don't think modesty is a suit you wear very often."

"That wasn't a compliment, was it? So is there something else you have to say?" Ben asked. He impatiently folded his arms across his chest. "Go on."

"No, it wasn't a compliment," Hayley said. "You seem to be so distant when you're in here with me. Did I do something to offend you? Are you angry at me for some unknown reason?"

"No and no."

Hayley sat up as straight as she could, albeit with discomfort. "That's it? No and no," she said, demanding an answer.

"Uh....You don't really know me, do you," Ben responded, again making a statement, rather than asking a question. "I've had my share of psychologists and, honestly, I've found them close to worthless. I'm not going to spend one additional second of my life having people trying to figure me out. What's worse is that even when psychologists can't figure things out, they can still tell me exactly what I need to do. As I said, you don't know me well enough to have any idea what's gone on in my life."

"I know enough from watching you come and go. People tell me I have a pretty good sense about these things."

"You don't know anything and I have to go," Ben said.

"Enough to guess, and it's just a guess, that you're angry, conflicted or afraid of something. And you've never talked to anyone about what's eating you."

"God, you're all alike. So full of yourselves. You don't know a thing."

"We do agree completely on one thing," Hayley responded.

Hunt shook his head, "Yeah. What's that?"

"I'm not going to ever treat you or tell you what to do."

"Thanks. It's the little things that help."

As Ben turned to leave, Hayley added, "Sarcasm pretty much describes you. Also, I heard from one of the night nurses that you hung Dr. Marshall on a coat hook so he wouldn't get in the way."

Hunt turned back and shook his head. "Urban legend and that's not entirely true. I did move him aside and had Dr. Boestom guard him. He wasn't being helpful."

"I've heard other things too. How about 'Attila." Hayley said. "Great nickname to have. A few of the nurses here are afraid to work with you, something about a short fuse."

"That's their problem and you're wasting my time," Ben said. "I'm just fine with things the way they are. I've got issues I think about all the time and then try to make sense of it all. Unless you're a robot, I know you think about your leukemia."

Hayley, surprised by Hunt's bluntness, ended by saying, "You can go now. I just wanted to thank you. I guess I owe you. I hope I live long enough to pay you back."

Ben relaxed as the focus of the conversation changed. "The medical oncologists are pretty good at treating leukemia," he said. "I'd take the high road and let's assume that you will pay me back someday. I really have to go."

Ben opened the door and left without saying good-bye. *How could she see into me or even through me?*

Exiting the door into the hallway, the "Hmmmmm" restarted.

"Zip it. Now," Ben barked.

All was quiet.

*_*_*_*

The next evening, the surgical team's visit to Hayley's room ended rounds. After a light day with free time available, expectations remained high that Ben would stop and grill the residents on some aspect of surgery. Yamamoto reported on Hayley's improving status.

Avoiding eye contact with Hayley, Ben told the team that she would likely be ready to transfer to Dr. Capland's care in forty-eight hours.

Ben then eyed his entire team. Normally, Ben asked questions in the hallways outside the patient rooms but he chose to quiz the team in Hayley's room. Ben also knew that Ralph Yamamoto had developed a relationship with Hayley..

"Dr. Yamamoto, Miss Green, here, lived because the biopsy needle didn't penetrate the right internal iliac artery. However, it could have and knowing its anatomy is crucial in a variety of surgical situations. Would you mind telling the group all the branches of that vessel, in order, from its origin?"

Hayley sat up and listened. She didn't know the name 'internal iliac artery', not to mention all its branches. *I thought the needle cut a vein?* Hayley thought, *Name all the branches of the Columbia River? Must be a zillion.*

Yamamoto stammered, "Oh, gee. I should know these. Uh. Gluteal, pudendal, uh…sacral, rectal, vesical, uterine, I think. I just don't remember them in order offhand. I'm sorry. I'll learn them tonight."

Yamamoto's incomplete answer triggered a reaction in Ben. His face contorted and the left side of his mouth angled towards his nose.

"Dr. Yamamoto," Ben raised his voice a decibel, "how in the hell do you think you're going to get a position anywhere in surgery with no knowledge of anatomy? You're a disgrace and an embarrassment to this program. I expect you to know the answer to this question by morning. You are so disappointing."

The venom held in the air like poisonous gas.

The entire team stood transfixed by the offhand dismantling of one of the most competent young residents, and the kindest, in the surgery program.

Yamamoto, unable to bear the tirade, collapsed backwards against the wall opposite Hayley's hospital bed, mumbling, "Dr. Hunt, I'm sorry."

Ben watched the slumping Yamamoto over his shoulder and headed for the hallway. As Ben exited, Hayley's mother entered the room holding a large, flower-laden vase in both hands. About to say hello to Ben, she raised the vase upward as a greeting, when he, unaware of her presence, knocked the vase out of her hands onto the floor.

Ben ignored the crashing glass, headed into the doorway, turned, and said without emotion, "From posterior to anterior, the iliolumbar, lateral sacral, superior gluteal, inferior gluteal, pudendal, inferior vesical or uterine, middle rectal, vaginal, obturator and umbilical. Okay, let's go, we've still got work to do."

*_*_*_*

Deidre sat at the bedside that evening as Hayley unfolded the details of the afternoon.

"I'm telling you, if I had the strength, I would have gotten out of bed and strangled him," Hayley said. "I swear."

"He seems so confident," Deidre said. "Why do you think he's like that?"

"How would I know and I don't care. Curious, I've seen him patiently teaching the residents and they hang on every word. So, I don't think it's just his personality. Something in his past triggered the outburst. That's my guess."

"I don't know," Deidre responded. "You've told me the stories about him but it's hard to believe he's all that bad. He did save your life."

"You sound like my mom now. He didn't even think about apologizing and Mom completely forgave him. I can't. Actually, what he did to Dr. Yamamoto was far worse. In front of the group of them, he just buried the poor guy. It was so horrible, so vicious. The next time he walks into this room, I'm going to let him know what I think."

"So is this your responsibility? Taking Dr. Hunt down a notch?" asked Deidre. "I'd say wait until you're out of his care, then say something."

Hayley sat up, her eyes narrowed and her jaw set tightly, as if she'd been born with an underbite.

"Uh-oh," Deidre said. "I've seen that look before. Calm down. I think you should let this slide. I agree with your mom. I wouldn't say anything to him."

"I can't wait," Hayley demanded. "Not my personality."

"That's for sure," Deidre nodded.

"I'm stressed to the max already. I don't want him taking care of me anymore. I don't want to see his face."

*_*_*_*

Not unusually Ben slept poorly that evening. He often slept poorly after losing control.

At three thirty a.m. he sat up, awake, dripping with sweat.

Into the dark room, Ben whispered, "Izzy, you okay? Izzy?"

*_*_*_*

Ralph Yamamoto did not return to Hayley's room that night or the next morning on rounds.

Hayley asked the group, "Where's Dr. Yamamoto?"

Hunt ignored the question and Watson answered, "He's busy, elsewhere."

The following evening, as the surgical team, with Dr. Yamamoto, started filing out of Hayley's room, Hayley, sitting up in bed and alert, said, "Dr. Hunt, would you possibly stay back for a moment and close the door."

Ben stood and nodded to the group as they filed out. No *Hmmmmms* this time. The last intern out of Hayley's room pulled on the door, meaning it to close but it stayed ajar.

"Yes?" Ben asked, impatiently.

"Dr. Hunt, I 'm not sure where to start," Hayley said, "or what to say. I hoped, in some way, that things I'd heard about you weren't all true. You wear the nickname 'Attila' well. It suits you."

"You trying to get me suspended?" Ben retorted, "If I say what I want to say, you'll report me. You don't have the right or experience to criticize me."

"First, I have no intention of reporting you and second, I have more than enough experience," Hayley responded. "What kind of a person treats people like you treated Dr. Yamamoto? Who runs into a patient's mother, knocks a vase filled with flowers and water to the ground, then acts as if she didn't exist or that nothing had happened? You're not human or, at least, you haven't one shred of compassion for other individuals."

"You don't know me," spewed Ben, "and I don't have time or inclination for your criticism or 'psycho-babble.' I am sorry about your mother. I didn't see her walking in."

"That's it. You didn't see her walking in? What about Dr. Yamamoto? You didn't see him as a human being?"

Ben spit back, "Dr. Yamamoto is my concern, not yours. I've got rounds to run and sick people to see." He reached for the door.

"Not yet," Hayley said, raising her voice a decibel. "You don't get it at all, do you? I know for a fact that Dr. Yamamoto had been up for thirty-six consecutive hours after working all night on two other sick patients in the ICU. He has been attentive to me ever since I arrived. He sees me first in the morning and I'm the last one he sees at night. He has been patient with my family and me and goes out of his way to make sure that we understand everything that has happened. I wish Dr. Yamamoto had saved my life, not you. Running into my mother, not acknowledging her presence and, mostly, not saying, 'I'm sorry,' immediately, catapults you into the stratosphere of total jerk."

Ben stood unmoved.

Hayley, continuing to rant, added, "If you've really ever seen any competent therapists and they haven't helped you, it's because you wouldn't let them into your sick head. You're hiding something for which you carry a ton of guilt or blame. You can't get helped until you level with someone about what really causes your outbursts."

Ben remained still but felt as if his head had been pushed against the wall behind him. *She knows. How does she know?*

"I'm done. You can leave now," Hayley said, "and please do not come and see me again. Have anyone else do my follow-up, but not you. Thank you again for saving my life. Now leave."

Ben said nothing, turned, realized the door was ajar and left the room. *She knew. How did she know?*

Transfixed to the wall outside the room, the team stood still as Ben exited and walked quickly towards the stairwell. Ben turned at the stairwell entrance, shook his head clear, and looked back at his team. "Why are you standing there? We haven't finished rounds. Move."

Ben looked at a smiling Sally Boestom, the sole female on surgical team. Sally had withstood the worst of Ben's wrath eight hours earlier for not knowing the venous pressure ranges in the portal vein. "What are you smiling at, Boestom?"

"Nothing, Chief. Nothing," responded Boestom. *Hayley Green, you're my new best hero.*

Ben's stare erased Sally's smile.

*_*_*_*

Ralph Yamamoto returned to Hayley's room at nine forty-five p.m. that evening.

"You okay?" Hayley asked.

"Yeah. Sure. Water off a duck's back," Yamamoto replied.

"Bull. No one is berated like that in front of their peers and shrugs it off. Is he like that all the time? What a son of a bitch."

"I've seen him worse than that more than a few times. We never know what'll set him off. It seems to occur when someone doesn't act on or know something that Dr. Hunt thinks they should know."

"He hasn't one shred of self-control. No one can learn when they walk around in abject fear," said Hayley.

"It's weird. He is an incredible teacher and so patient with us when he knows we're learning. As a surgeon, he seems light years ahead of all the other residents and much of the staff. He knows stuff that no one else seems to know. I know you've heard this before, but you and I wouldn't be talking now, except for what he did. Your rescue was surreal. Hunt made every right move for over two hours."

"He's still a first-class jerk, to me."

"Funny," Yamamoto said, "I really think he likes me. He's told me so. He's told me that I'll be a fabulous surgeon when I'm done. After my first year here, the Department wasn't going to offer me a position to finish the residency. Dr. Hunt, then just a Junior Resident, went to bat for me with every professor. I'm here only because of Dr. Hunt." Yamamoto didn't wait for a response and put his stethoscope into his ears. "Take a deep breath."

As Yamamoto tried to listen to Hayley's chest, she continued her polemic, "There's a screw loose somewhere. His anger response was so quick, like a trigger. He needs some help and you can be sure that it's not me that's going to help him."

Yamamoto stood back and watched Hayley start to softly weep.

Hayley sniffled and continued, "I feel like total crap. I'm scared to death and I'm probably going to die anyway and people around me are making one decision after another about my life without my input. I hate that. Ben Hunt is the worst of my nightmares. The last thing I need around me is some asshole-jerk-sonofabitch doctor who can't control his emotions. Saved my life or not, you remind Ben Hunt not to come around here anymore. I don't want to see him ever."

The next morning, Hayley transferred to Solomon Capland's medical oncology service on 13-South. Ralph Yamamoto saw her two days later to remove her staples.

Hayley reminded Yamamoto, "Make sure that Dr. Hunt doesn't pay me a social visit."

*_*_*_*

Dr. Capland ordered a myriad of tests and had a vascular surgeon place a central intravenous line with ports for giving chemotherapy and drawing blood. Hayley exited Seattle Med three weeks after her surgical misadventure.

Hayley returned to Dr. Capland's office three days later for a successful and uncomplicated bone marrow biopsy done on the opposite iliac crest.

Five days later, Hayley, with her parents in tow, sat on a large couch in Capland's suite. He entered the room, shook hands with Hayley's parents, and then pulled a chair in front of the couch.

Hayley, the psychologist, couldn't help noting the subtle

differences in approaches between Marshall and Capland. *Nothing separating us from him as did the monolithic desk in Dr. Marshall's office. Good.*

Capland reviewed the tests done to date. The bone marrow biopsy confirmed that Hayley had acute myelogenous leukemia, a disease normally treated with a bone marrow transplant from a relative or matched donor. Unfortunately, Hayley had an extremely rare combination of genes. Despite evaluating all of Hayley's relatives and a national pool of thousands of potential donors, no reasonable matches could be found.

"And here I thought I was a pretty normal person," Hayley said, trying to be glib. "So, now what?"

Capland then laid out a detailed plan. He would begin intensive hospital-based chemotherapy, or an 'induction phase,' in an attempt to change Hayley's bone marrow back to normal. Once over the effects of the chemotherapy he would perform another bone marrow biopsy to confirm that the marrow appeared healthy.

Then special medications would be given to stimulate Hayley's bone marrow to make 'stem cells,' which are special circulating blood cells that can repopulate bone marrow. Capland would then harvest the stem cells using a special blood separation device. The stem cells would be frozen and stored.

Hayley would then be readmitted to Seattle Med for intensive and potentially lethal doses of chemotherapy to destroy all of Hayley's bone marrow. Capland would then rescue Hayley with her own stem cells.

"We call this an autologous stem cell transplant" Capland said.

"Isn't that better, getting my own bone marrow," Hayley asked, "like an identical twin, rather than someone else's?"

"Yes, but mostly no," Capland responded. "The recovery from an autologous transplant is easier because it's your own marrow, you won't reject it. Unfortunately, the recurrence rate of the leukemia is much higher because we are technically transplanting marrow that has a high potential of becoming leukemic again."

"Damn... Excuse me," said Hayley.

"We don't have the luxury of waiting for a better match," Capland said, "which makes our decision easier."

"So what next?"

"Chemo. And lots of it."

"When?"

"Next week. We start the 'induction' phase. Two drugs, Ara-C and daunorubicin. Then….."

*Now he's using "we" too.* Hayley tuned out and remounted the merry-go-round.

Once Capland had finished the recap, of which Hayley ingested little, Rachel said, "Sounds pretty straight forward."

"Yes," Capland said, "but Hayley could die at any time."

The Green family let out a collective, "Oh."

*_*_*_*_*

Six days later, Hayley re-entered Seattle Med to start her induction chemotherapy.

As she sat with Deidre on her first night, Hayley could not stop staring at the IV tubing meandering over shoulder and then under her hospital gown into the semi-permanent catheter on her chest wall.

"How can I help you?," pleaded Deidre after twenty minutes of no conversation, "You're never this quiet."

"I don't know that anyone can help me. I'm just lost," Hayley said. "All my life's dreams and ambitions are merely blue smoke. I'm tethered to this bed by a ton of tubes and I'm waiting for this IV to kill me. That's how I feel."

"C'mon. There's got to be something I can do?" pleaded Deidre.

Not answering the question, Hayley continued, "I've lost all control. Different building, different floor, different room, different nurses, different aides and different beds. Dr. Capland and most of the nurses try to explain stuff, but I don't understand most of it. I'm scared. I'm so scared."

"Maybe it won't be so bad."

"Mom crying twenty-four seven doesn't help either."

Deidre persisted, "Knowing you - and I do know you - I think you need to be as involved as you can. That'll give you some comfort, even if you're not making any decisions."

"Probably right. I'll try."

*_*_*_*_*

As new drugs were added to Hayley's regimen, the expected side effects of the chemotherapy kicked in. The malaise began on day two, the chills and nausea on day three and the vomiting on day four.

On the fifth day, Dr. Capland's asked Hayley, "Are you really demanding to check every medication given to you?"

"Absolutely. It's my body," Hayley demanded, "and I need to know. It's my only way of keeping my sanity. I'm not going to reverse any orders, I promise. I just need to know what's going into me. I need a little sense of control."

Capland shook his head as he exited and turned around at the door, "Have it your way. The nurses are busy and some might be upset by what they regard as an intrusion into their job."

Regardless of how tired, how nauseated, or how cold or hot she might feel, regardless of the time day or night, Hayley checked every medication and IV dosage she received. The nurses quickly became accustomed to her routine and started announcing medications as they entered the room.

Hayley never changed an order, dose or drug.

After a week of therapy, Hayley's blood counts remained low, too low to allow a return home. But she rebounded nicely and by day ten, some of her appetite returned.

Cycle two of the induction chemotherapy started on day fourteen and the malaise, chills, nausea and vomiting commenced hours later.

Hayley did her best to pretend as if she only had the world's worst flu until the hair loss in clumps shattered her illusions.

On the sixteenth hospital day, Rachel Green entered the hospital room as the nurse's aide assisted Hayley into the shower.

"I'm here, honey," Rachel shouted through the din of running water and past the nurse's aide. "I'll sit until you come out. I bought a sweet roll on the way up. Doing okay?"

"About the same. Only puked twice so far today. Take that as a good sign."

"Hayley, please. I don't need the sarcasm."

Ten minutes later the aide walked Hayley out of the bathroom and Rachel jumped up to assist. Hayley, head wrapped in a towel, spa-like, wore a plush, terry cloth robe brought from home.

"Hi, Mom. I'm fine. Finish your sweet roll," Hayley said.

The hot shower and attire gave Hayley the glow of apparent normality for the first time in a few weeks. Rachel, smiling, approached and kissed her daughter's moist forehead.

"I love you."

"I love you too, Mom."

As the aide settled Hayley into bed, Hayley asked, "Can you remove the towel? I think my hair's dry enough."

The aide, a lovely young African woman, gently unwrapped the towel, folded it on her arm and turned to leave.

Standing at the bedside, unprepared for the buckshot swatches of baldness covering her daughter's head, Rachel's eyes widened and she exhaled, "Oh. Oh my God. What are they doing to my daughter? My beautiful baby." Rachel held her hand up to her mouth, mumbling, "I'm going to be sick," then rushed to the door of the room, stopped and vomited the sweet roll into the hallway.

Deidre arrived at the hospital in the early evening. Hayley's dinner tray, Jell-O and broth, sat undisturbed at the bedside.

"You going to eat anything?" asked Deidre.

"Probably not until you leave. I'll just vomit ten minutes after starting."

"I hate the gutter humor," said Deidre. "How's your mom doing now?"

"I guess she'll be okay tomorrow," Hayley said. "She knew my hair would fall out. She just wasn't prepared for the reality of it all."

"You gonna be okay?"

"I looked in the mirror after Mom left and I can see why she lost it. It was the first time I thought maybe I should just die and get it over with."

"You're joking?" said Deidre, worried that Hayley wasn't.

"I dismissed it. Honestly I did."

"That's better."

"I've always thought, or at least hoped, I would make an impact on the world. Help humanity in some way. I haven't done that yet. So I pulled out some more hair, looked in the mirror and said, 'Fuck you, leukemia. I'm going to fight you tooth and nail.'"

Deidre walked over to the bed and hugged her best friend longer than normal. "That's the Hayley I know."

*_*_*_*

Expectedly, Hayley received two units of blood and three platelet transfusions over the ensuing week. By day twenty-three, her blood counts returned to acceptable levels, her nausea and vomiting subsided and she started eating normally.

On day twenty-four, Capland discharged Hayley to home. Thirty-five days later, Hayley returned to Capland's office for another bone marrow biopsy.

Gone, at least temporarily, were the leukemic cells.

Dr. Capland seemed pleased, but pointed out that without the planned bone marrow transplant, the leukemia would recur quickly.

Capland began Hayley on special stem cell growth stimulating medicines followed by five days of six-hour-a-day blood collections to capture her stem cells, which were frozen and stored.

A week later, Hayley returned to the hospital and started on super lethal doses of chemotherapy to wipe out all of her current bone marrow. Forty-eight hours later, Hayley received her stem cells to repopulate the marrow.

Despite two bouts of pneumonia, three blood transfusions, ten days in an isolation tent, and two episodes of prolonged nausea and vomiting, Hayley exceeded the expectations of Dr. Capland and the transplant team.

As before, Hayley checked every medication, oral or IV.

Four weeks after transplantation, Dr. Capland came into Hayley's room in mid-afternoon expecting to announce her discharge for the following morning.

"I see you've had a bad day. What's up?" Capland asked.

"I don't know," Hayley said. "For the past week, every day has seemed a bit better than the one before. Then, this morning, I had little appetite, forced myself to eat lunch and then threw up everything. I'm no better now and my stomach is out of sorts. It's almost as if I had just received some more chemo."

"You know you haven't. We'll have to hold off on your discharge," Capland said, "until we've figured this out. The blood tests are difficult to interpret, but we'll see how they look in the morning."

Hayley's medical condition worsened every day over the next week. She stopped eating and Capland restarted her intravenous feedings. When healthy, Hayley weighed one hundred nineteen pounds. She weighed one hundred ten when the transplant was given, fell to ninety-nine pounds, then rebounded back to one hundred two. Despite the week of IV feeding, Hayley's weight continued to fall to her current weight of ninety-six pounds.

Dr. Capland obtained consultations from experts in infectious disease, lung, gastroenterology, general surgery and nephrology. Hayley's demands to understand everything annoyed each consultant.

Capland repeated blood tests, X-rays and varieties of scans, none of which gave clues to her malady. On day ten of her mystery illness, Hayley developed two episodes of irregular, fast heart rhythms, or tachycardias, but the cardiologists had no answers. Capland scheduled a repeat bone marrow biopsy, which revealed nothing.

Dr. Capland and the consultants remained perplexed. Capland said he would start the whole cycle of consultations and tests over again.

"We've got to find some answers quickly. I am concerned about weathering this storm unless..., well, just unless," Capland told Hayley, her parents and Deidre late at night. "I'll be back. I need to check your labs once more."

Thirty minutes later, Capland had not returned and Hayley's parents went home for dinner. Deidre sat with Hayley, holding her hand.

"Can you do me a favor?" Hayley asked.

"Sure. Of course. Anything. What?" said Deidre.

"Can you try to find Dr. Hunt and ask him to see me?" asked Hayley.

"What? You mean the person you railed about being an asshole and an idiot. The guy who thinks all psychologists are fools. You trashed him for an hour a day for a week after you last saw him."

"Yeah. I hate the thought. He's still an ass, but no one's coming up with answers. He's opened me up, damn it. Maybe he knows something."

"I'd call Adolf Hitler, Charles Manson, and Ted Bundy if I thought they could help," Deidre said.

"Go. Go before Mom and Dad come back."

*_*_*_*

"Dr. Hunt, this is Deidre Williams. I'm Hayley Green's friend. Do you remember me?"

"Sure," said Ben, "Not expecting to hear from you. You need a photo of me so your friend can throw darts?"

"No," said Deidre. "This is serious."

"Last I heard, she was doing okay."

"Not. She's dying. She got through the transplant okay and then ten or eleven days ago, just before going home, she got sick. No one's been able to find any answers. Dr. Capland said he's really worried that she's not going to make it unless someone can figure out what's wrong. Anyway, Hayley asked me to call you to see if you had any ideas."

"Is it you or her parents that want me to see her?" asked Ben.

"No. It's Hayley. I guess deep down she hopes you might be able to help, although I'd be disingenuous if I didn't tell you that she still thinks you're a bona fide jerk."

"She might have had that right. Sure, I'll come by. I've got a few patients to see. Maybe ten, ten-thirty tonight."

*_*_*_*_*

By the time Ben arrived at eleven fifteen p.m., Hayley was alone.

"You look like shit and your chart isn't helpful," Ben said.

"It's nice to see you too." Hayley let the sarcasm sit for a moment, then said, "I'm sorry to bother you," as she reached for the wig sitting on a small mannequin head at her bedside.

"You don't need to put that on. Actually, if I'm going to examine you, I'd like it off."

"You're the last person I wanted to see me," Hayley said, "but I'm desperate… I don't want to die..." The tears, diminished by the effects of the chemotherapy, hesitated in a slow stream, circling her nose and on each side of parched and dry lips. "I'm sorry for saying the things...." Hayley rolled over and dry-heaved into a small basin.

Ben wetted a washcloth and gently wiped Hayley's face.

Hayley didn't finish her earlier thought and said, "Thanks. Thanks for coming."

"Don't apologize. You're right. I have trouble with my emotions. I wish I were different. You psychologists, and I've seen a shitload of them, seem to think they have all the answers, but not for me. I hate to admit that you appear to be sharper than most."

Hayley struggled to sit up, holding on to the bed rail. "I'm not that good and, more importantly, I'm not going to treat you. That's a promise."

"You actually may be that good, we'll never know, but that's not why I'm here. I'm going to get a nurse so I can examine you," said

Ben.

Ben did a thorough physical. The pelvic exam was particularly uncomfortable for Hayley.

"I am concerned about some discomfort in your right deep pelvis," Ben said when finished. "Has anyone done a pelvic exam this week?"

"Who hasn't? Nobody said anything," Hayley quipped.

"I'm going to review your CT and PET scans, then call Dr. Capland. I have an idea."

Ben returned forty minutes later. "Dr. Capland thinks I'm crazy, but I think you have appendicitis. It hasn't ruptured but it's inflamed and walled in from the scar tissue after your surgery. Your white count and scans don't support my diagnosis, but nothing else fits. If I had to make a decision, I'd re-explore your abdomen."

Hayley sat up. "I don't want any more surgery," she demanded.

"It's not what you want that counts," Ben said.

"I'm not sure why I called you. Why do you think you're such an expert on everything and come in here….?"

A nurse came to the door, interrupted the disintegrating discussion, and said, "Dr. Capland is on the phone. I'm going to patch it through."

Hayley and Ben remained quiet until the call came into the room.

"Hayley, Dr. Capland here. I've talked to Ben Hunt."

"He's here in front of me, Dr. Capland."

"Maybe you could ask him to step out of the room?" Capland asked.

"Uh. Okay," Hayley said, then turned to Ben and asked, "Dr. Capland wants to talk to me alone. Is that okay?"

"Sure. I'll step out," said Ben.

Hayley lowered her voice and covered the phone's mouthpiece. "Actually, I don't want you to go. You might as well hear what he has to say." Turning back to the phone, which she placed on speaker, she said, "Dr. Hunt is gone."

"Hayley, I don't want you to listen to Dr. Hunt. He's only a resident," Capland said. "Fred Davis has seen you twice already. He is an excellent surgeon and I trust him. I'll call him first thing in the morning and have him see you again."

"Thank you, Dr. Capland."

After Hayley hung up, Ben said, "I'd say the same thing if someone called me in the middle of the night. The difference is, I'm right. You're on the wrong antibiotics as well, but let's see what Dr. Davis comes up with in the morning. Dr. Capland's correct, Davis is an excellent surgeon. He's just wrong about this."

"I'm sorry about what I was about to say earlier," Hayley said. "Well, not totally sorry. I don't like you and your being here and remembering what you did to my mother and Dr. Yamamoto riles me no end." Hayley rolled towards her nightstand and grabbed a towel and a small plastic bucket.

"Hey, I'm sorry if I nauseate you. Remember, I'm not that fond of you either," Ben said. "Never met a shrink that I liked or could trust. But, hey, that's only me."

"I wish it were just you that nauseates me." Hayley dry-heaved twice into the bucket and then spit out a mouthful of saliva. She then lay back onto her pillow. "I'm sorry."

Ben picked up a small washcloth, wet it, and gently wiped Hayley's mouth.

"The difference for me is that I want to live," Hayley said, "and if there is one chance in hell that you have an answer to why I'm sick, I'll take it. Will you talk to the other doctors and tell them what you think? Whether you see me again is up to you."

"I have a short case tomorrow morning. I'll be back here around nine."

"Thanks. Thanks, again. I'm sorry about what I said."

"You're probably not sorry about what you said. I deserved it," Ben said as he left the room.

The next morning, Ben arrived at eight forty-five as Dr. Davis perused Hayley's chart at the nursing station monitor.

"Ben, it's good you're here," Davis said. "You shouldn't be seeing my private patients without permission. I'll let it ride this time."

"I'm sorry, Dr. Davis," Ben responded, taking a step back and lowering his head. "You know I wouldn't see your patients without permission, but she specifically asked me to come."

"Regardless, you should have called me first."

"No excuse and again, I'm sorry. It was late last night and I saw no reason to bother you because I expected to find nothing. That said, I think she should be explored. I believe she has appendicitis."

"Believe what you want, that's enough. Go," Davis sneered.

"May I say something to Miss Green?" Ben asked. "I need to apologize for something that happened a few weeks ago."

"No. I don't want you talking to her. Ever. Don't call her, either. Am I clear?"

"Yes, sir. Perfectly." Ben departed the unit and headed back to the OR for an afternoon of hernia repairs.

Later that morning, Dr. Cassetti came into Ben's operating room. "Can you stir up hornet's nests, or what? Fred Davis called me, totally bent out of shape."

Ben explained that he had been called directly by the patient, late at night. "I saw Hayley fully expecting to add nothing. Chief, she's got appendicitis. Subtle, but there's a small inflammatory mass in her right pelvis. Besides, no one else has any ideas."

"Stay out of it," Cassetti demanded.

"Yes, sir. What if she specifically asks me to see her again?"

"She won't. If she does, don't see her," Cassetti demanded.

*_*_*_*

That evening, with Deidre present, Hayley asked Dr. Capland why Dr. Hunt had not returned to see her.

"Dr. Hunt is a resident," Capland said, "not a board certified surgeon. I know he saved your life because he was in the right spot at the right time. That doesn't qualify him as the guru of all gurus when it comes to diagnosis. Dr. Davis is an excellent surgeon and has asked that Dr. Hunt not interfere with your care. He told Dr. Hunt not to see or talk to you again. I agree with Dr. Davis and so does Dr. Hunt's chief, the chairman of the surgical department, Dr. Cassetti."

"I'm sorry if I caused a problem. I didn't mean to," Hayley said. "I felt that Dr. Hunt might have some kind of inside track on me. I don't like him personally. In fact, I dislike him intensely and the feelings seem to be mutual. But after seeing me, he seemed to think he knew what was wrong."

"Dr. Hunt believes you have subclinical appendicitis. No one else does. None of your tests suggest it, although many tests are difficult to interpret because of your transplant and the surgery for the punctured blood vessel."

"What's subclinical mean?" Deidre asked.

"A medical problem that's not severe enough to present definite findings. That means, it's difficult to diagnose," Capland responded.

"Dr. Capland, make me a promise," Hayley said, without hesitation. "I may not be strong enough to do anything about it later.

If I worsen, and no one has any answers, I want Dr. Hunt to take over my care."

"That's crazy," Capland responded.

"It's my life. If I'm not improving, whether I am mentally alert or not, I want Dr. Hunt to assume my care."

"I don't know about...," Capland started.

Hayley, making strong eye contact with Capland, interrupted, "I do know. That's my decision. Deidre is a witness to my feelings. And don't ask my parents. It's my decision. I'll sign something if I have to."

Capland acquiesced. "That won't be necessary. Let's try to get you better in the next day or so. I'm going to switch the antibiotics per Dr. Kramer's recommendations this morning. He's the infectious disease specialist."

The next morning, Hayley redeveloped irregular heart rhythms, which became increasingly unstable. Capland transferred her into a medical intensive care unit. After two bouts of transient, dangerously low heart rates, the cardiologists placed a temporary cardiac pacemaker through a vein in Hayley's arm. That evening, Hayley's temperature spiked above one hundred two degrees Fahrenheit and despite the use of pressors, her blood pressures became increasingly unstable. The nurses noted that Hayley would have episodic lapses of orientation.

Dr. Capland made afternoon rounds at four thirty p.m., then called Dr. Davis.

"Fred, Sol here. I'm calling about Hayley Green. We're losing her and we don't know why. She's not mentally all there, but two days ago, while she was competent, she specifically instructed me to transfer her care to Dr. Hunt if she didn't improve. I did everything I could to dissuade her but she made me promise and had it witnessed. Like it or not, I don't want you causing trouble for Dr. Hunt. He has not talked to Hayley, or anyone in her family, to have prompted her decision."

"If she dies, I don't want my name associated with this debacle in any way," Davis replied. "Is that understood?"

"Absolutely, Fred. You will not be blamed," Capland said. "I've just seen her, and in my opinion, she is going to die soon."

*_*_*_*

"Ben, this is Dr. Capland. I just got off the phone with Dr. Cassetti. Hayley Green wanted me to let you know that you are assuming her care as of this minute and......"

After Capland finished, Ben hung up and made three calls. He wanted the same surgical team that had saved Hayley's life the first time.

Roy Watson was available. Bob Feldmar was in New York interviewing for a plastic surgery residency. Bob Fink, the anesthesiologist, and the surgical nurses, Polly Sawa and Diane Hopper, were asleep at home. As a courtesy, Ben called Ralph Yamamoto. The entire team assembled in the OR ninety minutes later.

Fink evaluated Hayley's status in the pre-op area and counseled her parents that Hayley's tenuous situation meant that a life-ending cardiac arrest or arrhythmia might occur at any time.

Scar tissue that had formed around Hayley's intestines, adhering them to the repaired pelvic blood vessels, made Hayley's exploratory surgery demanding and time-consuming. After seventy-five minutes of tedious dissection, the intestines were freed from precarious scar tissue to allow Ben a better look at the cecum, the first portion of the right colon and the structure from which the appendix arises. Hayley's appendix had fallen behind the cecum and appeared normal as it attached to the cecum.

"I hope for her sake," Ben said, "we find something. We need to get a look at the entire appendix, so let's keep going."

Forty more minutes of additional dissection, millimeter by millimeter, led to the tail of the appendix and revealed an inflamed mass the size of a walnut, sealed off by Hayley's meager immune system. Ben removed Hayley's inflamed appendix.

Hayley's cardiac situation remained critical for the next four hours, then stabilized.

Late that night, Ben returned to Hayley's room to find her asleep with stable vital signs and no arrhythmias. He wrote a chart note but did not awaken her.

The following morning, only Ralph Yamamoto made rounds on Hayley. The effects of the anesthetic had mostly worn away and, despite the narcotic pain medication, Hayley was alert.

"What happened?" Hayley said. "I don't remember a thing. The nurses told me that Dr. Hunt operated on my last night. Is that true?"

"Yep. True. You've apparently been out of it for a couple of days," said Yamamoto. "Dr. Capland had Dr. Hunt assume your care yesterday afternoon. Hunt was right on. You had appendicitis. Tough going because of scar tissue."

"Where is he?" Hayley asked.

"He was here last night but you were out of it. He had an emergency surgery starting at six fifteen this morning and there wasn't time to come up here. He told me to say he'd be up tonight, unless you're going analyze him again."

"He really said that? If I'm going to analyze him."

"Uh, that's what he said." said Yamamoto.

"What's wrong with him. He's got more than one screw loose."

Yamamoto stood silent, not knowing what to say.

"I'm barely in control of my emotions as it is," Hayley continued. "I can't handle the way Dr. Hunt treats me. Tell him not to bother coming. I don't want to see him. You tell him that."

"He saved your life. Again. You're kidding, right?" Yamamoto asked.

"Not kidding."

*_*_*_*

Hayley's status improved dramatically over the next thirty-six hours and she no longer required blood pressure supporting medications.

On post-op morning three in the ICU, Hayley greeted her nurse with, "I'm starved. Can I get a glass of orange juice and some scrambled eggs."

Ben did not visit or speak to Hayley after her appendectomy, even once, per her request. Ralph Yamamoto took charge of her surgical care for the rest of the hospitalization. On four different occasions Ben pressed the elevator button to 13-South, Hayley's floor, but stayed in the elevator, returning to the surgical floors.

A night before discharge, Yamamoto said to Hayley, "You know, Dr. Hunt asks how you're doing every day. I can ask him to come up here, if you want?"

"I suppose I should thank him. Again. But.. But I don't know," Hayley said, clearly undecided.

"I'd think that'd be appropriate, really," Yamamoto said. "Dr. Davis wanted Dr. Cassetti to fire Dr. Hunt that night. If you hadn't had appendicitis, he might have."

"I don't know, I don't know. Shit, I don't know," Hayley said. "He just rubs me the wrong way every time I see him. Not to mention, he's never apologized. No one treats my mother, or you, like he did. I can't forget that. My emotions are all over the place and I suppose I'm being inconsistent, maybe even pissy, but you can tell him thanks for me. That's all I can handle right now."

"Uh. He can't apologize if you won't let him see you," said Yamamoto.

Hayley glared at Yamamoto, giving her answer without uttering a word.

Hayley resumed a normal diet and started gaining weight. Yamamoto and Capland discharged her to home from Seattle Med seven days later. Capland sent Ben a case of 2008 Chateau Lafitte Rothschild. Ben kept none and gave each member of his team two bottles.

## Chapter 5

Ben's intermittent anger outbursts occurred more frequently, despite repeated warnings from Dr. Cassetti.

Two members of the nursing staff and a Chief Resident in the Department of Medicine filed independent grievances against Ben. Ben apologized, formally, to all three. One nurse settled the complaint by moving to another city at the hospital's expense.

Dr. Cassetti considered suspending Ben but, as a Chief Resident, he was irreplaceable on short notice.

"Ben, you're way past three strikes with me," Cassetti said. "One more tirade and you're done here. I don't care what it does to the program. We cannot put the department in a position to be sued by a disgruntled resident or employee of the hospital. Am I clear?"

"I get it, Chief. I'm sorry," Ben said.

"You've said that before. Damn it. You are the best surgical resident I've ever trained but your outbursts are killing me. You are going to seek help until someone figures you out."

"I've seen plenty of therapists. They're all useless," said Ben.

"Great attitude." Cassetti softly pounded his desk. "What the hell am I going to do with you. You don't get it."

"I'm sorry, Chief."

"Here are two names, Wilford Cornelius and Robin Anders. Both are well-respected therapists in the local community. The hospital attorneys told me that I can't afford a conflict of interest by having you see someone on the staff at Seattle Med. See one and, if he or she doesn't help, see the other. If they can't help, we'll keep trying."

*_*_*_*

Ben's nightmares intensified. At least two nights of every week, he would awaken, drenched in sweat and whisper, "Izzy, are you okay? Izzy, Talk to me."

*_*_*_*

Ben entered the office of Dr. Wilford Cornelius for the third time in three weeks. Despite the brightly colored Chihuly glass and Joan Miro prints, Ben felt no sense of lightness. Ben sat on the couch and waited for Cornelius to assume his usual position on a chair opposite the couch.

Ben could only think of sick patients he needed to see as Cornelius droned on, "....I suspect you are blaming yourself for your father's suicide and perhaps your mother's alcoholism. You haven't opened up on your time in Afghanistan, so I'm discounting that as a source of your outbursts."

*He doesn't get it.* Ben merely said, "And."

"I believe that a two prong approach would be best. First, we will meet weekly or more and use in-depth cognitive therapy. I will help you understand and change how you think about your personal trauma and its aftermath."

*Bullshit.* "Okay," said Ben.

Cornelius continued, "I hope to help you understand that the traumatic events you lived through were not your fault."

"Secondly, I believe strongly that adding a medication is essential to control your outbursts. Selective serotonin reuptake inhibitors or SSRIs are a type of antidepressant medicine.

"These can help you feel less sad and worried. I've found them to be helpful, and are very effective in circumstances like yours. I'd suggest trying Paxil first. If the side effects are bothersome, we can switch to Celexa."

Cornelius quickly wrote out a script for Paxil and pulled a handful of samples from his desk drawer. "Ben, I am really encouraged by the progress we've made. I'll see you back in a week. Same time."

As Ben exited the office, he garnered the attention of Cornelius's receptionist, making certain she watched him throw the prescription and drug samples into the wastebasket.

*_*_*_*

Ben’s second appointment with Dr. Robin Anders was twenty-one days later.

“.......You really dumped the prescription in front of his receptionist?" Anders asked.

"Yes," Ben said.

"I believe that to be a mistake."

"We both know I can't afford to take any medications that might impact my decision making or ability to operate.".

"Perhaps, perhaps not,” Anders replied, “but we can see how they affect you, then decide."

"That's not going to happen,” Ben declared. “No way. It takes only one mistake in judgment or technique to hurt someone. I can't afford to take drugs."

"Have you considered taking a sabbatical and maybe reconsidering whether surgery is the right place for you?"

"No. Not likely that'll happen either."

"I'm not sure I can help you without medication,” said Anders, “but I'm willing to try. I'd like to start EMDR, which is an acronym for eye movement desensitization and reprocessing. I believe EMDR can help change how you react to memories of your trauma. While thinking of or talking about your memories, I'll teach you to focus on other stimuli like eye movements, hand taps, and sounds. I will move my hand, and you'll follow the movements with your eyes."

Twenty minutes later, in the middle of a hand movement session,

Ben stood and calmly announced, "This is bullshit," and walked out.

*_*_*_*

Ben entered an angry Dr. Cassetti's office an hour later.

"Sit down, God damn it. I just got off the phone with Dr. Anders. You can't just walk out on people," Cassetti said, shaking his head.

"Both psychiatrists wanted me on antidepressants," Ben responded, "and you and I both know that would possibly affect my surgical skills. Anders suggested I might find another job besides surgery."

Cassetti explained to Ben that the hospital's attorneys demanded that Ben be in therapy as long as he worked at Seattle Med.

"It is not an option to go this alone. You've created too many waves. Hell, waves. I meant tsunamis. Find someone to help you. This week. Find someone, anyone, who can figure out what's eating you."

Ben made a call that afternoon.

## Chapter 6

Three months after discharge, Hayley returned to her clinical psychology and social work employment at the Washington State Department of Social and Health Service, or DSHS, offices in downtown Seattle.

"I used to feel that I was at the exact place I wanted to be, but not anymore," she told Deidre two weeks after returning. "It's as if I'm on the wrong freeway entrance ramp, heading south, wishing to go in any direction but." Hayley repeated the exact complaint to her mother a week later.

Hayley's Monday clinical appointments would normally start at two thirty p.m. At one twenty p.m., the clinic secretary buzzed into her office.

"Hayley, your one thirty is here. Some guy."

"One thirty?" Hayley whined. "I'm not supposed to start until two thirty. I've still a ton of paperwork to do. Who scheduled this?"

"Don't get mad at me. Your friend Deidre called it in this morning. She said you'd understand. The patient isn't registered on our dockets and he won't fill out any paperwork. He won't even give me his name. But he's really good looking and...."

"Okay, okay, that's enough. Bring whomever this joker is back to my office." Hayley, having no idea who was going to walk through the door, grabbed the mirror in her top drawer to make sure her wig was in place.

Twenty seconds later, Ben Hunt stood in Hayley's office doorway.

"I need help," Ben said before Hayley could formulate an intelligent response.

"You? I can't see you here," Hayley said, confused.

"The woman at the front desk made that abundantly clear," said Ben.

"I don't work anywhere else."

"Then can you see me outside these walls?" Ben asked.

"N-O, no. Why should I? I don't even like you. You never even came to see me after the second surgery."

"You're whining," Ben said. "Very uncharacteristic of a psychologist. Besides, I was told not to visit, so I assumed you didn't want me to come."

Hayley folded her arms, then said, "You're right, I am whining and I didn't want you to see me, but I thought you should have come anyway. Just so you know, I don't owe you a thing."

"I agree. You don't owe me anything," Ben said.

"I thought you don't particularly care for psychologists?" Hayley asked.

"True," Ben replied. "I've not done well with any of them before now, but I think you can help me. I need help."

Hayley swiveled her chair away from Ben. *He saved my life. Twice.* Turning back, she said, "I might be able to help you but I don't want to. Maybe I can find someone who can. I'm busy here, have a full slate of patients this afternoon, and more importantly, I'm not supposed to do any counseling outside of DSHS. The best I can do is meet you for dinner one night this week. I'll listen to you for as long as I can stand it and then suggest who might be able to help."

"Sure," Ben said. "So you know, I want you to help me, not someone else."

"That's not going to happen."

Undaunted, Ben said, "We'll see."

"We won't see."

“How about Wednesday? I can pick you up here, if you like? Seven p.m., Italian?"

"Fine. As long as you understand, I’m not going to be your therapist and I certainly won’t treat this dinner as a therapy session.” Hayley banged her palm against her forehead, then said, “I'm crazy to do this."

"Yep, you're crazy to do this, but you are alive to do it."

Hayley's jaw tightened as she glared at Ben. "Hey, I don't owe you, remember.” *I'm going to kill Deidre.*

"I said you don't owe me. I was just pointing out the obvious. By the way, you look great."

"Right,” Hayley snickered. “Now I know you’re full of it. If I take this damn wig off I’d look like a pale, white, semi-fuzzy bowling ball. I'm thinking this might be a very short dinner."

"Sarcasm is the lowest form of humor. See you Wednesday at seven." Ben turned and walked out of Hayley's office.

Hayley swiveled back to her desk. *I'm going to kill Deidre.*

*_*_*_*

“Hey, best friend, most trusted advisor, how ya doin’?” Hayley started that evening’s phone call to Deidre.

“That bad? Come on. You owed him at least that,” Deidre responded.

“I didn’t owe him a thing. He was just doing his job. I hated him and he never came to see me.”

“You told him, and me, and Doctor Yama-whatever that you never wanted to see him, ever.”

“Whose side are you on?”

"The side of truth, justice and the American Way. So?"

"We're going out to dinner Wednesday night and I'll try not to be nice. I'll tell him to leave me alone."

## Chapter 7

The evening dampness, slight drizzle and brisk wind from the southeast that night would chill the soul of anyone, even a grizzled Seattleite. Ben picked up Hayley on time and, with little discussion, took her to Il Terrazzo Carmine, an upscale Italian restaurant in Pioneer Square. Ben found a parking spot on Jackson Street around the corner from the restaurant.

"Hold on, I'll get the door for you," Ben offered after parking.

"No need, I'm not sick and I can get out myself," Hayley replied, emphatically.

"Don't. My mother had a ton of faults, which you may hear about, but she always waited for my dad to open the door for her."

As they walked, Hayley realized that Ben dwarfed her and she had forgotten to bring a pair of heels to work. "You're as tall as my dad. I didn't realize that," she commented. "I must look like a pygmy."

"That's okay. I didn't realize you were so..."

"So short," Hayley interrupted. "Thanks for that. We can go home now."

"I didn't realize you were so pretty."

"That's not what you were going to say, was it?"

"You'll never know if you keep finishing sentences for me," Ben said with a broad smile.

"You're right. I'm sorry," Hayley said. "We're trained to listen. Although, as I've said before, I'm not your therapist and this dinner isn't therapy."

Ben said nothing.

The host seated the two quickly and a server came with water and asked if they'd like something to drink.

"I'd like a glass of white wine, a Sauvignon Blanc," Hayley said.

Already perusing the wine list, Ben said, "A glass of the Michel Cordaillat Sauvignon Blanc for her, I'll have iced tea."

The waiter turned as Hayley asked Ben, "You don't like wine?"

Ben didn't answer at first and lazily twirled a spoon in his glass of water. "Sure, I like wine but I never drink anymore," he said. "My mother was an alcoholic, actually remained an alcoholic until she died. In an oblique way, her drinking killed my father. I swore to myself, at age thirteen, that I'd never drink. I broke that promise a week later and kept drinking through my time in the Marines, but never since coming back stateside."

"Really. Where'd you grow up?" Hayley asked.

"Apple Ridge, Washington. Do you know where that is?" Ben asked.

"Sure. To the east, somewhere along I-90. I'm sure I've driven by it."

"North of I-90, halfway between Ellensburg and Cle Elum."

"Small, eh?" Hayley asked.

"Very, compared to Seattle. Not that I knew that growing up."

"Your parents moved there?"

Ben explained that he was third generation Apple Ridge. His grandfather, Harry Hunt, moved to Apple Ridge from Iowa in 1948 and married Ben's grandmother, a local schoolteacher in 1950. Ben's father, Curtis, was born in 1951. His grandfather shipped off to Korea in 1952 and returned to Apple Ridge severely impaired mentally.

"In today's world he'd be labeled as having PTSD," Ben said.

Ben related how his grandfather, misunderstood, became a town joke. He would walk around town mumbling to himself, holding his hands over his ears like he was awaiting an explosion."

"Why you telling me all this?" Hayley asked.

"I'm hoping you can help me," Ben said.

Hayley gave a subtle headshake. "That's not going to happen," she said.

"Please. I just want you to know about my life. Different than yours."

Hayley relented and gave a subtle nod. "Okay. Okay. I'm game for a little talking. The operative word there is 'little.' Are your grandparents still alive?"

"No, both died when I was eleven. My dad was the best student and the best athlete in his class. The only way to level the playing field for the other boys was to bring Dad down a notch or two by making fun of Gramps."

"Ouch."

Ben then talked about his dad's two friends growing up. Bill Carter was his Curtis's best friend. Bill was the son of John B. Carter, the biggest landowner and wealthiest man in Kittitas County. The Carters owned a large fruit processing plant and a good deal of the land in and around Apple Ridge. People in Apple Ridge worked for the Carters, one way or another. Bill wasn't book smart or a good athlete, but he had all the respect that came from wealth.

Curtis's other friend growing up was Ellen Lytle. Ellen, Ben's mother and the daughter of the town's pharmacist, was the only student smart enough to keep up with Curtis.

Curtis went to Washington State College after high school and excelled academically. Rush Medical School in Chicago offered him a full scholarship. After med school and a year of internship in Chicago, he returned to Apple Ridge to practice. He was one of only two docs in Apple Ridge at the time. The other, Dr. Donohue, was close to seventy years old when Curtis returned.

"When did your dad marry your mom?" Hayley asked.

"After returning from first year of med school. Mom had to make a decision. Bill Carter wanted to marry her, but she wanted out of Apple Ridge. She thought she was a big town girl after graduating from UCLA. Bill was rich and fun, but he wasn't leaving Apple Ridge with all the money and land he'd inherit. Mom was certain that Dad would practice in Chicago or some big city after training. She decided to marry him and moved to Chicago while Dad finished med school and internship. Mom worked at Sears in some advertising job. When Dad finished his internship, my grandparents needed him and he and Mom came back to Apple Ridge. Mom thought the move was temporary."

"That upset your mom?" Hayley asked.

"Big time," Ben said. "She railed about not moving back to Chicago or San Francisco or almost anywhere else, especially after my grandparents died. By then, Dad had a full practice. I was born the year after they moved back."

"So your dad didn't want to leave."

"Right. He loved being a small-town family physician. Mostly, he enjoyed the adoration and respect of the community. Adoration wasn't a big deal to him, but respect was addicting after growing up without it. My dad needed respect like the orchards around Apple Ridge needed water. Then, when Doc Donahue died, Dad couldn't move. The town needed him."

"Did they fight a lot, your mom and dad?" asked Haley.

"Not that much. Dad didn't care that much about Mom's drinking. Mom was only upset that Dad didn't drink."

"Did your mom ever leave you?"

"Mom left Dad and me three or four times, but she always came back. She couldn't make it on her own. In hindsight, when she returned after her second walkabout, she was a full blown alcoholic."

"Sorry about that. Brothers or sisters?"

"Nope, just me. Mom didn't want any more kids. I'm close to sure she didn't want me. Dad would have had ten kids, if he could. Mom snuck off to Spokane two years after I was born and had her tubes tied. That ended the fighting about having more kids. In fact,…"

Hayley interrupted, "Why do you think your mom wanted no more children?"

"It got in the way of her drinking."

"Dang," said Hayley.

"My dad and I were so close. When he had spare time, we'd play catch, do homework, make model airplanes, whatever."

"Sounds nice."

"There's more. My grandmother's family left Dad three hundred acres of forest lands just north of Apple Ridge in the foothills to the east of the Cascade Mountains. When Dad could get away we'd go there and hike, hunt, fish and camp out. Mom hated the forest and was only too happy to see us go because she could drink herself into a happy stupor for a whole weekend."

"Your dad sounded amazing," said Hayley.

"Those weekends were the best of my life. He told me the land would be mine someday and made me promise that I'd never sell it."

The server appeared and both ordered.

"What exactly happened to your dad?" Hayley asked.

"He committed suicide in 1993. My mother and dad's best friend, Bill Carter, caused it."

"Was your mom having an affair with the friend?"

"No. No. Not at all," Ben said. "Carter enjoyed my dad's company too much and had already been married and divorced twice."

"Okay, go on," Hayley said.

"My dad was the only working doc in Apple Ridge. Dad refused to drink alcohol, ever, because there was no one else to call if there was an emergency. Mom was an alcoholic and my dad's best friend, Bill Carter, liked to party too. Bad combination."

"Uh-oh. I can only guess where this is going," said Hayley.

"Yeah."

"I'm sorry. Go on."

"One night Mom, Bill Carter, along with Carter's girl friend of the month, harangued my dad to join in their drinking. Mom did that often, but this time Mom had Bill and his date as co-conspirators. Dad caved and got really drunk. Anyway, a pregnant women and her baby died that night and my dad felt responsible and took his life. I was the one who found him the next morning with the car engine running in a closed garage with a hose from his tailpipe into a window.

"You know that's not your fault," Hayley said.

"Maybe I could have stopped it," said Ben.

"What. You were eleven or twelve?"

"Twelve, almost thirteen."

"Not your fault."

"Maybe…Maybe not. Whatever."

Hayley watched Ben closely for clues as he finished this part of his story: forehead, eyes, mouth, posture, hands, and fingers. *He's not that upset. This is not the source of his emotional instability.*

The food arrived and Ben said, "Good, I'm starved."

*There's definitely something else.*

Hayley attempted diverting the conversation…

"This chicken dish is fantastic. You've been here often?…I don't have the energy I used to yet….Deidre is the only person that gets me..."

Ben showed little interest in Hayley's diversions and repeatedly asked, "Do you mind talking some more?"

Hayley finally accepted his plaints and returned to therapy mode. "Okay. Okay. But I'm not your therapist and never will be. I thought you understood that."

Ben's jaw jutted forward. "I trust you and I need help."

"You got that right. Did you ever talk to anyone professionally about you and your parents?"

Ben's shoulders relaxed. "Yes, well, sort of. We haven't talked about Afghanistan yet. There's stuff I never bring up and can't forget."

Hayley watched as Ben softly bit his upper lip and his grip tightened on the edge of the table. *This must be it and I don't want to go there.*

"No we haven't, yet," Hayley said. "And we're not likely to have time to talk about it."

"I hoped we would," Ben said.

"I only agreed to having dinner with you this one time. Did you ever talk to someone about your mom and dad?"

"After returning stateside, I had two or three short sessions with a Marine counselor about my battlefield issues and I mentioned my dad's suicide and mom's alcoholism. The lady shrink, a colonel, spent maybe ten minutes talking about my dad and jumped to the conclusion that my issues were all based on my family issues and had nothing to do with my tours. If so, she said, then they were not her problem or Corps' problem either. She didn't like me and I decided I didn't want to talk to her."

"Did you ever talk to your mom about your feelings?" Hayley asked.

"I did, but not for a while," Ben said. "Two years after my dad died, Mom married a travelling salesman named Victor Evans. I think she knew him even before Dad died. I never really asked. They were made for each other. Both liked to drink and party.

"Anyway, after high school and two years at Central Washington, which I pretty much tanked 'cause I was drunk most of the time and didn't give a shit, I had to join the Marine Corps."

"Your mom?"

"Getting there. The night before I left, Mom said she'd like to have a little family dinner as a going away thing. I knew there was a chance something could happen to me, so I decided to let my mom know how I felt."

"Never before?" Hayley asked.

"No. I assumed she knew but she continued to drink and with enough alcohol in her, I think she forgot. Anyway, with my stepfather and mom at the table, I said I wanted to talk to them about Dad's suicide. My stepfather went ballistic."

Ben lowered his voice to mimic his stepfather, "Son, God damn it. You're so fucking ungrateful. This isn't the time or place for that conversation. Your mother's spent all day cooking to make this dinner special for you."

Switching back to normal voice, Ben continued, "I hated when he called me son. I wanted to say I'm not your son and never will be, but never did."

"So what did you say?" Hayley asked.

"I said. 'Nope, good time to talk.' I told them that the night Dad got drunk, I sat at the top of the stairs and listened to everything. I told them that I heard Mom, Bill Carter and his date harassing Dad. I heard Dad say, repeatedly, 'I can't drink and work.'

"They kept pummeling Dad with 'you're no fun,' 'no one's going to call,' 'stick in the mud,' 'boring one,' 'Dr. Dead-Ass,' 'I'm never having any fun,' 'you gotta lighten up,' 'one drink isn't going to hurt you,' and 'I'm lonely here, it's not fair.'"

"What did your mom say?"

"She started sobbing and left the table. I thought my step-dad was going to slug me but he said 'Fuck you,' as he went to my mom's room. We didn't talk about it again, that night or ever. Anyway, Dad got drunk, a pregnant woman and her baby died and Dad took his life. End of story."

"I'm sorry," Hayley said.

"Worse than that, so many kids at school and storeowners told me that Dad was drunk and shouldn't have been. He had lost all the respect that he worked so hard to achieve. He must have known he'd never get it back."

Again, Hayley watched Ben closely for clues as he finished the next chapter. *He's not upset at all. Not a tear. This cannot be the source.*

"What happened to your mom?" Hayley asked.

"Mom died at the beginning of my second tour in Afghanistan from liver failure. I knew she was ill but she hid how ill from me. I heard about her death two weeks late after I received a condolence email from a girl I knew in high school. Victor sold the house and all their belongings, then moved to Yakima. I've never spoken to him."

"I'm sorry. I'm so sorry. Did you ever see any other psychologists after discharge?" Hayley asked.

"After discharge, I saw a slew of VA docs. They were all a bunch of clock-stampers and just wanted to give me anti-anxiety drugs. No one really wanted to listen."

Ben paid the check and escorted Hayley to his car. He turned on the engine to warm the car, but made no effort to drive.

"Thanks for hearing me out," Ben said. "There's more, I suppose you know."

"I'm sure there's a ton more," Hayley said, "and I've always felt you were hiding something. I'm even surer that I'm not the right person for your problems."

"Perhaps not, but I trust you."

"Trusting me has nothing to do with it. You've got to be willing to open up and then be willing to listen. Nothing you've told me explains why you treat people around you so terribly. There is no excuse for that. Have you taken any anger management courses?" asked Hayley.

"No, not really. The US Marine Corps wanted me angry. Angry at the Taliban, angry at Al-Qaeda, just angry. I started college and the workload kept me busy and I had no responsibility for others. So I had few issues. Same with med school.

"It's when I became a surgical resident and had the responsibility to keep others alive that my anger really came to the surface. I tried one anger course at the med school and lasted thirty minutes. Such bullshit."

"Not a lot of perseverance," Hayley said. "I thought surgeons would be different."

"I don't know," said Ben. "I couldn't handle situations where other people's lives could be impacted. Anger. I don't need someone to tell me I have issues."

"Spare me," Hayley raised her voice. "You're telling me you have issues. If nothing else, do you ever think about thinking before speaking? All you have to do is pause for a moment before reducing people to refuse."

"I don't always have the luxury of waiting before making decisions," Ben stated. "If I had contemplated your injury for three more minutes, or listened to Dr. Marshall, you'd be dead."

"Boy, are you dense," Hayley said, gesturing with a knock on the side of her head. "I get that surgery requires quick decisions at times. Educating other residents does not. Can't you see the difference?"

"Perhaps," Ben said. "I see it afterwards and feel badly. At the time it happens, I don't or can't. If the residents or nurses don't know something they should, or worse yet, not act on something they do know, I lose control."

Hayley shook her head. "You're too smart not to get it.

Ben nodded acceptance, then said, "I've tried. I can't always control my feelings."

"It's getting late," Hayley said, "and I have to go to work tomorrow."

Ben drove Hayley back to her clinic in silence. As they approached her car, Ben asked, "Can we meet again? I'm here for another four or five weeks."

"Where're you going?"

"Don't know yet. I wanted to talk about that too."

Hayley, arms crossed over her chest, looking straight ahead, said, "I'll have to think about it. Probably not. I promised myself I wouldn't see you more than once. I've got my own issues."

"Please."

"I'll call and leave you a message. Don't even think about showing up and expecting me to be civil. Give me your phone number. Most likely, the best I can do is make a list of local people who might help you."

Ben wrote out his number on a piece of paper. "I want you to help me."

Hayley took the number and put it in her purse. Exiting the car she said, "Thanks for dinner. Don't call me," and disappeared into the garage under her office building.

*_*_*_*

Ben would sleep soundly for five consecutive nights.

*_*_*_*

## Chapter 8

"So how bad was it?" Deidre asked as soon as Hayley called.

Hayley paused.

"Oh, so not so bad?" Deidre asked.

"Actually he's got an interesting psychological background" Hayley said. "Dad was a doc, mom an alcoholic. Mom drove dad to suicide, or at least that's his side of the story. He started drinking, tuned out and joined the Marines. That's about as far as we got. Obviously, he got his life together to get where he is now. There's more, something big, I think. I'm almost positive that his mom and dad aren't his problem, so there's some stress or trauma I didn't hear about. He needs help and I told him I don't have the experience to treat him."

"Is that true?" Deidre asked.

Hayley didn't answer.

"Deidre to Hayley. You there?"

"Yeah, I'm here. I was thinking," said Hayley.

"Is it true you can't treat him?" Deidre persisted.

"No. Not really, but I went into this dinner not wanting to see him. I figured telling him I wasn't capable of handling his problem was my way out."

"So, send him to someone who can help him."

"He's adamant that he wants me to take care of him. I told him twenty times that dinner was a one-time deal and wasn't therapy. I wasn't going to handle his issues and that I'd look for someone else for him and....." Hayley paused again.

"And?.......And?....You there?" Deidre asked.

"I don't want to see him," Hayley pleaded. "If you're my friend, and I know you are, please stay out of this."

"Okay, okay. You are so two-faced," Deidre responded. "You always say you want to help people with their emotional problems. You're not getting it at work. He's got real issues and wants your help. Get over your anger and help the poor son of a bitch."

"Me? You started this. I had almost forgotten his sorry ass until he walked into my office."

"Impossible. His sorry ass saved your life. Twice."

"You weren't there. I saw it and heard stuff from more than a few nurses. He was totally scary, out of control. Problems I can't deal with now. Or ever. I'm not going to call him."

*_*_*_*

Sitting in her office four days later, Hayley stared, frozen-like, at a stack of charts, unable to open any. The intercom buzzed.

"Hayley, line four. Says he's Chief of Surgery from Seattle Med. If he's lying, it's one of the best 'get-me-through-channels' lines in history."

"Hayley Green here."

"Miss Green, Armin Cassetti here. I'm Chairman of Surgery at Seattle Med. I don't know if you remember me?"

"I do remember you. What can I do for you?" asked Hayley.

"A favor maybe. As you know, Ben Hunt is nearing the end of his residency here. He's the best surgeon I've ever had the pleasure to train and the most difficult and volatile personality I've ever dealt with."

"I know from personal experience exactly what you're talking about."

"Good. Anyway, these last few days he's been calmer. Not wound so tight. It was noticeable enough that I asked him what's going on and he said he's talked to someone about his issues. Apparently, it's you. He said it was probably his only session."

"I'm guessing he put you up to this, calling me. Correct?" Hayley asked.

"No, Miss Green. Contacting you was entirely my idea. The only way he'll ever know about this call is if you tell him."

Hayley lied, "Dr. Cassetti, my training and experience don't make me even remotely qualified to handle his issues." Reverting to the truth, she said, "Not to mention the fact that I don't really want to take care of him."

"I can't speak to your qualifications, but we've sent him to an array of eminently qualified therapists over the past few years. He's never lasted more than two or three sessions with anyone, despite threats from me to throw him out of the surgical program."

"Why didn't you throw him out?"

"Because he was just too good a surgeon to let go."

"So what do you want from me? He's leaving town," Hayley asked.

"I'd really appreciate you continuing to counsel him. I just can't afford to have him melt down as he finishes his training."

"I didn't counsel him and it wasn't a 'session.' We went out to dinner. That's all. I owed him that."

"Call it what you want. He's better and it makes my life easier and all of the staff's too. It'll also keep the hospital attorneys off my back if he's seeing someone professionally. Please."

"I don't like him."

"I'm sure you don't like many of your patients, but Ben Hunt is special and, for what it's worth, you'd be helping him, Seattle Med and me tremendously. I mean it. Again, I'd appreciate you seeing him."

"I'll think about it. That's all I can promise," Hayley said. "I've got my own issues."

*_*_*_*

By the following Wednesday, Ben had not heard from Hayley. After work, he drove back to his apartment at nine thirty p.m. and parked in the underground garage. He sat, quietly, in semi-darkness, perhaps an hour or more, until he had enough energy to walk up twelve stairs to his unit. He knew he would sleep poorly.

At one a.m. the phone rang. Ben, assuming a hospital call, answered, "Dr. Hunt."

"Ben."

Ben sat up quickly. Hayley's voice was strong and forceful, "This is Hayley Green. I hope I didn't wake you."

"You didn't, actually. I was…."

"I couldn't sleep, so let me say my piece," Hayley said, interrupting Ben's response. "It's obvious to me that I can't make myself happy. My parents are no help. They cry twenty-four-seven worrying about me. Other than Deidre, my friends don't call because they don't know what to say and that hurts. My job, which used to give me intense satisfaction, sucks and I'm not even close to deriving or giving happiness there. So, it comes down to you, as much as I dislike you personally."

"I'm sorry and…," Ben interjected.

Hayley interrupted again, "Let me finish. Apparently, I do have the power to make you happy, or at least, try to make you happy. Seven thirty tonight. Text me where we'll meet. Don't say anything. Good night."

"I'm not looking....," Ben started.

Hayley had already disconnected.

"...for happy."

*_*_*_*

Hayley walked into the ultra-posh Canlis restaurant, said something to the maître d' and scanned the room. Ben, already seated at a window table, stood quickly and walked to meet her. Her head stood out dramatically with two inches of new, thin, brown and black stubbles of hair.

Hayley sat and absorbed the spectacular one hundred eighty degree view of Lake Union. "Nice. Haven't been here for ages. As if you didn't notice, this is my first day in public without the wig."

Ben smiled. "Looks great. I do remember from the first time I saw you. Long, black hair. It'll come back in time." After a small moment of uncomfortable silence Ben said, "Thank you again for coming. Our dinner last week helped me…."

Hayley interrupted, "Stop. I've done as much thinking as I can about you. I didn't want to be your therapist. I'm not equipped, trained or qualified to deal with your issues. Right now I've got more on my plate than I can handle. I used to feel that I had control of my life and now I have none. As I said this morning on the phone, I hate my job, I will probably die young, never fall in love, get married or have children. I don't know how or what to do with my parents. I live in fear every time I go back to see Dr. Capland. And that's just for starters. Your issues aren't even on my radar."

"You went into counseling because you wanted to help people and here I am asking you to help me," Ben pleaded.

Hayley rolled her eyes upward and shook her head.

Ben continued, "I know your concerns are real but..."

"But, what?" said Hayley.

"You don't know how long you might live or whether you're going to get married. Your parents are big enough and smart enough to figure out what to do, no matter what happens. Your fear of Dr. Capland's follow up visits and the batteries of x-rays and tests will never go away completely, but as time goes on and you're doing okay, the fear only gets bad from the time of the visit to the follow-up phone call from his nurse after the tests and blood work are completed."

Hayley's lower lip covered her upper lip for a moment and she said, "Thanks. We'll see."

"I'm leaving Seattle," Ben said, "in four or five weeks and I'm going somewhere that has no help for me, so I need you now."

"And where might that be?"

"I've been assigned to Apple Ridge."

"You're kidding me. That's gotta be the worst place for you to go."

"Or the best. If I can handle my emotions and get some kind of understanding from the people I alienated as I left, maybe I'll be okay. Besides, the forestland, where Dad and I used to hike and hunt, is still there and I own it. Maybe I can find some peace there. Maybe not."

"That's asking a lot," said Hayley.

"Probably, but I owe the government five years of service for student loans. Apple Ridge was one of the choices, so I took it. In any event, I'm outta here in little over a month and I need your help. So there. Please."

Hayley's eyes were glued to Ben. Any air of surgical swagger and confidence was gone. "You're serious," Hayley said. "I wasn't sure if seeing me was some kind of cruel joke."

As Hayley scratched her eyebrow searching for a bit of wisdom, Ben repeated, "Please."

"Jesus, you're persistent. What part of the word 'no' don't you understand." Hayley lied for the third time, "I have no experience in treating your problems. Just stuff I've read." She reached into her purse and pulled out a piece of paper. "I said that I'd see you until you left but I made a list of possible therapists in the community that can help you. I called each of them this afternoon. The ones on the list said they'd see you and would make room in their schedules for you as a favor to me. Robin Anders was on the list but apparently you've seen her."

Ben nodded, took the list, unread, and put it in his coat pocket. "Even our dinner last week helped me. I can't say why. Just that I thought you might be able to help. I slept better for two or three nights and the dreams weren't so bad."

"No. You're not trapping me with that load of crap. We'll talk some and enjoy dinner…if that's possible."

After they had both finished their salads, Hayley asked about Ralph Yamamoto and some of the residents who had helped in her care. Then, without hesitation or thinking, she slipped back into therapy mode. "What is it that sets you off? You know, a trigger."

"Doesn't happen always," Ben said, "but usually the same theme when it does. I think someone should know something, some fact or point. I can't handle it when they don't know it because they should and not knowing it puts patient's lives at risk."

"Like Yamamoto didn't know some obscure anatomy question?"

"Yes."

"I'm curious, how did you ever end up in the Marines? Not the usual segue into a surgery residency."

"One night, mid-summer after my worthless, give-a-shit, two years at Central Washington I got into some trouble Billy Jr., Tony Ramos and I got plastered and tried to steal the Apple Ridge hook-and-ladder. We planned to use the ladder to climb into Billy's girl friend's window. It didn't go well after we took out a light post on the first turn out of the fire station. Judge Harcourt gave all three of us the option of going into the Marine Corps or spending three months in jail. I guess he figured the Corps would straighten us out."

"Really?" Hayley said, incredulously. "You gotta be kidding me. A judge plea-bargained you three into the Marines."

"No. Just me. Junior and Tony refused and spent three months at the Coyote Ridge Corrections Center."

"What happened to your buddies? You guys still friends?"

"No. Not friends. Both were back in the pen at Walla Walla within two years. Junior was killed in a bar fight four years later in Yakima. Tony Ramos has been in and out of jail. The crazy thing is that Junior could have had all the money in the world. His family was rich. He just liked living on the edge."

"Hard to believe you're the least screwed up," Hayley said.

"Over time, so I've heard, the Carters and Ramoses have shifted all the faults of Junior and Tony Ramos onto me, and both families have made it abundantly clear that they don't want to see me back in Apple Ridge, ever."

"Then why go? Seems like another reason not to be there," asked Hayley.

"I wasn't to blame for Ramos or Junior, but as I got my life together, their families got madder and madder. I feel I need to clear the slate. I can try to make amends for the stuff in Apple Ridge. I can't undo what happened later."

Hayley caught the end of Ben's thought. *There it is again.*

Hayley's pan-seared sable fish and Ben's grilled halibut with a pistachio crust arrived. They shared a small portion of each other's entrees after disagreeing whose fish could possibly be better.

As an overly attentive waiter cleared the plates, Ben asked, "So why do you hate your job?"

"Maybe hate is too strong. I'm just disappointed with myself,"

Hayley said. “I wanted to help people and work in the public sector. Four years into it, I can’t say that I don’t feel useful most of the time by the people I’m supposed to be helping. I told the director of the clinic that I wasn’t happy and she wondered if I’d come back too soon. I told her that with leukemia, nothing is too soon.”

After dinner, waiting for their cars, Ben said, “Thanks again for coming tonight. I do really feel better talking to you. Would you see me until I leave? Next week, same time?”

“To what end? You're just talking and I'm listening. That's it.”

"I'm guessing most times therapists think they're helping and the patient's thinking the opposite. At least that's the way it's been for me. I've had a couple of them call to say they thought we had a connection and they'd like to see me a few more times. I wasn't always nice."

"I'm not helping."

"Actually, you are. You're thinking you're not and I'm saying you get it."

"What's it?"

"Me. You get me. You can see into me."

The valet stood impatiently by Hayley’s open car door.

"I can't," Hayley said."

"You do. Please, see me until I leave," Ben pleaded. “Please."

Hayley clenched her jaw while shaking her head no and sat in her car. The valet shut the car door immediately. After a moment she opened the car window and said to Ben, "Okay. Okay. I swore to myself I wouldn’t do this. Next Wednesday. Thanks for dinner." She drove off, not waiting for Ben to respond.

## Chapter 9

The next morning, Bev Bergreen, the local director of DSHS and Hayley's boss, knocked once, then walked into Hayley's office and sat in front of her desk.

"Hi, Bev. What's up?" Hayley asked.

"You doing okay?" Bergreen asked back.

"Sure. Why do you ask?"

"I dunno. Seems like you're mopey. I expected you have less energy but…" Mrs. Bergreen hesitated, looking for the right words. "Anyway, I can only imagine what you've been through in the past five months, but, as I've said before, I wonder if maybe you came back too soon."

"Jeez. Is it that obvious?" Hayley frowned.

"Actually, it is."

"I'm sorry. I'm trying. I really am, but I'm not getting the same feeling about helping people. Not like before I was sick. Funny, because I was truly looking forward to coming back, hoping it would give some normalcy to my life, but the glass is 'half-empty' rather than 'half-full' most of time. Most of my caseload is crap. People are just gaming the system rather than making any attempt to improve their lot."

"I'm sorry you feel that way," said Bergreen. "If you want to take more time off and come back with a fresh sense of purpose, I'd understand. Do you think you need to see someone?"

"No. I'm okay. I'll try to be a bit more positive, perky, upbeat or whatever. Curiously, the only person that really wants my help is some surgical resident that took care of me in the hospital. He's got some stress issues. He's pleaded with me to help him but I don't really like him."

Bergreen shook her head. "First, you shouldn't be doing any work outside of DSHS," Bergreen warned, "and I need all your energies here."

"I didn't see him professionally," Hayley interjected. "Just a couple of dinners, so far. He was just being persistent. He believes I'm the only one who can solve his problems."

"What you do on your own time is your own business," said Bergreen. "Watch out, the rescuer becomes the victim."

"That's not going to happen," Hayley said. "I've tried giving him a list of qualified people in the community but he's adamant that I be the one who helps. I owe him that. Probably a lot more after he saved my life – twice. Literally. Anyway, he's leaving Seattle in a month. He's been assigned to Apple Ridge for five years to pay off his government loans."

"Apple Ridge. Now there's a city in a big, black hole. Trust me that there's probably no one, public or private, in Apple Ridge who can help him. Olympia can't keep any qualified DSHS people there for more than two months. I think two different managers have quit this year alone."

"Why's that?"

"A small town with a large fruit processing mill that closed four or five years ago. Most of the town worked in the mill and the rest supported it. Half the town's on welfare and the other half should be. The stress levels are off the wall and jobs are non-existent."

*_*_*_*

Hayley and Ben met twice more for dinner. Ben described the varied situations and his responses surrounding his recent anger attacks. All were similar to the one Hayley witnessed. The trigger always seemed to be some piece of information that Ben expected the person to know.

*_*_*_*

Aromas of hummus and freshly baked pita wafted at the door as Ben walked Hayley into a small Madrona restaurant on Thirty-Fourth Avenue called Turkuaz Bistro. Ben had no idea that restaurants existed in this part of Seattle. "How'd you find this place?"

"Friend of friend, I think," said Hayley. "Has to have the best lamb, ever."

Waiting for a sampler of hummus, baba ghanoush and cacik with extra pitas," Hayley said, "This is our last meeting. You okay about Apple Ridge? Not that you have much choice."

"Yeah, not much choice," Ben said. "I got an email from a girl who knew me from high school. She said that more than a few people are already beating the drums of discontentment. Worst of all is Bill Carter, my dad's old friend. They've already written letters to the NHS to see if they'll send someone, anyone, else."

"You knew Apple Ridge would have been my last choice for you. By the way, you know your chief called me a while ago."

"No, really?" Ben asked.

"Really. He thought I was helping you after our first dinner. Am I helping you? Other than me listening to your crappy childhood and triggers, I don't know what I've done. I certainly haven't given you any suggestions or therapy options."

Ben sat still, spinning his dinner fork in a small circle on the table.

"Hello, anyone there? Am I helping you?" Hayley asked.

"The pita's fabulous."

"That's not an answer."

"You do, actually. Help, I mean. You knew I was afraid. No one, nobody, whom I've talked to professionally, seemed to make that connection. You did it without knowing a thing."

"I could tell you were hurting. I don't know why. I just knew."

"I know you knew and, at first, it made me angry. Now, with my addled mind, if I can tell you everything, maybe you'll understand and can help. That gives me hope."

Hayley shook her head, picked up the menu. "The pita is good," she said.

After Ben and Hayley ordered two entrees of braised lamb shank, Hayley asked, "Tell me about the Marines and Afghanistan."

Ben talked non-stop for most of an hour through dinner, two Turkish coffees and a split order of baklava. Boot camp, home on leave where Ben and his mother fought for seven days. After infantry training, Ben hope for some leave time to return home to patch up hurt feelings with his mother. That didn't happen as Ben's unit headed to Afghanistan the day after formal training ended. Ben re-upped after his first tour. He came back to Washington State after his second tour with a Distinguished Service Cross and restarted his junior year at Central Washington University. Ellen Hunt had already died.

Ben, sweating, was unaware that he was clenching a dessert fork most of the time he talked. He summarized the entire dialog with, "War. Death. Fear. Hate. College. Med School. That pretty much sums it up."

Hayley put her hand on Ben's clenched fist and said, "That's it? You know there's more. There's something really big you're not telling me."

*She knows. How does she know?* Ben bent the fork that he had weaved through my fingers before saying, "Guilt. I caused the death of my entire squad. It haunts me every day. I try but I can't forget."

Ben had never mentioned guilt to anyone, until then.

"Good, it's out. Now you can talk to someone about what's really bugging you," Hayley said as she looked at her watch. "It's late now, the restaurant is closing, and I have to work tomorrow."

"Can't we go somewhere and talk? I have so much more I want to explain," Ben asked.

"You don't wear pleading very well and, no, we can't. As they say, 'Your sixty minutes are up.' Besides, you're leaving town."

"Not for three days."

"I can't fix you in three days, or thirty days. You will need to find help in Apple Ridge or some nearby town. Maybe Ellensburg, Cle Elum, the Tri-Cities or Yakima has someone to help you. This is our last dinner."

"You're not being very sympathetic," whined Ben. "I really want to talk some more."

"I'm sorry. I shouldn't have started in with you in the beginning." Hayley hesitated briefly, then said, "I'm really sorry. We have to stop now. It's for your own good. I'm here in Seattle and you'll be east of the mountains."

"I don't want to see anyone else. I've never felt that anyone else could see my problems, but you do."

"That's bull. Anyway, I am not supposed to be counseling anyone outside of work. I could get fired."

"I doubt you'll get fired and I suspect you doubt that too," said Ben.

"Perhaps. What I'm trying to convey is that you can't drive back to Seattle every time you want to talk and expect me to be there for you."

Ben sat quietly, a bit stunned at Hayley's abruptness.

"It's better that we stop our relationship," Hayley said, knowing she'd hurt Ben. "Regardless, I need to get home. I will say, as much as I hate admitting being wrong, I don't think you're a bad person. I think your reasons for acting the way you do are discoverable and, hopefully, treatable. You have an incredibly bright future in medicine according to your chief. Let's hope you find someone to help you."

"Please, Hayley."

"Now. Home."

*_*_*_*_*

"How'd your last visit with Ben go?" Deidre asked.

"Okay. Well, okay for me. I finally got an inkling of what really happened to him. He said he's never been able to tell anyone what he wanted to tell me."

"And, then what?" asked Deidre.

"He wanted to talk more," Hayley said, "but he's leaving Seattle in seventy-two hours, so I acted a little abrupt at the end. I needed to end our relationship so he could move on to someone else."

"I guess the next question is: Did you want to talk more?" Deidre asked.

"I didn't think so until after he dropped me off. I know I was helping him. I told him that I wasn't doing anything but listening. He swore that I was the only one who has ever helped."

"If you hadn't been so judgmental in the hospital, you could have seen him months ago."

"Yeah. Too bad. You were right," Hayley said, with a touch of remorse. "It's just that he dismantled a resident and my mother in front of me. I just couldn't see past that at the time. I was wallowing in my own self-pity and I guess I needed to get angry at something or somebody for my leukemia."

"Shit. You're a mess," Deidre said.

"I know I was helping. That felt good, for a change. It's addicting to know that you're helping."

"Uh-oh. You're going to miss him, aren't you?" Deidre asked.

"Anyway, I did get him talking so maybe he'll find someone good in Apple Ridge or nearby to help. I hope so. I really hope so."

"You didn't answer the question, girl. You're going to miss him, won't you?" Deidre asked again.

"No. No. He needed to go," said Hayley. "He'll be fine."

"Do I know you, or what? Can't you be honest with me?" asked Deidre. She waited for a response and got none. "Hello. you there?"

"Yes. I suppose I do, I mean I will miss him. I liked being needed," Hayley said. "I liked our dinners."

"You gonna call him? See how he's doing?"

"No.  That would be the worst thing for him. He needs to find someone close by to help."

## Chapter 10

Three months passed before Bev Bergreen, Hayley's boss, again sat in the chair opposite Hayley.

"I know we talked a few months ago about your change in demeanor," said Bergreen. "I happen to like you. No, I love you. You were my best counselor and set a tone and attitude that everyone here tried to emulate. Since coming back, we haven't seen the old Hayley. You're edgy and seem so distracted."

"I'm sorry Bev. I'm trying. I just have so many things to worry about. Not to mention just living."

"You're right, you've been here every week for five months. I'd like you to take a short break. A week or two. Get refreshed and see if we can't find the old Hayley."

"I don't think I need a vacation. I've missed enough time already."

"Hayley. I wasn't asking. I'm telling," Bergreen demanded. "Go someplace with a friend. Puerto Vallarta, Cabo, Maui. I don't care. Sometime in the next month. Capish?"

*_*_*_*

"You have any free time coming?" Hayley asked, twenty minutes later.

Deidre jumped at the suggestion, "Sure. What'cha wanna do?"

"My boss thinks I need a change of pace."

"She's got that right. You're miserable, but I still love you. Where should we go?"

"I don't know. Hawaii?" suggested Hayley.

"Too far, too expensive. I just saw a travel program about hiking in the Sawtooth Mountains outside Sun Valley, Idaho. It's off-season and the prices are cheap-cheap. We could stay at the Sun Valley Lodge or rent a condo."

"What's there to do?"

"Hike. Bike. Massages. A little shopping. Vegging. Ice skating."

"Deeds, We don't ice skate," said Hayley.

"Never too late to try. I can get out of here week after next. Sound good?" Deidre said, hopingly. "We could stay in Walla Walla one night and do a little wine tasting. I've never done that."

"Book it," said Hayley.

*_*_*_*

Two weeks later, four days into Hayley's forced vacation, Deidre headed off to the Sun Valley Lodge spa for a massage.

Hayley phoned her boss in Seattle. "Bev. You asked me to check in. I'm having a great time but I'd be disingenuous if I told you I've had some kind of epiphany."

"Well, we tried. Maybe your mojo will come back on its own," Bergreen said.

"I hope so too."

"Oh, by the way. Weren't you seeing some guy from Apple Ridge a while back?" Bergreen asked. "A doc?"

"I wasn't seeing him, if that's what you mean," Hayley said. "I was just helping him out because he literally saved my life. Why'd you bring that up?"

"Oh, nothing, I guess. I was at the DSHS director's meeting in Olympia yesterday. Corinne Shermann, the Apple Ridge director, sat next to me during one of our sessions and then I had lunch with her. She's really nice. Her assistant agent in Apple Ridge is quitting, or actually asking to be transferred. Corinne has had three assistant agents quit in eight months. The assistant who's leaving wants back in Seattle. Corinne thought we might find a spot for her."

"She wants my job?" asked Hayley, thinking for a moment she might be fired.

"No, no, no. It's not about you," said Bergreen. "Anyway, to the point, Corinne told me about a young surgeon that came to town in July, working for the National Health Service. Apparently, he grew up there and left a trail of smoke on his way out of town."

"Yep, that would be him."

"Anyway, his return was not welcome by some well-positioned people, despite the fact that the town needed a surgeon badly. I guess he's gotten into a few tussles."

"Yep. Definitely him."

"Apparently, the city manager has called a town hall meeting to discuss his being there. They're trying to force the NHS to remove him."

"That's horrible. He's really not a bad guy."

"Whatever. See you back next week. Bright and chirpy."

"I'll try. Chirp."

Hayley disconnected, sat a moment, then googled "Apple Ridge city hall." In sixty seconds she learned that the town hall meeting would be the next day at six p.m. in the high school auditorium. The meeting had been originally slated for noon at the city council meeting room but too many people showed interested in attending. The venue and time were changed to accommodate the expected brouhaha."

*_*_*_*

"We're leaving first thing in the morning," Hayley stated as soon as Deidre returned.

"What's up? I thought we were going to stay until Saturday and stay two nights in Walla Walla?"

"I've got to see a man about a horse," Hayley said, already packing.

"What are you talking about?"

"We're going to Apple Ridge. I just got off the phone with my boss and..."

*_*_*_*

Hayley and Deidre left Sun Valley at seven a.m. much to Deidre's objections.

Every thirty minutes Diedre would ask, "Are you sure you know what you're doing?"

"No," was all the reply Hayley would give.

"Do you have a plan?"

"Don't know, but I have to be there."

Making good time, they stopped in La Grande, Oregon, for lunch, then straight through to Apple Ridge, arriving at four thirty that afternoon.

As Hayley registered into the Travelodge, Deidre checked in with the local sheriff's office. FBI protocol required her to let local police know she staying in town and carrying a weapon.

"What'cha here for FBI lady," the deputy sheriff asked, "if it ain't for police business?"

"I'm merely on my way back to Seattle from vacation in Sun Valley," Deidre said. "My travelling partner has a friend here in Apple Ridge. We'll be gone in the morning."

"'Scuse me. Why you telling me all this?"

"By federal law, I am required to remain armed even when I'm off duty."

"Hmmph. Well, I don't rightly remember any FBI through these parts before," said the deputy, "so I can't say that I knew that. I'll tell the sheriff. How's he gonna reach you, if need be."

Deidre gave the deputy her cell number and told him where she and Hayley would be staying.

At five forty-five, the high school parking areas were full. Walking in, Hayley garnered a few odd looks, but most everyone stared at Deidre.

As they followed the signs to the auditorium, Deidre asked Hayley, "Once more, I'm going to ask, what exactly are your plans?"

"Dunno," said Hayley. "I don't know exactly what's going to happen so I'm just going to listen. I know enough that if Ben is asked to leave town, he'll need a friend. I feel like I abandoned him."

"You really do care for this guy. I still can't believe you don't hate him."

"I told him that coming here was a huge mistake," said Hayley. "He just wanted to prove to everyone that the Ben Hunt who left here isn't the same guy as Ben Hunt, M.D. Apparently, some here have long memories."

As they entered, looking for two adjoining seats, Deidre whispered, "When I leave in the morning, one hundred percent of the blacks will be gone from this sorry-ass city."

"Same goes for miserable, somewhat spoiled psychologists." Both laughed.

Hayley and Deidre took seats on the back and side of the packed auditorium.

"I see Ben up front on the right." whispered Deidre.

Hayley nodded.

You think he should know we're here? Deidre asked.

"No. Let's just listen and see what happens," said Hayley.

At six o'clock, three men took seats behind a large table at the front of the auditorium's stage.

At exactly six ten, a walrus-sized, older gentleman, sitting in the center, banged his hand on the table, "Hello, everyone." The crowd quieted immediately. "I hope to make this meeting short and sweet. I'm not in favor, one bit, 'bout what's goin' on here in Apple Ridge, but rather than let bad blood simmer forever, maybe it's best we git it all out in the open."

The crowded auditorium collectively nodded agreement.

"There's a petition before us, signed by the required five percent of Apple Ridge's registered voters," the speaker said, waving a handful of papers. "It asks that the City of Apple Ridge demand that the National Health Service replace Dr. Benjamin Hunt."

Hayley noted that speaker didn't introduce himself. *Everyone knows who he is. Small town.*

The speaker continued, "Anyway, we'll begin by calling on Councilman Bill Carter to present the petition. After Bill has spoken, Dr. Hanratty, from Apple Ridge General, will speak for Ben, uh, Dr. Hunt. Councilman Carter, the floor is yours."

Bill Carter, sitting next to the speaker, stood. Carter, big, graying, ten years younger and twenty pounds lighter than the first speaker, carried his weight well. Carter approached the podium, exuding confidence. "Thanks, Harry," Carter said, nodding back to the seated man, "We're all lucky to have Harry Brown as the City Manager."

The crowd mumbled acknowledgment.

"Folks," Carter continued, "You all know why we're here. Ben Hunt left Apple Ridge thirteen years ago. He had been trouble for our police for years because of rowdiness and drunkenness. The last episode before leaving Apple Ridge was the worst. Ben decided to steal the town's hook and ladder truck and crashed it into a lamp pole forty feet from the station, drunk as a skunk. He dragged Tony Ramos and my son, Billy, Jr., with him. Long and short, Ben got Judge

Harcourt to let him go scot-free, while my son and Tony had to spend time in jail. It changed my son and when Billy returned from Coyote Corrections, he was never the same. In the end, Billy's dead and I blame Ben Hunt for all that. Tony Ramos didn't do much better. My family, and the Ramoses, won't forgive Ben Hunt and never will. He doesn't belong in Apple Ridge, got no family left here, and shouldn't have come back other than to say hello and good-bye."

Carter paused to see that most of the heads nodded agreement.

"Since coming back, he's already had two run-ins. One with my son, Joey, and another with Joey's wife at the Safeway. I don't see those problems goin' away. I don't think it's asking too much for all of you to support our petition to have him removed from Apple Ridge. It's the least we can do. Thank you."

The same heads continued nodding agreement. Bill Carter sat back down next to Harry Brown on the dais. Carter mumbled to Brown, "That oughta fix him."

Brown remained emotionless.

On cue, as Carter took his seat, Felix Ramos, Tony Ramos' dad stood from the middle of the auditorium and yelled, "Ben Hunt no good. He the devil. He gonna be trouble for all of us. Jus' like he got my son, Tony, in trouble. Bill Carter's right. We needs to send Ben back where he come from."

Harry Brown held his hands up and said, "Listen here, folks. From now on nobody speaks until I call him or her. We don't need a free-for-all." Brown waited for the room to quiet. "I'd like Dr. Hanratty to speak for Ben."

Dr. Hank Hanratty, tall, reed-like and long necked, came from the first row of the auditorium, mounted the stage and approached the podium. Already sweating, he started fidgeting with the microphone, which remained six inches too low when fully extended.

"Folks. I'm not much good at public speaking. I'm sorry we have to be here," Hanratty said, bent over and speaking in a halting monotone. "It's a shame, a damn shame. Apple Ridge has been requesting a full-time surgeon for four years now. It's just insane that surgical cases had to be sent to Yakima or the Tri-Cities. Ben Hunt volunteered to come back to his hometown to help us out. He's done his time, supported our country, like many of us, with honor and dignity and was awarded a medal for bravery. Not many of us can match that. He is well trained and came with the highest recommendations of the surgical department at Seattle Med. Short and sweet, we need him."

The audience remained silent.

Hanratty continued, "I can't speak to the run-ins he's had with the Carters. No arrests were made and the few people I've talked to tell me Ben did not cause those incidents. I say it's time to forgive and forget and let's get on with our lives. Thank you."

Hanratty, head down, sat back in the audience. The auditorium was abuzz with conversation as Harry Brown banged his hand on the table until the auditorium quieted. "Anyone have anything else to say."

Warren Kiffers, a local attorney and a known hunting buddy of Bill Carter, stood and raised his hand. "I've got some information to share." Kiffers mounted the stage and took the microphone. "Bill Carter asked me to see what I could find out from Ben's training at Seattle Med. I know a few people there. Anyway, from what I could learn, Ben had issues with anger management the whole time he was in Seattle. I admit this is hearsay because nothing official was filed with the City of Seattle or the State of Washington, but I suspect there's more than a kernel of truth."

The audience's silence continued.

"I think we should demand that Dr. Hunt sign a statement about what happened at Seattle Med and give us a release to investigate. If he was receiving treatment for psychological problems and is a liability to Apple Ridge, I think we have the right to know."

Kiffers paused as the auditorium nodded, then looked directly at Ben. "Dr. Hunt, are you willing to sign a release?"

Ben, sitting next to Dr. Hanratty, attempted to stand.

Hanratty put his hand on Ben's shoulder and kept him down. Hanratty whispered, "Don't answer," then stood and turned to address the audience from his seat. "This is a witch hunt. You all know it. Ben's a good man now."

"If there's nothing to hide, Ben shouldn't care whether he signs a release," Kiffers said.

"Warren, thank you for your comments, but...," Brown started, then stopped as a sea of noise drowned out his voice. The audience had started talking amongst themselves, some raising their voices to a mini-scream, advocating one side or the other.

Harry banged his hand on the table again and again, pleading for quiet. He semi-shouted over the din, "Ben, you have a problem signing something?"

The audience quieted quickly, waiting for Ben's response. Ben sat still. Even those on his side took the absence of acceptance as guilt. Kiffers returned to his seat.

"That's too bad." Brown shook his head and waited for the audience's attention. "Anyone else want to say something?" Brown said.

Brown then stood and scanned the auditorium, as everyone looked around. "I guess that's about it. We'll need to put it to a vote and…."

Hayley stood up and Deidre mumbled, "Uh-oh."

"I do," Hayley said loudly, from the back of the now quieted auditorium. "I have something to say."

Ben, confused, stood quickly, and spun towards Hayley's unmistakable voice. Hayley's first look at Ben's face since his departure from Seattle, etched with fatigue and defeat, told her exactly what she would need to do.

The audience turned towards Hayley as Brown said, "And who in God's name are you, young lady?"

"I am Dr. Hunt's therapist."

The room's silence seemed deathlike for a few heartbeats and then the talking quickly crescendoed to hard-rock cacophony.

Bill Carter stood next to Brown, which quieted the gathering.

"This is crap, Harry. Total crap," Carter said. "We don't know shit about who this lady is and what she knows. I'll bet Ben hired someone to say what he wants them to say."

Brown turned to Carter and said, "Sit down, Bill. This is an open forum; she's got the right to speak her mind. You can ask her questions, if you want. I expect you to be civil, and watch your tongue. We can decide afterwards how valid her comments might be. Now, please, sit down." Brown turned back to Hayley and said, "Come on up here Miss, or Mrs., and tell us who you are and what you know."

Hayley walked confidently to the stage and podium. She purposefully did not look at Ben. Hayley's erect posture, tilted head, eyes narrowed in skepticism, and tight jaw made it clear to Apple Ridge that this strange women had a mission. She climbed the stairs to the microphone.

"Thank you, Mr. Brown. My name is Hayley Green. I work for the Department of Social and Health Services for State of Washington. You know us best at the DSHS. I have been in the Seattle office as a case manager half time and a therapist the other half. I have a bachelor's degree from UC Berkeley and a Masters of Social Work and Counseling from Seattle University. I will be working as an assistant agent in the Apple Ridge DSHS office."

Hayley paused to let her credentials sink in.

"I have been treating Dr. Hunt as a patient for a while. Federal and state privacy laws, or HIPAA, protect his medical and counseling records. I've already breached that confidence by even saying that I've been counseling him. Before I can say anything more, he'll need to consent to release of any information by me."

"Ben," Harry Brown asked, "I assume you know this lady?"

Ben stood. "Yes. Yes, I do. I didn't know that she'd be here for this hearing. In fact, I'm quite surprised."

"We're not going to go through the rigmarole of having you sign forms," Brown said, "which we don't have here anyway. So, I'll ask you. Can this lady speak about your condition?"

"Yes. Yes, I believe she can."

Brown turned towards Hayley. "The floor is yours, Miss. Tell us what you know."

"Thank you," Hayley said. "I will let you all know first that I do not intend to speak of some details of Dr. Hunt's life which I believe to be personal and have no bearing on his ability to practice medicine."

Bill Carter, crimson faced with neck veins bulging to his temples, stood, and waved an accusing finger at Hayley. He yelled, "See. See. I told you. She doesn't know shit about what's going on here. A dollar to a doughnut she's sleeping with Hunt and he's paying her. It wouldn't surprise me if that black one that walked in with her isn't doing the same." Carter was pointing to Deidre, which turned every head in the auditorium.

Immediately, chaos reigned. Two hundred heads in the auditorium began popping up and down, swiveling front to back, and all the while yelling back and forth at each other.

Harry Brown stood and started banging the table with his fist as hard as he could, "Damn it, Bill. Sit down. Sit down, now. You're way out of line. And watch your tongue. Everyone be quiet."

When Brown finally quieted the room, he pointed at Deidre and asked, "Miss. I'd like you to stand and tell us who you might be before we go any further. We've had enough surprises this evening already."

Deidre stood, scanned the room and said, "My name is Deidre

Williams. I am an agent of the FBI or Federal Bureau of Investigation. I am here unofficially with Miss Green as a friend. I did check in with the Apple Ridge Police Department when I arrived in town per FBI protocol. By law, I am required to carry a weapon wherever I go."

Amidst the gasps, Brown asked, "You're armed?"

"Yes, sir." Everyone in the room knew that firearms were not allowed within a mile of the school by city ordinance.

Brown turned to the opposite corner of the room. "Chief Robertson, did you know about this?"

Charley Robertson, the city Chief of Police had been leaning against the back wall of the auditorium. "I did, Harry," Roberston said. "Eddie, uh, Deputy Stafford, called me two hours ago. Agent Williams told Deputy Stafford, that she was accompanying a friend who was visiting Apple Ridge. She didn't say nuttin' to Eddie about being at the town hall meeting. She certainly didn't say nuttin' about being colored, not that I care. She's right though, as an agent of the FBI, she has the right to be armed. In fact, I think she is obliged to be armed at all times. Anyway, school isn't in session right now and there aren't any students around."

"Thanks, Charley. Miss Williams, do you have any knowledge of Dr. Hunt?" Brown asked.

"Yes, I do." Deidre replied.

"How is that?"

"I met him when he was taking care of Hayley. He was her surgeon. That was more than nine months ago. I haven't seen him since, although I talked to him on the phone once."

Carter, his face beefsteak red, stood up again. Wagging his finger at Hayley, he yelled, "There it is. I told you. She owes him something. She's not going to tell the truth. She's just going to lie. She's gonna lie through her teeth. She doesn't know a thing about what's going on here in Apple Ridge and neither does that one." Carter's wagging finger had switched to Deidre. "All we're going to hear are lies."

Before Harry Brown could calm Bill Carter, Deidre spoke up. "Mr. Carter… Mr. Carter." The room quieted immediately. "Mr. Carter, I don't know you, but I do know Hayley Green. She is not Dr. Hunt's girlfriend, she's not sleeping with him and she's not a liar. I have a law degree from Seattle University and have passed the Washington State Bar. I am confident that you have just slandered Hayley, and possibly me, in front of two hundred witnesses. Unless you have some kind of proof, which I know you don't, I'm hoping that Miss Green sues you for slander and defamation of character. If you'd like a definition, slander is when someone tells one or more persons an untruth about another, which untruth will harm the reputation of the person defamed. Slander is a civil wrong and can be the basis for a lawsuit. Damages for slander are significantly higher if there is malicious intent, which I am sure there was. You may want to consider what I've said before you open your mouth again."

Carter, his mouth forming a large 'O', continued to stand, as did Deidre. Other than breathing, the room was cemetery-silent again as heads rotated back and forth waiting for the next salvo.

Hayley turned back to the table with Carter and Brown. In a calm, but strong voice, she said, "I have no intention of suing anyone for slander or defamation. Mr. Carter, I have the floor. I'd like you to sit your uninformed, ignorant, red-neck ass down so I can say what I have to say."

Carter knocked his chair backwards to the stage floor, and screamed, "I'm not a red-neck and I'm not ignorant."

"Exactly," Hayley responded. "Perhaps you're not. Now you know how it feels. And I'm not sleeping with anybody and I'm not a liar."

Carter knew he had been bested. He picked up his chair and sat. Hayley turned back to the audience, whose attention she now had completely. Rarely did anyone get away with putting Bill Carter in his place.

"As to what I know, let me start off by correcting some

statements by Mr. Carter," Hayley said. "The incident with the fire truck involved trying to use the ladder to gain entrance to Billy Carter's girlfriend's window. I find it hard to believe that Dr. Hunt, sober or drunk, concocted that plan by himself or coerced Mr. Carter or Mr. Ramos into joining their ill-planned scheme. I also know that the judge offered the same sentence to Mr. Carter's son, Billy, and Mr. Ramos' son. Serve time or join the Marine Corps. Only Ben, uh, Dr. Hunt, took that option. I am sure that the transcripts of the court proceedings will show that to be true."

Hayley waited and scanned the faces to see that most agreed with her opinion of the facts and that she clearly knew more than Carter had suspected.

Hayley turned to Bill Carter, now seated. "Mr. Carter, do you want to change your description of the court proceedings?"

Carter, looked to the ceiling with folded arms, acquiesced, "I got nothing to say to you."

"As I expected," Hayley said, turning back to the audience. "This is just an old-fashioned witch hunt based on false information and innuendo."

Hayley paused for a moment then began again. "As for Dr. Hunt. He was the surgeon on call when I had an emergency less than a year ago. His quick thinking and actions saved my life. We'll leave the medical stuff on me out of this. It also has no bearing. During my hospitalization, Dr. Hunt and I discussed some concerns he had. Three months after I was discharged, he sought me out and I started counseling him. We touched on an array of issues and have more to delve into, but here is what I know to be true."

Hayley paused again, the audience in her hands. "Dr. Hunt is an outstanding surgeon. In fact, the Chairman of the Department of Surgery at Seattle Medical School, Professor Armin Cassetti, told me that he was the best resident he ever trained.

"In addition, he served in the Marine Corps with two deployments to Afghanistan. He was discharged honorably and received a Distinguished Service Medal for bravery. That alone is enough to offer him the chance to prove himself worthy of this city. Shame on all of you for not finding out what Dr. Hunt has accomplished since leaving Apple Ridge. Instead of trying to ride him out of town, tarred and feathered, you should be thanking him for service rendered for his country. Shame on all of you."

Hayley paused to scan the audience. Heads were nodding yes.

"Your town has suffered some severe financial setbacks in recent years. Apple Ridge needs some breaks. You've just been given the gift of a talented surgeon, one of your own, and you're trying to throw it away.

"I will try to help the town with its welfare needs at the DSHS. While here, I will continue to counsel Dr. Hunt to see that he reaches the potential that I know he has."

Hayley turned back to the table. "Mr. Carter, Mr. Brown, do you have any questions?"

Harry Brown was smiling from ear to ear. Carter remained in a tight arms folded position and said nothing. The auditorium had no sounds other than people breathing.

"With that, I think I will take my seat with my friend, Agent Williams," Hayley said. As Hayley descended the stairs from the stage, she stopped and added, "Probably a good idea that no one get Agent Williams angry again." The lighthearted remark brought laughter and a resumption of normalcy.

Hayley sat and Brown stood at his seat. "Well. That was entertaining. I say we have a voice vote. All in favor of the petition to ask Dr. Hunt to leave Apple Ridge say aye."

Carter trumpeted, "Aye," as did a few handfuls of people in the audience.

"All those opposed and want Dr. Hunt to stay say nay."

One hundred fifty people resonated "Nay."

"I believe we're done here," Brown said, then banged his hand on the table, turned and walked off the stage.

Hayley and Deidre remained at the back of the auditorium. A handful of locals stopped on their way out to welcome Hayley to Apple Ridge.

Ben waited until the auditorium cleared before getting out of his seat and approached Hayley and Deidre.

"I had no idea you two were coming. Thank you," Ben said.

"You look like crap," said Hayley.

"I've felt that way for a while. I didn't think this would go well for me. It wouldn't if you hadn't come."

"Possibly," said Hayley.

"You know you can't stay here," Ben declared.

“Where exactly is here?” Hayley asked.

“Apple Ridge.”

"And why is that?"

"It's too dangerous for you."

"More dangerous than being stabbed in the ‘icicle’ vein with a biopsy needle?"

Ben smiled. "It's the iliac vein, and yes, more dangerous."

"I'm not scared."

"We'll see. When can I talk to you, the three of us?" Ben asked.

"Don't know, exactly,” Hayley said. “I've got to make sure they'll give me the job. I took a chance by saying it was mine. I need to call Bev Bergreen, my boss, and the local DSHS manager. I can’t remember her name right now. I took a chance that she wouldn’t be here at the meeting and doesn’t have a replacement already. I'll know more on Monday. If I'm going to stay, I'll have to go back to Seattle and get my stuff and close up my condo."

"I've got to be at work on Monday," Deidre said.

"I can drive you to Seattle," Ben said to Hayley. "On the other hand, anyone seeing me driving with you alone will get tongues wagging. Also, where were you going to live?"

"Don't know. I'll need to talk to the DSHS manager," Hayley answered. "I can stay at the Travelodge until I've found something. I think it best that I go back to Seattle with Deidre in the morning and return when I'm packed up."

"Can I at least take you two out to dinner tonight?" Ben asked.

As they walked out of the near empty auditorium, Chief Robertson stood at the exit. As big and broad as a SUV, with crossed arms resting on an impressive beer belly, he said, "Pretty impressive, young lady. Gotta hand it to you. Not many get the best of Bill Carter. Not many at all. I know Bill real well, so I'm sure he ain't done with Ben, or you. Not by a long shot. He's gonna try to even the score, someway."

Hayley turned to Ben and Deidre, "Why don't you two head towards our car. I'll meet you there in a second." She turned back to Robertson. Her eyes came level with his sheriff's badge, just above his folded arms. *He's got the biggest hands I've ever seen.*

"I know from experience that Dr. Hunt is pretty fragile right now," Hayley said, "and I also know he's had a couple of scrapes already. He'll be better once I'm back here which may take me a week or two. I'd really like you to look out for him."

"That's not my job, lady. I don't babysit," said Robertson.

"Ben, that's Dr. Hunt, will be fine as long as no one tries to push his buttons. He's got some war issues that he's not resolved. I'll fix them but I'm hoping you can keep any button pushers away from him, if you get my drift."

"The Carters and the Ramoses are the only people looking to rile him up. Tell him to stay away from restaurants. Any restaurant. There's a bunch of them Carters and Ramoses and they eat out a lot. Better to use drive-thru and eat at home or the hospital. If he can get somebody to do his grocery shopping, that'd be real smart too. He ran into Carter's daughter-in-law at the Safeway last week. Didn't go well."

"I heard. However, he's got to eat," said Hayley.

"Well, if you're gonna be back in a week, I'd go shopping with him tonight and buy enough stuff that he stays clear of anywhere that the Carters and Ramoses might be."

"Thanks. Tough town you got here."

"Lots of people out of work," said the sheriff, "so that makes some edgy. Ben didn't leave town on a positive note, ya know. Can't figure out why he chose to come back."

"I'm working on that. I asked the same question. I guess he figures that if he can square accounts here, he'll be at peace. Something like that."

"Shit, lady. You got your work cut out for you. I'd get back here quick if I were you."

"I'll try. Here's my card. Has my cell phone number on it. Call me if you think you need to."

"Sure. Just so you know, I ain't doin' no babysitting. Neither's my deputies. You tell Ben to keep outta trouble."

"I'll try. Thanks."

Hayley shook Robertson's hand. Her entire grip barely made it to the edges of his palm.

*_*_*_*

Ben walked into the office at the Travelodge at eight thirty p.m. and encountered Deidre jawing with the motel manager, trying to figure out the Wi-Fi, or lack of thereof.

"Hayley's up in the room. Number 207," Deidre said. "Second floor, first set of doors to the left. She's waiting for you."

The manager walked Ben to the door and stood there as Ben mounted the stairs. All the room doors were outside and faced the manager's office.

Ben knocked on Room 207 and remained in the doorway when Hayley opened the door.

"The manager's watching us," Ben said. "I don't think we should stay here for very long. He's probably a friend of Bill Carter. I expect he'll be on the phone twenty seconds after we leave."

"I understand. Anyway, come in for a second, Hayley said. "I just need to get my coat and purse and shut down my laptop."

Ben walked into the entry as Hayley grabbed her coat and purse then hit the sleep button on her computer. She turned and walked towards Ben. "Ready to go."

Ben seemed to be frozen place, took a huge breath and exhaled slowly. "I didn't know you were coming. I didn't know what to do. All I could think of for the past two weeks is that I'd like to talk to you. I wanted to talk to you so badly. Thank you. Thank you for coming."

Ben's emotional outburst reaffirmed the spontaneous and irrational decisions Hayley had made in the auditorium forty minutes earlier.

"It was so random. I only heard about the meeting last night. I knew you'd need some help," Hayley said.

"You can't stay here. It's too dangerous. You have to go back to Seattle," Ben said.

"I'm not frightened of Bill Carter or anyone," Hayley replied, defiantly, "and I won't leave you this time until you're better. I promise." *I'm not leaving.*

Ben wiped his eyes with his sleeves. "We'd better be going."

*_*_*_*

Once seated at the restaurant, Ben turned to Deidre. "Hayley can't stay here. No way. She's not listening. Apple Ridge is not a nice place. I didn't realize how many people Bill Carter and the Ramoses control. Losing their petition at the town hall meeting isn't going to stop them from trying to make my life miserable. If they think they can hurt me by hurting Hayley, they will. I can't put Hayley in the middle of all this."

Before Deidre could comment, Hayley said, "I'm not afraid. What are they going to do? Shoot me?"

"Sounds like that's a distinct possibility," Deidre said.

"Well, probably not," Ben said, "but that's only probably. I think they'll just try to scare you often enough so that leaving is the only option to keep your sanity. They'll hope that I overreact, which I will, and force another town hall meeting."

"Jesus," Hayley responded, "You two are talking without listening. I'm not afraid. Really, I'm not. They can't do anything worse to me than having leukemia."

"Okay. I'll make this clear. Do you own a gun?" asked Ben.

"No. Are you crazy? Of course I don't own a gun."

"Why is that crazy?" Ben asked.

"I don't own a gun, never have, never will. My parents have never owned a gun either."

"You're friend owns one," Ben said, pointing his thumb at Deidre.

"Don't get me started," Hayley responded as Deidre giggled.

"Who carries guns in Apple Ridge?" asked Deidre, "or need I ask."

Ben laughed. "Everyone. And I mean everyone. I learned to shoot when I was six and had my own shortened twenty-two rifle when I was eight. The second amendment comes before the Ten Commandments here. Trust me."

"So what do you want me to do?" asked Hayley.

"You might think about carrying a gun," said Ben.

"I'm not going to do that."

"Actually, both of you are right," Deidre said. "You don't need to carry a gun,  you just need to make people think you are."

"What are you talking about?" quizzed Hayley.

"I think she means, get a permit from Nate's Gun Shop here in Apple Ridge, buy a gun, go to a shooting range and then give the gun to me. Trust me. In thirty minutes, everyone will think you've got a gun in your purse."

"That's crazy. Insane," Hayley said, raising her voice in protest.

"You're crazy to be here, so it's not such a big leap," said Deidre.

"If my parents found out that I owned a gun, they'd shoot me."

"Good choice of phrases," Ben laughed.

"Not going to happen. I didn't realize that Carter was such a jerk. I thought you told me that he was your dad's best friend and your mom almost married him?"

"Right," said Ben.

"What happened? He's really got it out for you," said Hayley.

"And then some," Deidre added.

"He tried to be supportive after Dad died. He wanted to take me fishing and hunting. I wouldn't go. Anyway, I guess he figured out that

I blamed him, as much as my mother, for Dad's suicide."

"How'd he jump to that conclusion?" Hayley asked Ben.

"I told him. Maybe I forgot to mention that."

"This is getting way over my head," Deidre said. "I'm glad I'm not a shrink."

"He's madder than that," stated Hayley. "What else happened?"

"Not sure exactly. I was always good friends with Billy Jr. When we all got in trouble, Carter thought that I was responsible. Maybe he thought it was my way to get back at him. He was wrong. Junior was the source of most of our fuck-ups. Afterwards, Carter talked Ramos' dad into believing I was the instigator. Looking back at it all, when I left for the Marines at twenty, I don't think Bill was as angry as he is now."

"I'm not following this yet," Hayley said.

"Dad's will was explicit in giving me control of the three hundred acres of forest land. Mom and husband number two tried to sell it but couldn't without my permission. I refused, which didn't help an already shitty relationship."

"What's that got to do with Carter?" asked Hayley.

"Carter called me a some time ago and wanted to buy the land. I refused. He said he'd pay me twice what it was worth."

"I don't get it. Why'd he want it so badly?"

"Good question," said Ben. "I still don't know. Anyway, he called me two of three more times and kept raising the offer price. I didn't need the money and, if for no other reason, I wanted to do something with the land. I promised my dad."

"Yeah, you told me that before," said Hayley.

"Anyway, I got a call a year ago from a real estate broker in Yakima, a Peter something. He said he had a buyer for the property. I asked who and he said he couldn't say but that he represented a consortium of east coast developers. I told him to send me an offer, which he did. It was a bit more than Carter's last bid."

"Then what happened?" asked Deidre.

"I called the county planning office and asked if anyone had been looking at the property. I figured that no one was going to make an offer without investigating. Apparently, Bill Carter and Warren Kiffers were the only people looking at the property and had been doing so on a regular basis, including that week."

"Then what?" asked Hayley.

"I knew the broker would lie, so I called Carter's office and told the receptionist to tell Mr. Carter that I was Mr. Peter Something and had the deal signed."

"You lied," said Hayley.

"Of course. Bill Carter picked up the phone and said, "You really got that prick to sign?" I said, "Yep." That's all I said. Carter said, "Congratulations. I knew this would work." I then told Carter, "Oops, this is Ben," and that I didn't appreciate the trickery and that I'd never sell it to him. Not that nicely."

"What'd he say to that?" Deidre asked.

"That I should never show up in Apple Ridge again if I wanted to remain healthy."

Nodding her head, Hayley said, "Starting to make more sense to me now."

"That's when I started hearing from old friends how mad Carter, and in turn, the Ramoses were with me. He'd tell anyone who'd listen how bad I was."

"And still you opted to come here. Why?" Hayley asked.

"I didn't like being bullied and I still had the forest land."

"I told you back in Seattle that coming here was a bad choice. Hearing all this, your presence here was a terrible, miserable, awful choice," said Hayley.

"I'm here. So deal with it."

"You two stop it," Deidre interjected. "You're acting like you're married."

Hayley, needing to get in the last word, said, "Have you ever given any thought to making your life easier? Don't answer that. After dinner, we've got to go grocery shopping. I'll explain why."

*_*_*_*

Back at the motel, Deidre returned to their motel room while Hayley talked to Ben. "Remember," she pleaded, "you promised to stay away from anyone in the Carter or Ramos families. If you happen to see one, turn and walk away. I don't care if you've done nothing wrong, leave. If they follow you, run. Get in your car and drive away. You've got to promise me."

"I'll try," Ben said.

"If you want me to come back, you've got to do more than try."

Ben nodded.

"See you in a week or two. Don't call me. I can't help you over the phone," Hayley pleaded. "Stay out of trouble."

*_*_*_*

On Monday morning from Seattle, Hayley called the DSHS office in Apple Ridge.

"DSHS Apple Ridge, Corinne Shermann."

"Didn't expect you to answer the phone. I'm Hayley Green and…"

"The secretary quit last Friday," Shermann interrupted. "Anyway, I know who you are. It took all my fortitude to keep my mouth shut until I talked to you. Kind of gutsy to say you have a job here before talking to me."

"Yes," Hayley admitted, "I'm so sorry and I knew it was wrong. Honestly, the circumstances were such that I needed an excuse to say I was coming."

"Well," Shermann said, "if it's any consolation, I talked to Bev on Saturday morning. She clued me in on you, your work record and the relationship with Dr. Hunt."

"I'm sorry to have put you through that."

"Nah. It's okay. I'd have had a tough time finding anyone to work here. I know about your leukemia and I know you've had some motivation issues since returning. You think coming here is going to help that?" Sherman asked.

"I can't say for certain. I hope so. After the town hall meeting, I'm sure Ben, uh Dr. Hunt, needs me. And I don't have an official or unofficial relationship with Dr. Hunt."

"You know you can't see him through DSHS."

"Of course," Hayley said.

"In fact, ethically, you're not supposed to have any relationship with him."

"I understand. We've done nothing but have a few dinners and chats. I've been clear to him that I'm not his therapist and won't be. He does find comfort talking with me. He thinks I have some insight into his behavior. I know I'm helping."

"Good. I don't need the local powers any more upset than they already are," said Shermann.

"I promise not to cause trouble," Hayley said.

"Right. Oh, one more thing."

"Yes?"

"You're hired."

*_*_*_*

"You, what? Are you crazy?" Rachel Green said, after first hearing of her daughter's decision to move to Apple Ridge. "Wait till I tell your father. You've lost your mind."

"Mom, I'll be fine. It's not forever but I'm needed there. DSHS can't seem to find an agent to work in their office and..."

"And why do you think you're so different? There's nothing there. There's no one there that you'll have anything in common with."

"Actually, you're probably right. Regardless, Bev Bergreen thinks the move is worth the try. I wasn't happy here at the Seattle office anymore, but that's not the real reason. I'm needed in Apple Ridge and I haven't felt needed since my transplant."

"And why's that?"

"Ben Hunt's there."

"You mean the surgeon whose guts you hated even after he saved your life twice. Now he needs you?"

"I didn't tell you but I'd talked with him a few times before he left Seattle," said Hayley. "I tried to help him straighten out some issues that had nothing to do with me. He's really not such a bad person and, for some reason, I'm the only one who's been able to reach him. He wasn't doing well in Apple Ridge on his own."

"There's got to be other experienced therapists who could help him just as well. You're not Sigmund Freud, after all."

"He'd been to ten or twelve people here and elsewhere. He walked out on all of them He came to see me specifically before he left Seattle and I helped. Even his chairman called me to thank me for seeing him. I must have made a difference. And for some reason, it felt really good."

"Okay, then how long are you going to be there?" asked Rachel.

"Depends on how it goes. I don't know."

"There aren't any oncologists in Apple Ridge. Who's going to take care of you?"

"Mom, please, I'm not moving to the moon. I can drive back to Seattle for routine stuff and tests."

"You seem to have an answer for everything. Your dad and I need you to be close. We've almost lost you twice in the last year and we don't know what the future will bring with your leukemia. I'm going to be miserable."

"Visit."

"Oh, Hayley."

"Deidre's going to visit too."

"She has probably less in common with those people."

"I love you mom. I've got to finish packing up the condo. If I'm going to be in Apple Ridge for a definite period, I'll sublet. As for Apple Ridge, I'll send you my contact info. The last agent in Apple Ridge walked out on a twelve-month lease on DHSH's dime. I'm going to take over her place and then we'll see."

*_*_*_*

Bobby Mendez, Joey Ramos's second cousin, drove into the Shell station off Third Street in Apple Ridge just after ten p.m. Two friends accompanied Mendez after watching Impact Wrestling at Harrigan's Sports Bar. All three had blood alcohol levels over the limit.

Mendez looked over two bays and saw Ben filling his car with gas. Rolling down his window, Mendez yelled, "Hey, asshole. You ain't 'sposed to be here. You shoulda never come back. You lucky I ain't carrying or I'd pop you right here."

Ben ignored the comments and turned away. He then watched the gas station's attendant run into the restroom and lock the door.

Mendez, now out of his car, continued, "You listening to me, *hijo de tu puta madre*. You too pussy to face me?" Mendez turned to his buddies, "Let's teach this *culo* a lesson. You with me?" Mendez turned back to face Ben.

Ben had already opened his trunk and removed a thirty-four inch, thirty-one ounce, black maple Louisville Slugger bat, the Ken Griffey, Jr. model C271C. Mendez saw the bat and stared for a moment as their eyes met. Mendez turned back to his car and shouted to his friends, "C'mon. This asshole wants it." Mendez opened his trunk and pulled out a tire iron. Two other young Hispanic men jumped out of the passenger side of Mendez's car.

Ben yelled, "I can't do this." He threw the bat back in the trunk, quickly disconnected the gas hose from his tank and drove away quickly, losing a hubcap on the curb edge. Once he realized that Mendez and friends hadn't followed him, Ben stopped.

Pounding his steering wheel hard enough to crack the rim, Ben screamed repeatedly, "I can't do this. I can't do this…" When he finally calmed, he called Hayley's cell phone, which forwarded to voicemail. From that point, Ben limited his activity to the hospital and his apartment, bringing food and drink home from the hospital cafeteria.

Hayley texted Ben seven days later that she had arrived in Apple Ridge.

*_*_*_*

Corinne Shermann showed Hayley to her new office. Hayley sat alone for twenty minutes before starting to unpack her belongings.

Shermann put her head through Hayley's door at ten thirty. "I'm on my way to a meeting with Harry Brown and Bill Carter. Not sure why, but it can't be good. We'll re-run an ad for a new assistant in the paper tomorrow and get a hundred responses. None will be qualified. I'll be back after lunch."

Immediately after Shermann departed, the phone rang.

"DSHS. Hayley Green."

"Hi. It's Ben."

"I'm back," Hayley said. "I still have a ton of stuff to do in Seattle, but I thought you'd get in trouble if I stayed away too long."

"That's an understatement when sixty percent of my diet has been mac 'n cheese from the hospital cafeteria warmed in my microwave. I'm ready to kill for a hamburger."

"I'm sorry. At least you're in one piece and not in jail."

"You answered the phone. You're the front desk person too?"

"Yep. Just me. The secretary quit last week. I feel like I'm in a 1930's movie in black and white. The last agent left a key to my office with a note that read, 'Good Luck. You'll need it.'"

"Where're you staying?"

"A small split level house was leased by DSHS at 828 Merrimount near Crest. Three bedrooms and another on the lower level, opening onto the backyard. The last two assistants were single moms with kids."

"Great. When can we talk?" Ben asked.

"How about a fancy dinner? Like Canlis?" Hayley asked.

"That's not going to happen," Ben laughed. "How's Chinese food sound? It's not too bad, or at least I like it."

"Sounds okay."

"We'll need to keep our visits public. The Carters and Ramoses are still raising a ruckus. I had one almost run-in at a gas station while you were gone. Everyone'll be watching you and me."

"Was that when you left a message on my phone?" asked Hayley.

"Yep."

"I'm sorry. Anyway, Chinese is fine by me. How's tomorrow night? I'll be unpacking tonight."

"Okay. Seven p.m. We should take two cars. Seven Stars Chinese restaurant is on Jefferson and Second Street in a small strip mall."

"Got it."

"I'm glad you're back," said Ben.

*_*_*_*

Corinne Shermann returned at four p.m. She slammed the door to her office – hard enough to shake Hayley's desk and filing cabinet, twenty feet and two walls away.

Hayley caught the edge of her desk as she watched a pencil roll off the edge. *Bill Carter can do that to you.*

Moments later, Shermann, looking like the last disgruntled human in a thirty-person return line at Wal-Mart, entered Hayley's small office, said nothing, and plopped down in a chair.

"You okay?" Hayley asked.

"No. I've had run-ins with Carter before but today was over the top," said Shermann. "The son of a bitch accused me of bringing you here on purpose to rile him. Harry Brown, as nice as he is, could do nothing to stop Carter's ranting."

"Funny," Hayley nodded, "but I understand completely. The town hall meeting made it abundantly clear who thinks he runs this town."

"I didn't blow your cover and tell him that he and the rest of Apple Ridge found out you were coming before I did."

Hayley nodded, "Thanks. Again, I'm sorry. I did what I thought I needed to do."

"Yeah. I suppose," Shermann said. "Anyway, Carter and his lawyer friend have already made two calls to Olympia asking to have both of us placed elsewhere."

"Olympia called you?" asked Hayley, a look of disbelief across her face.

"No, Carter told me he'd done it. I haven't heard a word from Olympia."

"Will you?" asked Hayley.

"Maybe, probably not. Makes little difference. Carter's going to make our lives miserable, so I'm letting him win this one."

"How so?"

"I quit," said Shermann.

"You what?" Hayley shouted.

"I quit. Apple Ridge is yours to run. I should have never taken this post."

"I can't do this myself," pleaded Hayley.

"You'll have to. Olympia doesn't have a replacement and won't find one easily. Nobody wants to come here. You've worked at DSHS long enough to know the routines and protocols. I'm not going to have a heart attack because Carter's got a burr up his ass."

Hayley slumped in her chair. "I'm so sorry. I didn't want to cause trouble for you."

"Not your fault," said Shermann. "I was looking for an excuse to quit. You can call me anytime for advice. Good luck. You'll need it."

As Shermann departed, Hayley looked at the key and note on her desk. *That seems to be a recurring theme around here.* She then called Bev Bergreen.

"I'm not surprised, actually. Corinne told me she was going to retire as soon as she found a qualified assistant. You'll be fine, I hope," said Bergreen.

"At least you didn't say 'good luck' like everyone else," Hayley responded.

"You wanted this job," said Bergreen. "Good luck."

*_*_*_*

Hayley made it to her new house at eleven thirty p.m., exhausted and fell asleep on an unmade bed, fully clothed. She awoke at midnight to undress and brush her teeth and returned immediately to bed. At two forty a.m., heavy crashing noises shook her awake. Half asleep, Hayley thought the sounds might be thunder and rose quickly to make sure the windows were closed.

Stumbling into the darkened living room, Hayley chilled as she heard, then felt, whistling wind and rattling coming through the drawn Venetian blinds covering the front windows. Windows that she was certain could not be opened. Searching for a light switch in unfamiliar surroundings she took three steps towards the front door.

"Ow. Ow." A sharp pain from the sole of her right foot shot upwards. Still smarting, Hayley fell backwards onto the floor. Keeping her foot elevated, she slid backwards into the safety of her bedroom. She rotated on her rump to allow the door to close, then turned on the overhead room lights.

Blood. Blood everywhere. Blood on the door, floor and wall in front of her. She was no longer asleep.

*What's happening?*

Hayley quickly picked up her foot to inspect the pain and found a protruding half-inch chard of glass emanating from the middle of her sole. She pulled the chard loose which made the bleeding worse. Holding pressure with her left hand over cut, she then realized the only bandages she owned were sitting in a cupboard one hundred five miles away in her Seattle condo.

She slid back to her suitcase, still unpacked, grabbed an old, but clean, cotton tee shirt she had used as a pajama top. She then laid back, put her right foot over her left knee and used the shirt to hold pressure over the cut. She looked at the foot every minute or so until the bleeding stopped.

The tee shirt had a small worn hole just under the bottom hem and Hayley used the tear as a starting point to tear away a strip of cotton. She tied the ersatz bandage around her foot then stood slowly. She sat on the edge of the bed for a short time to make sure that blood wasn't coming through the bandage, hopped back to her suitcase and slipped her feet into a pair of unlaced sneakers.

She had heard no more thunder and couldn't hear rain pelting the house.

*What just happened? Did a picture frame fall off the wall and crash?*

Still uncertain, but her feet now protected, Hayley opened the door to the living room and, using the ambient light from the bedroom, found the living room light switch.

Glass chards were everywhere, heaviest towards the window at the front of the room. Only then did she see the eight inch ragged hole in the middle of the blinds. Walking over glass, Hayley approached the blinds and inspected and felt the edges of freshly snapped wood. Behind the blinds, two ten inch window panes were missing other than small, irregular, sharktoothlike edges that clung to the pane perimeters. The window edges, sills and the floor were dry. It had not been raining. Despite the warm night air blowing into Hayley's face, the chill intensified.

Hayley turned off the lights, ran back to her bedroom, locked the door and called Deidre.

"You up?" Hayley asked.

"I am now," Deidre said, used to middle of the night calls.

"Ben was right," Hayley started talking in triple time, "I'm scared."

"What happened?"

"Something broke my front window and glass is everywhere and a blind is shattered."

"I hope to hell you didn't open the door or stand by the window looking?"

"No. I couldn't see or hear anyone. I thought at first it was thunder but it hadn't rained and the skies outside my bedroom were clear went I went to bed and I stepped on glass and cut my foot and didn't have any bandages and pulled a piece of glass out of my foot and…."

"Hold on. You're rambling. How did the window break?. Did you see a rock or something on the living room floor?"

"No. I didn't, but I didn't look."

"You maybe should go back and look."

"I don't want to turn on the lights or go out there. It's still dark."

"Someone's just sending a message. If they want to hurt you they don't break windows. Go on out there and look."

"Okay, but I want to keep talking to you. Okay?"

"Sure," Deidre said.

Hayley walked back into the living room.

"Glass and wood chips everywhere." Hayley walked around the room looking mostly down at the debris.

"Okay. What do you see?"

"No rocks or bricks by the window or on the floor that I can see. But what a mess."

"I don't want to freak you out anymore than I have to but look on the wall opposite the windows and tell me what you see."

"Just a wall, with a couch and table and two lamps and a place where there used to be a picture because the rest of the wall is faded. Oh, wait. I see two finger-sized holes a few inches apart where the picture used to be."

"Now turn off the lights and go back into your bedroom," Deidre said. "Now."

"What's up?"

"Just do it."

Hayley hobbled back into her bedroom. Her foot ached. "Okay, I'm here."

"First, the good news," Deidre said. "Someone is trying to scare you and it sounds like they're doing a great job."

"I am scared."

"I know. I know. Now the bad news and try to remain calm. The two holes in the wall are probably bullet holes. Someone drove by, shot a few times at the window and drove off."

"Omigod!" Hayley screamed. "Are you kidding me? Should I call the police?"

"Probably, but you might want to wait until later this morning. The sun is up in an hour and most likely whoever it was won't come back again. You need some sleep. Call after you get up."

"I'll never sleep. I could have been killed. They could have shot me," Hayley yelled. "I hate guns."

"Try. I can go back to sleep and you should try. If they wanted to hurt you, they wouldn't throw a rock or shoot out a window. They're trying to scare you, that's all. How secure is your house?"

"I don't know. Locks on all the doors."

"Deadbolts or passage locks?"

"No deadbolts. Just regular door locks."

"I'll call you tomorrow," Deidre said. "You'll need deadbolts, window locks, good perimeter lighting that is motion activated, maybe an alarm or, better yet, a big dog."

"A dog. What am I going to do with a dog?"

"You'll be okay, I promise. Good night."

"How do you know that?"

"I just do," Deidre lied. "Good night. You'll be fine. You still sure you want to be there?"

Silence.

"You want to be there," Deidre repeated.

"I purposefully didn't call Ben last week and didn't answer the phone the one time he called," Hayley said. "I had to know for certain. I missed him and I want to help."

"And?"

"I want to be here. First thing that's made sense in a year."

"I love you. Be careful. Call me in the morning," said Deidre.

Hayley ended the call, "I love you back."

*_*_*_*

Hayley called the police station at six thirty a.m. and talked to the on-duty patrolman. Chief Robertson appeared at her door thirty minutes later. She had not touched a thing.

Robertson listened to Hayley's story including her conversation with Deidre. He then surveyed the room and walked into the laundry room which sat behind the living room and found two bullets imbedded in the far wall.

He returned to the living room and snorted a little laugh, "Not that I didn't warn you. Someone's trying to spook you. These look like twenty-two short slugs. Good for shooting rabbits mainly. Probably a kid's gun."

"Do you know who did this?" Hayley pleaded. "You need to arrest them."

"Not likely we'll ever find out unless someone saw them. We'll ask around but I'd be surprised if anyone says anything. Pretty dark out there at two a.m."

"They could have killed me," Hayley said, angrily.

"Nah, unless they were lucky. I'd say offhand that everyone in town owns a twenty-two. And these slugs are worthless."

Still angry, Hayley said, "You're going to do nothing? Honestly?"

"Yep," Robertson said. "To me it's just a bit of vandalism. Teenage boy gets mad at his girlfriend or her family and shoots out a window. Happens twice a year around here. If you want to get your FBI friend to open a federal investigation, be my guest. Not likely she's gonna do anything. You should probably get better lighting around the house and some deadbolts and maybe a big dog."

"God. You're all alike. That's what Deidre said."

"She must be a smart lady," Robertson smiled.

"What now?" Hayley asked.

"Get the window fixed. Get some new blinds and maybe put a picture over the holes in the wall. 'Bout it. If it keeps on happening, I'll talk to the Ramoses. Not likely it's Carter doing. Not his style. The Ramoses will know about this but deny everything. Like I said, they're just trying to scare you. I don't think they're stupid enough to do anything else."

They both stood for a moment until Robertson said, "Gotta go."

Hayley sat at her kitchen table watching her hands tremble and started to dial Deidre but cancelled the call. *I've got to be strong.* She took in a deep breath, showered, dressed, caught a cup of coffee and sweet roll at Starbucks, bought fresh bandages at Walgreen's and went to work.

*_*_*_*_*

Hayley joined Ben at a corner table at the Seven Stars Chinese restaurant..

As Hayley sat, Ben said, "You're limping. You fall or something?"

"No. I cut my foot on a piece of glass."

"Oh. Want me to look at it?"

"No," Hayley said. "Well maybe later. Corinne Sherman quit. I'm here alone."

"You're kidding me. She just quit," said Ben.

"Yep. One argument with Bill Carter and Corinne said she'd had enough."

"I'm guessing I won't be seeing much of you then."

"Luckily, the Spokane and Yakima office will do most of the paper work for me. They've been doing that for Corinne for a while. I think I'll be okay."

Hayley waited until the end of the meal to tell Ben about the broken window in an attempt to make light of it. Sipping tea, she said, "Oh, by the way, someone tried to scare me early this morning."

"What? You've got to be kidding. You haven't been here a day."

Hayley explained the incidents and the responses of Deidre and Robertson, including Robertson's guess that the Ramoses were behind the prank.

"Why didn't you call me?" Ben asked, obviously perturbed..

"I called Deidre. She told me what to do. Better lighting and locks. Maybe a dog. I made some calls, but nothing will be done until Monday. I found a locksmith, a housekeeper to clean up the mess and a handy man to fix the window and blinds."

"You should go back to the Travelodge."

"That's silly."

"Not silly. You're scared. They know it and they'll find another way to keep you up. I'm not going to let you go back to your house."

"Perhaps you're right."

“I am right,” Ben said.

“On another subject, what does Felix Ramos do?” Hayley asked. “I’m going to assume he’s not a neurosurgeon.”

Ben laughed. “Nah. But he’s a smart guy and tough as hell. He organizes pickers for the cherry and apple growers in three adjacent counties. Somebody needs a crew, they call Felix. He trains the pickers, treats them fairly and never gouges the growers. He also provides food and portable toilets at the sites. The sheriff lets Felix handle pickers who cause trouble. Nobody in the Hispanic community messes with him.”

“Maybe I should call on him?”

“Terrible idea. I doubt he’d listen to you unless you’ve got something he wants badly.”

“What would that be,” Hayley asked.

“Damned if I know,” Ben said. “If you do go, make sure it’s after nine a.m. From four thirty to nine his yard is disorganized chaos until the crews are dispatched. He usually goes out to the farms in the afternoon to make sure things are running smoothly.”

Ben trailed Hayley back to her house to pick up an overnight bag, checked her foot and then followed her to the Travelodge. Ben made sure that Hayley had the first floor room closest to the manager's office.

"I know he's a buddy of Carter," Ben said, "but he's not going to allow anyone bothering his motel guests."

Knowing that the manager was watching, Ben spent less than a minute getting Hayley's small suitcase into her room.

"I'm sorry about all this. I warned you" Ben said.

"I'll be okay, here," Hayley said, "…..I hope."

"I wish you could stay at my place." As soon as he spoke, Ben recanted. "That's not true. It wouldn't work."

"You'd better go," Hayley said.

Ben turned, allowing Hayley to peer out the motel room window. The motel manager had retreated into his office and couldn't be seen. Hayley grabbed Ben's coat to stop him. He turned thinking he'd caught his coat on the doorknob.

"I wish I could stay at your place," she said, then stood on tiptoes to give him a quick kiss on the lips. "Thank you for caring."

Ben, stunned, immediately turned to see that the manager had retreated to his office. Ben said, "I've got to go."

*_*_*_*

Hayley called Deidre to tell her of the move back to the Travelodge.

"Smart move to go back to the motel," Deidre said.

"Ben made me go and paid for it. He's more worried than I am."

"You really ought to think about getting a dog. A big dog."

"I'm not home enough. It wouldn't be fair."

"Yeah. You're probably right," said Deidre.

"I, uh, kissed him," Hayley said.

"You, what?"

"I wanted to thank him for caring."

"A kiss on the cheek doesn't mean diddly," said Deidre. "He's been nice. I'd kiss him on the cheek."

"I kissed him on the lips," Hayley said. "I don't know what came over me. I just did it. I don't think he really cares for me that way. He just turned and ran out of the motel room."

"You have to be the densest psychologist in the universe. Of course, he cares for you. It's written all over him. What's next."

"I don't know. I really don't. I think I scared him."

*_*_*_*

The first night back in her home, Hayley's newly installed, motion-activated, perimeter lights illuminated the entire block. When her next-door neighbor, Henry Anderson, took his dog out to pee at ten p.m. and then again at two a.m., night became day. Pleas from the neighborhood to tone down the sensitivity of the motion detectors balanced promises that everyone would be on the lookout for intruders. Mr. Anderson removed slats in the fence between their backyards to let Bivouac, his eighty-five pound German Shepherd, roam between houses at will. Anderson then took an old movie camera and mounted it over Hayley's door to give the look of twenty-four hour monitoring.

At eight thirty a.m. on Wednesday, Hayley parked outside Felix Ramos's office on the outskirts of Apple Ridge and watched. A huge yard surrounded a smallish one story office. Trucks and vans of all sizes were moving in and out while hundreds of Hispanic men and women milled inside and outside the gates. By nine a.m. the yard was dead quiet. Hayley walked into the building at nine ten and introduced herself to the secretary. Hayley sat in front of Felix Ramos five minutes later.

Felix Ramos, arms folded confidently across his chest, dispensed with pleasantries and said, "Lady, I know who are and I don't like your boyfriend. Don't know why you bothering me. I got nothing for you. And you got nothing I want."

Hayley responded, "I admit it's an impressive thing you got going here."

"So what you want, 'cause I'm busy?" Ramos demanded, reflecting the compliment.

"I understand," Hayley said. "I'll make it short and sweet so you and I can get back to work. We're both in the same business. We find jobs for people and help them out however we can."

Ramos nodded, unimpressed.

"So don't fuck with me," Hayley said, looking straight into Ramos's eyes, "and I won't fuck with you."

Ramos unfolded his arms and leaned forward on his desk looking straight back at Hayley. "Lady, you got *cajones* walking in here and talking to me like that. You better watch yourself. You got nothing I needs."

Hayley didn't blink. "You're forgetting who my friends are. If one blade of grass at my house is disturbed, I swear I'll have half your work force deported in fifteen minutes. You leave me alone and I'll leave you alone." Hayley didn't wait for an response. She stood and walked out.

Hayley had no more midnight runs.

*_*_*_*

Hayley dove into her job at the DSHS office. Thirty percent of Apple Ridge was out of work and, including children, forty percent of the population received some kind of aid from the state. If DSHS accounted for the people who moved to other parts of the state to find work or live with relatives, Apple Ridge had 'dust-bowl' levels of depression.

Hayley interviewed fifteen people for the assistant manager position. Former fruit processing workers, men and women, with little or no typing or computer skills, comprised the majority of applicants. Housewives tinkering with thoughts of two incomes made up the rest.

Bill Carter's daughter-in-law's sister, Katy MacArthur, had recently graduated from Eastern Washington University with a Bachelor's Degree in Business Administration and a minor in Psychology. Katy wanted to remain close to her family, but without local job opportunities in Apple Ridge, she, reluctantly, planned to relocate west to Seattle. The job description at DSHS appeared in the local newspaper and seemed to be a perfect fit. Katy, as did the rest of Apple Ridge, knew of the ill will with Hunt and then, Hayley Green. Katy called her sister's father-in-law for advice.

"You got zero to no chance of being hired if you tell her who your related to," Bill Carter told her. "Hunt's got it out for us now. Anyway, this lady's gonna hightail it out of town like all the rest of those Olympia blood suckers who've been here in the last two years."

"It's gotta be good practice to have a hostile interview. Can't hurt," said Katy, hoping for a word of encouragement.

"Total waste of your time," Carter said. "Do what you want. I gotta go."

Katy hung up and thought, *How did my sister marry into that family?*

*_*_*_*

Katy MacArthur appeared for her interview, having skills and education far above any other applicant. After two days of interviewing people, ill-qualified for the job, Hayley couldn't help smiling.

"Impressive resume," Hayley said.

"Thanks, Miss Green," Katy responded, "but I have to be honest and let you know that my sister is married to Bill Carter's son, Joey. That's not on the application but I thought you should know."

"Really. Did Carter send you here?"

"No. In fact, he told me not to bother applying. After what I heard happened with you and him at the town meeting, I can't see you wanting to get mixed up with us."

Hayley thought for a moment. "Katy," she said. "Thank you for your honesty. That says a ton already. Here's the deal though. The things that pass through this office are often sensitive and personal. Sometimes medical, sometimes financial, sometimes criminal. I know you're smart but I have to know that you can keep everything you hear or see inside this office private. What happens here stays here. I need to trust you. I don't tell Ben Hunt anything and never will. If anyone finds out that we're talking about him or her, good or bad, no one will want to be confidential with us. Bill Carter, the Ramoses, Joey and your sister are no exceptions. They used to say during World War II that "loose lips sink ships." I don't know if that really turned out to be true, but if you, or I, say things, even the littlest of things, outside the office, our ship is sunk. People are going to have to trust us. Can I trust you?"

"Yes. Yes, you can trust me. I swear," Katy vowed.

"Can you start tomorrow?" asked Hayley.

*_*_*_*

Ben and Hayley sat in at a window table at Bingo's Italian Restaurant and Pizzeria.

Ben asked, "Feeling more secure now?"

"Yes. I could light up the Grand Canyon if anyone comes within twenty feet of my porch and the whole neighborhood is watching out for me. I have electronic deadbolts on every door and slide bolt window locks. There's been no trouble unless you count a bag of dog poop in the mailbox."

"How's work?" Ben asked.

"Good. I hired an assistant agent," said Hayley.

"Who'd you hire?"

"Katy MacArthur. She's Joey Carter's sister-in-law. She was far and away the most qualified."

"You think that's a good idea?" Ben asked. "The Carters will be looking for any way to get back at you or me. They're going to pump her for information daily."

"I realize the risks, but you know the old saying about keeping your friends close and your enemies closer. She's smart. I think I can trust her."

Ben smiled. "You're not Michael Corleone, but the thought is there."

"I'm not planning to sleep with the fishes just yet," Hayley countered.

Ben looked down at his empty plate, then back into Hayley's eyes and asked, "Uh. What was with that kiss?"

"What kiss?" Hayley paused, "…Oh, that one. I don't know. It just came over me. I was merely trying to thank you for caring."

"A mistake then?" Ben asked.

"A big mistake. If I know anything about helping you, we can't change our relationship. Understood?"

"No, not really, but I'll try."

"Try, okay?" Hayley said. "So, back to you. The last time we had a serious talk you said that you left the Corps with guilt. Start somewhere."

"Isaiah Joseph Jones."

"Who?"

"Isaiah Joseph Jones. He went by Izzy, sometimes IzzyJo. Isaiah if I was pissed at him."

"Okay. First you've mentioned him. Who's Izzy?" asked Hayley.

"Izzy was a poor black kid from Detroit who had absolutely nothing in common with me. He joined the Corps to get out of an impossible life. I joined the Corps because I didn't want to go to jail, but mostly because I didn't give a shit. Izzy joined the Corps so he could breathe. He arrived at Camp Rhino, south of Kandahar, about two weeks after I did. He'd done boot camp at Parris Island in South Carolina and was assigned to our squad."

"Unlikely friend."

"You'd think so. Izzy was given nothing in life and was as poor as dirt. He didn't know who his father was and his mother was an on-and-off heroin addict. A maternal uncle and grandmother raised him. He had lost two older brothers to gang violence. He graduated from high school with a marginal education, although he said he went to school every day and tried. And he was the first person, since my father died, to teach me how to live. And he became my best friend."

"Where's Izzy now?"

"Dead. I killed him."

Hayley's eyes widened. "You killed him? I don't believe that," she said.

"I caused him to get killed; that's just as bad. He pleaded with me and I didn't listen. He and bunch of others died. A piece of me died with him."

"Tell me more about Izzy."

Ben's eyes misted a bit as he started reminiscing about his friend.

"Izzy was a shy twenty year old from Detroit and poor as dirt," Ben said.

Ben deepest and darkest story then slowly unfolded to Hayley.

Ben's squad, including his sergeant, believed immediately that

Izzy was stupid and didn't belong in the Marines, in Afghanistan, and particularly in their squad.

Ben's squad could barely discern Izzy's ghetto jargon, if and when he spoke at all. The battalion had many black men but Ben's squad of nine men had none. The overt shunning of their newest squad member and the lack of anyone who might be his friend drove the already quiet Izzy into a clamshell. When the squad's sergeant, John Wilcox, asked the company commander, Captain Jack Howsfield, to have Izzy transferred, Howsfield went ballistic and Izzy stayed.

"Go on," Hayley said.

"In the Corps, it's all about teamwork," Ben said. "We could only be as strong as our weakest link. And the nine of us, including Sarge, believed Izzy was a weak link and a liability."

"When did you find out that Izzy fit in?"

"Just after his second week. The squad was prepping an updated MK-19 grenade launcher. Sarge couldn't get it to function properly.

"Izzy told Sarge he could fix it. Sarge didn't like anyone showing him up. We all knew that; Izzy didn't. Sarge was so sure that Izzy wouldn't be able to fix the damn thing, he said, 'You think you're smarter than me, boy.' The tone of the word 'boy' was not nice. Izzy, acting like he didn't hear a thing, said, 'No, sir. Not smarter, but I can fix that thing. I'm real good at fixing things.'"

"Sarge gave Izzy the same shit when anyone called him 'sir.' 'Boy, I'm not a sir, I work for a living. It's Sarge to you. Got it.' Izzy said, 'Yes, sir, Sarge. I gots it.'

"Anyway, Izzy takes the grenade launcher, breaks it down faster than anyone I'd ever seen before, looks at the mess on the table, bends a small metal piece and then puts the whole thing back together. Couldn't have taken him more than four or five minutes. 'Here, Sarge. Should work plenty fine now.' It did.

"No one in the squad, including Sarge, ever used 'boy' again around Izzy. In fact, when anyone outside the squad used 'boy' or said something demeaning because of Izzy's speech, we'd all correct whoever said it, 'That's Izzy to you mister.' Izzy loved the respect. He earned it."

"Sounds like a great guy," said Hayley.

"Yes he was," Ben said. "After that we got closer and closer. Izzy could fix anything, weapons, engines, whatever. I'd say he was the most valuable guy in the squad. He'd talk about central Detroit. I'd talk about Apple Ridge. He'd love hearing about my dysfunctional family, for whatever reason. I had things handed or given to me that he'd never known. Family, money, school, love, opportunity. He thought I was the luckiest man alive. He just couldn't understand why I didn't appreciate 'the bounty of the Lord's gifts' that I had. Those were his words."

The salads and bread came. "I'm famished," Hayley said, as she picked up a piece of garlic bread and her fork at the same time.

Ben said, "I'd like to talk a bit more before we eat."

Hayley put her fork down and smiled. "Of course."

Ben restarted, "Izzy said he'd love to come and visit Apple Ridge someday. To him it sounded like the Garden of Eden. I couldn't convince him how wrong he was; not to mention he'd be the only black person there. He said that'd be just fine. Where he lived, there were only blacks. He thought if it was just Izzy, just the one black in Apple Ridge, he might be judged fairly. He said, 'As soon as I fixes somethin' that no one else can fix, they'll say I can stay long as I wants to.'"

Hayley interrupted, "You don't have to use Izzy's form of speech. I get it."

"I do, actually. Helps me remember him. I told him I couldn't promise how people would take to him if he came to Apple Ridge, but if he was forced to leave, I'd leave with him.

"Izzy told me that I didn't have to stay with him. He said, 'Ben, you smart. You can do anything you wants. I don't wants you tied down by my sorry ass.'

"Anyway, we pledged that we'd watch each other's backs extra carefully. For some reason, with Izzy at my side, I felt secure. He told me that he felt the same way." Ben paused for a moment,

"I haven't felt secure like those times with Izzy until now. Thank you."

"You're giving me too much credit," Hayley said with a faint smile, "but thank you."

"I suppose, but it's comforting to me to think so." Ben picked up his fork.

After dinner they said little as they walked to their cars in the parking lot behind the restaurant.

Ben asked, "How's this going to work?"

"Work? What work?" Hayley asked back.

"Long story or short story?"

"Let's try short and if that doesn't work, you can use long," said Hayley.

"I'm in love with you," Ben said without hesitation. "That short enough? Kissing me didn't help."

"Oh, dear. Remember, I'm a psychologist. I'm something you can't have, so you'll want me more. Besides, I've told you that changing our relationship will affect how your treatment goes. Not to mention it's unprofessional. Therapists have lost their licenses when they've...."

"Stop. I'm in love with you," Ben said.

Hayley stammered, "I don't know what to say. I'll see you next Wednesday." *Deidre was right.*

"I don't want to wait until next Wednesday."

"I'm sorry I kissed you. I led you on. I was wrong." Hayley opened her car, sat behind the wheel and closed the door. As Ben backed away to leave, Hayley rolled down the window.

"Yeah?" Ben said, trudging backwards to his car.

"I'm not sorry I kissed you. See you next Wednesday."

*_*_*_*

Hayley tucked herself into bed and dialed Deidre. "I'm so conflicted, I don't know what to do."

"How about hello, first, and conflicted about what? You wanted to stay in that hellhole of a city. Remember, you're the therapist; I'm just a FBI agent. Are we getting things backwards?"

"Are you my friend or are you going to give me lip?"

"I'm listening," said Deidre.

"I feel like I'm dying slowly. Every day, every hour, every minute, I feel like I'm closer to death. I try to fight it, but I can't."

"Your tests have been good so far, right?"

"Yes, but…"

"But what?" Deidre interrupted. "We both know what your story is. C'mon, what would you tell a patient in the same situation? You've got to start living fast, instead of dying slowly. Have you considered maybe it's time to do things without thinking so much? Act on your emotions. They're real."

"What are you talking about?"

"How are you getting along with Ben?"

"Good. I'm helping him. I can see that. He is so vulnerable through that veneer of toughness."

"Did you kiss him again?"

"No, but he did ask me why I kissed him."

"And?"

"At first, I told him it was a mistake and shouldn't have done it and it wasn't professional. Then I told him I wasn't sorry about kissing him but that I won't be able to counsel him if we get into a relationship."

Deidre shouted into the phone, "Dammit, girl. Talk about mixed messages. Does he like you?"

"He said he loves me."

"What did you say to that?"

"I told him that he likes me only because I'm counseling him and that it's not real. Also that it was unprofessional and I could lose my license."

"Are you dense, or what? If you've ever trusted me as a friend, listen to me. Go for it. Screw professionalism. You can always come back to Seattle. Get this guy in bed and don't call me back until you do. Don't think it out. Don't obsess over it. Just do it. Figure out a way. If it doesn't work, you've lost nothing."

Hayley was silent for a moment. "Except my license. It's late and I'm tired. I don't know what to do."

"I do," Deidre exclaimed. "Get this guy in bed. Trust me on this one. I'm giving you ten days. Now hang up and figure out how to make it work."

*_*_*_*

The next morning, Hayley asked Katy MacArthur to get Bill Carter on the phone.

"You sure you want to talk to him?" Katy asked, a bit stunned. "I know for a fact that he does not want to talk to you. The operative word there is N.O.T."

"Katy, try."

Hayley was on hold for fifteen minutes.

"Bill Carter here."

"Mr. Carter, this is Hayley Green."

"I knew who was calling," Carter said. "I thought I'd make you wait a while, just so you know the pecking order around here. You calling to rub more salt in the wound? You don't show up that night, Ben's gone. Ya know that?"

"Perhaps," Hayley said. "I'd like to come to talk to you, in person."

"We got nothing to talk about."

"How do you know until you hear what I have to say."

"Listen up, lady. I'm not, nor is my family or the Ramoses, gonna forgive Ben. That's it, plain and simple."

"I didn't ask you to and I won't. I'd still like to talk to you."

"You can come by my office after noon, but don't expect me to be nice. I have some meetings starting at one, so I can't give you much time. I may have Warren, Warren Kiffers, my attorney here, just in case you're trying to throw another curveball at me."

"You don't need an attorney for what I'm going to say."

"Well, we'll see now."

Hayley ended the conversation, "Have it your way. I'll be there just after noon." *God, he thinks he's so damn important.*

*_*_*_*

Hayley was ushered into Carter's office at twelve fifteen. Warren Kiffers was sitting opposite Bill Carter's desk. Only Kiffers stood when Hayley entered.

Before Carter could say hello, Hayley asked, "May I sit?"

"Sure. Don't know how long you might be here," said Carter.

"That was a mighty interesting show you put on at the high school," Kiffers said.

"I didn't mean it to be a show. It was pure serendipity that I was there. Corinne Shermann sat with my boss from the Seattle office at a statewide meeting the day before. Some of their discussion was about the happenings here in Apple Ridge. The upcoming town hall meeting was brought up and my boss knew I had been seeing, uh, counseling Dr. Hunt."

"He didn't call you?" Carter asked.

"No. I was in Sun Valley with my friend, Deidre, the FBI agent. I had just called the Seattle DSHS office to check in."

Carter shook his head, "Our bad luck, eh?"

"I can't answer that. Apple Ridge has a surgeon now."

"Okay, you two," Kiffers said. "Enough badgering. Miss Green what do you want from Bill?"

"First, everything I said that night at the town hall meeting about Dr. Hunt was true," Hayley said, "absolutely true. Other than the times Dr. Hunt took care of me in the hospital, the only contacts we've had, in Seattle and here, have been professional. He has some issues dating back to his father's suicide and his tours in Afghanistan and I've been trying to help him."

"We got that the other night." Kiffers asked. "So what exactly do you want?"

Carter spoke up, "I don't give a shit about Hunt's problems. I lost a son. Plus, I'm the biggest landowner in Apple Ridge and the economy is in the toilet. Most of my tenants can't make rent. I'm foreclosing on families that have been here for three or more generations. If you got a problem, lady, it's gonna be so low on my list of worries that I can promise you, before you open your mouth, that I ain't gonna help."

"I don't need your help and I'll try to never ask for it. Deal?" Hayley said.

"What do you want then?" Kiffers asked.

"Maybe I need to tell you a little about me. I hope you keep what I'm going to say confidential, but it's not a secret."

"We'll see," Carter said, "I'm not promising anything."

"Dr. Hunt saved my life at Seattle Med when a doctor put a bone marrow biopsy needle through my backbone into a vein in my abdomen. I should have bled to death but didn't, thanks to Dr. Hunt."

"How's that change anything?" asked Carter, "as if I care."

"I was having a bone marrow biopsy for leukemia."

"That's bad," Kiffers said.

"Yes, bad. A short time later, when I was finally healthy enough, I had a bone marrow transplant."

"You're here, so it must have worked," said Kiffers.

"Yes and no. They couldn't find a match for my marrow type, so as a last resort they used my own marrow for the transplant."

"How's that work?" Kiffers asked. "Seems like they're putting the same bad cells back into you."

"Yes, exactly," said Hayley.

"Sounds good to me," said Carter, "not that I know much about that shit."

"The problem, as Mr. Kiffers suggested, is that my marrow created the leukemia in the first place, so it's likely it'll do it again. Highly likely. When, we don't know. Hard to have a relationship when you can't buy six months of life insurance at age twenty-nine. Have I mentioned that the chemo probably destroyed my ovaries. Looks like getting married or having a family aren't on my to-do list."

"Sounds like you're screwed but how's that my problem?" asked Carter. "I've already told you, I got my own issues."

"I know no one here in Apple Ridge, except Dr. Hunt. And, although you don't care for him, I'd like to have a small amount of social life without you raising a stink. I'd like to be able to go to Dr. Hunt's house and have him come to mine for a meal without the hound dogs baying at the moon."

"I'll think about it. You've been planning this all along, eh?" Carter said.

"Nineteen hours, to be exact. I counseled Dr. Hunt last night for an hour at some pizzeria and then he left for home. He says we should not be seen together. But afterwards, I was lonely."

Hayley let the comment sit but neither Carter or Kiffers responded verbally or visually. Hayley continued after the uncomfortable pause, "By the way, Katy MacArthur is working out wonderfully. She is very talented and capable."

"You didn't have to hire her. Bill doesn't owe you a thing for her job," said Kiffers.

"You got that right. I don't owe you shit," said Carter.

Looking at Carter, Hayley said, "Yes, I did have to hire her. She was the most qualified. Owing or not owing you had nothing to do with it."

With a moment of silence, Hayley stood and said, "Thank you for your time. Oh, thanks for calling off the two a.m. greeters. I've got new blinds and they look great and I'm sleeping better."

"I have no idea what you're talking about."

Hayley shook her head in obvious disbelief and said, "Right," as she turned and walked out.

*_*_*_*

"What do you make of that?" Carter asked Kiffers.

"I don't know," Kiffers said. "You've lost a son and it sounds like her parents are going to lose a daughter. I'm not sure what's worse. Having it happen suddenly and unexpectedly like Billy Jr. or knowing it's going to happen but not when."

"I'm not forgiving Ben Hunt. Not now. Not ever."

"She didn't ask you to," Kiffers said. "She asked you to let her enjoy what life she has remaining."

"Fine. Shit. The only thing that bothers me is that asshole Hunt's likely to have a good time. Admittedly, she is pretty and that pisses me off."

Kiffers sat silent.

"Okay, okay. I won't bother her anymore," Carter bemoaned. "It wasn't working anyway. I heard she had it out with Felix Ramos. She's tougher than I thought. I gotta admit she's not afraid of me one bit." Carter smiled, "So far."

Kiffers changed the subject. "The Toppenish Indian lawyer and some manager types from Atlantic City will be here in an hour. I told them to wear jeans and T-shirts. We don't need people around here getting suspicious. Let's make sure we've got our numbers straight. We've just closed on the two foreclosed parcels giving us total control of the area except for Ben's parcel. If all goes well, we'll plan a trip east to meet with the big shots."

"Right. But we still need a way to get Hunt to sell his property. The whole casino and resort scheme goes down the tubes without it. You think this girl could talk some sense into him? Everyone's got a price."

Kiffers mulled over the question. "I may be reading her wrong," he said, "but she's on a mission. Unless you've got a cure for leukemia, and you don't, I'm guessing you've got nothing she wants. But that's a guess."

"Maybe Katy MacArthur can help us? We need to find something on Hunt's girl that we can use."

## Chapter 11

The smell of boiling oils and spices surrounded Ben and Hayley as they entered Annie's Fried Chicken House off I-90, south of Apple Ridge.

"I can't believe it's been a week since we had dinner," Ben said.

Hayley responded, "I'm sorry. I've been so busy trying to get up to speed. So many need help and so much has to be done. Uh-oh. I'm dwelling on my issues. How are you doing?"

Ben misunderstood the question and wished he could be busier at the hospital complaining that most doctors in town had relationships with Carter or the Ramoses and send business to Yakima or Cle Elum.

"That wasn't exactly what I was talking about when I asked how were you doing," Hayley said. She picked up the menu at Annie's Fried Chicken House. "Yikes. This has to be the unhealthiest place in the universe. Everything is fried in thirty weight oil."

"Probably, but once you've tried Annie's Cajun chicken, you'll be back. And, I'm okay, I guess."

After ordering two Cajun Chicken Dinners, Hayley said, "Okay. Izzy fit in, you became friends. Then what happened?"

"As I said, meeting Izzy was at the beginning of our first tour. At eight months, the tour was completed and we all had a chance to return stateside. Three quarters of our platoon came home. Izzy and I opted to re-up for another tour. Well, actually, I re-upped and Izzy wouldn't leave me.

"My mom was in a rehab unit in Yakima for her drinking. I just couldn't see going back. I didn't realize how severe her liver disease was. Anyway, another tour seemed like the best place for me. I was angry, drunk often and didn't feel like going back to Apple Ridge. Besides, some friends had written me a couple of times that the fruit processing plant was in trouble and there'd be no jobs. I promised Izzy that I'd only do one more tour. So we stayed. If I hadn't stayed in Afghanistan, Izzy would still be alive.

"Lots of guys stay for a second tour. Your re-upping didn't kill Izzy. He could have left."

"You're right, he could have, but he didn't want to leave me. That was our deal with each other. He had already decided that his best ticket out of Detroit was to stay with me. He had never had a white friend before and wasn't going to let anything happen to me. The second tour didn't kill him. I did that later."

"Golly, you're way too hard on yourself. I'm sure there's more to the story."

The Cajun Chicken arrived and didn't disappoint.

After dinner, Ben said, "I can't tell you how much you being here has helped me. I know we haven't really gotten to the place that will be hard for me to discuss. I think about it all the time. I'd like to be able to dream about good things. Fun times. A happy future. I can't. I can't forget."

"We'll get there," Hayley said, watching Ben's hands tremble, "We'll get there.

"I do think about you. I guess that's a good thing," Ben said.

"What do you see when you're thinking of me. May I ask?"

"Sure. You know how I feel about you. Mostly, I don't want you to hate me."

"I don't. I don't anymore. I did."

"I don't blame you for hating me. I deserved it. I probably deserved worse. I was certain when I came to your office that first time that you'd throw me out. You didn't. Why?"

"Don't know. If I had known you were coming, I would have stopped it. Perhaps, it was the first words you said in my doorway."

"I can't remember what I said exactly," Ben said, his head tilted in curiosity.

"You said, 'I need help.'"

"I don't honestly remember saying those words, but it was true."

"It's getting late. I think we're ready to discuss what exactly happened to Izzy. I'm equally certain we shouldn't be exploring Izzy's death in a restaurant. Any suggestions?" asked Hayley.

"Let me think on it. Obviously, our houses are out," said Ben.

Hayley smiled, let the comment slide, and said, "Yeah. We'll think of somewhere by next week."

*_*_*_*

Two nights later, a Friday evening late, Ben put a frozen lasagna in the microwave, then sprawled on his small couch, still in his scrubs, to read the current issue of the American Journal of Surgery. His cell phone rang.

"Ben, Hayley here. I'm in a little bind."

"How can I help? Ben asked. "I just got home."

"I wanted to go to Seattle to see my parents and pick up some stuff from my condo. My car broke down outside Cle Elum and got towed into a repair shop but the parts won't be here until Monday. I can't see myself staying in Cle Elum all weekend and was hoping you could pick me up and bring me back to Apple Ridge. I don't know anyone else to call."

"Why don't you rent a car?" asked Ben.

"Both rental car places were out of cars, other than a twelve-speed, two-ton truck. There's no bus service until tomorrow afternoon."

"Okay. I'll call Bill Harkins and sign out. Where are you exactly?"

"At the Best Western in Cle Elum. I checked in, thinking I'd stay, but the manager said I could leave early and pay only half."

Hayley filled in the directions and Ben said he'd be there in forty-five minutes.

*_*_*_*

Ben knocked on Room 232. As he knocked, the door, apparently unlocked and slightly ajar, swung open. Ben entered the room, dimly lit by a bedside lamp. He saw clothes on a couch next to an open small suitcase and Hayley's shoes on the floor nearby.

Ben announced his presence. "Hayley, I'm here. What's going on? You're not packed."

Hayley exited the bathroom wearing a cut off T-shirt and skimpy underwear. She took a deep breath and approached Ben.

Ben, a look of concern on his face, quickly scanned the room searching to see if others were present. "I... I'm confused. What's going on?" he asked.

"I'm not sorry I kissed you," Hayley replied.

Ben turned, shut the open door, and then turned on the room lights. "Are you okay? Have you been drinking, or something?"

"I'm stone sober and I'm not sorry I kissed you." Hayley walked past Ben, turned off the lights, circled in front of Ben and repeated, "I'm not sorry I kissed you." She grabbed Ben's hands and said, "I want you to kiss me back."

"I'm confused. Where's your car?"

"It's in the back of the hotel lot, behind a large SUV. My car is fine. Are you going to kiss me?" Hayley asked.

"You said, uh," Ben hesitated, at a loss for words. "You said this would make treating me impossible."

"I did say that. It's complicated. We'll find a way. Right now, I don't care. I want you to kiss me."

"Are..are you sure about all this?" Ben asked.

"As sure as I'll ever be. You said you loved me. Were you kidding?"

"No. I do love you. I love you enough for both of us. I just didn't expect you to love me back."

"For a doctor, you don't seem to listen very well. I want you to kiss me."

Ben smoothed the loose hair off Hayley's face and cupped both sides of her face. "Hayley Green, I do love you. Their lips met for the second time. Unlike the Hayley's first peck at the motel, Ben's kiss was deep, penetrating and mutual.

They stopped, took deep breath and opened eyes to see 'yes' bannered across each.

"Don't stop," Hayley whispered.

Ben picked Hayley up and she wrapped her legs around his torso and they kissed again as he walked towards the bed. He put Hayley down and sat next to her.

"Hayley. Are you okay?" Ben asked again.

"I hope so," Hayley said, taking a deep breath. "It's been a year since anyone but my mother held me in their arms. The chemo treatments wreaked havoc to my hormones. Dr. Capland suggested I start some hormone replacement but I never filled the prescription. He thought that I might need some lubricant. He wasn't sure. Anyway, I have some in the bathroom."

"That's way more information than I needed to know," Ben said.

"I thought, you being a doctor and all, that you'd understand and..."

Ben put his finger over Hayley's lips and said, "Shh. Let's figure this out together. Slowly. Real slowly. Without Dr. Capland in the room."

Hayley had already started tearing. A small tear hung on the inside of both lids, as if waiting for a race to start. Someone needed only to say 'go'. The right-sided tear won by half a second as Ben watched them roll down past Hayley's nose.

"What are you thinking?" Ben asked. “What are you really thinking?”

Tears now cascaded across Hayley’s face, one over another, in a steady stream. "I want to be normal. I want to feel normal. I don't want to be broken. I want to be loved. I want to be needed. There's more, but that's what I want now. Can you try to make me feel normal? Can you really love me?"

Ben didn't answer. He stood up and removed his scrub top, then sat back on the bed next to Hayley. His chest was firm and unblemished except for an irregular, raised, violet and red scar just over his left shoulder.

Hayley wiped her face with the bed sheet, then brushed the scar gently with her fingertips. "What's this?"

"Shrapnel. July, 2002." He outlined her face with both hands. "What's this?" Ben asked.

"I don't know what you mean." Hayley said.

"Your face. It's so beautiful. It takes my breath away."

Hayley smiled at the lame compliment. "Let me sit up and take off my top."

"No. I don't want you to move. I'll do it."

He slid his hands under the shortened T-shirt, stopping only for a moment to outline her breasts, and then slid the shirt off as Hayley raised her arms. She tried to bring her arms back, as a modesty reflex, to cover herself. Ben gently held both wrists and placed her arms on the bed.

"Don't move," Ben said. "You are exquisite."

"Right," Hayley said, dripping with her own special form of sarcasm. Arms are her side, looking down at her upper chest, she added, "Like the chemo port sites and IV scars on my neck are beautiful. I was thinking about putting some makeup on them and...."

Ben interrupted, "Yes. They are, in fact, beautiful. They show your courage to have faced adversity and won. They're your shrapnel wounds. And you are exquisite and you never need to cover them for me."

"I want to be exquisite. I don't want to be damaged."

"You are. I swear."

"Talk is cheap…but I do like hearing it again. I used to feel that way."

"This may come out wrong," Ben said, "but hear me out. You may think that I'm in love with you because I believe you are the only one that can help me. God, how I've thought about that question."

Hayley's lower lip quivered softly, her eyes open wide, waiting for the next sentence.

Ben continued, "Honestly, I don't know for sure, but I feel like I'm going to be better. No, I *know* I'm going to be better with your help. Not be so angry and when that happens, I'll be able to prove to you that I love you because of who you are and not because of what I needed."

Ben kissed Hayley on the lips softly and then slowly moved down, kissing her chin, neck, her chemo port site scars and finally her breasts. "Did you not know I've dreamed only that you might like me every day since I saw you at the back of the auditorium? They're the only good dreams I have."

"I didn't. I don't know why I was so blind. Pig-headed, I guess."

"I never thought for a second that it would happen," Ben said. He too had small tears in each eye.

Hayley grabbed Ben's head and pressed it onto her chest. "I'm so sorry I waited. I should have known."

Ben stood and removed his scrub pants and underwear. A large, irregular scar on his right thigh presented itself to Hayley, along with a full erection. She touched the scar gently.

"That must have hurt," she said.

"It did," Ben smiled, "but they kept missing the important parts." Ben's erection left no doubts.

Hayley arched her back then circled her thumbs under the elastic of her panties.

"Don't you dare, Ben said. "I don't want you to move." He sat astride Hayley and started kissing and caressing her breasts and then moving slowly down her abdomen, past her belly button and lower. He pulled down the elastic on her panties and continued to kiss and caress as Hayley purred in soft rhythmic breaths.

Ben gently circled his hands around to Hayley's back as she instinctively arched her back once again. Ben slid his hands under the elastic and slid the panties to her knees. With Ben holding the panties still, Hayley removed one leg and then the other.

"Be gentle," Hayley said.

"I will. I promise. I'll be gentle with you forever." *She's so scared.*

Ben lay astride Hayley, enveloped her in his arms and kissed her over and over until he felt the muscles in her back and arms soften. He descended slowly, stopping at her breasts, twirling one nipple gently with his fingers as he circled the opposite one with his tongue. Hayley's purring was deep and throaty as he descended past her belly button, spread her legs gently and moved lower. He explored everything as Hayley arched her back with each deep breath.

Hayley lifted Ben's head up then slid her hands under his shoulders and forced him up. She bent up and grabbed his firmness with one hand and directed it towards her open legs. “Now. I need you now.”

"Do we need protection?” Ben asked. “I don't have anything."

"Redundant. My ovaries are pretty much shot." She guided his erection in circles around her moistened and aroused opening until she knew she couldn't wait a moment longer and then guided him in. "It doesn't hurt, Ben. It doesn't hurt."

He kissed her deeply and passionately as their bodies moved together, eye to eye, each slow thrust another step further from their fears, to the end.

Both spent, they held each other, quietly, silently, interrupted only by the synchrony of their deep breaths followed by seconds of peace.

Hayley broke the silence. “You know how one plans something after they've dreamed it? You think, or at least you hope, it'll be the best day in your life, but it never seems to work out just that way. Something little, a blemish, a ding, the wrong word. The dream is never completely fulfilled. I dreamed of this; meeting you here.”

Ben remained still knowing Hayley had more to say.

“For two days I couldn't think of anything else. Every detail, every facet. How to do it. The room. The phone call. Your response. What I would wear. What would happen when you came. How I would feel. How I thought you would feel. How happy I could be again, really happy, even for a short time. It all came true, everything I dreamed. It was perfect.”

Ben smiled and kissed Hayley on the lips softly. “You were so far ahead of me. I would have never thought to have dreamed of this."

“Was it just pure dumb luck or coincidence that you happened to be steps from me when I was injured?” Hayley asked.

Ben paused a second and said, “I'm a surgeon so I have a hard time believing in coincidence, but it's even harder to believe in anything else."

Hayley smiled, "Maybe, but possibly this is some supreme being's way of remaining anonymous." Hayley cried softly into the nape of Ben's neck as she circled his chest with her free hand. "I want to live. I want to live so badly."

Ben knew enough to say nothing. He slid his head down to Hayley's damp cheeks and kissed away the tears. He then encircled her with both arms and hugged her until she relaxed.

"God, how I hate feeling sorry for myself. I'm sorry." Hayley mumbled.

"That's okay. I can only hope to understand."

"Thank you."

Ben relaxed his hug and said, "To change subjects, you hungry?"

Hayley moved her head back and smiled, "That's such a guy thing to say. Right out of a sitcom. We're only missing the audience's canned laughter."

Before Ben could formulate an apology, Hayley added, "Actually, I haven't eaten since lunch. I was too nervous. I'm starved."

"Let's shower, find somewhere to grab a bite, come back and try to do perfect again."

Hayley smiled, rolled on top of Ben, kissed him on the lips and said, "Let's."

*_*_*_*

At ten the following morning, after checking out of the motel, Ben and Hayley sat in a Starbucks in Cle Elum having coffee and pumpkin bread.

"This changes everything," Ben said. "How's this possibly going to work? I can't go a week without being with you. Clandestine meetings outside of Apple Ridge every time we want to be see each other?"

"Well. There's something I didn't tell you," Hayley said. "I didn't want to spoil perfect."

Eyebrows arched, Ben asked, "And that is?"

"I met with Bill Carter on Thursday."

"You're kidding," Ben said. "And?"

Hayley explained the meeting and conversation with Carter and Kiffers including the fact that she had leukemia with a high likelihood of recurrence.

"You mean he knew you were coming here before I did?" Ben asked. "Ouch."

"No. Of course not," Hayley laughed. "I hadn't formulated the plan yet. I just told him that I wanted to be friends with you. That's it."

"He'll figure someway to use this against me."

"No one at the town hall meeting asked if I cared for you. I did, you know," Hayley said as she grabbed a small crumb of pumpkin bread off Ben's chin and put it in his mouth.

"I didn't know," Ben said.

"I know you didn't."

"I have to ask you an honest question?"

"That is?"

"Did you make love to me last night because you're afraid?" Ben asked.

"Afraid of what? Having sex doesn't prevent the leukemia from returning," Hayley asked back.

"Of course it doesn't," Ben said. "I didn't mean that. What I meant was did you hurry into our relationship because you were afraid to wait?"

Hayley hesitated and softly bit her lower lip as she thought. "It's possible."

Ben started to say something but Hayley held up her hand, "Stop. Let me finish my thought. I can see why you might say that. When you left Seattle I was already conflicted. I was having trouble getting over how much I hated you in the beginning. After you left, I began to realize how much I missed you. How much I enjoyed our Wednesday dinners. When I heard you were in trouble, I felt guilty for abandoning you. Then, when I saw your face at the town hall meeting, that sealed the deal. I needed to be here. So my answer is, no, I didn't hurry up because I was afraid." *You don't need to know that Deidre helped push me.*

"Thank you. You know I can't possibly wait until Wednesday to see you," said Ben.

Hayley started playing with Ben's hands, "I don't want to wait either. Let's go out to dinner tonight."

"Can I come to your house for dinner? If I leave early enough then......" Ben asked.

Hayley interrupted, "Why not. Seven."

Ben, looking over Hayley's shoulder did a double take, slid his hands away from Hayley and looked down at the remnants of his pumpkin bread. "On another note, that man and woman behind you across the room are from Apple Ridge. Rob and Rhonda Anderson. We've already been IDed. Turn and wave."

"I'm not waving at someone I don't know. Will they tell Carter that we were here?" Hayley asked, with lines of worry etched on her face.

"They don't run in the same circles, but Apple Ridge is small and they'll tell someone, who'll tell another. Carter will know in less than forty-eight hours."

"Gee. Seattle's sounding better and better."

"Hayley. What can happen? They're not likely to convene another town hall meeting unless either of us screw up at work. Even if they did, what's the worst? They ask you or I to leave. If I knew you'd come with me, they could send me to Somalia."

"I'm sorry, Ben. I don't like it. I feel like I've been caught in a lie."

"Nothing's going to happen. Seven o'clock, your place. I'll bring a bottle of wine for you. You head home in the car that runs fine."

Hayley smiled broadly.

"I'll go over and chat with Rob and Rhonda," Ben continued, "and tell them we're here looking at antique furniture for your rental. They won't believe it and they won't ask about you. Small town people are like that. On the other hand, they will tell others. Small town people are like that too."

Hayley got up and left while Ben headed over to schmooze and lie a bit.

*_*_*_*

Ben arrived at Hayley's at six forty-five p.m. to find every light on and every window shade open.

After hanging Ben's coat on a rack near the door, Hayley said, "I've had goose bumps all afternoon waiting for you."

Ben surveyed the small house from the entry. "Nice place. Think you have enough lights on?"

"No secrets here tonight. I walked the perimeter of the house twenty minutes ago. The only blind spot is the hallway between the kitchen and my study. I'll show you." Hayley led, and Ben followed, into a small hallway. "Right here. No one can see."

Ben wasted no time spinning Hayley around, holding her face and kissing her on the forehead, eyes, nose and then lips. "If I tore your clothes off and made love to you in this hallway, would anyone know?"

"No one but me. I've made dinner and we have stuff to discuss.

We can't have it both ways, on the couch and in the bed."

"Why not."

"Because it doesn't work that way," said Hayley.

Ben moved his hands down to Hayley's waist and held her closer. He said, "Have you ever tried it?"

"No, of course not. I've never even touched a client."

"I think we went way past touching." Ben moved his hands lower.

"I can't be effective if I'm not objective. I can't be objective if I'm sleeping with you. We'll have to find someone in Yakima, Ellensburg, or anywhere, who can see you."

"I don't want to see anyone else. I'm so much better with you here. Can't we try for a while?" Ben pleaded.

"We have to until I, or we, find someone. We'll need to set parameters. Specific days for counseling. If it doesn't work, one of us will know. We'll have to be honest with each other."

"You're not sure it won't work. You and me."

"No. No, I'm not. I want to try to finish your time in Afghanistan. We were so close." Hayley tried to push away from Ben's hold on her butt. "You have to let go of me."

"Damn. Next time we don't get out of the hallway. What's so important?"

Hayley pecked Ben on the lips. "Izzy. That's what." Hayley moved Ben's hands off her butt, turned and started back to the kitchen. She turned to Ben, following her, and said, "I feel so alive."

Hayley baked a salmon filet and placed it on a bed of quinoa and black beans.

They ate at a small table in a bay window kitchen nook. Hayley had two glasses of wine; Ben, as usual, none. She talked mostly about her life growing up on Mercer Island and her friendship with Deidre. Ben listened, watching Hayley's hands, face, and large brown eyes tell her story.

"When you talk," Ben said, "your hands move like silk in a breeze. Can't we go back into the hallway, just for a second?"

"No," said Hayley, curtly.

*_*_*_*

Ben sat on a small couch in the living room and Hayley in a chair to the side.

"Okay. Forget about us for now. Izzy? You two re-upped."

"Can I hold your hand?" Ben asked.

"No. C'mon, this is serious," said Hayley. "Izzy and you re-enlisted for another tour and you didn't go home to see your mother. Then?"

Ben explained that coming home was too expensive and took too much travel time. He also didn't want to go back to Apple Ridge and see his mother or stepfather. So, he, Izzy, Sarge and two other guys from their squad went to Dubai and partied hard for two solid weeks until they returned to Afghanistan.

"On the second tour our platoon was used almost exclusively as support of the Afghan National Army or ANA," Ben said. "That's a whole other story. So much graft, so much patronage. Half the officers bought their rank. Some were good soldiers, most weren't. I never trusted them as a group, and Izzy was even more suspicious."

"Is this important about what happened to Izzy?" Hayley asked.

"Absolutely. I need to tell the entire story. That's how I dream it. Start to finish."

"Go ahead," Hayley said.

Ben lowered his voice. "'Ben, listen up.' Izzy always said 'listen up' if he wanted my attention. 'I don't trust these guys no way. They ain't no good. I giv'em equal chances of switching sides, running away or just putting their hands up if the Taliban sneezes. You and me gotta watch the bad guys, and these guys just as hard.'

"Our squad had been back about three months when the ANA moved east of Kandahar. Our whole platoon followed and set up Camp Hippo nearby. The Taliban were active in the surrounding hill country and our squad would accompany the ANA platoons on their patrols.

Coming back from an uneventful recon mission, Sarge tripped coming down a steep portion of the trail. He had been yelling at the ANA lieutenant to keep his troops alert and ready. The ANA soldiers, including the non-coms, were smoking and joking and Sarge didn't like it."

"What are non-coms?" asked Hayley.

"Non-commissioned officers or NCOs, mostly sergeants. The ANA lieutenant didn't like Sarge, even an experienced US Marine sergeant like Wilcox, telling him what to do. The lieutenant said something in Pashto, the local language, which got all the ANA guys laughing.

"Anyway, Sarge gets distracted, misses a step, falls and slid downhill for about ten feet and hits his head on a boulder. If it hadn't been for the boulder, he could have easily gone another sixty feet. I remember Izzy, who was just above me, saying, 'It be good Sarge hit his head. Gotta be the densest part of that man.' Our whole squad cracked up. Sarge was knocked unconscious for ten, twelve seconds, no more. He got up and walked down the rest of the hill, pissed because he looked weak in front of the Afghanis.

"That night Sarge had a terrible headache and started popping ibuprofens like they were Skittles. We didn't have much to do for the next forty-eight hours so Sarge stayed mostly in his bunk complaining of a headache. He refused to see the doc, who happened to be an Afghani guy trained in London.

"Whenever Sarge would get up to take a leak, he'd wobble a bit, grab onto the tent post before getting his bearings, then start swearing again about how bad his head hurt. We didn't think much of it though. Then we got orders to recon a mountain village twenty clicks away, without the ANA."

"What's a click?"

"Sorry. A click is a kilometer, two-thirds of a mile. Anyway, the ANA had been in the village two days earlier and told US command that everything was hunky-dory, but our intel had the place highly infiltrated with Taliban.

"Our platoon was to split into the three squads, Alpha, Bravo and Charley. We were Bravo. Sarge was given coordinates from the captain and Bravo was supposed to arrive at the coordinates at 1400, then radio the captain so we'd all enter the village at the same time from different directions. Bravo would come from the east over a couple of big hills and then down into the valley."

"You okay?" Hayley asked. "You're breathing faster than usual. You want a glass of water?"

"Sure. That'd be good. I think I'll lie down."

Hayley returned with a glass of water. Ben raised up, took a sip then laid back down, closed his eyes and continued his story.

## Chapter 12

## Camp Hippo. July 9, 2002, late morning

Ben, Izzy and the rest of Bravo were at the ammo depot checking and rechecking armaments for the mission.

Izzy whispered to Ben, "Sarge's not right. He don't belong goin' on no mission. He ain't thinking straight, two days now. You gots to talk to him."

Ben whispered back, "Why me, Izzy. He'll just rip my head off."

"You's the squad corporal, and you outranks everyone but Sarge. Should be you talking to him," demanded Izzy.

Ben reluctantly approached Sarge who was busily packing his gear. "Excuse me, Sarge, you okay? I'm thinking you're still loopy from that fall the other day."

Sarge grimaced. "What the fuck you talking about, Hunt? Get your gear packed. We're leaving in fifteen."

"I am packed," Ben said, "but I'm just worried about you being one hundred percent and...."

Sarge wheeled around, grabbed Ben by his ammo vest and pulled him nose to nose. "Back off, corporal. You're way out of fuckin' line. You even mention what you just said to anyone else, I'll have you in the fuckin' brig so fast your dick'll be in Timbuktu and your ass'll be in Kabul. You got me?"

"Yes, Sarge. I got it."

"You make sure the rest of the squad is ready in ten, asshole," Sarge said, jabbing his finger into Ben's chest.

"Yes, Sarge."

Ben told Izzy about their brief lack of conversation.

Izzy shook his head, saying, "I thinks you ought to go to the captain. Sarge ain't all there and you knows it."

"Izzy, I agree with you, dammit. What am I 'sposed to do? I thought he was going to kill me. If I go over his head, he will kill me."

"I dunno," Izzy said. "You better watch Sarge real close. You gotta make sure he's making good choices. You gotta promise you'll watch him. For me. Promise?"

"I promise, Izzy. If he even farts wrong, I'll correct him," Ben said. *No way I'm doin' that again.*

Ben and Izzy's Bravo squad, fully loaded, jumped into three Humvees and headed west-northwest towards Gereshk following the two other squads of Marines, Alpha and Charlie. After two hours on Afghan highway A1, the Bravo Humvees turned north northwest on a camel track road as Alpha and Charlie in the other six Humvees continued due west. Captain Howsfield, riding with Alpha, radioed from the lead Humvee to keep complete radio silence until all three squads arrived at their coordinates.

After another two hours of brutal, rutted-road travel, Sarge's lead Humvee came to a halt at the base of a range of small hills. The squad emptied out and instinctively formed an outward facing perimeter to reconnoiter the surrounding area.

"We walk from here," Sarge said. "The village is two clicks to the northwest, over two sets of hills. We'll stop half a click out and radio the captain when we're in position. When we get the signal that Alpha and Charlie are in position, we enter from the southeast. No chatter and eyes everywhere. Let's go."

"Oorah," softly chimed nine Marines.

Heading up the first hill, Sarge kept checking his GPS device every five or six minutes trying to get a bearing on their position. After thirty minutes and about two-thirds up the first hill, the squad halted when Sarge raised his hand.

"Let's stop for a second," Sarge mumbled. "This fucking, piece-of-shit GPS. The latitude keeps changing every ten seconds." He spanked the side of the handheld GPS, then re-read the output.

Izzy leaned over to Ben and said, "Sarge be lost. He don't know where the fuck we is. Maybe you needs to go over and help him."

"Sarge's fine and we ain't lost. I trust him," Ben said, without conviction.

"I'm glad you do, I don't. I says he's lost."

Sarge stood and pointed towards a small gap at the top of the hill. He said softly, "Eyes everywhere," then put his finger to his lips, flipped off the safety on his M-16 to show everyone to do the same and headed up.

The squad had climbed another fifty yards up the hill when a fist-size rock came tumbling down from the east side of the hill, narrowly missing Izzy.

Sarge yelled, "Down," as he motioned for us to take cover. Before Ben hit dirt, the first rounds of random automatic weapon fire whistled over Bravo's heads. Every member of the squad could tell from the familiar pop-pop-pop sounds that AK-47s, maybe twenty, were firing at intervals from above, right and left of their position. Everyone but Sarge looked back down the hill for a potential defensive position. Izzy and Ben had decent cover behind a modest sized boulder. The rest of Bravo lay exposed.

Pop-Pop-Pop.

Within the first minute, a handful of rocket propelled grenades, or RPGs, disabled Bravo squad's three Humvees parked below. Sarge never looked down, he knew down was never an option.

Pop-Pop-Pop. Then the firing stopped.

Brave squad looked to Sarge as he started barking orders. "Can't stay here. Fuller, radio the captain and tell him we're pinned down three quarters of a click from the target. Ben, Izzy, on my word, you two lay down covering fire and the rest of us head left to the jagged boulders over my shoulder. Up, right, and down are no good."

Izzy swore softly to Ben, "Shit, Ben. Sarge led us into a nest of these assholes. Musta had the coordinates wrong. Shit, I knew he wasn't all there."

"Quiet, Izzy," Ben demanded. "I'll lay fire over our guy's heads and you keep the guys up above busy. When Sarge says go."

Fuller, the radioman, yelled, "Left a message, Sarge. Don't know if they got it."

Sarge put a hand in the air and yelled, "Go."

Ben and Izzy started firing left and up trying to give the squad a chance to move.

Sarge and six men raised to a crouch and started traversing quickly to the left, a mere twenty yards of open space between them and adequate cover.

Immediately, the AK-15s let loose with a barrage of pop-pop-pop-pop-pops.

Sarge was hit first by a bullet through his right shoulder. The force of the penetrating shell lifted Sarge up and spun him around and he was hit with two more bullets to the neck and right leg. He was dead before hitting the ground. Fuller hadn't gotten his gear ready and when he saw the hailstorm of fire, he froze. The rest of the squad kept pushing to the left. The pop-pop-pop was then overridden by the staccato fire of two PKM Soviet machine guns. Both guns emptied their hundred round belts in thirty seconds. The 7.62 mm shells shredded all six moving men of Bravo.

Ben yelled, "Fuller, stay down. Keep radioing for help. Don't stop radioing until you get an answer. Keep an eye down the hill and make sure no one's below us. Izzy, you keep looking up and right. I'll do up and left. Don't waste ammo unless you've got a shot."

"We needs to see if any of the squad needs our help. Can't just let'em lie out there." Izzy yelled.

“Don’t you move,” Ben said. “I need you here. I need you alive. Nobody in the squad is moving and nobody’s calling for help. They’re dead, Izzy. They’re all dead. And you got no chance of making back if you go out there.”

“Why’d you let Sarge get us here?” Izzy shouted. “Why Ben?”

“Izzy, shut up. Can’t change anything now. It’s done. We gotta concentrate.”

The pop-pop-pop would stop every so often and fragments of voices of Pashto-speaking Taliban could be heard clearly. Ben and Izzy hadn't fired a shot for over three minutes, when Izzy said, "Two crouched over a rock at two o'clock."

Ben turned to the right. “Three shots each and then back down,” Ben said. “Now.”

Ben and Izzy raised enough to send six shells into the two open targets then slid down behind their rocky cover.

"HQ picked up my call,” shouted Fuller. “They'll tell the captain and try to get air support. They don't know where Captain, Alpha and Charlie are exactly."

Moments later, another Taliban RPG came down the hill, landing forty feet below Fuller. The explosion carried downhill and away.

Ben looked up and right twenty feet to Fuller, crouched behind a small boulder, and realized the Taliban could see that he had a radio. “Fuller, Fuller,” Ben shouted, “You gotta move. Leave the radio and get down here.”

Fuller nodded and turned to grab his rifle when the second RPG landed five feet in front of him. The blast blew the boulder, the radio and Fuller twenty feet down the hill. A piece of shrapnel glanced off Ben's left shoulder.

Smoke and dust was thrown up fifty feet in all directions.

"Izzy, we gotta move now," Ben yelled.

"Fuller needs help. He's hit."

"Fuller's dead, Izzy. Move now while there's smoke and dust."

The two remaining men of Bravo moved in a running crouch quickly to the left stepping over the Sarge and six dead squad members. As they neared the craggy formation that Sarge had been trying to reach, the smoke started to clear. Not thirty feet from the edge of the rock formation sat four unsuspecting Taliban trying to clear dust from their eyes. Izzy saw them first and killed three with short bursts from his M-16. Ben killed the fourth.

"Izzy, we're good here for now. Good cover. How much ammo you got left?"

"Forty-five rounds," Izzy said, "maybe fifty. You?"

"About the same."

Izzy pointed back to his fallen squad members. "You think we can sneak back and get some extra ammo?"

"Great idea. You'd be dead in five seconds."

"If they throw another RPG and kick up some dust, I'm going back."

"Big if."

"Why'd we listen to Sarge, Ben? Why'd we do it?"

"We did. We just did. I'm sorry. It's my fault. I should have known," said Ben.

The Taliban fired three RPGs in rapid sequence at the massive rock formation. Other than smoke, gravel and shrapnel in the air, Ben and Izzy were safe. After the third RPG, without asking Ben, Izzy dropped his rifle and ran fifteen yards to pick up two loose ammo vests and another M-16. He dove back next to Ben as the dust settled and the pop-pop-pop resumed.

"Good work, you lucky sonofabitch."

"What next, Ben?"

"We wait here and hope Captain figures out what's goin' on and helps us or maybe we'll get some air cover. I can't see us moving and making it anywhere."

"Sarge led us into this mess. I knew he wasn't right."

"Can it," Ben demanded. "We gotta stay sharp and alert. I figure twenty or so AK-47s and two PKMs. They're not going to waste ammo any more than we are. We keep peeking to see what's what. Don't put your head up at the same spot. Not likely these assholes will move below us, no cover for them either. We gotta keep checking."

The pop-pop-pop stopped for ten minutes.

"You thinks they gone?" Izzy asked.

"No way," Ben said, looking at his watch. "They may be waiting for dark to make a move. Sun's down in two hours. We need to move too. There's another set of protective rocks twenty-five yards to the left. Risky, but we can't stay here. Better they don't know where we are."

For the next two hours, Ben and Izzy saw and heard nothing, other than the occasional short burst pop-pop-pop.

As the sun set to the west, even the short bursts stopped.

"They're probably moving," Ben said. "Maybe on the backside of the hill. I guess they'll come from the west where we were heading. If we can get there first, then..."

"Then what?"

"I don't know. I think our best option is to get there first. They won't figure on us moving anywhere but down. Getting too dark for air support and it doesn't look like Alpha and Charlie are coming. I figure thirty minutes more and we move."

Thirty-five minutes later, quiet darkness had settled. A sliver of moon gave little light.

"Okay. Let's go," Ben said softly.

Each carrying a rifle and an extra ammo vest, Ben and Izzy scrambled low to the large boulders to the west. They moved quietly and steadily, rifles ready, fingers on the triggers. Only the soft steps taken by Ben and Izzy, the random shouts in Pashto and a short run of pop-pop-pops broke the silence. All the Taliban shooting bounced behind Ben and Izzy, off rocks at the position they had held all afternoon.

Ben and Izzy covered the twenty-five yards to the outcropping in thirty seconds. The moonlight gave no hint of Taliban outside the rocks. Shielded from the moon and pitch black, the small protected area within the rocks conveyed safety, or doom. The Marines hugged the outside of the rock formation listening for any noise or any movement within. Hearing none, Ben put a small flashlight, turned off, up to Izzy's eyes. Izzy nodded, both raised their rifles and Ben gave a short burst of light into the center of the rock formation. Empty. They quietly entered, put down the extra ammo vests and waited, Ben looking west and up, Izzy east and down.

Ben and Izzy waited, knowing that one sound, one shot would be all the enemy needed to know that the two beleaguered Marines had changed positions.

By five a.m., Ben and Izzy had run out of water and the few energy bars stocked in their vests. Both were weary from the constant listening and watching through the night. At five fifteen a.m., three RPGs were again hurled at the rock formation twenty-five yards to the east, their prior position.

Izzy stated the obvious, "They thinks we're still over there. What'cha think they's gonna do now?"

Following the RPGs, a constant chatter of pop-pop-pop started, aimed twenty five yards away.

Over the din of automatic weapons, Ben said, "Be sharp, Izzy. I think they're going to make a run at our old position and are laying down covering fire. They're not gonna waste ammo for too long, so I think they're coming. If I were those assholes, I'd come from the east and west. We won't see them to the east, but if it's the west, they've gotta go through us here. Be ready."

Forty seconds later, four scruffy Taliban, crouching low but moving quickly, approached the Marine's position. The four acted as if they wouldn't be seen until after clearing the rocky formation hiding Ben and Izzy.

Ben whispered, "Hold your fire until we're sure there's no more."

Ben and Izzy could already here pop-pop-pop coming from the east. Then they heard screams in Pashto. The gunfire stopped. The four Taliban stopped to try to hear what was being yelled, then one of them yelled back.

"They knows we moved," whispered Izzy.

Without hesitation, Ben and Izzy stood and emptied their M-16 clips into the four intruders.

"Gotta move again," Ben yelled. "Over there," pointing to the next rocky protection thirty yards to the west and up.

They covered the thirty yards in less than fifteen seconds. As they neared the rocks, a salvo of AK-47 fire burst around them coming from above. Both men dove for cover.

"You okay?" Izzy yelled.

Ben screamed something unintelligible then rolled over showing his right leg covered in blood. "I'm hit. Fuck. Fuck."

Izzy turned quickly to see the front of Ben's right pants leg torn away with a freshly bleeding hunk of skin hanging by a flap over the wound, exposing raw muscle.

Izzy pulled a wad of gauze out of his vest, put it on Ben's open wound and then flipped the skin flap over the gauze. "Hold it there. I gotta keep looking," shouted Izzy.

Ben, breathing heavily with sweat pouring down his face, sat against a rock holding pressure on his leg. "I don't feel so good," he cried.

"Ben. You gotta stay with me. We needs eyes everywhere," pleaded Izzy.

Ben removed a strap from his vest, cinched it tightly around the bandage on his leg and attempted to stand up. "Fuck this hurts," he yelled and slid back down.

"Ben, I needs you."

Screaming in pain, Ben stood using the butt of his M-16 as a crutch. Ben looked back to the four dead Taliban sprawled on the rocks to the east. "I'm with you, Izzy. I'm with you."

The firing ceased and the Taliban voices to the east started yelling what sounded like Muslim names towards Ben and Izzy.

"They're looking for those four dead assholes," Ben said.

After a minute of yelling with no response, the pop-pop-pop starting bouncing off the rocks hiding Ben and Izzy.

"They knows we're here. Should we move again?" Izzy asked.

"I can't move anywhere. Fuck'em," Ben said through gritted teeth.

The hill became quiet again.

After five minutes of no noise, Ben's ear perked up after he heard strange gunfire from above and none of it coming anywhere near the two Marines. "Izzy. Izzy. Something goin' on up top the hill," Ben said.

After another thirty seconds of intermittent fire, Izzy said, "Those be M-16s up above. I think the Captain done found us. Praise, Jesus."

"Good and bad," Ben said. "If it's Alpha and Charlie, the towelheads will be coming down the mountain as fast as they can. Be ready."

Intermittent shouting in Pashto surrounded the hills. The Taliban that had overrun their previous position to the east started scurrying down the hill and Izzy turned his M-16 towards them. Ben yelled, "Leave'em alone, they're not coming back. Eyes up."

Twenty or more Taliban appeared scattered all over the hill above them, carrying AK-47s, the two PKM machine guns and a few toting RPGs.

"They know we're here," Ben said, "so I think they'll move to the east."

The sounds of friendly M-16 fire was clearly distinguishable. Izzy yelled, "I sees them. I sees some Marines way up there."

As soon as Izzy finished his sentence, an F1, World War II, Soviet style hand grenade, called a 'limonka', because they resembled lemons, landed just behind Izzy. Ben saw the grenade a half second before Izzy, dropped his rifle, dove, picked up the grenade and tossed it just over the boulder protecting them. Izzy had already lowered his head as the grenade exploded before it hit the ground on the opposite side of the rock.

Izzy yelled, "I'm okay. I'm okay. I owes you for that one."

Ben rolled over, grabbed his rifle and stood on his one good leg to watch to the east and then up the hill. Ben yelled, "Izzy, I see the captain up there and guys from Alpha."

Ben and Izzy, using the rock formation as a fortress, emptied half their remaining clips of ammunition into the unprotected Taliban fleeing down the hill.

Exchanging clips, Izzy yelled over the noise of gunfire, "We're gonna make it, Ben. We're gonna make it."

As Izzy started to laugh, two 'limonkas' clunked to the rocks behind the two Marines at the same time. Izzy saw them first as Ben turned a second and a half later. Izzy knew instantaneously, as did Ben, that there wasn't time to toss both grenades to safety. Without hesitation, Izzy bent down, grabbed one grenade, then the other, and curled into the fetal position over the grenades. Ben dove with his one good leg out of cover. As Ben was airborne, both grenades detonated simultaneously. Parts of Izzy were spread over the rock formation and twenty yards right and left. Ben, blown ten feet downhill by the blast, hit his head and shoulder on the rocky terrain, rendering him unconscious. Gravity rolled him another fifteen yards downhill. His shoes had been blown off and his leg wound started bleeding again.

*_*_*_*

After a long pause, Hayley said, "Oh, God. That's awful."

Ben lay face up on the couch, eyes shut, color drained from his face.

Hayley moved off her chair, knelt on the rug next to the couch and kissed Ben's forehead. "I'm so sorry," she whispered.

Streams of tears cascaded across Ben's face once he opened his eyes. He looked at Hayley, a combination of fearful and sad. Hayley kissed his forehead again and moved back to the chair.

"How long was it until you realized what had happened and where you were?" Hayley asked.

"Couple of days, maybe. As soon as they got me to Kandahar they had to operate on my shoulder and thigh wounds to remove Afghan dirt, grenade fragments and pieces of my pants. I think they cut down the narcotics the next night and by morning, some officers started asking me questions. At first, I couldn't remember much of anything. Then, stuff came back quickly. I kept asking how Izzy was doing and they kept telling me he was fine."

"Why would they lie to you?" asked Hayley.

"I dunno. I guess I was really agitated on and off and they thought knowing Izzy was dead would make it worse."

"Sooner or later they had to be honest with you."

"Yeah, only when it suited them," said Ben. "I lost track of time, but Captain Howsfield came in four or five days afterwards to see how I was doing and reconstruct the events for his report. He started off by telling me I was the only one to survive. I said, 'No way, sir. How's Izzy? They told me he was okay.'"

"Howsfield told me that Izzy, Sarge and everyone in Bravo was killed on that hill except me. He thought I knew. Then started asking me questions to fill out his report."

"Gee. That seems a bit insensitive. What did you say?" Hayley asked.

"He was a Captain and I was a grunt. I said, 'Yes, Sir.'"

"And?" Hayley said, waiting for Ben to resume.

"I told Captain Howsfield everything I could remember. I know I was crying, on and off, during my recollections. He didn't seem to care that much, but I don't know. He just wrote shit down and asked questions."

"Did the Captain have any explanations?" Hayley asked.

"Captain went on to say it took four hours for HQ to reach him by radio. They headed straight for the village. No men, or at least no men of fighting age remained when they got there. The women just pointed up the mountain towards our position. Captain couldn't reach us by radio and neither could HQ. By then it was dark, so they stayed put.

"Captain told HQ to call off any airstrikes because he didn't think they'd be able to tell Bravo from the bad guys. Alpha and Charlie started up the mountain, double time, at first light, hoping we'd be okay.

"Did you tell your captain what you and Izzy thought about the sergeant?" Hayley asked.

"Yes, at the end. I told him that Izzy and I thought that Sarge was confused before the mission and had led us into an ambush."

Hayley asked, "What did he say to that?"

"That didn't go well. The captain told me that Sergeant Wilcox was an outstanding US Marine in every way and that I needed to keep those thoughts to myself, or else. He repeated that a few times until I said, "Yes, sir."

"Have you ever told anyone?" asked Hayley.

"No. Never. Not until now," said Ben.

"Captain then said, 'I'm thinking you've had a head injury, Corporal, and aren't thinking straight. We ended up killing a bunch of Taliban thanks to you and Private Jones. You've earned a Star or DSC and a Purple Heart, unless you pop off about Sarge. Got it? Keep your mouth shut, forever.'

"I just said, 'Yes, sir,' just like I was supposed to. I've tried to block out everything that happened on that hill, but, of course, I never can. I can't forget. I can't stop blaming myself for Izzy and the rest of the squad. I often find myself saying 'I'm sorry, Izzy. I should have known.' Sometimes I say 'I should have known' over and over until I fall asleep. I should have known. I should have done something."

"I'm sorry. I'm so sorry," Hayley said, as she wiped her own tears with her sleeve.

Tears continued streaming down Ben's face. "I can't forget. I'll never forget. I just can't forget. Anyway, I was evacuated back stateside to heal."

"You blame yourself for Izzy. Right?"

"Yes, him and the whole squad. I've blamed myself every night since then that I didn't go to the captain before we left that afternoon to tell him that Sarge wasn't up to the mission. I owed that to Izzy.

"In surgical hindsight, I am certain that Sarge had a concussion, maybe even a subdural hematoma. That's a blood clot around the brain. I still hear Izzy asking me to do something about Sarge and I can still see Izzy diving onto those grenades and...."

Ben stopped and sat up quickly. "I don't feel so well."

Hayley stood quickly and said, "Can I do something for..."

Ben rose quickly off the couch, held his hand over his mouth, ran to the bathroom and collapsed, putting his head over the toilet. Minutes later, after Hayley had helped him clean up, Ben laid flat on the bathroom tile, next to the toilet. Ben's salmon filet found itself flushed into the Apple Ridge sewer system.

"Let me get you back to the couch," said Hayley, holding out her hand.

"No, no. I'd feel better here. I'll just lie on the floor. It's cool."

"I'll get you some water. Little sips. You've got to get that taste out of your mouth."

Ben nodded. After fifteen minutes of staring at Hayley's bathroom ceiling, he said, "I think I feel better now."

"I've got one more little question. Did you ever reach out to Izzy's family after you got back stateside?" asked Hayley.

"No. I thought about it a few times but I was afraid that I'd break down and tell his family, a grandmother and an uncle, the truth that I killed him. It's so sore, his memory. All the plans we had. Seeing his family. Trying to explain. Lying about what happened. It all seemed too much for me to handle. I still don't know that I have the strength or courage to face them."

Hayley helped Ben back to the couch, then ran into the kitchen and returned with a wet washcloth. "This is just the first step," she said, gently wiping his brow. "A huge one. We've got it out on the table. Now we can deal with it."

"I'm so tired," Ben said. "I want to go to bed but I'm afraid to close my eyes. Everything will come back."

"For a time, you're probably right," Hayley said, "but we're going to make it better. You and me. Do you want me to drive you home?"

"No. I'll be okay," Ben said. "Boy, that was intense."

"I'm figuring you'll get little rest tonight. Do you need a sleeping pill? I've got some Ambien in my cupboard."

"No. I'm on call. I could have two scotch and waters to get the same effect. I'll be okay. When can we talk again?" asked Ben.

"How's tomorrow night? I'm free every night. No friends here and I'm all unpacked."

"I have a full surgical schedule tomorrow. I doubt that I'll be free before seven, seven thirty and that's if I don't have any emergencies."

"Twenty-four seven service here," Hayley said, smiling. "You call me when you leave the hospital. I'll bring something to eat to your place."

"One question before I head home," Ben said, "Was last night at the Cle Elum Best Western real, or did I imagine it?"

"What do you think?"

"I don't know what to think. Funny, isn't it?"

"What?" asked Hayley.

"I'm as scared that Cle Elum wasn't real as I know that Kandahar and Izzy were real."

Hayley kissed Ben on the lips. "See you tomorrow after work."

*_*_*_*

At eight forty-five p.m., Ben called Hayley. "I'm sorry it's so late. Just finished," Ben said, "and I'm exhausted and you were right that I wouldn't sleep very well and..."

Hayley interrupted, "When will you be at your place?"

"Twenty minutes. Max."

"I didn't sleep much either. I'll be there in twenty-two minutes."

The National Health Service provided Ben a sparsely furnished, bottom floor, one bedroom unit in a two level apartment complex. Hayley entered #104.

"Nice, simple," said Hayley.

"You don't lie well," said Ben. "These units are cheap and the walls, paper-thin. I can hear noise two doors down and if anyone flushes a toilet above me, you'd think the ceiling was collapsing."

Hayley, smiling at the litany of complaints, said, "Then we'll have to be quiet. Put some dishes on the table in case anyone is looking in. They'll think we're eating."

Hayley threw her coat on a small couch while Ben searched the refrigerator. He placed two glasses, two forks, a bowl with day-old pasta and some dishes on the small dinette table in the kitchen. They sat at the table for a moment, then Hayley stood up and closed the blinds.

As Ben wrapped her in his arms, she said, "Tonight, we work on dispelling any notion that the Cle Elum's Best Western was a mirage. Yin and Yang."

Between breaths, Ben asked, "Is this Yin or Yang?"

"Does it matter?"

"Yes, absolutely. I want to know what to call it." Ben swept Hayley off her feet and carried her into his bedroom. He flipped off the light switch, putting the room into total blackness. "Uh-oh. Too dark?" he asked and turned the lights on and set Hayley at the bed's edge.

Hayley removed two candles and a book of matches from her purse. As she lit the candles, Ben turned the lights off again. As the two candles gave exactly the correct amount of sensuous light, Ben and Hayley started undressing each other. At first, sensuously slow and deliberate but, like children with free reign in a candy shop, they quickly reached warp speed.

As Ben explored Hayley's abdomen and lower, Hayley purred back, "I couldn't wait. I couldn't wait another day."

Ben, still unsure about Hayley's responses after chemotherapy, slowed down to ensure that Hayley was excited before he rolled over onto his back. Hayley moved between Ben's knees, massaging his abdomen with both hands as her mouth brought Ben to states he could only imagine existed.

Ben pleaded, "Let me…"

Hayley immediately put her fingers on his lips. "Nope. I'm in charge."

Moving up, Hayley straddled Ben's erection and slowly settling down, hands on his chest, and then moving with a slow purposeful rhythm until they both collapsed.

Lying side-by-side, face on his chest, her hands rolling gentle circles on his stomach, Hayley said, "I couldn't wait. I couldn't wait another day."

They showered together, unable to keep their hands off each other. Ben toweled Hayley dry then wrapped his arms around her, looking into the mirror.

"How lucky am I," Ben exclaimed. It was not a question.

Hayley smiled. "How lucky are we." They dressed, reentered the kitchen, opened the shades and shared a cold pasta salad. "Tomorrow, we talk," she said.

*_*_*_*

The next night, after a quick dinner out, Hayley and Ben returned to Hayley's living room. Ben started to close the curtains.

"Don't close them. I said we needed to talk," Hayley said. "We're not mixing Yin and Yang."

"You're not fun. I don't even remember what we had for dinner twenty minutes ago. I could only think of you and me wearing nothing. Besides, you've still not told me which one is Yin and which is Yang."

"Not for you to know, only me. I've been looking for someone to take over your counseling and I have a lead."

"Who?" Ben asked.

"You wouldn't know him," said Hayley.

"Test me. I know everyone in Apple Ridge."

"Jon Brander?" said Hayley.

"Don't know him," Ben said with a wrinkled brow.

"He owns a chicken and dairy farm five miles out of town. Been there a couple of years."

"That's helpful. You're not serious," said Ben, "and I hate feathers,"

"Not funny."

"Funny to me. How's a chicken farmer going to help me?"

"He's the retired Chairman of Psychology from Portland State. One of my professors from Seattle U knew him and said he's a great guy. He left academia, somewhat suddenly, three years ago after his wife died and moved out here."

"Why would he be any different than anyone else?"

"I don't know yet. I talked to him for a few moments this morning. He said he was busy and couldn't talk. That said, he's coming into Apple Ridge on Monday to buy some supplies. He promised he'd stop by the DSHS office and have lunch as a favor to my ex-professor."

"I want you," pleaded Ben.

"I'll just have to see what he says and whether he's willing to see you. He did say that he is up to his eyeballs in eggs and didn't think he'd have time for anything else."

"Why would I want to see someone who doesn't want to see me?"

"We'll see."

"Whatever. I don't want to see anyone else but you. You know that."

"I know, but I want you to try?"

"It's not going to work," Ben whined.

"With that attitude, I refuse to sleep with you."

"That's not fair."

"Absolutely, not fair. I agree. Hopefully you'll get the point as to why we need someone else to counsel you. I'm human. If I felt that you didn't value my work or you weren't trying, I'd have a hard time feeling for you the way I do. So it comes down to either I counsel you or I can love you unconditionally and be your support, the rock you lean against. I can't do both."

Ben thought for a moment. "Believe it or not, I'm getting the picture," he admitted.

"We don't have him yet. So I like to try some exposure therapy," said Hayley.

"That's a joke, right? I've already said I wanted us naked."

"Not a joke. I'm trying to be serious," said Hayley. "Exposure therapy is meant to give you less fear about your memories. By talking repeatedly about the events that caused your emotional trauma, we might be able to desensitize you so that when you have those memories, they're not so painful."

"I dream about the events in Afghanistan all the time. That certainly hasn't desensitized me," said Ben.

"Dreaming, or more accurately 'nightmaring,' about it is completely different from talking about it. You were uber-emotional when we broached the subject two nights ago. I want you tell the story again and again, in detail. It'll be hard at first. You will feel strange, bringing up painful memories on purpose, when you've been trying to suppress them for years. You're likely to sleep little and have more nightmares in the beginning, but each time it'll be easier. With time, and knowing that I'll be on this journey with you every step of the way, you'll feel less overwhelmed."

Ben put his feet up on the couch and recounted his last week in Afghanistan. When done, he was wet with perspiration.

"I feel like a limp dishrag. I'm not sure I can stand up right now," Ben said softly.

Hayley stood and returned from the kitchen with a clean towel. She knelt in front of Ben and dried his face. His eyes remained closed as she kissed him on the eyes, nose and mouth. "Sorry to put you through that. I love you."

Ben started to cry. "Why? Why can't I forget all this?"

Hayley put her face on Ben's shirt, soaked with perspiration, and said, "You can't. Hold me. I'm not leaving you."

Ten minutes went by before Ben spoke. "Thank you. I don't know what I'd do without you."

"Me, neither."

Ben sat up, hugged Hayley and said, "I have an idea. I can sign out Saturday morning until Sunday night to the surgeons in Cle Elum. Let's go camping."

"Bad idea. I don't camp," Hayley said, quickly.

"Everybody camps," declared Ben.

"Not this girl from Mercer Island. In my family, camping meant staying at the non-ocean side of the Mauna Kea Resort in Hawaii."

"You were deprived as a child."

"I didn't think so at the time. I'm certain that neither of my parents ever camped."

"More deprived people."

"I'll try anything. Don't expect me to enjoy it," whined Hayley.

"You like walking?" asked Ben.

"Yes, of course," responded Hayley.

"You like eating?"

"Yes."

"You like beautiful vistas?"

"Yes."

"You like peaceful surroundings?"

"Get to the point."

"That's pretty much camping."

"Shopping? Theaters?" said Hayley. "No. Are there toilets? No. Get my drift?"

"Does this mean you won't go with me. My best memories in life, until meeting you, are the times spent camping and hiking with my dad."

"I understood that and, of course, I'll go. I'm just preparing you for the possibility that I might not like it as much as you. Hedging my bet."

*_*_*_*

Ben picked up Hayley at eleven a.m., Saturday. Hayley looked into the back seat of his car as she sat.

"The back seat is empty. Don't we have to bring a bunch of stuff?" asked Hayley, a slight quizzical frown across her brow.

Ben smiled. "Not too much. I have two backpacks in the trunk. It's enough. You're gonna love it."

"I dunno. We'll see. Oh, I didn't think to ask. Where do we sleep? Did you bring a tent and sleeping bags?"

"Nope, no tent."

"C'mon you're kidding. Sleep out in the open?" asked Hayley.

"Just walk. You'll see. I have surprises." Ben squeezed Hayley's hand.

"A surprise would be a Travelodge or, better yet, a Four Seasons."

Ben, laughing, said, "It'll be better."

Two minutes out of Apple Ridge in late September, the sun beamed across the east side of the Cascades as the temperature hovered above seventy. The scenery changed to low green rolling hills, dotted with groves of pine trees. Fifteen minutes later, Ben parked around the back of a small store that appeared to have been built at the time of Bonnie and Clyde. An old, dull and rusted, red Mobil gas pump, sans hose, stood proudly at the front. Ben popped the trunk and handed Hayley the smaller of two backpacks.

"Hey. This is heavy," Hayley said.

"Not so bad. It'll toughen you up," responded Ben.

"Well, on the way back, it'll be lighter. I'll try looking for the good."

"Not so. Whatever we pack in, we pack out. That includes garbage."

Hayley frowned.

Ben donned the other backpack, then pulled out a rifle from the trunk and slung it over his shoulder.

Hayley's mouth popped open at the sight of the gun and her two hands shot up in the 'STOP' position. "Wait, wait, wait a minute. What's with the gun? You're not going to shoot something, are you?"

"Not planning to," said Ben.

Keeping her hands up, biting her lip and shaking her head no vigorously, Hayley asked, "Then why bring it? It, it freaks me out."

"I can think of five good reasons."

"Name just one," demanded a clearly perturbed Hayley.

"Mountain lion. Need another?"

"You're joking. Right?"

"Wolves, bears, coyotes, angry moose or elk. Want me to keep going?"

"My mom, dad and Deidre are going to shit when they hear this. They know how I feel about guns."

"I'm going to check in with Mr. Greavy in the store and leave the car keys in a special hiding place near his back door," said Ben. "Always good to let someone know where you are."

Ben returned in two minutes, carrying two plastic bottles of cold water. "We're off."

At fifteen minutes, Ben asked, "You tired? We can stop for a minute and rest."

"I'm fine," Hayley said.

Fifteen minutes later, Ben repeated, "You tired?"

Hayley responded, with attitude, "You're annoying, I'm fine." Hayley looked at her cell phone, found no coverage and pocketed the phone.

Twenty minutes later and five minutes after starting up an elevation, Hayley admitted fatigue, "How much farther? It's hot and I'm sweating like a pig."

"I thought girls don't sweat," said Ben. "You want me to carry your pack?"

"No and shut up."

"It is warm," Ben said. "I'm guessing about seventy-five or eighty. But we're almost there. Can't stop now."

They hiked over the rise, down into a valley and walked around a third of a small lake before reaching a clearing. Unseen until reaching the clearing, facing the lake, stood a small log cabin with two windows on opposite sides of a heavy-looking wood door. Metal grating covered the windows. A brick chimney stood proud on the left side. A huge maple tree, its trunk wider than the cabin door, shaded the right side of the cabin.

"Hey. Whose place is this? Are we stopping to meet someone?" asked Hayley.

"Nope. This is it. Casa de Hunt. Built by yours truly."

"You built this? When?"

"Actually my dad built most of it. I helped."

"It's amazing. So we're staying here?"

"Yep."

"I thought you hadn't been around here for years. It's not run down at all."

"I've been coming every couple weeks or so since I got back to

Apple Ridge. The first time I came, the brush and grass were so thick I couldn't see the cabin. I thought the place had burned down."

"You cleaned it up yourself?"

"Not totally. I hired two migrant pickers standing on a corner outside Apple Ridge Hardware on a Sunday morning. We hiked in with rented power tools and spent the entire day clearing out the debris. The inside was filled with small animal droppings. I guess the iron bars over the windows kept out anything big."

"I'm not going in there; it probably stinks," Hayley said.

"It's okay. I swear. We came back a second time two weeks later and scrubbed it clean. The kerosene lanterns and old potbelly stove work, as does the fireplace for cooking and more heat. There's a small trap door and a cellar to keep things cool. Natural refrigerator of sorts. Trust me."

"I do trust you." Hayley spun around, hands in the air, and said, "I've never felt this isolated in my life. New experience. Amazing."

"We're not alone. Look," Ben declared, pointing fifty yards away to the lake edge. "Dad, mom and two kids."

A huge buck with an impressive rack, a large doe and two fawns. Mother and kids drank at the lake edge while the buck concentrated on Hayley and Ben.

As Hayley started towards them, the buck, followed by the doe, then the fawns, raised their heads.

"If you go any closer," Ben said, "they'll bolt. We'll leave out some salt and carrots. After a while they'll get comfortable. I've been seeing them for six weeks. The fawns are growing quickly."

Hayley backed up slowly, then smiled, pointing two fingers at the large doe, then back at herself. "You and me, babe. We'll watch over these guys."

The one-room cabin was sun-heated warm and spotless, albeit, a little dusty. A pair of twin beds had been pushed together in the corner. A potbelly stove centered the room with a metal chimney threading its way through the cabin roof. The fireplace in the corner had a grating with logs stacked nearby. Hayley picked up a small trap door to inspect a stone-lined cellar going down five feet with a small ladder.

Ben dropped his backpack on the floor, then took off Hayley's pack and laid it beside his. "Thank you for coming. Means a lot to me."

Hayley kissed Ben on the lips, then rescanned the cabin and asked, "Probably silly, but bath, shower, wash, toilet? I'm so dusty and sweaty."

"Bath is the lake, we have a makeshift shower around back near the well, wash in the lake, and toilet is anywhere."

"You're kidding," said Hayley.

"It was just Dad and me, sometimes Bill Carter and Junior. We didn't care much for an outhouse. After Dad died, my mom and stepfather wanted nothing to do with the cabin, but couldn't sell it unless they had my consent after I was twenty-five. I would have never consented, ever."

Hayley looked bewildered and leaned on the side of the potbelly stove.

"Probably don't want to lean on that," laughed Ben. "It'll burn you if it's hot and it'll leave black soot on your pants, hot or cold."

Hayley stood quickly, then watched Ben brush off the soot marks off her backside.

"Let's go down to the lake," Ben said. "The water is still warm this time of year. We'll wash our clothes out, soak in the lake, come back and make lunch." Ben took Hayley's skeptical hand, grabbed a towel and bar of soap from a shelf and walked Hayley to the lake edge.

Hayley slowed as they neared the water. "I don't know about this.

I'm out of my comfort zone and I didn't bring a bathing suit."

"The only things watching us are the deer and a few birds."

As Ben started shedding his clothes, Hayley took off her shoes and socks, walked around a few small rocks and dipped her toes. "Nice." She then waded in a few feet. "Oooh. The bottom is all squishy and muddy."

Hayley spun around as a naked Ben sped by and dove into the water. He came up standing ten feet away, water up to his mid chest, and yelled, "It's marvelous. Come on in."

Hayley, ankle deep in the water, scooped up a handful of water and washed her face. "What the hell." She quickly removed her clothes, threw them back onto the shore and dove in after Ben, staying down for ten seconds. She surfaced next to Ben with the water up to her shoulders. She wrapped her arms around Ben's neck, pulling herself up out of the water and kissed him.

"This is other-worldly. I don't know who I am," Hayley said. She slid back down along Ben's body until her feet touched bottom. She kissed his chest as her hands went down to his full erection. She dipped her head in the water and came up quickly. "I just told 'little' Ben that he might have to wait until after lunch."

Ben smiled and said, "He has no patience." Ben waded out, returned with the bar of soap and each washed the other. They exited the water, toweled off, then washed their clothes with the bar soap. They wrung out the clothes and hung them on tree limbs at the edge of the clearing. They had been completely naked for twenty-five minutes, in and out of the water.

"I never thought I could feel so free and uninhibited. It's just eye-popping amazing. Who knew?" exclaimed Hayley.

They returned to the cabin and unpacked some hard cheese, Italian bread and a bottle of Aqua Fina carbonated water. Ben offered Hayley a tee shirt, the only piece of dry clothing in the cabin.

Hayley responded without hesitation, "Unbelievably, I'm good."

Ben put lunch in a basket, grabbed two coffee cups, a large blanket and walked Hayley out to a flat shady area under the maple tree. They each had a cup of water, a snippet of cheese and bread.

Ben, fully erect again, begged the obvious, "Little Ben can't wait much longer."

Hayley recapped the water and put the cheese and bread back in the basket. "Can't have that, now can we." She rolled Ben on his back and knelt over his abdomen and leaned over to kiss every part of his face as Ben's hands explored her already moistened labia. Hayley murmured, "Don't stop."

Ben grabbed Hayley on each side of her rib cage and elevated her enough that his head slid between her legs, then let her down slowly. As his thumb and finger twirled each of her nipples, his tongue, penetrating and exploring, brought Hayley to places seen in dreams.

"Oh, my God. Oh, Ben."

The stream of Hayley's soft cries were Ben's only guide, as the four deer watching with prurient curiosity. Hayley unable to dream any further, slid down and guided Ben into her. Together, they watched each other as maple branches moved with them in breezy rhythm until the tree could take no more.

Afterwards, Hayley and Ben laid quietly, on their backs, hands held, looking up at the ever-guarding maple. Ben coaxed Hayley up after a few minutes and back into the lake. No toe-dipping, no wading, only uninhibited frolicking, like two otters who had just found a cache of oysters.

When Hayley went to check on their clothes, Ben grabbed a fishing pole and within fifteen minutes had caught two large trout. Hayley stood in utter amazement as the fish were cleaned and filleted. Ben started a fire in a pit at the front of the cabin and placed two large Idaho russets wrapped in tin foil into the base of the fire. He waited thirty minutes then cooked the fish on a skillet. As the night air chilled the cabin, their now dry clothes and a sweater gave them warmth as they fed each other pieces of trout and potato.

By eight p.m., the temperature had dropped into the high forties. Ben lit kindling in the fireplace, added logs, shuttered the windows and bolted the door. The cabin heated quickly.

Ben had two large sleeping bags, one on each bed.

"I've never been this happy or exhausted," Hayley said. She slipped into one of the bags and removed all her clothes. "No way you're not sleeping in here with me." Little Ben didn't need a second invitation as Ben moved into the bag and zipped it closed.

As they hiked out the following morning, Hayley said, "Amazing weekend. When can we come back?"

"Anytime you want. It's going to get colder now. By November we might have freezing weather and snow. December for sure."

"With you and me in the same sleeping bag, I feel like I could melt Alaska. Would you be upset if I told Deidre?"

"Tell her what?"

"Everything. Absolutely everything."

"Kind of personal, isn't it?"

"Not between her and me. Everything. Absolutely everything."

*_*_*_*

Jon Brander walked into Hayley's office at eight fifteen a.m. on Monday. Katy MacArthur walked him directly into Hayley's office.

The two psychologists gave each a quick look-over.

*He's sixtyish, ruggedly handsome, tanned and muscular from working outdoors. He's exhausted.*

"Thank you so much for coming. You know, Dr. Slater thinks the world of you," said Hayley.

"Bill Slater is a top-notch academician. His research on adolescent behavior in divorce or separation was seminal."

"Actually, I didn't know that. He gave the classes on interviewing medically ill patients."

"Between you and me," said Brander, "his skill was in research, not at the bedside."

Hayley smiled. "That's what we figured."

"Before you start," Brander said, "let me tell you that I have no free time. Running a farm is a ton more work than I remembered growing up in Michigan. So how can I help you?"

"I have a special client, very special. He has PTSD with two identifiable separate incidences, his father's suicide and, more importantly, two tours in Afghanistan, one of which ended in the deaths of everyone in his squad, except him. We were making great strides but I can't see him professionally anymore."

"Why's that?" Brander asked.

"I'm sleeping with him," Hayley stated.

"There's a big no-no," Brander said. "You should know better. You get reported by someone, like his wife?"

"No. No. He's not married and it just happened."

"He's okay with this?"

"No. He wants me to keep counseling him. I told him that won't work."

"Well, you got that right. How'd this happen?" Brander asked. "You should have seen it coming and nipped it in the bud. These things don't usually work out so well."

"I know. In the beginning, I didn't like him. No, that's too nice. I hated him. I pleaded with him to find someone else. He kept coming back. I guess he's been in love with me for a while, but I didn't see it."

"Patients frequently fall for their therapist, particularly ones as pretty as you. You're not supposed to respond. Counseling 101."

"I know all that too and couldn't help it. I have leukemia and had a bone marrow transplant. It's in remission but the chances of me living very long aren't so good. As my friend put it when I was complaining about my lot in life, she told me to stop dying slowly and live life fast. For the first time since I was diagnosed with leukemia, I'm happy and I can't go back. Ben - that's the patient - Ben Hunt, needs help. He's a surgeon with the National Health Service stationed here for at least five years."

"You followed him here?"

"Yes, but only to help him, if you can believe that. When he was in trouble in Seattle, big trouble, I seemed to be the only one that could make a connection."

"You really that good?" asked Brander.

"No, definitely not. I've had minimal experience with wartime PTSD. He had seen ten or fifteen other therapists, all more qualified. He walked out on all of them. From our first visit, he said I was different and I was helping. I even got a call from the Chairman of Surgery at Seattle Med telling me whatever I was doing was working. He had never seen Ben so calm. I had no clue what I was doing differently. I saw him maybe five, six times, once a week, when he had to leave Seattle."

"You know this is a lifelong problem. Rescuer becomes the victim, yadda, yadda."

"Dr. Brander, it's complicated. He had helped me out when I was sick and when he got into trouble here, I felt I needed to come. I don't know for sure that I loved him when I decided to come, I just knew I was helping. I didn't know it would change and, honestly, I don't know that I wanted it to change. It did and I can't go back. I love him."

"Compelling argument and I know of no one in this city who could help him. Too bad. I'm just too busy with the farm."

"That is too bad. Why'd you retire?" Hayley asked.

"Personal reasons," responded Brander, crossing his arms, suggesting he didn't want to talk about it.

Hayley decided not to give up. "Dr. Slater did allude to the fact that your retirement was somewhat precipitous. I would have guessed you'd come to Mason County to relax and run a small farm."

Brander, misty eyed as he answered, "If it were only that easy. My wife died after an eighteen month, mostly downhill, rollercoaster ride with cancer of the pancreas. I became depressed and was having a hard time concentrating on my job, running a department."

"I'm sorry for your loss."

"Thanks. I grew up happily on a farm in Michigan and had enough money to buy this farm. I thought that'd be a great way to spend the rest of my life. It was great in the beginning, not so now."

"How so?" Hayley asked.

"You know what. This is all personal. I have reasons for not being able to help you out."

"We're both professionals," Hayley declared. "Nothing leaves this office. Ever. I've already told you stuff about me that could technically cause me to lose my license."

"Okay. A month ago, my only child, a daughter, Angie, who's had addiction problems since high school, deposited my fourteen year old granddaughter, Amber, on my doorsteps. Angie left a note saying she couldn't take care of Amber anymore and left for parts unknown. Angie didn't even stop to say hello. Dumped her daughter and left."

"Yikes," said Hayley.

"Anyway, with the cutbacks to school bus service, I've been forced to drive Amber to school every morning and pick her up every afternoon. I don't have time for all this. There's too much work to do on the farm. I'm exhausted and Amber is difficult, which is an understatement. Angie and Amber were living in the Oakland area for the past two years and Amber became goth. You know what that is?"

"Black, black and black. That's all I know."

Brander slipped effortlessly into lecture mode, "Modern goth culture is largely dominated by dissatisfied youths hailing from the middle classes with a strong feeling of instability and ..."

Hayley tried to smile, but failed. Brander realizing none of his history lesson had relevance to Hayley, stopped in mid-sentence.

"Sorry. Amber's only fourteen and I don't think she's bought into any of that. She just wanted to dress differently and try to be unique. She doesn't fit in here in Apple Ridge at all, has no friends and doesn't want to change. She wants to go back to Oakland and won't listen to reason. There's nobody in Oakland to take care of her. As much as I'd like to help, I don't have time for you or Ben."

"Wow," Hayley said. "You really are up to your eyeballs in alligators. Anything I can do to help?"

"Nope," said Brander. "Anyway, it was nice meeting you. I gotta get going. Too much to do today to sit here chatting. I need to get the supplies back to the farm. I've hired two extra hands to clean the coops. I have to come back at noon to pick up Amber for a dental appointment. Good luck on your quest." Brander stood, shook hands with Hayley and left.

*_*_*_*

At dinner that night, Hayley told Ben about the conversation with Brander.

"Sounds like he's got more on his plate that you do. Granddaughter is probably a piece of work," Ben said.

"Perhaps. Brander seemed really nice. I know you'd like him."

"You say that about all the therapists. Remember when you gave me a list of names. You just wanted to get rid of me."

"I did. I didn't like you and I was absorbed feeling sorry for myself."

"And now?"

"I can't get enough of you. That make you feel better?"

"Of course. Anyway, I'd be willing to see this Dr. Brander. You want to feed chickens while he sees me?"

"Not in this life. I'm a city girl. I thought eggs appeared on the shelves of supermarkets courtesy of the gods. I had no idea it took work."

"I give up then," said Ben.

"And we keep looking," said Hayley.

*_*_*_*

Hayley continued to counsel Ben on Yin days, mostly having him repeat the stories about Izzy and his father's suicide.

After handful of sessions, Ben said, "This is getting a bit boring. Don't take it personally. It's just how I feel."

"I won't. It's boring to me as well. I don't know what else to do. Until we find someone else to help, we have to keep on going."

*_*_*_*

Three weeks later, driving east on I-90 coming back from Ellensburg, Ben saw a young female across the highway with multi-colored hair, a black hoody, black vest, black backpack, and arms wrapped in black straps. She stood at the highways edge, thumb out, trying to hitch a ride west. Ben exited at the next ramp, two miles further east, and headed back. Five minutes later, as Ben arrived, a semi-truck trailer was parked on the side of the freeway. The semi driver had his window down conversing with the girl in black. Ben parked in front of the truck, blocking its path. Ben exited the car and confronted the driver. The girl had already circled the semi and entered the cab on the passenger side.

The truck driver yelled, "Get the fuck out of my way, asshole. I gotta go and I can't help you with nothing."

"You're ten seconds from me calling the Washington Highway Patrol," Ben yelled back. "That girl in your cab is underage and needs to go back to Apple Ridge."

The truck driver, two days from shower and shave, said, "She said she's nineteen. Just giving her a ride into Seattle."

"She's fourteen and has no business in Seattle or anywhere else. As to what you were going to do, I can only imagine. She gets out of your truck now or I call the cops."

The truck driver turned to the girl, now animated, and started arguing. He turned back to Ben and said, "She says she's nineteen and doesn't know who the fuck you are. So move."

"Her last name is Brander, she's fourteen and lives with her grandfather, Jon Brander, on a chicken farm north of Apple Ridge. The only ID she might have is from Apple Ridge Middle School."

The truck driver looked back to the girl, apparently stunned by the comments, all accurate. He turned back to Ben. "Hey. No harm, no foul. I didn't know nothing. You're not going to report me, are you?"

"Not if she gets out of the cab and comes with me."

Ben and the truck driver forcibly removed the kicking and screaming teenager from the truck and put her in Ben's passenger seat after throwing her backpack in Ben's trunk. The truck driver held her in place until Ben had the car locked, started and moving.

Amber Brander minced no words or thoughts, "Who the hell are you and how do you know who I am? You're kidnapping me." Amber opened the window of the moving car and started repeating loudly, "Help. Help. I'm being kidnapped."

After a minute of screaming to an empty landscape, the tired, and somewhat hoarse, teenager quieted.

"Well, hello to you. I am Dr. Ben Hunt. My girlfriend, Hayley Green, is a friend of your grandfather. Remind me your first name."

"Screw you. Let me out of here. I have to get to Oakland."

"I'm sure you do. I have to make a call first." Ben dialed Hayley's cell phone and put it on speaker.

Hayley greeted the call, "Are you on your way back?"

"Yep. Guess who I just found hitchhiking on the 90 westbound. I pulled her out of a semi as she was about to leave."

"What are you talking about?"

"You know anyone around here who's goth?"

"Jon Brander's granddaughter."

"Right. Her backpack has 'Amber' stitched on the front."

"Yeah, that's her." Hayley said.

Amber yelled, "I don't know who you are."

"Amber, where's your grandfather?" Hayley asked.

Amber replied, "He went to Portland two days ago to settle something about grandma's estate. He said he'd be back that night but got delayed. He said he'd come back if I wanted him to. I knew he'd have to go back again, so I told him I'd be okay. After the first night, I didn't like being alone out there and couldn't go to school. So I left."

"Amber, please listen," Hayley said. "You're safe now. The man driving you is a doctor and my friend. He's going to bring you to my house in Apple Ridge and we'll wait for your grandfather to return."

"What if I don't want to go to your house?"

"Not an option. What's your grandfather's cell phone number?"

"You find it if you're such good buddies," demanded Amber.

"Okay. Have it your way," Hayley said, calmly. "We'll see you in a bit. Amber, you're safe and nothing bad is going to happen to you. I promise."

Amber folded her arms and banged her head on the back of the seat. She said nothing.

"I assume from her posture that she's resigned to coming to your place. Be there ASAP," said Ben.

Hayley called Brander's farm number, which went to voicemail. She then called the farm supply store Brander frequented and sweet-talked the owner into giving her Brander's cell phone number.

"Dr. Brander. Hayley Green here."

"Yes, Hayley. I'm in Portland. Heading back tomorrow morning. What's up?"

"Have you talked to Amber?"

"No. I've called every hour since this morning. I assumed she wasn't answering because she's mad I left her at the farm. Is there a problem?"

"Not one now. My friend, Dr. Hunt, found her trying to hitchhike west on the 90 towards Seattle."

"Oh. I'd hoped that wouldn't happen. She's okay?"

"She's fine," Hayley said. "I'll keep her here tonight and see that she gets to school tomorrow morning."

"Thank you. I'm at wits end with her," bemoaned Brander. "She's so unhappy and I don't entirely blame her, isolated and all. I don't know what to do."

"I'm not sure I have any answers for you. Let's get through tonight and tomorrow first. What does she like to eat?"

"Anything Italian. Pizza, pasta, calzones. Italian sausage and mushrooms are her favorites. She likes tacos too. Hey, thanks again."

Hayley made a call then redialed Ben. "Stop at Antonio's Pizzeria on the way home. The order should be ready."

"She might run."

"Doubt it. Keep her backpack. Besides, she likes pizza and has to be starved."

*_*_*_*

Amber and Ben walked into Hayley's house fifteen minutes later. Ben toted a large pizza box and Amber's backpack.

Hayley gave Ben a kiss and turned to Amber. "Hi, Amber. I'm Hayley. I'm a friend of your grandfather."

Amber, lower lip jutted to its full extent, arms folded across her chest and fists clenched, said, "I don't care. I don't want to be here or my grandfather's stink farm. I'd like to eat and then have you take me back to the farm. And I want my backpack."

Ben and Hayley looked at each other. *She'll run away again.*

"I promised your grandfather that you'd stay the night here and I'd take you to school tomorrow," said Hayley.

"I'm not going back to school here. I hate it. I have no friends. No one likes me. I miss Oakland." The first tears started running down Amber's cheeks.

"I'll tell you what. Let's all sit and eat dinner. I'm hungry enough to eat that whole pizza. We can talk. I'd like to hear some more about you. Do you want to wash up?"

"Just my hands. How do you know my grandfather?"

"We're both psychologists."

"Figures."

"Ouch. That didn't sound like a compliment but I would have agreed with you a year ago," opined Ben.

Hayley's stare quickly stopped Ben from going further.

Amber, quick to respond, said, "Wasn't meant to be a compliment. Where's the bathroom?"

Hayley and Ben again looked at each other, took a deep breath, pursed their lips and exhaled as Amber headed into the bathroom and slammed the door.

Hayley said softly to Ben, "Let her do the talking. Anything you say may, or will, be used against you."

"Amen," Ben responded.

As they all sat to eat, Hayley said, "Amber, I hope you like Italian sausage and mushroom. It's my favorite."

As Ben squirreled his face into a what-are-you-talking-about look, Amber said, "I like it okay."

"I'm glad," Hayley said, smiling broadly at Ben.

They ate quietly for three or four uncomfortable minutes. Finally Amber asked, "How long have you two lived in this terrible, awful place?"

"I grew up here," Ben said. "Left Apple Ridge when I was eighteen and just moved back."

"Why? Why would anyone want to move here?" Amber asked.

"Fair question. I owed five years to the National Health Service for paying my way through school. This place was one of the options and since I grew up here I figured what the heck. Plus I own three hundred acres of woodlands just west of here. I have tons of great memories hiking and camping with my father."

"Your dad lives here too?"

"No, he died."

Before Amber could ask how Ben's father died, Hayley intervened, "I came two months ago. I'm running the Washington State welfare office here."

Smiling, Amber said, "Was that a punishment?"

"I think so," Ben interjected.

Hayley looked back and forth at the two smiling jokesters. "Funny, you two. No. I came because Dr. Hunt was here. We're close."

"When I heard you knew Gramps, I thought you might be his girlfriend or something. I mean he's so lonely out there, but you have a boyfriend and you're way too pretty for him."

"Thanks. I'll keep that to myself. I actually think your Gramps is pretty good-looking," said Hayley.

"Maybe so. He's just old, grumpy and tired."

"How long did you live in Oakland?" asked Ben.

"Four years. We, mom and I, moved from LA. Mom had a job when we got there and we were living pretty good. I had started dance lessons in LA when I was eight and continued dancing in Oakland. I was good. I mean I was good at dance. At least the teachers told me I was. Anyway, mom lost her job two years ago and then everything turned to shh.. uh."

Ben added, "Shit."

"Yeah. Shit. Gramps doesn't like me swearing."

"I don't like it either," Hayley said. "Both of you, end it now."

Ben and Amber looked at each other, smiled, and then grimaced. Ben and Hayley waited for Amber to continue.

"Mom lost her job because she started doing drugs again. She'd deny it, but I know she called in sick too many times after partying. She promised she'd stop but never did. We got thrown out of apartments twice when Mom used the money that Gramps sent for rent to buy drugs.

"The dance lessons stopped and Mom would disappear a lot. I started spending more time with my friends, skipping school. Childhood Protective and the cops found me on the street three times. They told Mom that she'd go to jail and I'd be fostered out. Anyway, Mom wasn't going to change, so she called Gramps and he sent us bus tickets and a little money to come here. We got to the outside of his farm in a cab and Mom let me off, turned around and left. She didn't even come in to see if Gramps was there. Just left."

"Where do you think your mom is now?" asked Hayley.

"No idea," Amber replied, "and she hasn't called, even once. Not even a crappy post card. Gramps says she'll get in touch when she needs something. He didn't say but I guess that means money."

Hayley, changing the subject, said, "Why do you think you have no friends here. You seem nice."

"I'm all alone most of the time. I get to school just as it opens and Gramps picks me up just as it ends. It takes forever to get there from the farm. We have to get up at five a.m. to do chores to make it to school on time. I can't sign up for any activities because Gramps picks me up and then hurries back."

"If you had the time, what would you like to do activity-wise?" Ben asked.

"I dunno," Amber said, shrugging. "Nothing, I guess. Well, maybe. I think they have something called 'dance team.' That might be fun. Tryouts are in a month. Practices are before school and after school, so I can't do it."

"I hate to ask but..," Ben started.

Hayley interrupted, "If you hate to ask, then don't."

"Why do I dress and look like this?" Amber said, looking at Ben. "Everyone starts off with 'I hate to ask.'"

Ben, tail firmly between his legs, nodded yes.

Amber sat up straight, defiant, like an animal ready for a fight. "I can dress anyway I want. I can be my own person. I can have any color hair I want. Nobody can take that away."

"I'm guessing lots of kids your age dressed goth in Oakland. Not so many here, eh?" Hayley asked.

"Yeah. Most didn't dress like me, but enough that I wasn't unusual. Here, I'm the only one. They all stare and say things behind my back. I'm not making it up. The vice-principal told me so. She told me I should change if I want to fit in."

Hayley subtly nodded with her eyes to Ben not to ask any more questions. "Do you have homework?"

"I did. Two days' worth. My books are at the ranch."

"Is there a website where you can download assignments?"

"There is. I could do that."

"Good," said Hayley. "There's a computer in the study and I have a guest bedroom downstairs. I think you should call your grandfather and tell him you're okay and you'll see him tomorrow after school."

"I 'spose so," Amber said. "Is he going to be mad at me? I don't want to be yelled at."

"Can't say for sure," Hayley responded. "I'm guessing he won't be too angry. He'll probably just be happy that you're safe. He told me he felt awful about leaving you alone."

Ben departed after dessert. Amber helped clear the dishes without being asked, called her grandfather, did her homework and went to bed.

Hayley called Ben early the next morning after hatching a win-win plan. Ben concurred. Hayley then called Jon Brander and asked him to come by her office before picking up Amber from school for some 'negotiations.'

That evening, Brander and Amber arrived at Hayley's house to collect her belongings. Hayley asked them to stay for a taco dinner. Ben arrived as they sat down to eat.

Hayley presented the plan to Amber. Brander, acting surprised at first, relented as part of the ruse and by the evening's end, a mutually beneficial pact was set.

Amber would stay at Hayley's from Sunday night through Thursday or Friday night depending on activities. Ben now had a therapist. Amber and Brander understood that Ben would be around Hayley's house, often. The private bedroom on the lower level would be Amber's.

The following Monday, Hayley asked Katy MacArthur if she knew anything about the Apple Ridge Dance Team.

"Absolutely. I was on it," Katy replied.

"Really. I need to know what it takes for someone to get on the team."

Katy explained that Dance Team was the most prestigious group a girl could join in Apple Ridge. The team comprised of five eighth-graders and ten each from grades nine through twelve. Forty perform, five were in reserve. Elspeth Goodrich, the high school music and arts teacher and the totalitarian Czar of the dance team, made all the decisions. No one, not even the principal, gave Goodrich advice.

Goodrich made selections based on three criteria: dance ability, grades and demeanor, which included dress and comport.

"What's first?" Hayley asked.

"Dance," Katy replied. "All the students know, 'if you can't dance, you have no chance.' If you're a good enough dancer, grades and demeanor come into play. Anyone whose GPA falls below three point two is off. No exceptions. During the year, don't get into trouble, in or out of school, dress modestly, no makeup except when competing, no jewelry except small earrings and a small necklace. One mistake and you get a warning. Two and you're out. No one gets back on Dance Team. No exceptions."

“Who'd want to be on something like that?" queried Hayley.

"Every girl in Apple Ridge,” Katy said, “and I mean every. We travelled all over the West Coast performing. When I was a senior, we marched in the Rose Parade. The guidance counselor told us that colleges knew about our dance team and it was like adding half point to our GPA. We all walked around like the *crème de la crème* because we were the *crème de la crème.*”

Hayley told Katy about Amber and asked if she'd meet her.

"Sure, but if she's wearing black strapping, piercings, colored hair, black nail polish, whatever, she won't even get into the tryouts. Trust me."

"Will you tell her that?" Hayley asked, “and be blunt.”

*_*_*_*

Amber walked into Hayley's office after school the next day. Katy's expression was not lost on Amber.

Ushered into Hayley’s office, Amber said, "What's with your lady out there. She didn't like the way I looked, I guess."

"Probably not,” said Hayley. “Anyway, Katy grew up in Apple Ridge and was on the Apple Ridge Dance Team. She said she'd talk to you about it."

"Sure. Why not." Amber sat and went into the I'm-locked-and-not-receptive position with her arms folded tightly across her chest and her jaw locked.

Katy came back to Hayley's office and brought with her a

scrapbook of pictures and newspaper articles....."Here's me at the 2010 Rose Parade in Pasadena...at the Apple Cup in 2011...in Eugene for the Oregon State game. We were invited to march in the New York Macy's Thanksgiving Day Parade in 2010 but after the mill closed we couldn't raise enough money. Every member of the dance team my year, every senior, was accepted to college."

Amber, still locked, asked, "What's it take to get on the team?"

"Can you dance? Move well?" asked Katy.

"I think so," said Amber. "I've taken ballet, modern, jazz, hip-hop, a little tap."

"You're better prepared than ninety percent of the girls already."

Amber smiled and relaxed her arms.

Katy erased the smile quickly, "The tryouts are a month away and most of the students with a chance have been working on the routines for three or four months. Honestly, it's not worth your time. You'll never make the team."

"Why?" Amber asked, now curious.

Katy explained to Amber, as she had to Hayley, the other components.

"That's not fair," said Amber. "It's a free country. I should be able to wear whatever I want."

"I didn't say I liked the rules," Katy said, "or that they were fair. I felt them oppressive at times, but the benefits far outweighed the rules. We travelled; we loved being with each other because we all felt special. Lots of people, jealous ones, would try to see if they could get anyone of us to break the codes. We watched each other's backs to make sure that didn't happen. The girls on the team are still my best friends. I felt like I had forty-four sisters. Still feels that way. Elspeth Goodrich makes the rules. They are unbendable and you won't be considered."

"Then I don't want to do it. I don't think it's fair," said Amber, back in lock-down mode.

Hayley and Katy said, simultaneously, "Life isn't fair."

Hayley thanked Katy for bringing in her scrapbooks after Amber headed home.

"If I know anything about this girl, she has to come to a decision herself," Hayley said to Katy. "I think she's a good kid with a terrible family history. I can tell she's smart. Will you help her if she changes her look?"

"Sure, but I don't get the same warm and fuzzies you get," Katy said. "I doubt she'll change."

"Let's wait."

"Not too long. The tryouts are coming up."

Hayley agreed, "I got it, but she's got to decide this for herself."

*_*_*_*

Rachel Green yelled into the phone. "You took in a thirteen-year-old boarder, for free? Have you completely lost your mind?"

"Mom. Wait…," Hayley pleaded.

"Don't Mom me. Moving to that God-forsaken hole of a city with not one redeeming feature other than a guy you hated, then liked, made little sense. This makes none. Do you have any idea how difficult a teenage girl is?"

"I was wonderful as a teenager," Hayley opined.

"You weren't so easy, trust me. Still aren't. Is there anything I can do or say to talk sense into you?"

"Not really," said Hayley.

*_*_*_*

Two nights later, during dinner, Amber asked, "You haven't said anything about dance team. How come?"

Hayley knew the question would arrive, "Why waste your time and mine? Katy said you can't make the team no matter how good a dancer you are. Maybe you can find something else to do."

"I'd like to dance."

"And," Hayley said.

"I don't think it's fair. Do you?"

"Do you want some more spaghetti?" asked Hayley, purposely ignoring the question.

"You don't think I can make the team, do you?"

"I have no idea. I was given two left feet. I even walk funny. I don't have the gift of movement like you. Do you want some more spaghetti?" Hayley asked.

"You don't think I can make the team, do you?"

"No. I guess I don't."

"Why?"

"You'd have to give up too much. I don't think you're willing and I'm certainly not going to force you."

Amber sat quietly for a few moments. She then stood and looked at her reflection in the kitchen window. She spun around and said, "Will you help me?"

"With what?"

"Help me change my look and dress and get someone to help me with the routines?"

*Bingo.* With Jon Brander's blessings and four hundred dollars, Hayley's shopping, and Katy's suggestions and connections, Amber's look and dress were redone in forty-eight hours. Katy arranged dance lessons from two senior members of the dance team for an hour a day. Hayley had Ben put up two side-by-side full-length mirrors in Amber's room and she practiced routines one to two hours a day on her own.

When Amber wasn't dancing, she studied. Hayley and Katy tutored her and reviewed her schoolwork.

"I wouldn't have believed it. Amber's a different person," Katy told Hayley, as the dance tryouts approached. "God, I hope this work pays off for her. She's done everything you and I have asked of her."

The night before the tryouts, a Saturday, Hayley watched Amber practicing routines. "Do you want Katy, your grandfather and me to come and watch the tryouts?"

"I wasn't going to ask you. What if I fail?" Amber responded. "You and Katy have put in so much work. I don't want to let you down. Besides, I don't think Gramps cares that much."

"For one thing, you're wrong about your grandfather. He cares big time. You can't even imagine how proud Katy, your grandfather and I are at your efforts. No matter what happens, we'll still be there for you."

"Would Katy come?"

"She'd love to but only if you ask. Katy's more nervous than you are. She's invested."

*_*_*_*

Amber's dancing was superb, clearly better than any other girl who attended the tryouts. Hayley, Katy and Jon watched with pride. The results would be posted Monday after school.

Katy made some calls on Sunday and reported back to Hayley. Elspeth Goodrich had not heard of Amber Brander and was calling each of her teachers and the principal at the junior high. Goodrich didn't like uncertainty but she did appreciate promise.

On Monday at three forty-five p.m., hearing a ruckus outside her office, Hayley rushed out to find Amber crying and hugging an equally tearing Katy. Upon seeing Hayley, Amber, face wet with tears, couldn't stop the litany of hugs and 'thank yous'.

Amber's life changed and Jon Brander would be eternally grateful to Hayley.

## Chapter 13

Jon Brander had little difficulty taking over Ben's care. Ben, now able to tell his entire story without becoming emotional, found Brander to be the perfect solution.

Brander, with considerably more experience than Hayley, added a new wrinkle. "Misery loves company." Brander made a series of calls to the VA and American Legion and found two older men, Bart Gruett and Harvey Gordon, to meet with Ben. Bart, in his eighties, had been in the first waves on D-Day, June, 1944, and Harvey, in his seventies, had been in the Chosin Reservoir campaign in Korea in 1950. The three ex-soldiers found common ground quickly and would lunch twice a week at the Apple Ridge Hospital cafeteria. Ben, now, had little difficulty telling his story about the hills outside Kandahar to someone other than Brander and Hayley.

Slowly, Ben healed. Better yet, the Yang didn't diminish. Hayley and Ben made two more trips to the cabin, the last traipsing through snow. They never left the cabin other than to get wood for the fire and water from the well, now almost frozen.

In the following months, Amber spent more and more weekends in Apple Ridge as dance team activities became all consuming.

Jon Brander, fed up with work and now lonely, sold his farm in the spring. He and Amber selected a small house in Apple Ridge, two blocks from Hayley. Brander opened a small office to start counseling and Ben Hunt became his first official patient.

Amber's mother would call every six months, asking for money. Her enticements to Amber to join her in Northern California fell on deaf ears. As Amber said to Hayley, "Why would anyone leave forty-five sisters and you and Katy? Apple Ridge is home."

*_*_*_*

Bill Carter made two more calls to Ben asking him to consider selling his forest property.

"I don't think we'll ever sell. Don't take it personally. We love it there," said Ben.

"Who are we, Ben? You own it free and clear, your mom and dad are dead. Who are we?"

Ben, realizing his mistake in bringing Hayley into the equation, said, "Actually, there's three of us. Me, myself and I. None of us want to sell."

"You're such an asshole."

"Bill, coming from you, I'd take that as a compliment. Good day."

Carter immediately called Warren Kiffers.

"Shit, Warren," Carter said. "That goddamn woman is all of a sudden another clog in my getting that property. I knew we weren't tough enough on her when she got here, leukemia or not. She's now a major pain in the ass. We've got to think of something and soon."

"You gotta be prepared that the casino deal may fall through," Kiffers said.

"Maybe, maybe not," said Carter, "but I'm gonna keep trying."

"Just don't do anything too stupid."

"It's not stupid if it works," Carter said, ending the conversation.

*_*_*_*

Ben and Hayley hiked to the cabin on the second weekend in April.

"I remember the first time I hiked in," said Hayley. "I had so many misgivings about coming. I knew I'd hate it."

"And now?" said Ben, who knew the answer.

"I can't wait to get to there. All my troubles seem to melt."

The sun warmed the crisp mountain air, but the surrounding

mountain peaks remained laden with snow while the valley temperatures hovered in the forties, still too cold for swimming in the lake or resting on a blanket under the shaded maple tree.

After forty-eight hours of too much sex and too little eating, the two exhausted lovers started the hike back to Greavy's store and their car.

Just after the rise before the valley, Ben stopped suddenly. *Footprints, male, fresh.* Ben quickly shifted his rifle off his shoulder and scanned the periphery.

The footprints headed up towards the hill behind the cabin. The elevation on the hill represented the only spot where an onlooker could watch most of the cabin and the lake without being seen. Ben had scouted the area as a child for years. From the hill, he always had a sight to the activities below.

"What's wrong?" asked Hayley.

"Oh, nothing. I thought I heard something."

*Who the fuck's been here? If Hayley weren't with me, I'd head up the rise, gun ready.*

Ben watched the trail carefully and saw fresh prints heading away from the cabin.

Ben remained quiet. *Same shoes, paralleling their current path away from the cabin. I'm glad I didn't scare Hayley. Maybe Greavy knows who was around.*

After a few more minutes, Ben relaxed and shouldered his weapon.

Once back at the Greavy's market, Ben waited for Hayley to use the restroom. Mr. Greavy had seen no one other than the usual locals and no one heading towards or away from the cabin.

*_*_*_*

Ben called Bill Carter the next day.

"Hello, Ben. You thinking about selling?" asked Carter.

"Not why I called. I was up at the forest property this weekend and someone's been snooping around. The prints were fresh," said Ben.

"I don't have the slightest idea what you're talking about. You're wasting my time."

"I know you know the property as well as I do. You and Dad went up there all the time. Anyway, I was armed and followed the prints up the rise behind the cabin. I just want to remind you that someone could get hurt trespassing."

"You're full of shit. I didn't go up there," Carter spat into the phone.

"And you didn't send anyone else?"

"Go fuck yourself. I have no idea what you're talking about."

"Good. Sorry I bothered you." Ben hung up.

Carter called Kiffers. "Warren. Not sure if it spooked his girlfriend, but Ben's really pissed."

"I've said it before and will say it again," said Kiffers, "Ben's got anger issues and killed a slew of Taliban. I don't think you want him mad, particularly with a rifle in his hands."

"I'll take that chance if it gets us the property. If it means taking a little risk, so be it. Anyway, wasn't me going up there."

"Listen, it could come back to you. Be careful."

"Yeah, yeah."

*_*_*_*

Ben brought up his fears with Jon Brander at his next session.

"If not Bill Carter, then who?" said Brander.

"That's it, no one else knows the property," Ben said. "The tracks went right up the rise to the high ground above the cabin and then back down. You're probably right, though. Bill Carter's not stupid enough to go there. Still, someone was there around the time Hayley and I were there. Someone who's been there before."

Two nights later, Ben remembered that the two migrant workers knew the cabin property. He drove by Apple Ridge Hardware every day for a week until he saw one of the men he had hired for the clean up.

Ben exited his car and approached. "Hey, Miguel. How ya doin?"

"Bueno, Señor Doctor. Que pasa? J'you need some work up at the cabin?"

"Not today, amigo. Maybe later, but I was out there last week and found footprints heading up the rise above the cabin. You don't know who made them, do you?" asked Ben.

"No. Not me. I was doing some work at Señor Mullen's."

"You seen Humberto?" asked Ben of the other man who had done work for him.

"No. Humberto was 'sposed to help me but he no show up. I go to his house after I get back and his nephew tell me he got another job. Anyway, he paid enough money from this job to leave for Guatemala to see his familia. I upset he didn't ask me to help whatever job he find."

"Gracias, Miguel. You tell Humberto when he gets back that someone could get shot coming onto my property without being invited."

"You thinks Humberto come on your property?"

"No se. I'm not certain, but I trust you two to stay away unless I ask you. I'm the only one that can ask. Comprende?"

"Claro, señor."

"Miguel, here's twenty for your time."

"I didn't do nothing, Señor Doctor."

"You'll tell me if you find out something?"

"Sí."

*_*_*_*

A week before Hayley's quarterly return to Seattle for routine tests, her stress levels reached uncontrollable levels.

Hayley admitted to Ben before leaving, "I can barely breathe right now, I'm so nervous. Instead of getting better about the follow-ups, I'm worse."

Ben hugged her and said, "You know, I can have some of the tests drawn here in Apple Ridge so that...."

"No. Absolutely not. No. No." said Hayley, shaking her head. "The tests have to be done by Dr. Capland in Seattle and Doris has to draw my blood. I'm superstitious. I'll wait to go back home. It's just that I can't concentrate on anything else. Please understand."

"I'm trying. Really, I'm trying."

"I'm so much more agitated than I've ever been. I know it's because I'm so happy right now. I don't want it to end."

"I know. I know." Ben continued to hug Hayley until a bit of the tension dissolved.

*_*_*_*

Forty-eight hours later, Hayley called Ben from the car. Still in clinic seeing patients, Ben had been anxious, waiting for her call.

Ben excused himself, rushed into his office and closed the door. He merely said, "You okay?"

Intermittent heaving deep breaths interrupted Hayley's speech.

"Yes -- All the tests were negative -- I was so scared waiting for the results -- I'm still shaking -- I meant to stop at my parent's house but I need to get home -- Can you be there?"

"How far out are you?" asked Ben.

"An hour. I know I'm driving too fast. I just want to get home."

"Slow down, please. Pull off the freeway and call your mom. Don't call while you're driving. I'll be at your place before you get there. I can do my dictations later tonight. Do you want me to get some dinner for us?"

"No. I just want you."

"Okay. Drive slower, please."

Ben reached Hayley's house forty-five minutes later. As he sat at her kitchen table dictating charts from that afternoon's clinic, he heard Hayley's car pull into her parking space.

Ben hurried to complete the note he was dictating. Before he could finish, Hayley, jacket on and her purse still on her shoulder, rushed through the door and fell into his arms, forcing him back on his chair.

With tears flowing down her face and then onto Ben's neck, she cried, "I'm trying to hold things together. I couldn't breathe waiting for Dr. Capland to talk to me."

Ben gently pulled her face from his neck and kissed her on the forehead. "The news is good," he said. "You're here. I'm here. I think we should celebrate. Maybe go out to dinner."

"No. I want you to make love to me. I want to believe that everything will be all right. I want you to lie to me so I believe it."

With Hayley arms encircling his neck, Ben stood and carried Hayley into the bedroom. Only a small lamp by the bedside lit the room.

"Do you want me to run a bath for you? It might relax you." asked Ben. As he held her, he pulled down the cover and sheets on the bed.

"No. No. I need you around me and over me. I need you in me. I want you to smother my fears and put them back inside me. I know I'm not making any sense but…"

"You're making complete sense," said Ben. "I had so many years when I wished someone, anyone, could smother my fears."

As Ben removed Hayley's clothes, she closed her eyes and repeated over and over, "I'm so scared. I'm so scared…."

Ben undressed and slid under the covers beside Hayley.

"I love you so much," Hayley said, as Ben slid his right arm under her chest and rolled her towards him.

"First, open your eyes," Ben said.

Hayley did, the tears continuing, her eyes bloodshot.

"I love you more than life," said Ben. I will be here with you and for you, no matter what, no matter when, no matter how."

"I'm so scared. I don't want to be sick. I don't want to be afraid every time I go to the doctor."

"You know I can't tell you what's going to happen but I can tell you that you're all right now and I love you."

"My heart is still racing. I can feel it pounding against my chest."

She rolled away to free Ben's left hand and placed it under her left breast. "Feel my heart racing?" she asked.

"Yes."

"It's been that way since I arrived at Dr. Capland's office."

Hayley held Ben's hand in place until he said, "You're okay now. Shhh."

Ben kissed her lightly on the lips. "I'm going to slow down your heart."

Starting with Hayley's forehead, Ben kissed, nipped, and caressed every inch of her face, down to her neck. Moving lower, he teased both nipples with his tongue, right and left, back and forth. She spread her legs and lifted her hips up, then down, waiting, asking, demanding his hands to move lower.

Ben's fingers found the place and together with his tongue on her nipples, moved rhythmically with each of her breaths and each "I love you."

Hayley's skin felt searing hot, the frenzy of the day's news and the euphoria that followed, melded into her excitement. She could feel her wetness flowing onto the sheets.

She cried, "Ben. Ben. All I could think about on the ride home was you inside me. I don't know if I can wait much longer."

Hayley rolled on top of him and reached for his erection, only to be lifted up so that her legs spread over his chest. Ben slid down, sensing the moisture and sweet muskiness of her unique scent. Her thighs tightened over his face and she gasped at the deepness of his tongue and her pleasure.

Her sounds were incredible, deep and throaty, until she rasped, "I can't take it anymore."

Ben held her tighter and deeper. Despite her pleas, she didn't resist.

"Ben. I'm so alive. I'm so alive. I never want this to end."

Ben slid Hayley down over the wetness on his chest then rolled over, smothering her face with kisses.

She spread her legs to each side of the bed and pleaded, "Please, Ben. Please."

He lifted her legs and pinned her knees back. As he lowered his head, she pleaded again. "Please, Ben. Please."

He obeyed, lifted his body up and felt his tip against her throbbing and wet invitation and entered quickly and deeply.

Deep enough to smother her fears, if only for a moment. Each penetration deep enough to make her forget, if only for a moment. Each penetration deep enough to keep her sanity, if only for a moment.

Until they both collapsed, sweaty, fulfilled, and spent.

Ben got to his dictation at five-thirty the next morning.

Hayley's next follow-up was scheduled sixteen weeks into the future.

*_*_*_*

Three weeks later, Hayley told Ben that she'd be gone from Friday to Sunday, returning to Seattle for Deidre's twenty-ninth birthday and to see her parents.

Rachel and Mel Green had visited Apple Ridge only twice since Hayley's arrival. The first visit, as disgruntled and disbelieving parents, helping her to move-in. A few months later they returned even more disbelieving. Hayley's new relationship with Ben changed everything.

"Can I come with you?" Ben asked.

"Not to the party. Only old friends from high school."

"I can sign out, then drive you in and drive you back. Okay?"

"Sure. Why? It'll be boring?"

"I'm off this weekend, I'm up for boring and I want to be with you."

"You can hang with my mom and dad or see some old friends from Seattle Med. You sure you want to do this?" Hayley asked.

"I'm coming."

*_*_*_*

Saturday night, after Hayley departed for Deidre's party, Ben asked Rachel and Mel to sit and talk.

"Is everything okay with Hayley?" Rachel asked.

"The cancer tests were good, as you know," Ben said, "but I'm worried about her emotionally. Hayley's anxiety got out of control before her recent set of tests. Then, when the tests came back good, her euphoria was over the top. I don't think she can keep going up and down like this."

"I know," Rachel said. "She called me three times a day for a week, before and after her follow-up. I know that part of the euphoric ups and downs is her relationship with you. Going into the tests, she's afraid it will all end. Afterwards, she's as happy as a three-year-old finding out about Halloween for the first time."

"It would be nice to find a way to even things out a bit," Ben said.

"So, what do you suggest?" Mel asked.

"Don't know, actually. I'm not the psychologist," said Ben. "There may be nothing we can do about it, but that's not what I really wanted to talk to you about."

Mel and Rachel's eyebrows arched simultaneously as Rachel asked, "Uh-oh. I hope it's not bad?"

"Depends how you look at it, I guess," said Ben. "I want to ask Hayley to marry me."

"Wow, didn't see that coming," said Mel.

"I can't see living without her, so why wait and..."

Rachel stood and came over to Ben and gave him a hug. "Thank you. Thank you so much for giving us our Hayley back."

"I promise to take care of her," Ben said.

Mel Green stood and walked to the window looking out to the backyard. Facing the large and majestic Ponderosa pine tree that filled his view, he said, "How's that going to work. We've always thought she'd marry someone from around here. She's our only child and the thought of her living elsewhere is too much for Rachel and me."

"I'll probably end up wherever Hayley wants me to end up," said Ben. "I still don't know if she'll say yes. I thought I'd ask you first for your blessings."

Still gazing through the window, Mel said, "I don't know. I'm not sure how I feel. I don't know what she'll think and..."

Rachel came behind Mel and put her arms on his enormous shoulders. "Honey. Say yes. Just say to Ben, 'Of course, she'll say yes.' Then say, 'Welcome to our family.' Say it."

Mel turned, kissed Rachel on the forehead, approached Ben and started to shake his hand. Mel hesitated, then gave Ben a hug. "Thank you, Ben. Thank you for everything."

"Did you buy a ring yet?" Rachel asked.

"Well actually," Ben said, "I thought I'd give her my mother's ring, if I could find it. I tracked down my stepfather on Thursday in Yakima. First time we've spoken in years. I was going to try and buy my mom's ring back. He told me that he sold her ring the day after she died to pay for the funeral. I don't know if it's the truth or not. He didn't hesitate to tell me what he thought of me."

"I guess you two can go out and pick out something together," Rachel said. "For now, I'd be honored to give you my ring." With a bit of twirling and tugging Rachel slid her own wedding ring over her arthritic knuckle then held it towards Ben.

"I wasn't expecting that," Ben said. "It's my responsibility to buy a ring and I'm sure that your ring has years of sentiment for you two."

Rachel looked hard at her husband. Mel, picking up the Rachel's cue, said, "Giving the ring to Hayley is all the sentiment we need. We'd be honored if you used it."

Ben nodded and said, "Thank you. Thank you so much."

"When exactly were you going to ask her?" questioned Rachel.

"At first, I thought I'd do it at our cabin. She loves it there."

"She's told me that," Rachel said. "I never would have believed my daughter would be happy in a remote cabin in the woods and Deidre's told me it's even better than that. Not sure I get what she means. What happens at the cabin?"

*I'm not going there with Hayley's parents.* Ben, eyebrows raised, ignored the question and said, "Beats me. Anyway, I think I'm going to wait to tell Hayley."

Rachel asked immediately, "Wait for what?"

"For her to walk in the door tonight."

*_*_*_*

At twelve forty-five a.m., Hayley tiptoed into her bedroom to find Ben reading a medical journal.

"I thought you'd be asleep," Hayley said.

"Nope. Waiting up for you. Did you have a good time?"

"Wonderful. Too much wine. Deidre, her sister and four friends from high school. Mostly non-sensical giggling. We were only missing the pajamas and I would have said I was thirteen again."

Hayley started shedding her clothes and throwing them haphazardly on a chair near the bed and put on an old tee shirt, cut off below the lettering. "Mom and Dad asleep?"

"Dunno. Your dad for sure."

When Hayley slid into bed, she threw her arms around his chest.

"Deidre said something to me as I left. She said that we've been jealous of each other's accomplishments back and forth for twenty plus years. She'd win a basketball game, I'd have a recital. She'd get asked out to a dance before me, I'd get a date with a football player. Mini-competitions that we'd joke about. Like sisters. Anyway, she said it's been more than year and a half since she's had any pangs of jealousy until she realized how happy I've been recently. She said to say thank you to you for all that."

"You're welcome," Ben said.

Hayley caressed Ben's ear with her tongue as her hand slid across his abdomen and down. "So why'd you wait up for me or do I really need to ask?"

Ben answered, "Actually, I need to do some counseling tonight."

"Jon is your counselor now. Anyway, the counseling I was thinking about had no talking. I was planning to wake you up and...."

"Stop. The counseling isn't for me, it's for you."

"Oh. I don't get it?"

"Lie down on the bed and I'll sit on the chair." Ben got up, moved Hayley's strewn clothing and sat.

Hayley put her head on the pillow and crossed her arms onto her chest. "I'm waiting for you to pour water on me or do something stupid. Go ahead."

"Better yet, sit at the side of the bed," demanded Ben.

"Honestly, can't this wait until morning?"

"Nope. I'd never get to sleep."

Hayley sat up, legs dangling over the side of the bed and put a pillow in her lap. "Okay. Now I won't sleep until you get to the point."

"Miss Green, or may I call you Hayley?"

"Pretty soon you're going to call me 'adios' and I'm calling Deidre to tell her not to be jealous."

Ben laughed. "Okay. How long have you had this hidden desire to get married?"

"What. Are you joking me? I've not even given...."

Ben interrupted, "Answer the question. How long? And answer honestly."

"I'm a woman, girl, whatever. I probably thought about it in Cle Elum. I think a lot of things."

Ben stood and walked to the edge of the bed. "I'm a guy. We aren't so quick thinking. I've been thinking about it for a week." Ben kneeled in front of Hayley, whose hands went up to her mouth. He took out Rachel's ring and said, "Hayley Green, will you marry me?".

"Um. Uh. I'm confused. What are you doing with my mother's ring?"

"That's not an answer. I asked your mom and dad if it was okay to ask you to marry me. They said 'yes' and then demanded I use your mom's ring until we get our own."

"They know?"

"Yep. Aren't you supposed to say 'yes' or 'of course.' Or 'no.' or 'I have to think about it.' Something?" asked Ben.

"You don't care about my leukemia?" Hayley asked, still confused.

"Did you really have to ask? We both know what's going on. I could care less about your leukemia. In fact, I...."

Before Ben could finish the sentence, Hayley hurled herself at him forcing him onto the bedroom floor. "Yes. Yes and yes. Of course." Tears had already started down her cheeks as she got down to her knees and kissed Ben. Hayley then popped up and said, "Yes."

After they stood, Ben hugged Hayley and said, "Your mom said she probably wouldn't sleep tonight. You may want to see if she's awake and tell her."

Hayley kissed Ben on the lips, put on her underpants and scooted down the hallway towards the master bedroom and entered without knocking.

Rachel, totally awake, said, "I heard you come in and……."

Hayley hurled herself onto the bed and crawled between her mother and sleeping father. Hayley buried her head in her mother's neck and chest. "Oh, Mom. After last year, I never thought, hoped or believed I would be happy again. Oh my God, Mom. I am so happy."

"Me too. Me too," said Rachel, as she kissed her daughter's forehead. "Now I can sleep and tomorrow we'll talk. I'm so happy for you and we love Ben."

Ben stayed awake, which paid dividends until three a.m.

*_*_*_*

Ben sat silently the next morning, as did Mel, while the two women, plus Deidre, who had come over as soon as she heard the news, plotted a course. The triumvirate selected a date six months ahead.

*_*_*_*

On the following Monday, back in Apple Ridge, Hayley called Bill Carter and went to his office at lunchtime.

"What now? Hopefully, you're going to tell me you're leaving Apple Ridge?" Carter said with a huge smile.

"No one knows what I'm going to tell you," said Hayley. "Ben asked me to marry him and I said 'yes.'"

"You're kidding me? Pretty quick. He must be after your money."

"I don't have any money. My life is like one of those movies where a huge asteroid is heading towards earth and no one can stop it. Anyway, you know first."

"Lady. That doesn't change shit, far as I'm concerned. I don't like Ben and I'm getting not to like you either."

"Fine with me, Mr. Carter. I could care less what you think. Anyway, you know."

Carter asked, "Why do you keep telling me everything about you and Ben? As if I care."

"I like control," said Hayley.

"You made that abundantly clear that first night in the high school auditorium."

"I want you to know the truth. I don't want you misinterpreting stuff you hear second hand."

"So."

"Ben's doing well. That's it. I don't want you making his life miserable. You can't spread rumors if you know the truth."

"Actually, I can spread anything I want."

"Yes, but you won't."

"We'll see. I hear you've been spending time up at Ben's cabin. Not your big city style, eh. Can get scary out there."

Hayley, the therapist, was smart enough to think about her response. *I don't know what he's looking for.* "I have no idea what you're talking about. Scared of what?"

"Sorry," Carter said. "Just wondered what a city girl is doing out of her element."

Hayley shook her head in disbelief, said nothing more, stood and walked out of Carter's office.

That evening, Hayley told Ben about the conversation and Carter's unusual comment about being frightened.

"I don't know what he's talking about. We've been snug as bugs out there. He's just being an asshole," said Ben. *I know exactly what he's talking about.*

*_*_*_*

Small town, big gossip. Ben heard his first congratulations from an orderly at the hospital on Tuesday morning.

"Dr. Hunt, Congrats. Seems like you're happy as a five-year-old with a Popsicle ever since that Green lady came to town. Nice to see somebody so happy."

"You're so right. I am."

## Chapter 14

## Corporate Headquarters of CasManUS

## Atlantic City, NJ

Victor Rossi, CEO of CasManUS, sat behind a massive desk in an oversized, paneled, heavily decorated office. Rocking slowly back and forth, he faced his family's consigliore, Angelo Bruni. William Backmon, managing partner of Backmon Kurland Barak, a four hundred-man Manhattan law firm, sat next to Bruni.

CasManUS stood for Casino Management United States, which owned, ran, or managed Indian casinos throughout North America. CasManUS's ties to organized crime were well known on the street, but never proven. Victor Rossi ran privately held CasManUS with an iron hand and closed books, except for the IRS, which audited CasManUS every year. A much younger, brash Victor spent four years in the federal penal system for tax evasion when he helped run a waste management company in Trenton for the Ponti mob. Since then, Rossi had beaten four other raps, including tax evasion and money laundering.

Twenty years later, Victor Rossi was smarter, largely thanks to Backmon's firm and some well-placed bribes. Rossi had also artfully dodged a handful of FBI stings. The last time, in 2004, when the snitch disappeared a mere twenty minutes from the safety of the Federal Witness Protection Program.

All twelve of CasManUS's casinos made money, for Rossi, for the American Indians they represented and for numbers of other legitimate investors. Apple Ridge, Washington, sat more than fifty miles from the nearest casino and a popular gas stop on I-90 heading to and from Seattle. CasManUS had no casinos in the Pacific Northwest and, to Rossi, Apple Ridge represented pure gold.

Potential for a major winter ski resort, summer golf and hiking areas added to the Apple Ridge site possibilities. CasManUS already managed three casinos near Lake Tahoe. Each could be described as cash cows from Day One. Apple Ridge looked to have the same setup, sans competition.

CasManUS had approached Bill Carter, the region's major landholder, seven years earlier. At the time, Carter understood the feelings of the community and neither he, nor the city, needed the money. Apple Ridge would certainly have not tolerated a casino near the city and had the ordinances in place to reinforce those feelings. CasManUS was cordial enough and said, "Call if you change your mind."

When the fruit processing plant in Apple Ridge closed, everything changed. As families began to leave Apple Ridge for work elsewhere, Carter saw land values plummet. He had already foreclosed three parcels of land near the I-90 exit when he asked Warren Kiffers to approach CasManUS and see if interest in a casino still existed. CasManUS returned with a tentative proposal to make Carter more money than he ever thought possible.

The Apple Ridge City council and the county commissioners knew nothing of Carter's plans. Aware that current zoning would not allow a gambling establishment within a thirty-mile radius of Apple Ridge, Carter also knew the depressed local economy, without prospects for recovery, would be enticement enough for the council to become more flexible.

The only feasible and economically sound siting for a casino and ski resort was just outside Apple Ridge. Bill Carter already owned ninety percent of the land. Situated in the center of his holdings, the ten percent Carter needed, was the three hundred acres owned by Ben Hunt. Development of the planned resort could simply not go forward without Ben's property.

"I haven't met these three hicks," Rossi asked, moving his finger back and forth between his consigliore and lawyer. "What's your take?"

"They're small-town but not stupid." Bruni responded first. "Carter's family has owned most of the land in and around Apple

Ridge for decades. His attorney talks little and doesn't ask many questions, but when he does ask, they're insightful. I get the feeling he knows what's happening."

William Backmon nodded agreement. "I would concur, Victor."

"How about the Indian chump?" asked Rossi.

"The local tribes already have a couple of two-bit casinos that aren't doing well," said Backmon. "I'm pretty sure that if we swing this deal, they'll let CasManUS manage everything. Their guy doesn't understand much."

"He's not going to cause trouble?" asked Rossi.

Bruni interjected, "No way. He's just listening and will do anything we ask."

"My financial guys have gone over this time and again," Backmon said. "The demographics are incredible. Seattle, a backwater town thirty years ago, is thriving and growing like crazy. Boeing, Microsoft, Starbucks, Costco, and Amazon are all headquartered there. A world-class casino, winter and summer resort, without competition, can't fail. We figure it'll double the return from all three Tahoe units combined. I've got legitimate investors from JP Morgan, Wells and UBS drooling and queuing up around the block."

"I can taste this," Rossi said.

Rossi pointed to one of two, thick-necked, impassive men standing quietly in opposite corners of the room like enormous bookends. "Carlo, bring 'em in." Carlo, the larger of the two bookends, turned and went to the door.

Bill Carter and Warren Kiffers entered the Victor Rossi's office followed by John Two Rivers, representing the Toppenish Indian Tribal Offices. Everyone was standing other than Rossi who remained seated behind his fortress of a desk.

Bruni, who had met Carter and Kiffers in Apple Ridge, now

introduced Victor and William Backmon. Carlo, the bookend, resumed his furniture pose in the corner. Neither Carlo, nor his partner, were included in the introductions, but their presence set an unmistakable tone. After a few comments of greeting, Rossi invited everyone to take a seat.

"I shouldn't have to remind anyone in this room that what is said here stays here," Rossi said, starting the meeting. "With regard to CasManUS and the Apple Ridge Casino plans, you don't tell your wives, kids or anyone. You don't write or email anything to anyone. If you're discussing this between yourselves, do it in person at random locations like crowded and noisy fast food restaurants. No cell phones. Capish?"

The room nodded yes.

Rossi continued, "Mr. Carter, are you any closer to getting the property you need to close this deal?"

Kiffers started to answer Rossi's question. "Mr. Rossi, the remaining...."

Rossi nodded him off with the flick of a finger. "I want to hear what Carter says, not you."

Carter spoke up immediately, "Yes. We're really close. We need only one parcel, three hundred acres."

"I know that," Rossi said. "Am I missing something? Offer more money."

"Believe me, I've tried. The owner has a little vendetta against me and won't sell on principle."

"Use a dummy buyer."

"We tried that and got caught," said Carter.

"You must be a dumb fuck. The FBI can't pin shit on me, hard as they try, and you get caught by a minor league joker."

Carter knew Rossi had done some jail time but thought better of reminding him. "Don't worry. We'll find a way. I've got ideas."

Backmon, quiet until then, said, "Maybe we can partner up with this doctor? Give him a piece of the action."

Rossi, gritted his teeth and looked at Backmon, "You're here to listen. That's what I pay you to do. The last thing I want, or need, is another partner."

"He'd never go for it in a million years," said Carter. "Plus, he'd tell everyone what we're doing. Terrible idea. We need to get him to sell."

Rossi said nothing, which meant he agreed. After a brief moment of silence, Rossi said, "I want this casino bad. It plays just like Tahoe. Seattle's growing and has money."

Backmon interrupted, "I agree and….."

Rossi's glare stopped Backmon cold.

"So this is how it's going to work," Rossi said. "We start drawing up plans now. I've got an architecture firm here in Jersey that does all my work. Backmon will help the Indians start an application but we'll leave the exact location out of it for now. They'll start putting papers together. When you get control, I want to be ready to go the next day. I don't like delays."

The room nodded agreement in lockstep.

"To make sure that we're all on board, I'm going to hire you three," Rossi continued, pointing at Carter, Kiffers and Rivers, "as consultants. As such, we will open private and untraceable accounts for each of you in the Cayman Islands.

"Before you leave today, you will each create an ID and a password. By the end of the week, there'll be a half million in US dollars in each account. I don't need to say what is obvious. With the lawyer, architect and consulting fees I'm paying, this casino is going to be built. Mr. Backmon will meet with you three in the boardroom to work out details. Remember, for your own health, nothing leaves this room."

After Carter, Kiffers, Rivers and Backmon exited, Rossi turned to Bruni. "Angie, who can we get to look around this backwater, piece-of-shit town and see what's what. I need some eyes in there. Real quiet, so we don't scare the natives." Only Rossi called Angelo "Angie."

"I was thinking that myself," Bruni said.

"And I don't want another partner."

"And we don't want anyone who looks or sounds Jersey," Bruni added, they'd stick out like my hemorrhoids. I've already figured out who me might call."

"Who ya thinking of?" asked Rossi.

"Bobby Francisco's got a son working for him in Portland, Oregon. The kid's running Bobby's waste business. Doin' real well. He's got men working for him. He'll have someone who can take a peek."

"Good," Rossi said. "I want to know how, when and why people take a shit in Apple 'Fuckin' Ridge, especially Carter, his jerk-off lawyer buddy and the doctor who's got a bug up his ass about Carter. Capish?"

"I'm on it, Victor."

"If Carter can't make this happen, we'll do it. I want this bad."

*_*_*_*

Three days later, Bruni sat in Victor Rossi's office. "Bobby Francisco's son, Gino, has somebody on his way to Apple Ridge. Don't laugh. Guy's from Detroit."

"Detroit," Rossi said. "You're kidding me. They'll spot him in fifteen seconds."

Bruni laughed

"What was so funny?" said Rossi.

"Turns out there's a town in central Oregon called Detroit," Bruni said. "One stoplight town. Go figure."

## Chapter 15

Two weeks after formally announcing their marriage plans and six weeks from Hayley's last check-up, Ben received an unexpected, early afternoon call from Katy MacArthur.

Katy explained that Hayley, visibly upset, had rushed from their offices twenty minutes earlier without an explanation other than "I've got to go home."

"She's never been this way," Katy said, "so I thought you ought to know."

"Thanks Katy. I'll try and reach her," Ben said.

Ben called Hayley's cell phone four times. He then called Katy MacArthur to see if Hayley had returned to her office. She hadn't. Having no explanation, Ben cancelled his afternoon clinic and sped over to Hayley's house.

Parked askew in the driveway, with the door ajar, Hayley's car screamed trouble. Ben entered an unlocked front door, another departure from Hayley's usual behavior. From the living room, Ben called out. No answer. Hayley's purse lying on the dinette table suggested otherwise. He called again as he moved towards the bedroom. An open, but yet empty, suitcase on her bed chilled an already frightened Ben. He called again and heard a weak voice from the bathroom.

Entering the bathroom, Ben found Hayley wedged back against the wall, next to the toilet, wearing only a bra and underwear. Bloodshot eyes and a mascara stained blouse draped over the bathtub portended doom as she looked up at Ben with the facies of utter agony and sorrow.

Ben knelt in front of her. "What's wrong? What happened? Talk to me."

She nodded towards the toilet bowl.

Ben looked inside to see toilet paper soaked with blood. "Your bleeding. From where?"

Hayley, barely able to speak between sobs, cried, "I've been spotting for two hours… I was just sitting in the office interviewing a family when I felt moist… I excused myself and went to the bathroom… My underwear was bloody… I wiped myself over and over but the spotting didn't stop... I am so scared, Ben. This was how my nosebleeds started. I want to go back to Seattle."

"Maybe it's just a period."

"I haven't had a period since the transplant. Dr. Capland said I probably wouldn't."

Despite knowing that Hayley was obsessively superstitious about having her blood work drawn only in Seattle, and more specifically by Dr. Capland's office nurse, Doris, Ben persevered, "We can do some tests here and..."

Ben knew immediately those were not the words Hayley wanted or needed. Before Hayley could answer, he said, "No. Of course not. Let's get you to Seattle. We can be there before four o'clock, if we leave now. I'll sign out to the surgeons in Cle Elum from the car. "

Hayley nodded assent.

"I don't need anything," Ben said. "You grab some toiletries and a change of clothes. We can call Capland's office and your parents from the road."

Silence persisted until they got onto I-90 heading west towards Seattle.

"I know you want to tell me that everything is going to be all right," Hayley said, "and that there are many reasons for spotting and this doesn't mean my leukemia has returned. Don't tell me that. I know we don't know for sure, but until I know what's going on I can't talk about it. Please just drive."

Ben remained silent.

Hayley curled up in a ball, looking out the passenger window and stayed that way for most of the next ninety minutes. Ben called Rachel Green, then called Dr. Capland's office and spoke to his nurse, Doris.

Doris knew Hayley and her medical idiosyncrasies as well as anyone. "You tell Hayley that Dr. Capland and I will be here whenever you arrive."

Ben and Hayley arrived at Seattle Med at three forty-five and went up to the second floor offices of Dr. Capland. Hayley stopped at a restroom outside Dr. Capland's office. The spotting had ceased.

Waiting at the front desk, Doris escorted Hayley and Ben back to an exam room. Dr. Capland turned the corner and saw Ben standing outside Hayley's room.

"Hey, Ben. Long time, no see."

"Hello, Dr. Capland."

"I'm surprised to see you here with Hayley. She likes to come alone. Superstitious, like many of my patients."

"That's an understatement," said Ben. "But surgeons tend to be a superstitious lot, so I get it."

"Anyway, I need to talk to her and do an exam. Does she want you in the room? Doris told me she's spotting and it's new. I hope it's nothing."

"Yes. Started four or five hours ago. She freaked out. I know she wants me not to play doctor right now. I'll just wait here."

Twenty minutes later, Capland exited, followed five minutes later by Doris, carrying four tubes of freshly drawn blood and a urine specimen. Ben had not budged from his position against the hallway wall outside Hayley's exam room.

"Ben, you might as well sit in the waiting room," Capland said. "Hayley will be out in a few minutes. Her exam was normal and the blood work will take forty-five minutes to an hour. You know the drill."

Ben sat on a couch in the waiting room. Hayley came moments

later and sat next to Ben, curled her knees to her chest and put her head on his shoulder. Ben wrapped his arm around her as she whispered, "Thank you."

A few minutes later, Rachel and Mel Green came into the waiting room. Hayley stood, gave each a hug and kiss, and then returned to Ben's side.

The four sat silently.

Forty minutes later, the clinic's secretary spoke up, "Miss Green. Doris is busy but Dr. Capland would like to see you alone in his office. Do you know where it is?"

"Yes," Hayley said, "but I'd like Ben and my parents to come with me."

"Hold on. I'll ask Dr. Capland again what he wants to do. He did say alone."

The secretary hung up the phone and walked around the desk, and stood in front of Hayley. "Dr. Capland said he needs to speak to you alone, first. Then you can decide if the others can come."

"I don't need the privacy. Ben and my parents can hear what he has to say," Hayley responded abruptly.

"Dr. Capland was very specific that he wanted to talk to you alone."

Hayley already unwrapped from Ben, stomped back to Dr. Capland's office and sat in her usual, previously lucky, chair.

Dr. Capland entered the room a few minutes later with lab printout sheets in his hands. He sat in a chair next to Hayley. His face was unreadable.

"I really don't think we needed to exclude Ben or my parents," Hayley said, as Capland took a seat, "and they know what's going on. I can get them."

"No. I need to speak to you alone," Capland demanded. "You'll understand."

Hayley sat back in her chair, crossed her arms and tightened her jaw.

"First, the good news," Capland said. "All your blood counts are normal. Every one. Platelets, red and white cells, differential. Everything. You do not have leukemia, but not all the tests are normal."

"I don't understand. What other tests were you running?" asked Hayley, clueless.

"Spotting is not a disease and can be caused by a number of things."

"I'm confused."

"I'll un-confuse you. You're pregnant," said Capland.

"What?" Hayley, confused, stood quickly and then sat back down.

"You're pregnant. Like having a baby-pregnant," said Capland.

"No way. You said that was unlikely to ever happen and..."

"Unlikely is just that, unlikely, but not impossible," interjected Capland. "You're pregnant. I didn't want to announce it in front of Ben or your parents. I didn't know how you'd react. It's your call first."

"Could the test be wrong?"

"No. They rechecked it."

"Now what do I do?" asked Hayley.

"I have to ask. Do you want to be pregnant?"

"Will the baby be normal?"

"No one can promise a normal child, in any pregnancy, or ever," Capland said, "but I surmise that if you carry the baby to term, he or she will have an excellent chance of being normal. Whatever normal is." Capland smiled at his own mini-joke.

"Could this pregnancy cause my leukemia to return?"

"I don't think it will be a factor. The leukemia can return at any time, pregnancy or not."

"I want this child," Hayley said without hesitation. "I want it more than you can ever know. What do I do next?"

"Actually, I don't do this much," Capland said, now broadly smiling. He recommended that Hayley find a high-risk OB practice at Seattle Med, and start prenatal vitamins. "Whomever you see, have him or her give me a call."

Hayley smiled, stood up, walked around the desk and gave Dr. Capland a huge hug and kiss on the cheek. "Phew," Hayley exhaled. "I'm so excited. Thank you."

Dr. Capland watched Hayley exit the office and scurry to the waiting room. The yells of joy rolled through the clinic corridors.

*_*_*_*

The following Monday morning, Rachel Green cancelled the room she had booked for the wedding and started making calls to the guests and relatives to no longer 'Save the Date.'

Rachel's lame excuse seemed to work. Using the explanation that with her leukemia, Hayley didn't want to wait and neither Hayley nor Ben wanted a big to-do. Rachel slept well, despite a hundred lies. Only Deidre knew the truth.

The following Tuesday, Ben and Hayley left work and drove west to Ellensburg. At the Kittitas County Auditor's Office they paid sixty-four dollars for a marriage license. The following Saturday in Seattle, joined by Mel, Rachel, Deidre, and Rachel's sister, Aunt Leah, Ben and Hayley were married at the office of Anthony Kintraw, a Superior Court Judge and long time friend of Mel and Rachel. The group had dinner at Il Terrazzo Carmine, the site of Ben and Hayley's first meal together.

Before Hayley and Ben departed, Hayley drew Deidre aside. "You told me to stop dying slowly and live life faster. How am I doing?"

Deidre laughingly responded, "I didn't think you'd take me so literal. I've never been as happy as I am now for you. You deserve everything you can get."

On Sunday afternoon, Dr. and Mrs. Benjamin Hunt drove back to Apple Ridge. They considered stopping at the Cle Elum Best Western but opted out. Ben moved into Hayley's house over the next few days.

Hayley sought out a family physician in Apple Ridge and made an appointment with a high risk OB, Judy Kimel, M.D., at Seattle Med.

Kimel ordered an amniocentesis with prenatal genetic testing at sixteen weeks. Hayley received a call a week later.

"Hayley, Dr. Kimel here. The baby has forty-six chromosomes and all look good." Responding to Hayley's demands about her child's future during the amniocentesis, Kimel added. "I can now guarantee with certainty that the baby will be President of the United States, or at the least, a Nobel Prize winner in Physics."

Both laughed, as they had when the original demand by Hayley had been made seven days earlier.

## Chapter 16

Angelo Bruni sat in Rossi's office smiling. "Gino Francisco's guy from Detroit is back."

"Detroit, Oregon," Rossi laughed. "Somebody must have gone to the bottom of the barrel looking for a city name. So?"

"Kid's name is Richie Porto. I talked with him for an hour this morning. He seems sharp enough and Gino says we can trust him to keep his mouth shut. Using phony ID, he picked up a temp job for three weeks at a restaurant doing dishes. He scouted out the bars at night for most of the info."

"I'm listening," said Rossi.

"Bill Carter used to be best friends with a local doc named Curtis Hunt. Hunt popped himself twenty years ago. Curtis leaves Ben, his only kid, the three hundred acres Carter needs, bypassing the now dead alcoholic wife. Ben's best friend was Carter's son, Billy, Jr. Ben and Junior were in trouble all the time through high school, mostly booze and rowdiness."

"Go on."

"Ben Hunt joins the Marines on a plea bargain, two tours in Afghanistan, decorated, gets his shit together, finishes college, med school and surgical training. He comes back to Apple Ridge, courtesy of Uncle Sam, for five years to pay off school debts."

"And."

"Meanwhile, Carter's son, Junior, nixes the plea bargain, never turns it around despite having family money. Dumb ass gets himself killed in a bar fight four, five years later. For some reason, Carter blames Ben for Junior's death. The whole town knows about the feud, but Porto thinks it's Carter not liking Hunt. Most think Hunt doesn't give a shit one way or another."

"Sounds like one of my wife's soap operas," said Rossi.

"Anyway, Hunt's got a short fuse, real short, couple of run-ins with Carter's family after coming to town. The city council holds a meeting to throw Hunt out, but the girl friend, a city-girl shrink, shows up, takes a job and keeps him out of trouble."

"Shit. It is one of my wife's soap operas," smiled Rossi.

"Yeah. Hunt and the girl, name is Hayley Green, get married, all of a sudden a few months ago, and she's expecting a kid in four to five months."

"Okay. Okay. A real love story. As if I give a shit," said Rossi.

"There's more. The girl, by rumor, has some illness but nobody seems to know what it is. She keeps going back to Seattle for tests. That said, she's a looker, seems normal and everybody likes her. Apparently, Hunt and the girl go up to a cabin on Hunt's property in the forest a couple a times a month for a weekend. No one else ever goes there, ever."

"What'cha think?" asked Rossi.

Bruni, ready for the question, said, "Here's how I see this. Carter owns all the property we need, except Hunt's. Carter wants this casino, but not as bad as we do. We need him friendly, property or not, because he's the only one who can sway the city council to rezone."

"What if Hunt were to have an accident?" Rossi asked.

"It ain't New York, boss," said Bruni. "This is a small town and everybody knows everybody else, warts and all. If Hunt gets hurt, everyone points a finger at Carter because of the feud. Carter could get nervous and start pointing fingers at us and that'll screw the pooch."

"I'm not liking what I'm hearing," said Rossi.

"Actually, I think there's a wrinkle," said Bruni. "We get the girl to leave. She's a big-city girl from an upper-class Seattle burb and expecting a kid. I'll bet a duck out of water in Podunk, USA. We get her to leave and, presto, Ben leaves when his time is up."

"I don't like it," said Rossi. "We have no guarantee you can scare her or she'll leave, no guarantee he'll leave with her and no guarantee he'd let the property go. Not to mention I don't want to wait five fuckin' years."

"No, but we'll scare the shit out of her, especially with a kid coming, so she runs back to mommy and never wants to come back."

"I don't like. Too many ifs. What if something accidental were to happen to her or, better yet, both of them?" asked Rossi.

"That's Plan B," Bruno said. "In Newark or Chicago it'd be Plan A. It's got to look like an accident and we can't let them implicate Carter or Kiffers. That's an absolute. We don't want this coming back to us in any way."

Rossi nodded assent. "I understand, but I'm tired of waiting and you should be too. Tell Carter he's got six months to close the property. If he can't, we'll do it for him."

Bruni sent Bill Carter a cryptic note: "Six months, max. Then it's in our ballpark."

*_*_*_*

Carter and Kiffers had no trouble deciphering the meaning of the 'it's in our ballpark' message.

"I'm not liking this. These guys think on a whole different level than we do," said Kiffers. "We don't need this aggravation. These are not nice people."

"You're probably right," Carter said. "I'll approach Ben a couple more times. If he won't sell, we'll give Rossi his money back and call off the deal."

"I agree. Problem is, I don't know if we can call off anything with these guys. In for a penny, in for a pound, as they say. In this case, I fear it's a pound of flesh."

"You worry too much," said Carter.

Kiffers shook his head. "I'm thinking you aren't worrying enough. In this case, you should."

Carter merely laughed.

*_*_*_*

Bill Carter called Ben twice more, six weeks apart. Offering three and then four times the worth of the land. Ben refused politely both times and told Carter that the property will never be for sale and that his refusal to sell had nothing to do with their relationship.

Carter told Kiffers that they should start thinking of ways that they could get out of the CasManUS deal and out of Rossi's hair.

Kiffers reiterated his sense of the tone of the conversations with Bruni. Kiffers felt that getting out of the deal would not be simple.

*_*_*_*

Hayley, now seven and a half months pregnant, made another visit to Bill Carter.

"What now? Haven't I been nice enough to you two?"

"Actually, you've been great. Better than I expected. Thank you again for not telling everyone about my leukemia. At least no one has ever said anything other than 'How ya doin'?'"

"You need something?"

"I'm going to move back to Seattle in two weeks."

"Breaks my heart," Carter smiled.

"I bet it does," Hayley said.

"Permanent move? Apple Ridge not your cup of tea."

"It's only for the rest of the pregnancy. I'll be back after the baby is born."

"Oh." Carter stopped smiling.

"I was just hoping you'd leave Ben alone while I'm gone."

"He's not going with you?" Carter asked.

"No. Not until I go into labor. He can't leave work and my moving to Seattle for the delivery is optional, at least to the National Health Service."

"I can't promise anything."

"There's another thing. Ben and I don't keep secrets. He tells me you keep pestering him about selling the land his father left him."

Carter's eyebrows went up. "Yeah. And?"

"He's not going to sell and, from his therapist's standpoint, he can't."

"Why's that?"

"Oww." Hayley grabbed her stomach, death-clenched her jaw and shook her head.

"You okay?" asked Carter.

"This kid's kicking field goals twenty-four seven. I can't wait for this to be over."

Carter laughed. "I remember my first wife's pregnancies. Been there, done that."

*That's the first time he's ever laughed around me. Maybe he's human.* Hayley exhaled deeply, held her breath and waited a moment to see if the baby would strike again.

"Anyway, it's the only place he can remember his father in peace," Hayley said. "He's only got good memories when he's there. Surprisingly, I love it too. When we're there, he talks of mostly about his dad. Many of those memories include you and Billy, Jr. You know, he's not mad at you. He has a difficult time figuring out why you're so mad at him."

Carter thought for a moment before responding. *If he had sold me the property, I'd be as happy as a pig in shit.* "We had some good times there. Just so you know, I need that property."

"You need the property?" asked Hayley. "I don't think you need anything. Lots of people need things around here, like jobs. Not you."

"I have a deal in the works. Something that would bring a ton of jobs back to Apple Ridge, but I need Ben's land, or it doesn't work."

"You've not said that to Ben. He thought you just wanted the land because it was his."

"I'm sure he wouldn't have approved what I was planning. Besides, I'm trying to get out of the whole mess. It's not that easy."

"Tell me."

"I can't and won't," said Carter.

"If you're getting out of the deal, what's the difference?"

"I can't. Trust me."

Hayley smiled. "You forget that when I came here, someone shot out my living room windows to frighten me. And now you're asking me to trust you?"

Carter nodded. "You're tough. Are we done?"

"Yep. I enjoy our little get-togethers," said Hayley.

As Hayley, holding her belly as leverage, stood to leave, Carter added, "I assume you're not naming the baby Bill."

"We don't know the sex yet," said Hayley. "and I'm superstitious as hell. The bone marrow transplant did that to me. If you could promise a healthy baby and that my leukemia won't come back anytime soon, I'd name the baby Bill Carter Hunt, whether it was a boy or girl."

Carter laughed again and nodded his understanding of Hayley's tenuous hold on her sanity, "I hope everything goes well with the delivery and all."

"Thanks."

After Hayley left, Carter called Warren Kiffers. "We've got to call the CasMan people and tell them the deal is off. We're not getting the property. Hayley was just here and she's told me, in so many words, that Ben's not going to sell the property to anyone, ever."

"Rossi's not going to be happy," said Kiffers.

"I got that," Carter said, "but I don't see an option. Better to give Rossi his money back and try to extract ourselves."

"As I've said before, it may not be that simple. That's the feeling I got. I'll call Two Rivers at the reservation office and let him know first. He'll be pissed and may not want to part with the money. Shit, he may have spent it already."

"I don't think Rossi's going to let him keep it," said Carter.

"You got that right. I'll get back to you after I make the calls."

"On another score, I'm getting to like Hayley," said Carter. "She's got spunk and she's honest with me. I'm even starting to feel sorry for her, not knowing one day to the next what's going to happen."

"Does that mean you're going to send her a fruit basket when she has the kid?" quipped Kiffers.

"Warren, you're such a dickhead. As long as this deal is never going to happen, maybe I can make peace with Ben too. I know that he wasn't totally at fault about Billy, Jr. Probably more on me than anyone. Hayley said Ben's not really mad at me. He talks about the good times at the cabin with his dad, Billy, Jr., him and me. I think I blew this one, getting mad at Ben and all."

Kiffers added, "I hear he's doing a great job at the hospital. I'm guessing he's here for the long haul."

"Make the call to Rossi and get back to me. When this is all over I'll figure a way to make peace with Ben, but not 'til it's over."

*_*_*_*

Thirty-four weeks into her pregnancy, Hayley sat in her office finishing last minute details before heading to Seattle. Hayley had already promoted Katy MacArthur and informed Olympia and Spokane that Katy would be able to handle the office during Hayley's maternity leave.

"Sid Grahmel is waiting to see you," Katy said. "He said it'll just take a minute and he wouldn't tell me what for. I put him in your office."

Sid Grahmel owned a large pizzeria in Apple Ridge and would often find short-term work for some of Hayley's out-of-luck welfare recipients. Grahmel was on Hayley's short list of people she could trust in Apple Ridge.

Hayley entered her office and sat quickly, "What's up, Sid?"

"Nuttin' much," Grahmel said, "but I have something curious to tell you."

Grahmel then told a story about young man who had walked into the pizzeria a month earlier looking for work at minimum wage and willing to do heavy lifting. The man, who gave his name as Thomas Smith, claimed he was from Bozeman, Montana, and needed cash as he worked his way west and south. Grahmel hired Smith on the spot as a dishwasher although Grahmel thought him too sophisticated for a dishwasher.

Smith lived in a low-rent boarding house walking distance from the restaurant, never complained and did everything asked of him.

Grahmel became suspicious when Smith started asking detailed questions to the pizzeria staff about Ben Hunt, Hayley Green, Bill Carter and Warren Kiffers. Smith frequented local bars after work, spent freely, and Grahmel heard that Smith asked the same questions of patrons and bartenders.

Smith quit suddenly three weeks later but was seen by one of Grahmel's servers driving out of town in a newer BMW.

Hayley, curious, said, "I have no idea who Thomas Smith is or what he could have wanted."

"Anyway, I thought I should tell you," said Grahmel. "It was like he was doing some sort of investigation or writing a book."

"Thanks. I guess. Don't know what to do with the information. I haven't upset anyone that I know of. Olympia's been happy with the work that Katy and I do."

"Smith gave me no home address or social security number. He just wanted cash," Grahmel said. "I know it was wrong to hire him, but I did. Anyway, now you know."

Hayley wrote 'Thomas Smith, Bozeman,' on a piece of paper, put it in her desk drawer and forgot about it. Two days later, she moved back to Seattle to prepare for the delivery.

*_*_*_*

Kiffers called Bill Carter. "Bad news," Kiffers said. "Joe Two Rivers has a new house outside of Yakima. He's already spent half the money."

Carter thought a moment and said, "He can sell the house and we'll make up the difference."

"I was thinking that too, but Rossi's guy says he doesn't want the deal to go away yet."

"Did you tell him that we're not getting the property from Hunt?"

"Of course," Kiffers said. "He wasn't listening, didn't care, or, worse yet, he wants to deal with Hunt himself."

"That's not going to fly," Carter responded. "Hunt's gonna tell them to get fucked, not knowing that these guys aren't so nice. Not to mention, Hunt will believe we're behind it. We gotta get out of this."

"I agree," said Kiffers. "We've walked into a one-way swamp with alligators. Shit, I told him three times we're done. He'd just say, 'We're not.'"

"How'd did you leave it?" asked Carter.

"I told him that we'd make up the money from Two Rivers and gave them the passwords for our two accounts so he can withdraw the money and interest."

"Bruni said he's leaving the money as is and didn't care about Two Rivers. He then said CasMan wants this project and we're in it, whether we like it or not.""

"And."

"That's how it ended."

"What'ya think? Should we tell Hunt what's going on?" Carter asked.

Kiffers thought for a moment. "You're joking, right?" he asked. "I can see Hunt calling Rossi and telling him to get fucked. That'll go over real big. I wouldn't say anything to anyone just yet. I don't know what to do."

"Okay. We sit tight for a while," said Carter. "You tell Two Rivers not to spend one more red, fuckin' cent."

"Sure, but I'll keep the word 'red' out of the sentence."

"It was just a figure of speech."

"The first time you met with Two Rivers, he asked you if the deal was on the level and you responded, 'Honest injun.' You might wanna think before dropping figures of speech."

*_*_*_*

Richie Porto, Gino Francisco's spy from Detroit, Oregon, came back to Apple Ridge only to find Hayley gone, and not to be back for two to three months. Bruni told Gino to have Porto return to Apple Ridge in three months.

*_*_*_*

Hayley's anxieties and superstitions worsened as her due date approached. Knowing that superstitions ran her life and made no reasonable sense, she still insisted that all blood be drawn by Doris at Capland's office.

Dr. Kimel, Hayley's high-risk OB, did everything she could to calm Hayley's fragile psyche. Kimel pointed out repeatedly that Hayley's pregnancy had progressed normally and expected the baby to be born on schedule.

Hayley told Deidre, "I'm not nervous at all about the blood work. No God could be cruel enough to have my leukemia come back while I'm carrying."

"Then why do you have to go to your oncologist to have a blood sugar for perinatal diabetes," asked Deidre, "which hasn't a thing to do with your leukemia?"

"Because, and don't ask me again."

Hayley's water broke at eleven p.m., the two nights before her actual due date. Ben arrived at her bedside in Seattle Med's OB ward, four hours later.

Hayley's first words to Ben, "I am so scared. I've been so happy that I know something bad is going to happen. You have to promise me everything will be okay?"

Ben expected Hayley's state of mind and knew exactly the words Hayley needed. "Of course," Ben said, raising his right hand. "I absolutely promise, without question or hesitation, that you and the baby will be perfect."

"I don't care about me," Hayley said. "I just want the baby to be normal. Please promise."

"No. Never. I will only promise that both of you will be perfect. And that I promise."

Hayley made Ben repeat his promise between every contraction for the next three hours, using the promise as her Lamaze mantra.

Seven hours after her water broke, Hayley delivered a healthy seven-pound, fourteen-ounce boy. Ben remained above the bed talking constantly in Hayley's ear and holding both hands.

The baby started crying immediately and Kimel, holding the baby up with the cord attached, announced, "He's perfect, look at him."

Hayley's eyes remained squeezed tightly shut and she held Ben's hands in a death grip.

"I can't look," Hayley cried, "I won't look until Ben tells me the baby's okay."

Kimel shook her head in modest disbelief, divided the umbilical cord, and handed the baby to a circulating nurse. The nurse took the baby, now quiet, to a warming table to wash him.

"I can't look at our son unless you let go of my hands," Ben whispered in Hayley's ear.

Hayley loosened her grip and Ben left Hayley's side, her eyes still tightly shut.

"Ben, tell me he's okay. Tell me."

The baby, now cleaned, appeared perfect, other than matted hair, closed eyes and a small mark on his right forehead from the delivery suction. Ben, gloved, touched the baby's foot. The baby opened his eyes revealing light blue eyes and started to cry.

Ben returned to Hayley's side, her eyes remained forcibly shut. "Do you hear him? He wants you. He's perfect."

"Do you swear?"

"Yes. I swear."

Hayley slowly opened her eyes as Ben held her head up and turned it towards the warming table and her son. The nurse, watching Hayley's histrionics end, held the screaming baby up, moved his hand in a waving motion and said, "Hi. Mom. I'm here."

Hayley's head went back to the delivery table and the tears started. "Ben. Ben. Thank you so much. Thank you. I can't believe it. I don't believe it. Is it real?"

"As real as the Cle Elum Best Western," chuckled Ben.

No one but Hayley had a clue what the comment meant. Her bawling continued on and off for the next hour until she was back in her room with the baby in a warmer next to her bed. Hayley and Ben then got to watch her parents and Deidre continue the bawling of happiness.

"You have a name yet?" Rachel, between tissues, asked.

Ben answered immediately, "Hayley wouldn't let us talk about names until the baby was here. My first choice is Agador Spartacus Hunt from the movie *Birdcage*."

Deidre and Rachel gave Ben a look of disgust as Hayley started to laugh. "Mom, Ben's just… " Hayley stopped in mid-sentence.

Ben, arms crossed, winked at Hayley and said, "It's perfect."

"You know, I agree. It is perfect. We'll call him Aggie, for short," Hayley said, looking at her mother's uncertainty.

Deidre and Rachel swiveled their heads back and forth between Hayley and Ben until Mel realized the joke and started laughing, followed by Hayley and Ben, and finally Deidre and Rachel.

"I needed that," Hayley said. "but Ben and I will decide the name alone, just the two of us. No suggestions from the peanut gallery. Maybe tomorrow."

*_*_*_*

Later that evening, Ben tried to get comfortable on the cushioned seating area under the hospital room window, a marginally reasonable substitute for a bed. He opened his eyes to find Hayley, on her side, looking back at him.

Hayley, fully awake, said, "I love you. Thank you."

"For what?"

"You know. My life. My fairy-tale rebirth. Thank you."

"You know I've had a name for a while," said Ben, sheepishly.

"I know you do. Not a name that I would have ever picked in a million years."

"You knew what I was thinking?" asked Ben.

"Izzy."

"Yes," said Ben. "Although, I know your family wants to name the baby after someone who had a long, fulfilling and meaningful life."

"That's about right," said Hayley.

"Izzy did not have a long or fulfilling life by anyone's definition," said Ben. "Aside from the fact that yours truly wouldn't be here if he hadn't sacrificed himself, his life had huge meaning to me. I'll never be done grieving for him, and I'm not sure that having my son named for him will help, but I'd like to try to honor him in some way."

"I owe you that. Isaiah Joseph 'Izzy' Hunt."

"Really?" asked Ben.

"Really."

"Your parents aren't going to like it."

"They will, in time. I think I had a great uncle named Isadore. I can always tell them Izzy was named after him."

"I don't like telling them a lie. Izzy is named after someone very important to me. I'd like to keep it that way."

"You're right," said Hayley. "Besides, names just seem to fit people in the end. If Izzy doesn't like his name later in life, he can use whatever he wants."

Ben got off the makeshift bed and gave Hayley a kiss. "Thank you." He returned to the bed and asked, "What would you have named him, if I weren't around?"

"Bill Carter Hunt."

Ben laughed. "Izzy's sounding better already."

The next morning, when the technician from the lab came into the room to draw a routine blood count from Hayley, Ben shooed her out.

Ten minutes later, Doris, the nurse from Dr. Capland's office, entered the room. She swooned over Izzy and gave Hayley and Ben a hug and kiss. "Who would have thought all this wonderful stuff could have happened?"

"Not me," Hayley proclaimed.

"He's got more hair than you had a while back," Doris chuckled. "Did you think anyone else would dare draw your blood except me? No way."

Hayley looked at Ben and mouthed, "Thank you, again."

Ben returned to Apple Ridge five days later. Hayley, planning to stay in Seattle for a month, returned to Apple Ridge when Izzy was ten days old.

"I miss you," Hayley said, arriving home. "You miss your son. It's not fair to be away."

*_*_*_*

Victor Rossi was impatient. Very impatient.

*_*_*_*

Back in Apple Ridge, with unemployment reaching fourteen percent, Hayley had no problem finding a full-time nanny. Audrey Ward, a fifty-five-year-old mother and grandmother, lived close, had excellent references and badly needed the work. Hayley returned to her job when Izzy was three months old and sold her condo in Seattle. With the money from the condo sale, Ben and Hayley purchased an unoccupied four-bedroom house around the corner from Hayley's rental and moved in immediately.

Amber, now an unofficial member of Hayley's family, came to Hayley and Ben's home every day after school if she wasn't busy with school activities, and would stay until her grandfather returned home after work. Amber played with Izzy and often helped Mrs. Ward prepare dinner, frequently staying to eat. Izzy's second spoken word after "mommy" would be 'Ambo,' preceding 'daddy' by two weeks.

*_*_*_*

Victor Rossi was crazed.

Richie Porto returned to Apple Ridge six months later. His instructions were to tail Ben and Hayley's movements, looking particularly for times and places where 'special negotiations' could take place. Porto needed no additional explanation.

Porto returned to Portland three weeks later and called Angelo Bruni.

"Hunt's at the local hospital most of the time, even weekends when he's on call," Porto reported. "His wife's a machine. Work, baby, groceries and the rare dinner out. Only thing out of the ordinary were two weekend trips to a remote forest area that has a cabin. They went both times with their baby. The trips were two weeks apart, arriving Friday night and returning Sunday afternoon. From what people have heard, no one else is invited there. They just disappear for two or three days. I tailed them to an entry point behind some grocery store in the middle of fuckin' nowhere."

"Interesting," Bruni said.

"I figured you'd want more info on the cabin," Porto continued.

"Absolutely," Bruni said.

"Anyway, I went back on a Wednesday, parked quarter of a mile from the store and hacked my way through the forest until I got to a rarely used path. Leads to a little lake and a small log cabin, three miles in, about an hour walk. Cabin sits in a clearing off the lake. There's a small hill behind the cabin, with rocks, some trees and a good vantage point over the back of the cabin to the lake. No cell phone reception, no Internet, no electricity, no satellite dishes. Might as well have fallen off the end of the earth."

"How do ya know when they're going to this cabin?" asked Bruni.

"Yeah. I called the local hospital on the Friday night that I followed them to the entry point. I asked for Dr. Hunt. He was signed out for the weekend to a doctor in Cle Elum. My guess is that he'll sign out when he goes to the cabin. Makes sense since there's no connection to the outside world."

"Anything else?"

"The property boundaries are a quarter of a mile north and west, up over the hill behind the cabin. Outside the boundaries are public hunting regions. Someone, with difficulty, could approach the cabin, up, over and down the hill, looking for large game, like bear or elk, maybe get lost. Get my drift."

"Of course. Can you send me maps?" said Bruni.

"Done, already. Maps, entry and exit points. Hunting season for large game is September seventh to October fifteenth."

"You did good, Richie," Bruni said. "Best you stay away from Apple Ridge from now on. I'll tell Gino you did good. I wouldn't tell anyone about these trips."

"You can trust me, Mr. Bruni. I'm not gonna tell no one."

*-*-*-*

Angelo Bruni sat with Victor Rossi at a busy, local Starbucks and explained everything he now knew about Apple Ridge, Hayley and Ben.

"Bottom line, what do you think?" Rossi asked.

"This cabin, in the middle of nowhere, is perfect. So many possibilities. If we can get a couple of guys in and out of there from the hunting area, they could be gone by Saturday night, Sunday morning. No one finds either of them for days. At some point the property becomes available and either Carter buys it or we buy it."

"Almost too convenient," said Rossi. "We've got to get guys that can't be traced," said Rossi. "I'm thinking those two Columbians that we used in Guadalajara eighteen months ago. They're expensive but good. We can have that kid from Portland get them outfitted. Can we trust him? He knows too much already."

Bruni responded, "Doubtful Gino will have all the stuff the Columbians need in Portland. They like those German rifles. I'll get gear shipped, real quiet. As to the Gino's kid, he'll keep his mouth shut. We can deal with him afterwards, if you want."

"Too risky not to deal with him. He knows too much already," said Rossi. "Too bad, eh?"

"I suppose so, not a bad kid," said Bruni. "I'll talk to Gino later about it. We'll make it right for him."

"Problems? Think of anything else?" asked Rossi.

"Carter or Kiffers, his attorney," said Bruni. "They may have an idea we're involved but won't be able to prove jack shit. They're also smart enough to know that if they implicate us, we can implicate them just as easily. I'm guessing they'll say nothing. Also, there's no guarantee that they'll go to the cabin any specific weekend. Our guys may be there a week or two. That'll cost."

"We also gotta make sure that Carter and Kiffers aren't wandering about that weekend," Victor added. "They need airtight alibis without knowing a thing. Offer them some rooms and free stuff in Vegas as thanks for trying. The Indian's no problem. He's already spent half his wad."

"We do need a plan if this turns to shit," Bruni said, "although I don't see how. The Columbians would have to screw up and get caught. Then, Carter or Kiffers go to the cops."

"Yeah. We'll put a couple of guys near Apple Ridge. Can't have those jerk-offs talking. I like the plan. First, let's see if you can get those Columbians."

"Got it." Bruni said.

"Angie, baby, I want this so bad. Make it happen," demanded Rossi.

*_*_*_*

Bruni, smiling broadly, sat in front of Rossi four days later at the same Starbucks. "Those two bags of Columbian coffee you like are being shipped. Should be here by the end of August."

Rossi smiled.

"Also, I called the hospital and they publish the on-call list months in advance," said Bruni. "Hunt's signed out first and third weekend in September."

Rossi smiled. *I can taste this.*

*_*_*_*

Sid Grahmel called Hayley. "Just wanted to let you know that dishwasher I told you about, the guy from Montana, was spotted again in town. I don't think he worked anywhere. Stayed for a while, then left. Asking questions about you and Dr. Hunt."

"What kind of questions?" Hayley asked. "Maybe he's working for the National Health Service or Washington State."

"Not about your work or Ben's. Only where you go and what you do."

"Should I call the sheriff?" Hayley said, asking for advice.

"He didn't break any laws, far as I know," said Grahmel, "so I'm not sure the sheriff would care."

"I suppose so. Next time anyone sees him, let me know. Ben and I need to meet him and find out what he's up to," said Hayley.

"Will do."

*_*_*_*

Angelo Bruni called Kiffers and Carter to offer them a free week in Vegas, all expenses paid, for trying to make the casino deal work.

Kiffers called Carter. "I wouldn't have believed it but these guys were pretty generous in the end. I was wrong."

"Usually it's you that's skeptical," said Carter. "I smell a rat. I just don't know what kind of rat yet."

Kiffers took the offer and left Wednesday, September third, two days before hunting season's opening on a private jet chartered by CasManUs. Carter refused and told Kiffers he should have as well.

*_*_*_*

Richie Porto met two men at Portland International Airport on a flight from Houston on Thursday, September fourth.

Porto had no trouble identifying the two as they entered the baggage area. Handsome, mid-thirties, dark, nervous, searching eyes.

"You guys have some coffee for me?" Porto used the password phrase given to him by Bruni.

"Only dark roast," said the taller of the two men, giving the correct response.

"I'm Richie," Porto said.

"I'm David," the taller man continued, "This here's Emilio. That's what our ID says. All you need to know."

Porto nodded. He was impressed that David's English was perfect. "You got bags?"

"Just some clothes in these carry-ons. Nothing else. You're gonna give us the stuff we need?" David asked."

"Yep. Already in the back of my car."

"Good."

Porto added, "I've never opened the boxes sent from…."

Emilio interrupted, speaking for the first time, in a heavy Hispanic accent, "Amigo. Don't say no names. You understand?"

Porto answered, "Yeah. Yeah. You pick up your rental and follow me."

David shook his head no. "We're not going to follow you," he said. "We'll meet you outside the airport. You pick an exit and find some parking lot that has no cameras and text me an address only. No calls." David wrote his text number on a piece of paper and handed it to Porto. "Learn the number and toss it."

Twenty minutes later, Porto texted David from the side of a small strip mall with a dry cleaner, a small Mexican restaurant, a Subway and four empty storefronts. David pulled up in his rental ten minutes later. Each popped their trunk open and Porto put two boxes in David's trunk. The transfer took less than twenty seconds.

"Here's the address of a hardware store in Cle Elum, Washington. They won't hassle you getting a hunting license," Porto said.

David, eyes focused intensely at Porto's forehead, said, "We'll find a place to stay tonight and tomorrow night ourselves. Better if you disappear."

Porto nodded and listened.

"If the stuff in the boxes isn't right, I'll text you and ask where I can deliver the coffee. You'll tell me where to meet. No phone calls. You don't hear from me, we're good. Erase any contact information you have, even though it's phony."

Porto nodded again. *These guys are scary.*

*_*_*_*

Forty minutes later, David and Emilio checked into a Travelodge outside of Troutdale, Oregon, east of the Portland airport. Once in their room, they opened the sealed boxes given to them by Richie Porto. Both nodded approval as they extracted two Heckler and Koch MSG90 sniper rifles with five 7.62 x 51 mm NATO rounds in the cartridge and two extra cartridge clips taped to the gun barrel.

The second box contained two sets of orange reflective hunting gear and two sets of army style camouflaged gear. The box also contained a DeLorme InReach SE Satellite Messenger GPS tracking device with the coordinates for the cabin and exit and entry points and maps of the region, backpacks, rope, and two folding shovels. The box contained two body bags.

"Me gusta mucho," said Emilio, smiling.

David shook his head. "Hey, cabrone, you might want to think about speaking English while we're here."

"Fuck jyou. Is that English enough?"

*_*_*_*

Ben checked the weather forecast in the Apple Ridge area for the weekend - partly sunny and sixty-five degrees. Ben confirmed plans on Wednesday to sign out that weekend to the surgeons in Cle Elum. Ben knew that hunting season opened that Saturday, but his only concern, not shared with Hayley, was for the health of Buck, Bella and the two fawns. He hoped they wouldn't stray far from the lake and wander into harm's way.

On Thursday afternoon, Bruni called Bill Carter to re-offer a trip to Vegas.

"Nah," Carter said, "I don't like Vegas and my wife hates it. Besides, we would have gone with Warren but he left yesterday morning."

"No big deal. It's CasMan's jet. We can have it back to the Cle Elum airport in two hours. We'd really like to treat you and the Missus to a week in Vegas," said Bruni, pushing hard.

"Nope," said Carter. "Hunting season starts this weekend. I think I'm going to shoot pheasant."

"You going with a bunch of friends?" Bruni asked.

"No. I have a special place I go," Carter said, "usually with my son, but he's busy. So, I'll probably just go it myself."

"Carter, that's not a good idea. You shouldn't do that."

"And why not? I've been going opening week for my whole life. I'm not going to stop going for you."

"Trust me, Carter," Bruni demanded, "you don't want to go shooting alone. It's important to us and I don't want you to ask why."

"I don't get it," said Carter.

"You don't have to get it. Listen up real careful," Bruni said, raising the tone of this voice. "I'm only going to say it once. You are not to go hunting this weekend. Please don't ask me to say it again."

"Fine, I hear you," Carter said. *Screw you. I'll do what I want.*

"I'll talk to you next week," Bruni said. "Stay busy this weekend at home with a bunch of friends and family."

"I got it," said Carter, ending the conversation.

Carter immediately called Warren Kiffers in Las Vegas, "I just got off the phone with that Bruni guy. We had the strangest conversation, that I didn't understand. He asked me……." Carter echoed the entire conversation.

"I don't get it either," Kiffers said. "Anyway, I'm having a great time here. Front tables at all the shows and my meals are free. They won't even let me leave a tip. CasMan's got a ton of traction. You should have come."

"It's okay. Not my style. You enjoy yourself," Carter said.

"They're flying me home late Sunday night," Kiffers said. "I'll talk to you Monday. That said, if I were you, and I don't know why exactly, I wouldn't go hunting."

"Hmmph. We'll see. I don't like people telling me what to do."

## Chapter 17

Late Friday afternoon, as Ben, Hayley and Izzy motored to the entry point for the cabin, Ben fiddled with his son's foot. Izzy appeared to care less, concentrating on Hayley's right breast.

Ben asked, "Do I really need to keep seeing Jon? Seems like a waste of my time and his."

Hayley, switching breasts, said "No changes. Life is too good now. So there."

"Okay, boss. Whatever."

The feeding completed, Hayley said, "I've been meaning to tell you something. Sid Grahmel, the guy who owns Pizza Heaven, told me that some guy has been in Apple Ridge asking questions about you and me. He was here six months ago and worked as a dishwasher for three weeks and left driving a Beamer. He was here a month ago, again asking a bunch more questions."

"What's his name?" asked Ben.

"Sid said Thomas Smith from Bozeman. Ring a bell?" asked Hayley.

"No. Maybe we can research it a bit more this week when we get back."

Hayley nodded.

The overcast sky muted the Cascade foothills.

"The forecast was for sunny with some clouds. I hope it clears," said Hayley. As they parked at Greavy's store, she looked at her watch and said, "It's still ninety minutes to sunset."

Hayley quickly switched Izzy to a cloth diaper as Ben left a note for Greavy. Ten minutes into the hike, the sun broke through and the temperature rose quickly to the mid-seventies.

"That's better. What a great day," Hayley trumpeted to the trees.

Izzy sat comfortably on Ben's chest in a soft kangaroo pouch.

By the time they reached the cabin, the mountaintops, bathed in fall sun, glowed like fresh paint. As Ben opened the cabin and started a fire, Hayley donned the chest pouch, grabbed Izzy, ran to the lake edge, threw off her shoes and dipped her toes in the water.

She yelled back to the cabin, "Ben. Still nice. I'm guessing at least seventy. I can't wait to go swimming tomorrow. Izzy's going to be in seventh heaven." Izzy was already squirming, trying to get into the lake.

As Hayley and Izzy walked back onto the shore, Hayley heard loud crackling branches to her right. Turning quickly to see rustling in the bushes at the edge of the lake, she reflexively put her hands around Izzy's head to protect him. She didn't know if she should stand, run or scream for Ben, when four deer walked into the clearing and approached the north side of the cabin.

Hayley relaxed and beamed. "Hey, you guys scared the dickens out of me." She spun Izzy in the pouch to face the new arrivals. "Look, Izzy. Deer. They're here to say hello. There's Buck, Bella, Kiddo and Bambi." Hayley waved Izzy's hand at her old friends. The family of deer had come to trust Ben and Hayley and now, Izzy. As Hayley walked back to the cabin, Izzy started to giggle as Buck, the large ten point stag, lowered and raised his head, as if to wave hello back.

Hayley talked to the stag is a low monotone, "Don't worry big guy, you're safe here. I have some salt and carrots for you and the family. Let me put Izzy down first."

The deer picked up their heads quickly as Hayley spun around to find a sprinting, naked Ben dive into the lake.

He surfaced quickly and yelled. "I was so sweaty from the hike and I'm too tired to heat up the shower. The little rat's getting heavy. It's not so cold."

Hayley needed no encouragement. She put Izzy down, shed her

backpack and clothes onto the ground, picked up Izzy, threw his diaper and shirt onto the ground and waded confidently into the water. Ben kissed Hayley sweetly and took Izzy. Hayley dunked herself for a moment, surfaced and said, "Oh, that feels soooo good."

Ben kissed her again. "I bet the cabin is warm by now."

Three naked butts rushed back to the cabin. The deer watched with interest, motionless, hoping Hayley would remember to put out stuff for them. Ninety seconds later, Hayley exited the cabin, wearing only a tee-shirt, and sprinkled a generous amount of table salt on the wooden table in front of the cabin along with a handful of unpeeled carrots, then hurried back inside.

Hayley breast fed Izzy and put him in a small, wooden, swinging crib Ben had built. She sang a soft lullaby and watched sleep come peacefully. Hayley kissed Izzy's forehead and murmured, "I love you so much. Sleep tight."

Ben watched in awe at the budding mother-son relationship. Once Izzy had clearly found sleep, Hayley turned to Ben. She looked at Ben, then at his full erection, and smiled. "Not very subtle are we now?"

"I was trying to be subtle. Honestly, I was. It's hard," Ben said.

"That's for sure," Hayley laughed at the double entendre.

Ben swooped Hayley off her feet. "You're as light as you were when we first met."

"Actually, three pounds more." Hayley said, cupping her breasts, "All in my boobs. These things I'd never had before." Her tee shirt had small rings of milk stains on each side.

"I love them. I love everything about you," Ben singsonged. He laid Hayley on the bed and starting with her forehead kissed his way down.

"Be careful," Hayley said, "Milk is going to start pouring all over our sheets."

"I could care less. I'm going to enjoy all of you."

Fifteen minutes later, Hayley's guttural screams of enjoyment only heightened their excitement.

"Shh. You're going to wake Izzy," whispered Ben.

"No. No way. I know my son," Hayley, breathing heavily, responded, "He'd sleep through a thermonuclear explosion. Although, I may scare the deer away for weeks."

Sweaty, tired and fulfilled, Ben and Hayley lay cradled on their sides, heads turned towards a sleeping baby.

Hayley broke the silence, "If you would have told me three years ago, I'd be prancing around naked in a log cabin, in the middle of nowhere, totally in love, sexually aroused most of the weekend, looking at my child and husband, I would have had you committed for total insanity."

"Thanks to you," Ben said, "I'm naked in a log cabin, totally in love, sexually aroused all of the time, looking at my child and wife, and at some semblance of peace with myself." Ben started nibbling on Hayley's ear, and then picked himself up onto his elbows. "However, I take umbrage at your insinuation that we're in the middle of nowhere. This cabin holds memories dear to me from childhood. Admittedly, those memories pale in comparison, to what I'm looking at now."

At ten p.m., after Izzy had been fed again, Ben blew out the two lanterns, retreated to bed and curled around Hayley. "When will you need to get up to feed him?"

"Four hours, maybe longer. If my breasts are aching, I'll get up earlier. Hopefully, he's going to start sleeping through the night any time now."

At six a.m. a screaming and hungry baby woke up his parents.

*_*_*_*

David and Emilio checked into the Cle Elum Best Western on

Friday afternoon. They paid cash for four nights and told the manager they didn't want to be disturbed and specifically, didn't want housekeeping coming into the room under any circumstance until they left the following Tuesday morning.

The Columbians had no intention of staying past Saturday night.

The Cle Elum Home and Garden store, two blocks away, closed at six p.m. David and Emilio entered the store, purposely, at five fifty p.m. and purchased non-resident licenses to hunt elk for four hundred ninety-seven dollars each. Again, they paid in cash. For the clerk, anxious to close for the night, they produced perfect ID from Plano, Texas and certification of passing an online, hunter education course. The clerk gave each a cursory look, then handed the two Columbians all the licenses, tags and stickers they would need for the next day's shoot. Happily, the clerk closed the store at five after six.

The two Columbians, awake at five a.m., on the road at five fifteen, reached the entry point parking lot to hunting area #342 at ten to six, just as the sun crested from the east. A camper, already parked at the entry lot, had no movement suggesting the occupants were asleep or had already headed out. The satellite GPS put David and Emilio five miles, as the crow flies, to Ben's cabin. They donned their regulation, orange, hunting gear jackets, shouldered their rifles and backpacks and began hiking at a brisk pace.

Emilio asked, "Cuanto tiempo?"

"Two and a half hours, maybe three," said David. "Depends how rough the terrain is."

*_*_*_*

Bill Carter arose at seven and said to his wife, "We'll be back before four." We meaning Carter and his dog, Pancho, a six-year-old, eighty-five pound, Chocolate Labrador.

Carter drove leisurely towards his favorite hunting spot. As usual, he stopped into the local McDonald's for a coffee and two Egg

McMuffins and bought a third Egg McMuffin for Pancho.

Rosie, the McDonald's cashier, knew Bill Carter well, and asked, "Where ya goin, Mr. C? First day of hunting, eh?"

"Off to shoot some pheasant near Yakima River Canyon, Rosie. One of these days I'll bring you one."

"That's a deal, Mr. Carter," Rosie chirped, then asked, "Ya goin' alone?"

"Yep. Just me and Pancho."

Rosie's question immediately reminded Carter of Angelo Bruni's caution against hunting by himself.

"You be real careful now, Mr. C," Rosie added. "Lots of hunters out there today. Some of them pretty stupid."

Carter nodded thanks and turned to walk back to his truck. Pancho's head was out the truck window, tongue out and drooling, as Carter held up a bag containing the treat. After feeding Pancho, then settling in the driver's seat, Carter stopped and thought again about Angelo Bruni's and Rosie's warnings.

*Why didn't Bruni make a big deal about hunting until I said I was going alone? Why would I be in danger going alone? Why was Bruni so desperate for me to go to Las Vegas with Warren? ……..*

*……Oh my God, it's not me in danger. Shit. Shit.*

Carter called Apple Ridge General. "Is Ben Hunt there? It's Bill Carter and it's important."

"No, Mr. Carter, sir, Dr. Hunt is signed out for the weekend. Don't know where he might be."

"Thanks." Carter then dialed his daughter-in-law and asked for Katy MacArthur's phone number. Carter dialed Katy.

"Katy, Bill Carter here. Where is your boss this weekend?"

"Why do you ask?" said Katy, unable to hide her suspicion.

"I need to ask her something very important," Carter pleaded, "and very private. I swear I'm not hassling her, I promise."

"It's not likely you'll be able to talk to her until Sunday night. I'm certain she went up to Ben's cabin with her son and Ben."

"Thanks. That's what I thought. Thanks again."

*Shit, shit.*

Carter turned back onto the highway, then speed-dialed Warren Kiffers.

"Warren, sorry to wake you. I figured it out. Bruni wanted you and me to have alibis. Vegas was perfect. He was fine with me hunting, except alone. They're going after Ben and Hayley."

"You're delusional. You woke me up to tell me that?" Kiffers mumbled, still half asleep after a late night, huge meal and a bottle of wine.

"I'm not delusional, God damn it. It makes sense," Carter yelled into the speakerphone. "Why would Bruni be so adamant that I not hunt alone? It's got to be the answer. We needed alibis."

"So what are you going to do?" asked Warren, now fully awake.

"I'm going to their cabin. I don't have time to call Sheriff Robertson and explain everything. I need you to do it. The entry point and trail is behind Creavy's market out on Highway 424. Charley will know where it is."

"Listen to yourself, Bill. You're way overthinking this."

"Maybe," Carter replied, "but I can't take a chance. If I'm wrong, what's the big deal? If I'm right…well, let's hope I'm wrong. Get your butt out of bed and call Charley."

Carter headed his Range Rover towards Creavy's Market at breakneck speed and arrived twenty-five minutes later. A large red

'CLOSED' sign hung on the door, so Carter pinned a cryptic handwritten note on the door.

> *Creavy*
>
> *It's 8:30 on Saturday morning. I'm concerned about Ben. Sheriff should be here within the hour. I'm heading towards the cabin. I'll mark the trail with broken branches.*
>
> *Bill Carter*

At eight thirty, rifle on his back and Pancho by his side, Carter headed towards Ben's cabin.

*_*_*_*

By eight forty-five a.m., the Columbians had reached the upper ridge, high above Ben's cabin. From the ridge they could see the far side of the small lake and the second ridge below that would give them a clear view of the cabin.

They shed their bright orange reflective gear and donned camouflage fatigues.

"Move slowly," David said, "and try not to make noise. I don't know if we might create an echo that'll give us away."

"No way we're bringing bodies out," Emilio said, shaking his head.

David acknowledged the obvious, "Right," then started down the steep slope slowly followed by his partner.

Just after nine, Emilio and David had descended to the lower ridge. A clear view of the lake and two-thirds of the cabin showed them what they needed to know. A man and a woman were at the lake edge, pants legs rolled up, washing small white cloths. A small baby, clad only in a shirt, sat on the lake edge slapping mud with both hands.

Deer, seemingly unfazed by the three humans, grazed comfortably twenty-five yards from the lake edge.

Without conversation both men quietly unpacked their rifles. David attached the riflescope, set up a low tripod and mounted the rifle. The range finder measured one hundred fifty-four yards to the man. David kept the rifle's safety engaged.

Emilio waited for David to set his gun site, then deliberately and quietly started down the ridge. He shouldered his rifle with a bullet in the firing chamber and the gunlock disengaged.

When the woman turned back towards the ridge to check on the baby, Emilio froze against ridge wall. The woman laughed, never looking up towards the ridge, and turned back to the lake. Emilio, unnoticed, continued his slow descent towards the cabin and the lake.

*_*_*_*

Down at lake edge, Hayley reaffirmed the obvious. "Are you sure you don't want to consider bringing in disposable diapers and burying them? When it gets cold, we won't be able to do this."

Ben laughed, "I'm not carrying out ten pounds of shit, even my son's. We won't be able to bury it deep enough to keep the animals from digging it up, not to mention, when the ground freezes, we won't be able to dig at all. I can't even imagine what the natives did."

"I'm guessing the tepees smelled like poop," Hayley laughed.

Ben stood up laughing and looked to the deer grazing on the grass twenty yards away. "Buck's not laughing and neither is........."

Ben halted in mid sentence as Buck's head and tail went straight up to full extension. Bella followed a second later, then Kiddo and Bambi. Buck, neck muscles straining, stared intently over the cabin towards the ridge. Bella and her two youngsters immediately turned and fled at full speed into the forest away from the ridge. The large stag looked at Ben for a second, lowered and raised his head, then turned to follow his family.

Ben yelled, "Hayley. Something's coming that scared the deer. Could be a large animal. Cougar or bear. Drop everything and start swinging your arms and yelling at the top of your lungs and get into the cabin. I'll grab Izzy. Now. Yell and run."

Ben started screaming, while Hayley, seeing nothing of concern in her vision, thought Ben's histrionics were ridiculous. Still, she swung her arms, half-heartedly yelled and went directly towards the cabin front door. Meanwhile, Ben angled towards a stunned and frightened Izzy. Ben scooped Izzy up, and then followed Hayley to the cabin, screaming all the while.

Emilio, halfway down the lower ridge and shielded by pine trees could not see the sprint, but he heard the yelling. He continued down the hill in double time. David, up above and surprised by the sudden movement and yelling, had to flip off the gunlock on the rifle before aiming. The woman had already disappeared into the cabin. David sighted the running man and took one shot that whistled by Ben's neck on the side opposite Izzy's head.

Ben saw the muzzle flash as the bullet sliced quickly through the top of his shirt taking skin from his left shoulder. Ben, already screaming at the top of his lungs to scare away a large animal, knew immediately what had happened but continued to run. Hayley had already opened the cabin door shielding her from the site of the sniper above. She saw the blood spurting from Ben's neck and started to scream, in earnest.

Ben flew into the cabin, rolled onto the floor protecting Izzy and yelled, "Lock the door. Lock the door."

Hayley locked the deadbolt and turned. Izzy, blood stained from Ben's wound, was howling.

Hayley grabbed Izzy and spun him around looking for bleeding. "Is Izzy okay? Is he hurt?"

Ben stood and grabbed his bleeding shoulder. "Izzy's fine. I'm bleeding."

Hayley was yelling, "What's happening, Ben? What's happening?"

"Someone just shot me. I don't understand it. A drunk hunter, maybe. I just don't know." Ben tore off a pillowcase from the bed and applied pressure to his shoulder wound. He moved quickly to the window south of the door, closed and bolted the wooden shutter.

Ben yelled, "Close and lock that shutter."

After Hayley secured her window, she bent to pick up Izzy. A bullet whistled over her head after penetrating the shutter, sending splinters through the cabin.

"What's happening? Who's doing this?"

Ben listened but didn't answer as reflexes from two tours in Afghanistan kicked in. In seconds, he grabbed his Winchester Model 70, a rifle first owned by his father, loaded five rounds of .270 Win, as the second bullet came through the opposite shutter. Ben filled his pocket with another ten shells. As Ben donned his boots, he instructed Hayley to do the same.

Hayley screamed, "Who's doing this?"

Ben, with eerie calm, directed the hyperventilating Hayley, "You have to stop yelling and listen to me. Someone's trying to shoot us. Hold Izzy and sit. Don't move unless I say move."

Ben went to the window, put his rifle through the hole in the shutter created by the first bullet and fired two rounds randomly towards the lake, whistling through the branches of the Ponderosa Pines surrounding the cabin.

Hayley, close to hysteria, yelled, "Did you see someone? Did you?"

"No, but whoever's out there knows we're armed. It'll stop them for a moment. You and Izzy will be safer down in the cellar. Try to keep Izzy quiet. I need to be able to listen carefully. Voices, footsteps, anything." Ben threw a blanket and clothes for Hayley and Izzy into the cellar.

Hayley could not contain her fear, "What are we going to do? I'm scared. What's happening?"

Ben implored, "Please, I don't know what's going on. I need quiet. I need to get you two down in the cellar. At some point, I may need to go out there and…"

Hayley screamed, "You're not leaving me here, even for a second."

"Okay. Okay. For now, we stay put and do nothing but listen. There has to be at least two of them. The shot that hit my shoulder came from the low ridge above the cabin. I saw the flash before I was hit. The shot through the shutter came from the front of the cabin fifteen seconds later. No one could have made it down from the ridge in less than thirty seconds. I don't think they'd be stupid enough to rush the window; the bars will keep them out. "

"What are we going to do?" pleaded Hayley.

"I don't know yet. I'm not leaving you. You were right, I can't just go out there. The rifle on the ridge was probably surprised by our dash. He won't be again. I expect he'll stay up there and wait for us to make a move."

A bullet then ripped onto the roof and hit the top of the chimney sending ash into the cabin.

"Yep," Ben said. "That's the guy up on the ridge. We're just going to have to wait."

"Wait for what?" Hayley cried. "What if they put fire to the cabin? We can't be in here."

"Not likely they'd do that. The Forest Service copters are all over the place today and would see the smoke from fifty miles. There'd be rangers here in minutes. They won't draw attention. I think we surprised them by getting into the cabin so quickly. We were easy targets in the lake. We'll just wait and listen."

Hayley dressed herself and Izzy, then created a makeshift bed on the floor of the cellar. Within minutes Izzy fell asleep and all was quiet.

"Shhh," Ben whispered. "I think the guy down below is walking around the cabin. He won't find anything. I expect he'll go back out front and wait. I don't know what to do. We're in a vice."

The right hand shutter was partially blown off its hinges by two rapid-fire shots sending splinters of wood throughout the cabin. A large splinter embedded in Hayley's left shoulder as she stood on the ladder from the cellar. Hayley stared at the four-inch piece of wood penetrating her shirt but was too stunned to say anything.

"You okay?" Ben asked, quietly.

Collecting her senses, Hayley started to weep, "No, I'm not okay. Someone's trying to kill us."

"Please, Hayley. Are you hurt?"

Hayley stared at the splinter of wood and moved her hand to touch it. "No, not really. I didn't even feel it until I looked."

"Don't touch it," pleaded Ben. "I'll deal with the splinter later. Get down and close the cellar door. He may be stupid enough to rush the window."

Hayley lowered herself but kept the trap door ajar.

Ben listened closely as he could hear creaking on the porch steps. Hearing small rocks thrown onto the porch below the window to the left of the door, Ben moved his aim to the opposite right side. *A ruse.* A hunting cap flashed in the right window between bullet holes in the shutter. Ben fired just below the holes, knocking the hat away from the cabin.

"Mierda. Mierda," echoed through the cabin. The yelling continued moving away from the porch.

Hayley's head popped up from the cellar, "What happened?"

"I think I just shot someone in the hand. Whoever it is, he's Hispanic. He kept screaming 'shit' in Spanish."

"Who hates us enough to do this?"

"I don't know. Bill Carter?" Ben seethed.

"No. He'd never do this," Hayley cried.

"I don't know. Somebody."

"What do we do now?" asked Hayley.

"We wait," said Ben.

"For what?"

"For them to do something. They don't want to be here any longer than they have to. We wait."

The temperature and humidity in the unventilated cabin rose quickly. Ten minutes, which felt like an eternity, elapsed before Hayley, head just out of the cellar, said, "I can't take this. I broke off the jutting part of the splinter."

Ben, nestled to the side of the right window, said, "Shh. I need to listen. I thought I heard a dog bark in the distance a second ago."

A few seconds went by.

"There it is again," Ben said. "A dog's out there and is closer. Someone's coming."

Hayley repeated, "Someone is coming." Then added, "We're gonna make it."

The déjà vu of Hayley's remark, identical to Izzy's hearing the Marines coming down the mountain, made Ben shudder. He visualized a hand grenade, a limonka, thrown into the cabin. Ben calmed and repeated, "Shh."

Emilio heard the dog too. He stood and looked to the north. He whistled, got David's attention, on the ridge and yelled, "Perro."

Pancho, Carter's dog, barking loudly, bounded into the clearing and headed towards the crouching Emilio twenty feet in front of the cabin. Emilio stood and fired a shot hitting Labrador's right front shoulder. The dog rolled over from the impact and started whimpering.

Emilio and Ben could both hear a man's voice yelling, "Pancho, Pancho. Are you hurt?" Carter had reached the edge of the clearing.

"Otros, otros," Emilio screamed loudly.

Ben moved close to the semi-shattered shutter and listened. He heard a voice from above. The man on the high ridge acknowledging that "others" were coming. Ben moved close to the semi-shattered shutter and listened.

Ben understood the meaning of "otros" and from the rapid footsteps, he was certain the man near the cabin was running northward towards the voice and away from the cabin.

Ben yelled to Hayley, "Down and lock the cellar." *Someone's walking into a trap.* Ben counted on the shooter above moving his attention to the "otros".

Luckily, Ben guessed correctly.

Ben quickly unbolted, then opened the door, and hurled himself off the porch. He rolled once and assumed the prone position, five feet from the porch, with his rifle in front of him, ready.

Ben knew immediately that he needed to be closer to the porch and the cabin roof to shield him from the shooter above.

Bill Carter, rifle in his hands, entered the clearing at a semi-trot from the north. Ben hoped the shooter above continued his attention to Carter.

Carter saw his dog lying on its side bleeding and began screaming, "Pancho. Pancho." Carter did not see either shooter. Carter, moving forward and well in the open, quickly scanned the clearing when he was hit in the side with a shot from the crouching Emilio. Carter spun around and hit the ground screaming.

Ben fired once, hitting Emilio in the side of his chest, hurtling him forwards. Ben knew instantly that his target would die. He rolled quickly towards the cabin as two shots from the ridge above hit the dirt where he had been. Ben continued rolling until the porch and roof of the cabin shielded him. Ben turned to his left and saw Bill Carter sitting up aiming his rifle up the ridge.

Carter fired three rounds at the upper ridge before a shot from the ridge knocked the gun out of his hand and a second shot entered his right upper chest. Carter was slammed backwards by the shell and then rolled prone towards his injured Labrador.

Watching Carter's plight unfold, Ben knew he had an opening, stood and moved away from the cabin to see the shooter continuing to watch the prone Carter. Ben fired once hitting the man in the left shoulder and knocking him back. Looking down at Ben, the man rose onto his knees holding the rifle in his right hand trying to site the rifle with his remaining good arm. Ben's second shot hit the man just under his breastbone and blew him against the back wall of the ridge.

Ben quickly stood, bullet in the chamber, and approached the first shooter. He found Emilio, lying face down in a pool of blood, breathing, but barely. Emilio's rifle lay to the side. Ben knew the man would die quickly. Aiming the rifle at the man's head, Ben rolled Emilio over with his foot to ensure he had no other weapons. Ben grabbed Emilio's rifle and then ran towards Bill Carter.

Ben could hear the sounds of a helicopter approaching and looked up to see the US Forest Service chopper heading towards the clearing.

Ben got to Carter, a portion of his right hand missing, his shoulder partially torn and three bleeding entrance wounds on his side and back.

Ben knelt in front of Carter's limp body and rolled him onto his side. Carter opened his eyes and whispered loudly, "I'm sorry, Ben…. I'm so sorry….. I didn't mean….. this to happen."

"What happened? Who was after us?" Ben asked.

"Victor. Victor..... Rossi.... He wanted..... your... land," Carter whispered. Each phrase spoken between feeble attempts at breathing. "We had a deal... but we needed.... your property.... I told him... that the deal.... was off ...but he wouldn't listen... I'm so sorry."

The increasing noise from the helicopter's rotors made Carter's next few words unintelligible. Ben put his mouth next to Carter's ear and yelled, "Who is Victor? Who is Rosy? Tell me." Ben then moved his ear next to Carter's mouth.

Carter whispered, "Victor Rossi. ...I'm so....."

Carter closed his eyes.

Ben laid Carter's head down gently and started a run to the cabin to check on Hayley and Izzy as three US Forest Rangers exited their helicopter with weapons drawn.

"Drop the gun and get down on the ground," the three screamed in semi-unison.

Ben knew better to keep moving with a rifle in his hands. He stopped, threw his rifle to the ground and went down to his hands and knees.

The lead officer approached quickly, his handgun aimed at Ben's chest.

Ben picked up his head towards the officer and yelled, "My wife and child are in the cabin."

The officer screamed back, "Get down on the ground. Now."

Ben knew Hayley and Izzy were in no danger. Ben put his face to the ground, spread-eagled and waited. A man stood over him as the other US Forest Service officers looked at the two dead men, Emilio and Bill Carter.

"There's another shooter up on the low ridge behind the cabin," Ben yelled, with his head down. "I'm pretty sure he's dead but I'd be careful."

The officer yelled to the others, warning them. One of the rangers, gun drawn, inched slowly up the ridge. Another ranger stood in front of the cabin and trained his rifle on the ridge above.

Minutes later, the ranger yelled down from the ridge, "Another guy up here. Dead."

Charley Robertson and a deputy entered the clearing, guns drawn, out of breath. Robertson scanned the clearing, mouth agape. He saw two dead men, including his friend, Bill Carter, and Bill's whimpering Labrador. All three lay in pools of blood. The dog, clearly in pain, labored trying to inch his way closer to Carter. Twenty paces further, Robertson saw Ben Hunt on the ground, spread-eagled, with a gun pointed at his head by a US Forest Ranger.

Robertson yelled, "Oh my God. What the hell happened here? Ben are you okay?"

Ben raised his head and yelled, "I'm fine, Charley. Hayley and Izzy are in the cabin's cellar. Get them. Tell them it's safe."

Robertson holstered his handgun and said something to his deputy who ran into the cabin.

Robertson then approached the ranger guarding Ben. "You can let him up. He's not the problem."

"Sorry, Sheriff," the ranger responded. "This man had a rifle in his hands when we landed and there's a two dead men on the ground. This area is part of the National Forest System. You can help by cuffing him for me."

"Dumb ass. Fine with me," Robertson said. "Ben, I'm going to cuff you. It's just a formality until we get things straightened out."

"Do what you need to do Charley. Just make sure Hayley and my son are okay." said Ben.

Robertson finished putting cuffs on Ben when Robertson's deputy reappeared.

"The lady in the cellar wouldn't let me open the trap door. It was bolted from within," the deputy said. "She wants her husband and no one else."

The ranger said, "This man's not moving."

"Ben, I'll get your wife," Robertson said. "She'll listen to me."

"Sheriff, listen," Ben said, "this land is outside the forest area. I'm sure of it. I have title to the land and pay taxes to the county."

"Good to know," Robertson replied.

Robertson then turned and walked into the cabin and knelt over the bolted trap door to the cellar. "Mrs. Hunt, you there?"

"I'm not coming out until Ben is here. Who are you?" Hayley yelled.

"It's Sheriff Robertson. Ben is okay but the Forest Ranger won't let him up. You have to come out now."

"I can barely hear you and I'm not opening the door. How do I know it's you? You could be anyone. I want my husband."

"It's me. I watched you dismantle Bill Carter at the town hall meeting and then told you I wasn't going to babysit Ben while you were in Seattle. That proof enough?"

A latch clicked and the trap door to the unlit cellar opened slowly. Hayley was blinding by the light and Izzy started to cry. Once focused, she recognized the sheriff.

"Is Ben okay? Is he hurt? I need to know," Hayley said.

"He's fine and uninjured. Come out now."

Robertson held the crying baby while Hayley climbed out. She immediately took Izzy back.

"Where's Ben now? Hayley asked."

"He's just outside but.." Robertson started.

Before Robertson could explain that Ben was still handcuffed, Hayley, baby in hand, bolted from the cabin. She ran past the armed ranger to Ben, still prone on the ground with his hands cuffed behind his back.

Hayley, holding Izzy in one arm, ignored the ranger and kneeled on the ground next to Ben, sobbing, "Ben, are you're okay? We're fine. We're fine. Izzy and I are okay."

"I'm okay too," Ben said. "Don't worry. I'm okay."

Hayley then turned to the ranger. "Why is my husband handcuffed? What the hell is wrong with you? Men were trying to kill us. Why is he handcuffed?"

Hayley stood, Izzy in her arm, and started to approach the ranger.

"Back off, ma'am. Back off," the ranger yelled, turning the gun towards Hayley.

Robertson, following Hayley from the cabin, stepped between Hayley and the ranger and extended his arms towards both. "Stop," he yelled, "before someone does something really stupid."

Robertson turned to the ranger and in a calm voice said, "Put your gun down. This is getting out of hand. I am the sheriff of Apple Ridge. I know for a fact that this property is outside the Forest Service area and is within the jurisdiction of Apple Ridge. I know all these people and have a good idea of what just happened. The man on the ground is no threat, nor is his wife. I take full responsibility. Now let him up and holster your weapon."

The ranger backed down and holstered his gun.

Robertson then yelled to everyone within earshot, "Nobody touches anything until we get a forensic team here."

Robertson asked his deputy to uncuff Ben who immediately stood and turned to Hayley and Izzy.

Hayley appeared disoriented, her eyes scanning the surroundings, unable to discern meaning. Her bloodshot eyes, dirty face, disheveled hair and irregular breathing was the remaining shadow of two hours of hell.

Ben protectively held Hayley and Izzy together. He cried, "I'm okay. We're okay."

Hayley asked between sobs. "That's Bill Carter?"

"Yes. He's dead." Ben said.

Hayley continued to cry, "Why, Ben. What happened?"

Ben loosened his hold and held her by the face and kissed away her tears, softly repeating, "We're all okay. We're all okay."

Hayley wailed, "What happened? Why did this happen?"

Ben, re-embracing Hayley and Izzy, said, "I don't know. I don't know why."

Robertson stood behind the couple and as soon as Hayley stopped crying, he said, "Ben. We gotta talk now. I gotta make some sense out of all this."

Ben nodded and told Hayley to go back into the cabin and stay with Izzy. "I'll get you in a bit and we can start packing up to go home. Okay?"

Hayley nodded and walked unsteadily back into the cabin, clutching Izzy in her arms.

The rangers loaded the Carter's wounded Labrador onto the helicopter and took off for the veterinary hospital in Cle Elum with instructions to return with a forensic team.

Ben started his recollection of the morning's events to Robertson and the head ranger. Within a minute, the three could hear Hayley crying in the cabin.

"Let me try to calm my wife first," Ben said. "I won't be able to think if she's crying."

Ben entered the cabin to find Hayley and Izzy back in the cellar with the trap door open. Ben got on his knees in front of the trap door and held out his hand. "Come on back up. We're okay."

"Ben. Oh. Ben. Izzy could have been killed," Hayley cried, "You could have been killed. What happened."

Hayley handed Izzy to Ben and climbed out of the cellar. As she took Izzy back in her arms, she said, "Did Bill Carter do this?"

"No… I don't know yet," Ben said. "He saved us and gave his life for it. I just don't know. I don't understand what exactly happened. All I do know is that we're all okay. I need you to be strong right now for Izzy. I've got to talk to the sheriff. They'll need to interview you too, at some time. Try to relax here in the cabin."

Ben closed the cellar door and turned back to Hayley. "You shouldn't go back into the cellar. It'll just make you relive the events."

"I want to go home," cried Hayley. "I want to go away from here. I never want to come back."

"I do too. I want to go home, but the police need some answers first."

For the next forty-five minutes, Ben explained to Robertson and the rangers what had happened, including his conversations and disagreements with Carter over the past decade about the forest property. Ben mentioned Carter's last garbled words about being sorry for the trouble and about someone named Victor and another named Rosy.

Robertson added his conversation with Warren Kiffers from that morning, the call that prompted the Forest Ranger helicopter and the sheriff coming to the cabin. Robertson interviewed Hayley separately, who added her conversations with Carter and Warren Kiffers.

As Robertson finished interrogating Ben and Hayley, the county's helicopter returned with a staff of forensic investigators from Yakima.

Ben told Robertson where he had hidden the keys to his car parked at Greavy's store. The helicopter returned to Apple Ridge with Ben, Hayley and Izzy. The hospital's ambulance, waiting at the police heliport, took them to Apple Ridge General where Ben removed the remnants of Hayley's splinter. The ER staff cleaned and dressed Ben's neck wound.

Early that evening, Robertson and his deputies hiked back out of the forest to Ben's car. Robertson's repeated calls to Warren Kiffers' cell phone went to voice mail. Robertson had already sent deputies to Bill Carter and Warren Kiffers' offices to secure the contents.

As Robertson drove back to his office in Apple Ridge, the deputies called to report that both Carter's and Kiffer's offices had been ransacked. Locked filing cabinets had been pried open, papers strewn everywhere, computer hard drives missing and a wall safe from Carter's office had been chiseled out of the wall and removed. Robertson had still not been able to reach Kiffers.

After returning home, chaos reigned. Hayley handed Izzy off to Mrs. Ward, then headed over to Robertson's offices for additional interviews. Hayley contacted Deidre, already en route to Apple Ridge with two other FBI agents, after hearing of the incident.

As the interviews with Ben and Hayley ended, a deputy interrupted Sheriff Robertson.

"Chief, Warren Kiffers was found dead in a hotel room in Las Vegas. The Vegas PD thought it was routine murder by a prostitute's pimp for failure to pay."

Robertson shook his head in disbelief. "Warren was gay. Not many people knew. Not likely he'd hire a hooker. I'll call those idiots. Ya can't teach stupid." Robertson looked to the ceiling and wiped tears from his eyes. "This day's turned to total shit."

At eight p.m., Deidre Williams and two other FBI agents arrived at the Apple Ridge Sheriff's office.

Hayley, then Ben, recounted the entire incident again, including Bill Carter's dying comments about Victor and something akin to Rosy.

Deidre and her two partners said immediately, "Victor Rossi?"

"Definitely could have been," Ben said.

The agents told Ben what they knew about Rossi and none had heard about any Rossi activity in the Northwest. Deidre, on a hunch, immediately had the passport of Victor Rossi pulled and placed a "flight risk" status on him.

Hayley told Deidre of her conversations with Sid Grahmel about the man who had been snooping around Apple Ridge. Robertson called Grahmel at home and he arrived up at the sheriff's office twenty minutes later. Grahmel repeated what he knew about Thomas Smith of Bozeman.

"It's probably phony, given the story," Deidre said. "Did you or anyone who works with you ever take a picture of this Smith guy?"

"I didn't," Grahmel answered, then hesitated. "Wait, we did have a party for the real estate people in town and all the cooks and washers came out for a toast at the end. May be a picture there."

"Find out, ASAP," Deidre demanded.

Ben, Hayley and Izzy returned home accompanied by Deidre for added security.

***-*-*-***

For the next two hours, Ben and Deidre tag teamed Hayley, trying to keep her emotions intact. Ben, now desperate, called Jon Brander for advice.

"Did you hear?" said Ben.

"Unbelievable. Here in Apple Ridge. Simply unbelievable. How are you doing?" Brander asked.

"I'm doing fine, so far, but I have to," Ben said. "Hayley's completely out of sorts. I don't think she's going to get any sleep and she refuses to take a sedative. She's alternating between fits of crying and shaking. I've never seen her this agitated and that includes her recurring anxieties about her leukemia tests. It's scary."

"She needs rest. You do too. I'll be available all day tomorrow, for either of you. I told Amber not to come over, unless you need her." Brander said.

"We don't need her now, but I'll let you know. Hayley's friend Deidre is here and her parents will be here tomorrow."

Brander promised to be available the next day to see Ben and Hayley.

At eleven thirty p.m., with prodding by Ben and encouragement from Deidre, Hayley turned off her phone and tried to sleep. Ben reached Katy MacArthur to tell her that Hayley was not coming to work the next day and probably longer.

Deidre pointed out the obvious. "You both need sleep. The interviews and the police aren't going away anytime soon."

By two a.m., Hayley hadn't slept and still refused any medications. She would jump out of bed every thirty minutes, sometimes running, to make sure Izzy was secure. She then returned to bed, saying, "I'm sorry. I can't help it," toss and turn, cry some, then return to Izzy's room.

The semi-hysteria continued the next morning as Hayley started making breakfast at five thirty a.m. for Ben and Deidre. Rachel and Mel arrived at nine a.m. and Hayley demanded to make breakfast for them as well. Rachel had no success in calming her daughter. A team from the FBI came to the house at ten a.m. to begin re-interviewing Hayley and Ben. Despite Rachel's pleading, Hayley never rested. At two p.m., Rachel forced the police and FBI, except Deidre, to leave.

Hayley again attempted sleep but would exit the bedroom every thirty to forty minutes believing that Izzy, out of the house with Deidre, was calling for her.

Jon Brander, with Amber in tow, arrived after three p.m. After talking to Hayley for ten minutes, Brander took Ben aside. "Hayley's going to crash," Brander explained. "She's on the cusp of a sleep-deprived psychosis. She's already hallucinating. She needs rest and she needs it now."

"What do you suggest? Ben asked. "We've tried everything."

"First," Brander said, "get everyone out of the house that doesn't need to be here. Your in-laws can stay in a motel, as can Agent Williams. Mrs. Ward and Amber can take care of Izzy once Hayley's asleep. You can't let her decide whether she needs a sedative. Hayley's one-half step from a hospitalization."

Ben explained the situation to Rachel, Mel and Deidre. The three silently packed and left. With Amber and Mrs. Ward holding Izzy, Ben told Hayley that Brander demanded that she needed to sleep, if only for a short while, and that a mild sedative would help. Hayley finally relented and Ben surreptitiously gave her full doses of Ativan and Haldol. Ben got into bed and wrapped himself around her.

Hayley slept for fourteen hours.

Before she awoke, Rachel and Mel had returned to Seattle. Deidre stayed in a motel with the rest of the FBI agents until she returned to Seattle four days later.

*_*_*_*

On Monday evening, agents from the Newark FBI office arrested Victor Rossi and Angelo Bruni at the Teterboro Airport, north of Newark, as they attempted to board the CasManUS private jet. The plane's listed destination was Chicago, but an aggressive interview of the pilots revealed their intended destination would have been the Cayman Islands. Rossi's suitcases contained twenty-four million dollars in US currency, Euros and German Bearer Bonds.

Another strange report came to Apple Ridge from the Toppenish

Indian Reservation. Joe Two Rivers had been murdered, his home office ransacked and his computer hard drives taken. A quick check by the FBI revealed that Joe's cell phone number appeared often on Warren Kiffers' phone records.

The FBI called all three Thomas Smiths residing around Bozeman, Montana. All three were over the age of fifty-five and none had ever heard of Apple Ridge, Washington.

Jo Beaumont, from Apple Ridge Realty, arrived with a notebook full of pictures from the party held at Grahmel's restaurant. Grahmel was able to identify the alleged 'Thomas Smith' in three of the pictures. Once enlarged, the photo was sent back to FBI headquarters in Seattle and distributed throughout the FBI network.

The Portland office IDed Richie Porto twenty minutes later, but had no luck finding Porto over the ensuing forty-eight hours.

Gino Francisco, known to be his local capo, played dumb. "I'm looking for the son of a bitch too. For his sake, you'd better find him before I do," Francisco said, glib as always.

The FBI had CNN, Fox, MSNBC and local Portland TV stations post pictures of Porto on the evening news. At eleven thirty p.m., four days after the shootings, Porto used a payphone from Medford, Oregon, to call the FBI office in Portland and ask for protection.

Teams of agents from the FBI and IRS worked tirelessly for two weeks gathering information. Zoe Halpern, a United States Attorney from the Western District of Washington State, presented evidence to a grand jury in Seattle and obtained indictments on both Bruni and Rossi. Six weeks later, both were extradited from New Jersey to Washington State to stand trial.

## Chapter 18

The effects of the killings in the forest outside Apple Ridge, Washington, did not pass easily or quickly.

Used to small town triviality and not prepared for the chaos that ensued, Apple Ridge life quickly became uncontrolled mayhem. Reporters from all the major news services interviewed anyone that had a comment, which meant all the inhabitants of Apple Ridge over the age of twelve.

The madness lessened significantly in two weeks and Apple Ridge returned to normal within a month as the story became stale, although half the US population now knew Apple Ridge, Washington.

Ben continued seeing Brander, but no more often than before. Old wounds resurfaced briefly after the shooting. Knowing Hayley and Izzy were safe and not likely to be targets in the future, Ben, surprisingly, shrugged off the experience at the cabin quickly.

Hayley didn't fare as well. She tried returning to her job at DSHS three weeks after the shootings. Katy MacArthur, saying little, had shouldered most of the work in Hayley's absence. Hayley lasted three days but could not concentrate. Katy and Hayley mutually agreed that her return was premature.

Hayley started seeing Jon Brander twice a week. Vivid nightmares kept Hayley from having any meaningful sleep, other than with drugs. Hearings, depositions, intrusive reporters and finally a three-week trial in Seattle six months later unnerved an already fragile Hayley.

Hayley's blood work remained normal.

The trial of Rossi and Bruni, held in Seattle, re-elevated Apple Ridge to national news. Reporters in droves returned to the small town on days when court was not in session.

Richie Porto, now in the U.S. Witness Protection Program gave convincing and riveting testimony. That and scatterings of evidence left behind by the two assassins, Carter, Kiffers and Two Rivers proved ample to convict Angelo Bruni and Victor Rossi for accessory to the second degree murder of Bill Carter. The money found in the possession of Rossi and Bruni added tax evasion convictions. The judge sentenced Rossi and Bruni to consecutive thirty-year terms without parole.

The identification of the two hired assassins, known only as David and Emilio, remained unsolved. Reports from the streets of Cali, Columbia, filtered through the CIA to the FBI, suggested that they were Donaldo Ramirez and Edgar Santos, well-known, professional Columbian hit men. Both had been associated with murder-for-hire cases throughout South and Central America. The assassinations of Joe Two Rivers and Warren Kiffers remained unsolved.

On a Sunday, three weeks after the trial's completion, Hayley awakened after a rare good night's sleep without drugs. She rolled towards Ben and said, "I feel good. Really good. I only thought about my leukemia. That's gotta be a plus."

Ben laughed at the gutter humor and asked, "Izzy's not up yet. It's been more than forever and I'm horny as hell and I was hoping...."

Before finishing his sentence, Hayley kissed Ben softly, rolled out of bed and closed the door to their bedroom. She removed her nightgown as she returned to bed and straddled the already erect Ben.

Izzy wailed for twenty-seven minutes before being picked up.

Over the ensuing few months, Ben seemingly dismissed the entire event. Izzy, too young to know, was completely unaffected by the ordeal. Hayley started to relax and stopped seeing Jon Brander.

Ben longed to return to the forest but Hayley adamantly refused.

"I can't go back there," Hayley said. "The memories are still too fresh. I don't know if I'll ever be able to go there again. I know that hurts you but I could have lost Izzy and you. I just can't."

Hayley would not let Ben stop seeing Brander.

*_*_*_*

Amber, a senior in high school, now spent more time helping care for Izzy. "Ambo," Izzy's name for Amber, refused to be paid despite constant pleas from Hayley and Ben to accept some money.

One evening in mid-March after heading home, Amber returned to Hayley's house, entered and ran up to Hayley to give her a bear hug. "I got into the University of Washington for next year. That never would have happened without you. Thank you for everything."

Ben, Hayley, Amber and Izzy toasted Amber's success with a glass of apple juice.

## Chapter 19

Bev Bergreen, Hayley's old chief from the Seattle DSHS office, had become the head of DSHS for the State of Washington. Bev and Hayley, always good friends, remained in touch with each other, weekly, during the entire ordeal.

"Bev. I think I'm finally ready to go back to work." Hayley said, during their usual Monday morning phone call.

"Katy's been doing a bang-up job in your absence," Bergreen said.

"I know," Hayley said. "The fact that she's from here and knows just about everyone has helped. I've had lots of free time and, admittedly, I've enjoyed being a full-time mom. That said, I'm ready to work again, but not as many hours."

"What are you saying?" asked Bergreen.

"I'd like to work for Katy, part-time."

"Didn't see that coming. I think it's a perfect solution."

"Let me tell Katy. I know she'll be pleased," said Hayley. "Also, I have some ideas about helping Apple Ridge on a broader scale."

"What exactly are you suggesting?"

"Let me bounce it off some people here and I'll get back to you."

"A deal. Great to have you back. I remember our conversation before you headed off to Sun Valley. I suspect the real Hayley Green is back."

*_*_*_*

The next day, Hayley entered the DSHS office in Apple Ridge unannounced, knocked on Katy's door and entered.

"Got a second?" Hayley asked.

Katy stood and gave Hayley a hug. "For you, of course. What's up?" Katy asked, as they both took a seat.

"I'm ready to work and I'd like to know if you'd consider hiring me for a part time job here at DSHS?" Hayley asked.

"What are you talking about," Katy said. "This is your office."

"Not anymore. You've earned the job. Besides I don't think I want to work as hard or as many hours. I'd like to work for you, if you'll have me. I've talked to Bev Bergreen and she's agreed."

Katy caught her breath, stood and walked over to Hayley's chair and hugged her old boss again. "Sure. Of course. I'd love for you to work with me."

"I also have an idea how to help Apple Ridge. In all this free time, I've been looking at the numbers of how much DSHS spends here and……"

*_*_*_*

Oven the next three months, Hayley, with the help of Katy MacArthur, Bev Bergreen, Harry Brown and Joey Carter, made impassioned pleas to the Governor and local state representatives of the Washington State Senate and House of Representatives for tax incentives to return businesses to Apple Ridge.

Hayley and her group showed the politicians that jobs created locally in Apple Ridge would save Washington State seven million dollars annually in welfare payouts while costing only three million in tax incentives.

Hayley made four subsequent trips to Olympia to present data at hearings held by the Washington State Senate and House of Representatives.

Three months later a special bill passed both houses of the Washington legislature to offer tax incentives to corporations wishing to relocate to Apple Ridge and two other communities hit by recession. The governor signed the bill immediately.

Within days, two large fruit processing companies started bidding on the empty factory.

*_*_*_*

Ben and Hayley relaxed on their back porch three days after the signing of the tax incentive bill.

"You know," Ben said, "I only have nine more months on my Health Corps contract. We could leave and go back to Seattle or anywhere. Dr. Cassetti has told me every time I see him that he'd always have a position for me at Seattle Med."

Hayley thought for a second. "I never, ever, thought I'd say this, but I could stay here. Not that I don't mind the adulation about the processing plants coming back and all, but it's just that I feel so needed here. That's not going to happen anywhere else. You could easily start your own practice. Everyone knows you and loves you. It'll be difficult to leave. Only Deidre, and my mom and dad will be sad. They've always thought we'd come back to Seattle."

"We don't have to make a decision for a while," said Ben. "Let's not say anything to anybody."

## Chapter 20

Despite Ben's pleas, Hayley continued to refuse to return to the cabin. Equally frustrating to Ben, Hayley would not let Izzy accompany him.

Undaunted, and keeping Hayley out of the loop as much as possible, Ben took out a mortgage on the forest property. Using local contractors, he had a one-lane dirt road leveled past the cabin site using a different entry point out of sight from Creavy's store. Next, Ben had the existing log cabin leveled. At the end of the dirt road, two hundred yards further around the lake's edge, he cleared a one-acre site and had a three-room cabin constructed. The new cabin included a well, septic system and dual electric generators.

Ben insisted Hayley and Izzy return, if only for a look-see.

As they drove towards the cabin, Haley remained quiet, her arms folded across her chest as if she was cold.

"I know what you're thinking," said Ben, "and if, at the end of the day, you don't feel comfortable, I'll sell the property."

"I know how much the property means to you. I do but I could have lost you and Izzy. I just know it'll bring back thoughts and feelings I don't want to have."

"Try. That's all I'm asking."

Hayley nodded assent but kept silent.

Ben surprised Hayley by approaching the cabin from the new side road, bypassing Creavy's store. As they approached the lake, Hayley saw that nature, with the help of some pine tree plantings, had already erased and reclaimed the old cabin site. Most dramatically, the new cabin and site didn't remind her of the old one in any sense. The three exited the car and Izzy waddled quickly to the lakeshore. Despite Hayley's fears, Izzy's instant response to the lake melted her reluctance.

"Thank you," Hayley said. "It's beautiful and I know you did this for me."

Three hours after arriving, Buck, Bella and a single new fawn appeared at the forest edge.

Buck's ten-point rack moved up and down, welcoming his old friends.

Hayley picked up Izzy and walked to within ten yards of Buck. The large stag's head came up to full extension. Hayley sat on the ground, hugged Izzy and started to cry.

Wiping her tears with Izzy's T-shirt, Hayley said to the big buck, "We're back. I never thanked you for warning us that day. Ben doesn't think we'd be here if not for you. We owe you big time. Thank you. Thank you so much."

Hayley stood, took Izzy's hand and walked into the new cabin and came out with a carton of salt and a bag of carrots.

## Chapter 21

"Apple Ridge Surgery. Rhonda speaking."

"Rhonda, it's Hayley. Is Ben free?"

"I'll get him. How you doing?" asked Ben's assistant and sometime friend of Hayley. "Can't believe it's been more than a year since the ordeal.  Seems like yesterday."

"It always feels like yesterday to me," quipped Hayley.

A moment later, Ben picked up the phone. "Hey."

"Got a second."

"Sure. What's up?" Ben asked.

"My period's late," said Hayley.

"Your periods are never regular," said Ben.

"I know. Anyway, I had a little spotting today. Not like a regular period."

"And?"

"It's the exact kind of spotting I had when we found out that I was pregnant with Izzy. It's already stopped."

"So let's do a pregnancy test," said Ben.

"You know me. I'm so superstitious. I want to go into Seattle and have Dr. Capland do the tests."

"Hayley. I'm busy."

"I know. I know. It's just..."

"Don't say it," Ben interrupted. "I've got three small cases scheduled for this afternoon. Can it wait until tomorrow? I have a light day in the office and no surgeries scheduled. I can move the patients to Friday afternoon."

"That'd be great. Mom can take care of Izzy for the day and we can take Amber out to dinner, if she's free. I'll call Doris at Capland's office to let them know we're coming."

Ben called three times that afternoon. "You okay?"

"Stop calling me. It's annoying. I'm fine. Really, I'm fine. I'm sure it's nothing."

*_*_*_*

They arrived at Dr. Capland's office at eleven a.m. after dropping Izzy at Rachel's house. After Hayley's exam and blood drawing, they went to the International District for a dim sum lunch at the Harbor City Restaurant and returned at one p.m.

Doris came into the waiting area and said, "Hayley, Ben. Come on back."

"Did Dr. Capland say anything?" asked Hayley.

"Nope. Just bring you both back."

Hayley stood, turned, hugged Ben and grabbed his hand as they walked towards the consultation suite. "I remember the last time," Hayley said. "He wanted only me to come into his office."

The two sat in Capland's office and he arrived moments later with printouts in his hand. Hayley, still relaxed, had a moment of déjà vu.

*I'm pregnant.*

Capland sat, put the papers on his desk and looked at Hayley. The look was not what she expected. Capland looked crushed.

"Oh, oh. I'm not pregnant am I?" Hayley said.

Capland nodded no. "I'm sorry. The leukemia is back."

*_*_*_*

Capland admitted Hayley to Seattle Med that night and started her on chemotherapy the next afternoon. Ben made a call to the NHC explaining the situation with Hayley. The NHC found a temporary replacement in twenty-four hours. Izzy's care shifted to Rachel and Mel Green with the help of Mrs. Ward, who unhesitatingly relocated to Seattle and lived in the Green's basement guest room. Amber, at the University of Washington and only fifteen minutes away, came as often as she could.

Lying in a hospital bed on the first evening after the therapy, Hayley seemed withdrawn. Her parents and Deidre had left with Izzy an hour earlier.

"A penny for your thoughts," Ben said.

"Funny. I would have guessed I'd be sad, scared or angry or all three, but a strange sense of peace has come over me. I can't explain it. You and I both know that the chemo isn't likely to put me back in remission for very long. They'll try and then they'll switch drugs and try again. I promise I'll fight for every last breath but if it doesn't work, I'm okay."

Ben pulled his chair next to the hospital bed and kissed Hayley's hand. "I won't be okay. I don't know how I'll live day to day. I'll be lost."

"You can't be," Hayley said. "Izzy needs you. My mom and dad will need you too. Maybe more than Izzy. Deidre will help, but she'll be lost for a while too."

"I say we take the high road and assume the chemo will work fine. Maybe they'll find a suitable donor."

"Dr. Capland says they probably won't. Bad gene pool."

"I can't talk about this," said Ben.

Hayley sat up. "Give me both hands."

Ben sat on the side of the bed and softly caressed Hayley's

fingertips. "I love you."

"I know you do," Hayley said. "I remember you telling me, more than once, that your friend Izzy would say 'listen up' if he had something important to say."

Ben smiled and nodded.

"Well, listen up. I'll tell you this as many times as I can in the upcoming days. I'm not afraid to die. I've had a great life. I've helped people. I've had the greatest love one could ever hope to have. There hasn't been a week in the last four years that I don't think about that night in a Best Western in Cle Elum. Stuff of novels. I have a son that I know, with your help and guidance, will be successful. I may not have lived as long as many, but I've accomplished so much. You made that happen."

Ben was crying, openly and loudly. "You've given me life and peace when I had only fear and anger. You've given me a son. I can't let you go."

"Come here. Lie next to me," Hayley asked. "I'll be in an isolation tent in a day or two. I want to be held."

Hayley scooted over in her hospital bed and Ben lay next to her. They assumed a fetal cuddle together, Ben's arms wrapped around her chest, knees up. Within seconds both relaxed.

"You know," Hayley said, "without this leukemia, I never would have met you and Izzy wouldn't exist. Not all bad."

"Shhh," Ben said. "I would have found you."

"Maybe. Maybe not."

*_*_*_*

Hayley's white blood count fell quickly, but within four days the counts rose again.

Dr. Capland switched to another chemotherapy protocol, more aggressive and dangerous. The second set of drugs dropped Hayley's blood count quickly. With the drop, her resistance to infection disappeared. Dr. Capland hoped to see a rebound of Hayley's remaining marrow within a few days.

Five days later her counts remained low. That evening her temperature rose to one hundred four and broad spectrum antibiotics were started. Hayley was in and out of consciousness for much of the next eight hours before finally lapsing into a coma. Her white count remained close to zero and Dr. Capland told the family what they suspected. Hayley would not likely survive another thirty-six hours.

By midnight, Hayley's heart, kidneys and liver started to fail and two additional IV drugs, or pressors, were used to keep her blood pressure stable. Ben asked if the isolation tent could be removed. Dr. Capland agreed. Ben sat by her bedside, holding her hand and cried.

Hayley Green Hunt died in Ben's arms at two twenty-four a.m., just short of her thirty-third birthday.

## Chapter 22

The elder pastor of the Mercer Crest Presbyterian Church, Daniel Winegar, met with Ben, Rachel and Mel to express his sorrow and to help plan the words he would say at the funeral. Winegar had a brief remembrance of Hayley twenty-eight years earlier when she attended pre-school but had seen little of Hayley since, other than the random funeral or wedding.

"How many people do you expect will be present?" Winegar asked.

"We have a small family," Rachel said, "and Hayley hasn't been living in Seattle for five years. I would think not more than fifty or sixty people, less than a hundred for sure."

"I've called a few people in Apple Ridge who were close to Hayley," Ben added, "and I put an obituary in the Apple Ridge newspaper. I don't know who might come from Apple Ridge. Not many I suspect."

Mercer Crest Presbyterian had two sanctuaries: one small, one large. The bigger auditorium sat eight hundred seventy-five people and held services for major holidays and large weddings. Funerals and Sunday services were usually conducted in the small sanctuary with a capacity of one hundred eighty people.

Ben, Rachel, Mel and Deidre came early and met briefly with the pastor in his basement office to review the proceedings. When they ascended the stairs to the small sanctuary, the church administrator stopped them.

"Pastor Winegar, you might want to hold on a second. There are cars and school buses outside crammed with people. They're all from Apple Ridge. Hundreds of them. We're going to have to use the big sanctuary."

Nine hundred people had come from Apple Ridge for the funeral including the entire Apple Ridge City Council and a majority of the city employees. Apple Ridge had officially shut down for the day. The city had commandeered the school system's buses to transport all those wishing to come. The funeral service commenced twenty minutes late to allow time to install folding chairs along the sides to accommodate the overflow.

Winegar spoke on his memories of Hayley. His words were poignant but generalized about anyone who dies young. He did not know Hayley.

Deidre took twenty minutes to deliver eight minutes of memories, mostly funny. The other twelve minutes were spent trying to collect herself to speak.

Amber Brander spoke next. "I don't know if I'll be able to keep myself together any better than Deidre, but I'll try." Amber wiped the tears from her eyes, stood straight and scanned the huge auditorium.

"I'd like to tell you all the wonderful and amazing things that Hayley did for me but it would take forever. Suffice it to say, I was a lost soul when I came to Apple Ridge at age fourteen. With my grandfather's help, Hayley saved me. Hayley was my sister when I needed one. Hayley was my role model when I had none. Hayley was my surrogate mother when she needed to be, but most of all, Hayley was my friend. To me, that's the highest compliment I can pay anyone. She was just simply my friend.

Amber made a half turn on the dais, then turned back to the lectern. "Hayley, wherever you are, I will dedicate my life to helping others, in some fashion or form, as you did for me. I promise this to you."

Harry Brown had asked permission to say something, representing the City of Apple Ridge.

"Most here from Apple Ridge know exactly the moment they met Hayley Hunt. She appeared suddenly, almost mysteriously, at a town hall meeting 'bout four years ago. We were gathered to discuss her husband, Ben. It was not a friendly meeting and it was not going well for Ben. The reasons aren't important now and looking back, weren't important then.

"Out of nowhere stands this small and beautiful young woman that no one knew. She was ready to take on the most powerful men in Apple Ridge. She didn't waver or flinch. She stood, immovable, like a large boulder in a turbulent river. She won that day, but in the end it was Apple Ridge that truly won. It came to pass that her presence helped saved Apple Ridge. Was she a good person? I believe so. I don't know much about her faith but I do know that everyone of us felt her presence, in one way or another. Her loss cannot be measured.

"There will be a hole, a deep, black hole, in Apple Ridge left by her loss. She will be remembered. I know her parents, Ben and little Izzy will never forget her. Apple Ridge will not forget her either. I can promise you that."

Winegar stood and said, "What wonderful words. Thank you all. That concludes the service. There will be another short service at the graveside at the All Saints Cemetery on Queen Anne Hill. Directions are printed in sheets at the front door, if you need them. I want to thank`…"

Interrupting the pastor's instructions, Ben stood, placed Izzy in Rachel Green's lap and walked onto to the dais. Winegar stopped talking, not sure what Ben might be doing. Ben approached the microphone and Winegar stepped away.

Ben wiped the tears from his eyes and cleared his throat. "I've got to say something. I wasn't going to say anything because I didn't think I'd have the strength, but more needs to be said."

"Hayley told me twelve days ago that she did not fear death. That gives you only an inkling of her incredible inner strength. She told me she had a great, wonderful and fulfilling life. Her goals and aspirations in life were simple. She wanted to help people to give meaning to her existence, however long that might be. She touched and helped so many. Your presence here is testament to that. She also wanted to be in love, get married and have a family. I can tell you that she and I had the greatest love one could imagine.

"Without getting specific, she told me our love affair was the stuff of novels. We have a beautiful son, Izzy, who will carry her legacy and pass it on to his children and their children. I swear by all that is holy, he will know who his mother was. Izzy and I will not let her memory die.

"Hayley told me that she may not have lived as long as most, but she'd accomplished most of the things she wanted to accomplish. She wanted you to mourn her death, but more importantly, celebrate her life. Hayley Green Hunt was a woman of distinction, consequence and significance. She will be missed, but she will be celebrated as well. Hayley, I love you and always will."

## Chapter 23

After Hayley's death, Ben returned to Apple Ridge with only months left to fulfill his National Health Service contract. He would then be free to relocate anywhere.

Ben told the National Health Service not to send a replacement and that he would remain in Apple Ridge and start his own private practice. Apple Ridge had already started to awaken from its ten-year slump as the old food processing plant started hiring and another processing plant was being built. Families started moving back as jobs became plentiful.

After his decision to stay in Apple Ridge became public knowledge, Ben called on Harry Brown at the city office.

As soon as Ben entered Brown's office, Brown jumped up, then came around the desk and gave Ben a huge bear hug.

"Ben, I can't thank you enough for all you've done for Apple Ridge. You'll be so successful. I know it, everyone in town knows it, and I hope you know it."

"Thanks, Harry," said Ben. "but I've come to tell you my long term plans, just between you and me."

"And that is?"

"Just between you and me?" Ben reiterated.

"Yeah, yeah. Doesn't leave this office. Go on." Brown said.

"I don't plan to stay in Apple Ridge forever," Ben stated.

Brown surprised, his brow furrowed and arms crossed over his massive chest asked, "Then why stay at all?"

"I owe it to Apple Ridge to leave it with top class surgeons before I leave."

"I don't get it?" asked Brown.

"I've no family here anymore. I need help raising Izzy the way Hayley would have wanted her son raised. I need the help of Hayley's mom and dad and her friend, Deidre."

"You all planned this?"

"No one knows but you and Dr. Cassetti at Seattle Med, who's offered me an academic position. I haven't told my in-laws or Hayley's friend. I won't until I'm satisfied that Apple Ridge is set. Hayley's family believes I'm here for good. I'll leave it that way for now."

"The National Health Service isn't sending anyone else?"

"Don't know, probably not. I told them I planned to stay. If they do, you'll never know what kind of surgeon you'll get."

"They sent you, didn't they?" said Brown.

"I guess they did."

"We were lucky to get you and then Hayley."

"You're fifty percent right on that," said Ben.

Brown laughed, "Hundred percent right by my calculations, although if Hayley didn't show up at the Town Hall meeting, it would have been zero."

Ben smiled, "Thanks. Anyway, I will grow my own practice until I can take a partner, someone good. Someone who will want to stay in Apple Ridge, whether I'm here or not. Once I've found that surgeon, and he or she has established themselves, and all the local docs are happy, only then will I announce that I'm leaving."

"How long do you think?" asked Brown.

"Open ended. Three months, three years, thirty years. Whatever it takes," Ben said.

*_*_*_*

Ben opened his practice in Apple Ridge twenty-four hours after his National Health Service contract expired. Six months later he started advertising for an associate. Apple Ridge, by then bustling, had two food processing plants and a third planned. By twelve months, Apple Ridge needed almost two full-time surgeons.

Ben signed off every other weekend to the surgeons in Cle Elum. He and Izzy would alternate free time between the cabin and returns to Seattle to spend time with Rachel, Mel, Deidre, Deidre's new husband and Amber. Deidre had married another FBI agent and selected Izzy as the ring bearer, just after his fourth birthday.

Fourteen months into his private practice, Ben hired Daniel Reed, a graduating surgical resident from the University of California, San Francisco. Reed, an avid hunter and fisherman, and his wife, Susan, both from Spokane, Washington, were eager to relocate back to Washington State from the Bay Area. Allowing the Reeds access to Ben's cabin when he wasn't using it sealed the deal.

Six months after arriving, certain that Reed was qualified to be on his own and that he and his wife would stay in Apple Ridge forever, Ben call Armin Cassetti.

"Your position here is still available. You can start whenever you arrive," said Cassetti, delighted.

Ben then sat down with Daniel and Susan Reed. Ben told them of his plan to relocate and the reasons for doing so.

"I don't know," Susan Reed said immediately. "We don't have the money to buy your practice. Daniel's just begun here and we still have loans to pay back. We'd like to start a family and we need to buy a house first and…"

Ben interrupted, "I understand. Susan, you and Daniel can have my house for the same rent you're paying for the apartment you're in now. When Dan is financially solvent, you can either find your own house or buy mine at fair market value. As for the practice, I'm selling it for one dollar. You two can pay me for the office furniture and equipment whenever you can. If the asking price is too steep, I'll loan you a buck. I give Daniel three months before he starts looking for an associate. As for the cabin, Izzy and I will come when possible but most of the time it'll be yours to use and we can share expenses."

A single US dollar emerged from Daniel Reed's pocket before his wife could formulate a response.

*-*-*-*.

"Mom. Ben here." Ben had long before started calling Hayley's parents "Mom" and "Dad."

"Hey. How's Izzy?" Rachel asked. "How's Izzy" was always her first question.

"He's great. Talking up a blue streak. Mrs. Ward says we may need someone younger to handle him pretty soon. She'd like to start using a child leash when they take walks."

"You're kidding. I don't want to hear about my grandson on a leash."

"Mom, I was kidding."

"I'd hope so. You and Izzy are coming next weekend? Right?"

"Don't know. Things here are changing," said Ben.

"Oh. Is something wrong? Please don't tell me…"

Ben interrupted, "Everything's fine. I quit my job here in Apple Ridge."

"You what? You quit. You've only just started. That makes no sense."

"I've taken a new job. You're now talking to Benjamin Hunt, M.D., Assistant Professor of Surgery at Seattle Med."

The phone fell silent for a moment. "You're just k..k..kidding me, right?" Rachel said, sounding a bit disoriented. "That's also not funny."

"Wasn't meant to be funny. Can we stay in the guest wing until I find a permanent home?"

"You aren't kidding. Really?"

"Really. Actually, it was always my plan. I want you and Dad to help me raise your grandson."

"When will you start?" Rachel asked.

"Whenever the guest wing is ready."

"It's ready now. Tonight. This minute. C'mon, Ben. I can't take any more kidding. Is this all on the level?"

"Mom. I've got to get packed and all. Let's say we'll be there in two weeks. Mrs. Ward says she'll come and stay at her brother's house in Issaquah. She'll move in with us when I find a house. Amber can help a little too if she's not too busy at the U Dub. Mrs. Ward says she'll stay in Seattle until Izzy starts school. By then we should be set. By the way, where did Hayley go to pre-school?"

"The Community Center Day School here on Mercer Island."

"Call whomever you need to get Izzy enrolled. I'd like him to go there."

"I'm getting dizzy from hyperventilating. I'm so happy."

"I'm happy too," said Ben.

"Wait till Mel hears this. He'll go crazy. I gotta go. I gotta go and tell Mel," Rachel semi-shouted, in double time. "Bye."

## Chapter 24

Ben sat in his office at Seattle Med six months later preparing a lecture on penetrating injuries to the chest when his intercom lit up.

"Dr. Hunt. Phone call on line one. The gentleman says it's not medical. He said his name is Brigadier General Jack Howsfield."

Ben picked up the phone. "General Howsfield. Ben Hunt here."

"Dr. Hunt. Do you remember me?"

"Of course. You were a captain then. I see you've stayed in the game."

Yes, although I am retiring this August. I was diagnosed with Parkinson's disease six months ago, so I'm getting a medical discharge. That's not why I called."

"I'm all ears," said Ben.

"I made a to-do list a month ago," Howsfield said. "As it turns out, I've done almost everything. The last item was getting hold of you. Amazing how easy it is to find someone when you're a general in the U.S. Army."

"Strange how that works out," chuckled Ben.

"Yes, it is. I have had thoughts of you, and Private Jones, off and on since that battle on the hills outside Kandahar. In all my years of command, the fiasco to Bravo that day was my biggest and worst disappointment, although to the military it was a huge success."

"I guess that's relative to whom you're talking to," Ben said.

"I suppose you're right. I know we talked before you were shipped back stateside to recover, but I never had a chance to contact you about what really happened. I'd forgotten some of the details, so I went back and researched the DOD and Corps records and looked at my personal notes. I remember vividly that you left the Corps blaming Sergeant Wilcox for putting Bravo in harm's way. I remember telling you to keep that to yourself, forever. Corps and all. I wrote that in my personal notes."

"That's exactly how I remember our last conversation," said Ben. "I'm surprised you remembered it."

"I have forgotten little about that mission. At the time, I wasn't privy to classified information regarding the ANA and activities of ANA informants. I wasn't able to tell you what really happened because I didn't know. That information has now been unclassified for eight years and…."

"General Howsfield, before you go on," Ben interrupted the conversation, "I had eleven terrible years of posttraumatic stress because of that battle. I finally found two psychologists who could help me and I spent three years in therapy trying to reprogram those memories. I still see one of the counselors occasionally and I'm in a good place now. I don't need to have old wounds opened."

"I won't or, at least, I'll try not to. Sergeant Wilcox did nothing wrong. In fact, he did everything right."

"How so? That's not how I remember it."

"It turned out that one of the senior Afghani officers was an informant to the Taliban," Howsfield explained. "His wife, mother and two children were being held hostage until he could provide intel that was worthwhile.

"Before Alpha, Bravo and Charlie left Camp Hippo, the enemy knew exactly when we were coming. The Taliban wanted no part of us and hoped to be miles away before we arrived. They figured Alpha and Charlie would come from the south and west as they did. The informant didn't know Bravo was approaching the village from the east. Unfortunately, the enemy's route of escape was up, over and through your hill. They started towards your position before we ever left camp.

"Sergeant Wilcox had you in exactly the right place. Our plan would have put your squad on top of an unoccupied hill outside the village, dug in and safe. In the end, we lost everyone in Bravo, other than you. Nine good Marines killed. We killed seventy-five Taliban that day after Bravo held up their escape. I'm guessing you and Private Jones killed a third of them before Alpha and Charlie arrived. The Taliban have never returned to that area."

"It would have been nice to know all this then," said Ben.

"I didn't know the whole story either. Wilcox had your squad exactly where it was supposed to be. Bravo was just unlucky."

"That doesn't bring back Izzy or the others."

"No it doesn't," said Howsfield, "but the Corps thanks you for your service. You were a brave soldier. Anyway, I thought you should know."

"Thank you, General. Good luck on your Parkinson's."

Ben ended the call, leaned back in his chair and stared at the ceiling. *Izzy, did you hear that? Life is too strange. I wonder if I'll ever forget.*

## *Epilogue*

"Dr. Hunt. Your friend, Deidre, is holding on line four."

Ben picked up the receiver in his office, "Hey, Deeds. How's the pregnancy going?"

"Great. I was used to shooting basketballs, not swallowing them."

"Amen. What's up?" asked Ben.

"I've got two things to ask. First, Don and I caved last week at the OB's office and asked the sex of the baby. Anyway, it's a girl. I've discussed this with Don and we'd like to name the baby Hayley if that's all right with you?"

"Of course. You needn't have asked me."

"I assumed so. I cried for an hour when Don said it was fine by him."

"You might want to bounce it off Mel and Rachel."

"I will, but I wanted to ask you first."

"You said there were two things?"

"We'd like you to come to dinner on Friday."

"Celebrating what?"

"Nothing." Deidre hesitated for a moment and said, "We'd like you to meet someone."

"Kind of weird coming from you after you just asked me if you could name the baby, Hayley," Ben said.

"Well, maybe a little weird."

"How about a lot weird," Ben said.

"It's actually weirder than that," Deidre said. "The meeting was Hayley's mom's idea. She says it's time."

## ABOUT THE AUTHOR

James Gottesman M.D. is a Urological Oncologist who has been writing most of his adult life. He has authored more that a 100 scientific papers, medical book chapters, research grants, operative consent forms, and computer programs written in BASIC and HTML. His first book, *The Road Back Isn't Straight* was published in 2013. *The Search of Grace,* his second novel, was published in 2014.

He graduated from UC Berkeley and UC San Francisco Medical Center and did his Urology training at UCLA. He was Clinical Professor of Urology at the University of Washington. He lives on Mercer Island, Washington, with his wife, Gloria, three sons, seven grandchildren and dog, Biscuit. He plays golf and has traveled much of the world.

39565673R00191

Made in the USA
San Bernardino, CA
29 September 2016